JEWEL

Julia Graziano

978-1-965552-11-7 (Paperback)
978-1-965552-12-4 (e-book)

admin@bookwrightshouse.com
12211 W Washington Blvd.
Suite 110, Los Angeles CA 90066

CHAPTER 1

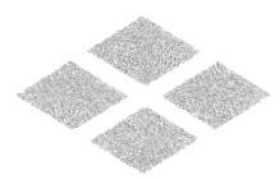

"Celia, Celia, Celia, okay, okay, you win. I give in!"

"Good. It isn't as though I am asking for the moon. It's just an hour of your time. The cocktail party is set for seven thirty, and their dinner reservations are set for nine o'clock. So by the time they arrive—and of course will be fashionably late—and have one cocktail, it will be time for them to leave to make it to the Four Seasons. It's time, Jewel. You can't keep living like this. It's time to let go. It's been well over two months. Kenneth, darling, please say something. I am right, aren't I?"

"Yes, my darling, you are right. Jewel, it's time. You can mourn for just so long. You know how much we care for you. Celia's right this time, Jewel. She wouldn't ask you if she didn't think it would be good for you to talk to someone other than us or the people at work. Come on, it's just an hour."

"Okay, you guys, I give in. So what exactly am I supposed to do at this party?" asked Jewel.

"Well, as I tried to explain, the dinner is to present an award to the partner who made the largest contribution, and that translates into the most money brought into the firm, and this year, as last year, it just happens to be Justin Angelis. That's why it is so important, and because he just happens to be the partner who has been acting as my mentor. He is unbelievably eccentric, but the most brilliant corporate attorney in New York. He can meet with a client and just write the entire prospective for the corporation in his head. It's amazing! He makes things happen that would take others weeks to formulate. I have learned more in six months from him than I have in the last four years with three other partners."

"All right, Celia, I get it. This guy is important to you, and you want to earn some brownie points with this party. I get that much, but what am I supposed to be doing with a room full of lawyers? I don't know anything about the world of corporate law. I'm not even sure I know what you all do. How am I expected to talk to all these stuffed shirts?"

"They are not all stuffed shirts. Some of them are really quite nice. Most of them will be with their wives, but Mr. Wilson's wife died last year, and Mr. Sawyer has never been married. It's no wonder, with his foul breath from the cigar that's always in his mouth, lit or not—ugh. Mr. Underwood's wife is in Europe with her sister, who just got divorced. She's pretending to drown her sorrows spending some of the twenty million she got in the settlement along with the house in the Hamptons and the apartment in New York. No kids, so it's all hers. Kenneth, if we divorced, would, I expect, get twenty million in a settlement?"

"My darling, if we divorced, you would have to support me." Kenneth laughed.

"Just as I thought." Celia laughed. "It's a good thing I love you so much." "Okay, back to you, Jewel. You'll be fine, darling. You can talk to anyone—and don't deny it. I've seen you talk to people who can't even speak English, and somehow you communicate, so you will be fine. Where were we? I think you should wear that adorable little black number you designed, you know, the one my very clever husband let slip by him. The one I could be wearing from his exclusive line."

"Let it go, Celia," snapped Kenneth. "It isn't funny anymore."

"I'm sorry, darling, you're absolutely right. And I think you'll be safe in your black pumps. We don't want you towering over all our guests now, do we? I think the only men over six feet are Mr. Underwood and Justin Angelis, man of the hour. Mr. Underwood is just a real sweetie when he isn't with his witch of a wife. You won't have to worry about him, though, and he makes any room come to life just by walking in. What I need you to do is to make sure the rest of the poor souls aren't holding up the walls or hiding behind a potted plant. They may be wonderful at the office, but when it comes to small talk, they can't put two words together. That's why most of their wives do all the talking. So in the event they get separated from their wives or for the men who will be here alone, I just need you to make sure they are being taken care of. You know, see if they need a drink or would like theirs refreshed, chitchat."

"Chitchat," said Jewel, "about what? Oh, wait, don't tell me. 'Gee, Mr. So and So, what's doing around the old corporate watering hole? Heard any good stock jokes lately?'"

"Jewel," snapped Celia, "now you're acting like a complete jackass. You know exactly what I want you to do, so stop acting like a child. I'm counting on you for an hour, and I would think you could at least do that much for me. Really, Jewel, sometimes you can be exasperating."

Exasperating, yes, Jewel knew what that felt like; that was the word she would choose to describe her entire life. From the time she was small enough to remember, it seemed her life was a contradiction. Exasperating, yes—being told you were smart but couldn't act too smart at times, being empathic but not showing it too often people might think you were strange, only kindness and service to others. Those were the parts she was allowed to show at all times. As a child, she found it so frustrating keeping it all in order. Living in a house or, really, over a restaurant and bar with your mother; aunt (mother's older sister) and uncle; two male cousins, one five years older, the other a year younger; and your mother's youngest sister just ten years older than yourself, plus the housekeeper, a simple black woman who possessed more wisdom than she was given credit for, nor did she ever covet it. Her advice to you was always the same: keep your mouth shut and just listen; you will learn much more that way. But that was what she wanted, to learn. To learn everything she could and excel at what she learned. She never planned to enter a cooking contest, but she wanted to learn how to make the best biscuits. She never planned to become a world-renowned botanist, but she wanted to learn how to grow the finest flowers. Everything went into the learning; the end product was not as important as the learning of how to create the best.

Thinking back on her early years, when she was two or three, she knew she had no say in being born bright. Words came to her easily; whole sentences came easily. Her natural curiosity made everything fun, and learning was fun. Then they moved to Upstate New York, where her mother was needed to help out in her brother-in-law's restaurant business. Jewel's uncle—that was when her education started to become confusing, exasperating, to say the least. At times, when she found herself alone with her uncle, who was also her godfather and whom she loved wholeheartedly, he would tell her that she was so special, she was smart, and she liked to learn and there was no reason she couldn't do whatever she set her mind on. He would tell her that it was sad to admit that she was smarter than either of his boys but that shouldn't stop her from learning all she could, but when the boys were around, especially the older one, she was expected to act dumb, not so much dumb as just not more clever than he was, not more clever then either of them, actually. Was she supposed to act this way in front of all men or just her male cousins? Was she supposed to not like competition because her cousins never won? It was all right to compete against herself and be better each time; just don't be better than them. Being smarter meant she had to act the role of a servant when they were around, or anyone else, for that matter. Little girls who grew up in an Italian household were trained early on in the role of the servant.

Her uncle told her she was special, that she had empathy for everyone, even the animals, but when she felt another's pain or loneliness and tried to comfort them or aid them in some way even before they knew they needed it, she was told not to use her gift, that people would not understand and think her strange. Was it better to sit idly by and watch the suffering? What did they expect of her? Be smart, not be smart. See how you could help, but don't help. Feel others pain, but offer no comfort. These conflicting thoughts banged around in her head, making her role in life seem utterly useless. Aunt Grace, their housekeeper, saw what these conflicting orders were doing to her, and her advice to this little child was to always be kind and do what was asked of her. So that was what she was doing now. Celia asked, and she would accommodate.

"I'm sorry, Celia, you're right. I swear I will make sure your guests are taken care of. No one will be leaning or hiding. All will have a drink in their hand and an hors d'oeuvre in their mouth, or vice versa. They will be engaged in titillating conversation, and by the time they are ready to leave, they will think they have just been to the finest cocktail party ever. How's that?"

Celia shook her head. "Jewel, sometimes I think you spend too much time with Michael and Jonathan. I expect conduct like this from them—they're only eight—but you, honestly?"

"I love you too, Celia, and I promise to do you proud."

"All right, if we can be serious just for a moment, I need to give you some background on Angelis, just in case you see him leaning or hiding. As I mentioned, he is brilliant and a little eccentric. Tall… I'm guessing around six four. You'll definitely notice him when he arrives. He is quite wealthy, I'm told. Family is from Connecticut, father is deceased, mother still lives in Connecticut, and he is an only child and socially awkward. What else do you need to know?"

"Bank account number would be nice," quipped Jewel.

"Really, Jewel, take this seriously or don't bother coming."

"I'm sorry, Celia. I'm just trying to get you to lighten up a bit. The night will take care of itself. You have it all covered—the best caterers, splendid ambience, no kids, and it's only an hour. Kenneth, have I missed anything?"

"Nope, I think you got it. Relax, Celia. Jewel and I will make sure it's a great evening."

"I know you will, it's just that I need it to go really well. This could open new pathways for me, especially with the senior partners. Very few associates get to rub elbows with the partners, especially in a social setting, and having Angelis as my mentor gives me an extra advantage. He said he would be here, and I know the partners will have to show up if they know he is coming. Oh, Kenneth, you know how hard I've worked these last three years. Sometimes I feel so guilty not spending more time with you and the boys, but with them in school and all their extra activities, I don't see them anyway, so this is the best time to try to make senior associate, and with Angelis's continuing support, junior partner could be a dream come true for me. You had your dream, and we made it come true.

Now I'd like mine. I love you, Kenneth, and I'd do it all again for you, but now I need this for me, for all of us."

Jewel usually had dinner with Celia and Kenneth and the boys on Monday night, and now, after listening to Celia go on and on about the cocktail party on Friday night, she decided it was time to go. Her head was aching, and she still had to read the boys the next chapter in *Moby-Dick*. Having read to the boys, Jewel said good night and called Rocky. The little dog bounded down the stairs even though the boys begged him to stay with them. Nothing could keep Rocky from being with Jewel. Since the day they found each other, they had never spent the night apart. Jewel clipped on his leash and said good night.

She was lucky tonight and quickly found a cab. She gave the driver the address and was surprised when the driver asked if she was sure of the address. Did she know that that was a very deserted area this time of night? She assured him she knew where she was going and agreed it was not where she would like to go but that the apartment she was staying in was in the same building where she worked. She doubted if the cabbie had ever heard of Kenneth Dolan or of the fact that he was a rising star in the fashion industry, but she mentioned it anyway. She was right; he hadn't heard of him. He asked what she did. "I am one of the lucky few who get to design clothes for Kenneth." She didn't mention that she probably made patterns and sewed more than she got to design, but she had been doing more and more designs and Kenneth was very generous when he liked something and bought it. He had even hinted that with next year's line, he might have her name mentioned as an associate designer.

As the cab pulled up to the curb at the address given, Jewel asked the driver if he could wait until she got the door open. "Sorry, lady," said the driver. "I don't get paid to wait." And off he went. Most of the drivers had been good enough to wait until she opened the door, knowing that the neighborhood was not the safest. Jewel always had her keys out so she could open the massive door as quickly as possible. She put the key in the lock and turned it. It clicked open. Jewel rushed Rocky inside. She looked up at the corner, where there was always a half-dozen people hanging out.

Most looked homeless. She assumed it was a good spot for drug dealers. What she was looking for was a person in a blue hooded sweatshirt that seemed to be there every time she was coming in or going out. She felt as though he was stalking her. She took one more quick look and then quickly closed the door, making sure to set the three rods that made the door virtually impenetrable. She also set the alarm. She took the huge elevator up to the third floor, where the apartment was. She never felt quite safe until she was in the apartment with the door locked; even then, the sounds of the old building creaking and groaning made the hair on the back of her neck stand up.

She was grateful to Kenneth for letting her use the apartment when she came back from upstate after Chris's death. Kenneth had the apartment put in a few years back so that he could stay overnight if he worked well into the night, which he did whenever he was getting ready for a show. He also stayed in the winter, when the streets were icy or there was too much snow and all the streets hadn't been cleaned. Jewel knew it was a big imposition for him, but he was gracious as always. She knew she needed to find something soon, but finding something she could afford that was in a decent neighborhood was proving to be difficult. Her friend Shelby wanted her to stay at her place, but her boyfriend had just moved in, and Jewel felt it would be too awkward. She would find something soon; she had to. She let Rocky out the door that led to the roof. Kenneth had made a small sitting area complete with potted plants, table and chairs, and a chaise lounge to relax on. Rocky did his business on a small patch of artificial grass she put down for him. It took him a while to learn to go there since he was so used to going in real grass. But Rocky was a very smart little dog and soon caught on, especially since he got a small reward when he did it right. Rocky only had to pee, and Jewel quickly washed it off with the hose Kenneth used for his plants. She locked the door, and she and Rocky went to bed. It was already eleven o'clock, and she usually was up at six thirty to get ready for the day.

The week flew by, and before she knew it, it was Friday. Dreaded Friday. Jewel was not looking forward to Celia's cocktail party. She even thought about calling and telling Celia she wasn't feeling well but knew she would go. "Just keep telling yourself," she said, "it's only an hour, only an hour." Kenneth had planned to leave early, so Jewel made sure her things were packed and ready to go when Kenneth said the word. Celia told her to come home early with Kenneth so she could play with the boys and keep them out of the way.

Kenneth called her at three and said he was ready to leave. Jewel put her things away, got her bag, and met him at the elevator. Rocky was coming to because she had planned to stay overnight, and Rocky would keep the boys company while the party was going on. They were going to have a pizza and had strict rules to stay down in the family room until someone told them otherwise, which was fine; the boys had just about every new electronic game you could want. Plus the TV was there, as well as a computer, so they were set for the night. That was where Jewel found them. Michael and Jonathan were great kids. Jewel found it hard to believe that with all their advantages, they never acted spoiled. They were really a pleasure to be with. The boys ran to Jewel and gave her a hug, then one for Rocky. She kept them entertained for a few hours, then told them she had to dress for the party. Sighs all round, but she said if things went right and everyone left early, she would play with them again.

Jewel readied herself for the party, wearing the outfit Celia told her to wear, which was fine, because the dress was comfortable, and so were her pumps. She went downstairs to find Celia and Kenneth. The catering crew had almost everything set up. The bar and bartender were on the right side of the long living room so that after the guests arrived and coats were taken, Celia and Kenneth would greet them and suggest they have a cocktail. The bar was set up for a few popular mixed drinks as well as some fine wine or something on the rocks. After everyone had their drinks, the trays of hors d'oeuvres were paraded around by two of the servers. Celia had selected a lovely variety of finger foods, and the bar she left to Kenneth. All systems were a go. Now all they needed were the guests.

Celia began pacing. "Celia, relax," said Kenneth. "They'll be here. Just relax."

"I can't," said Celia. "It's ten to eight already."

"I know," replied Kenneth, but before he could finish his sentence, the doorbell rang.

Several of the partners with their wives walked in. Their coats were taken, and Celia and Kenneth began to greet everyone. Celia introduced them to Kenneth and politely made some small talk and directed them to the bar. Another ring of the doorbell, and a flood of people walked in. Again, coats and wraps were taken, and the same process began again. Jewel had positioned herself a few feet behind Celia and Kenneth in hopes of catching some of the names, but by the time the first group had walked by, she had already forgotten most of them. No matter; Jewel was not the hostess of this party, so it didn't matter much to her. She knew she could bluff it. Celia was right about Jewel; she had an unexplainable knack for talking to just about anyone and putting them at ease in any situation. Jewel always possessed great empathy for people, and when she spoke to you, you could feel her focusing directly on you and not gazing about the room while she was speaking to you. This ability was always a big help to Kenneth when he was dealing with new buyers or sales reps. Now she would use it to help Celia pull off the best cocktail party. Jewel made her way around the room, introducing herself as she went and making sure everyone had a cocktail and everyone was chatting with someone. Most of the women were grouped together, talking about their recent trips to Europe or of their recent vacations to their homes on some island or another. Jewel wasn't needed there.

Jewel spotted someone in the front corner of the room, looking out the window. Time to put on that happy face, she said to herself. She made her way quietly toward the elderly gentleman. "Good evening," said Jewel. "Rather gloomy night, isn't it?"

"Yes, yes, it is," replied the man, who Jewel recognized as Mr. Wilson, the man who lost his wife last year.

Jewel introduced herself and explained her connection to Celia. Mr. Wilson smiled. "Do you also design some of the garments?" asked Mr. Wilson.

"I do, and anything else that needs to be done, from patternmaking to sewing or just making a new pot of coffee," answered Jewel.

"I guess we could call you Jewel-of-all-trades." And having said that, Mr. Wilson laughed.

"That's very good," said Jewel. "I guess you're right." Jewel felt relieved; she first thought she would have a difficult time trying to have a conversation with this man. Most men who had had a long and loving relationship with their wives were more often than not suffering from depression. She felt that with Mr. Wilson but was pleased to see he didn't seem terribly depressed, only very saddened. Jewel knew that most people, if given an ear, would immediately start talking about their deceased partner.

"Celia told me you lost your wife last year. I'm so sorry for your loss," she said, giving him an opening to start pouring out his heart.

"Yes, my Marjorie passed last November, bless her soul. We were married fifty-two years, you know. The only woman I ever loved. Met in high school, we did, and married while I was still in college, much to our parents' objections, but we did it anyway. She was the best, at most things, anyway. Had an awful fear of doctors, you see. So by the time she started feeling the pain and went to the doctors, it was too late. The cancer had already spread throughout her body. She went quickly, though. She didn't suffer a long time like some. A real trooper, she was. Right to the end, all she worried about was me." Mr. Wilson hung his head and shook it back and forth. You could feel his sadness.

"I know you are feeling a terrible sadness," said Jewel, "but my mother always told me that when the people we love pass on, they never leave us. They are always by our side. And I'm sure your Marjorie is right here with you, sharing this and every moment with you."

"That's a great thought. I hope you're right," replied Mr. Wilson.

"I know I am, Mr. Wilson. Just believe it, and you will make it through the hardest times."

"Thank you, Jewel. I would like to believe that."

"Now, Mr. Wilson, please come and talk to some of your colleagues while I fulfill my duties and make sure everyone is having a good time."

"If they are talking to you, Jewel, then they are."

"Thank you," said Jewel as she led him back into the room toward several of his colleagues. He quickly became engaged in whatever they all happened to be talking about. As Jewel began to walk away, she saw Mr. Wilson give her a wink and a smile. Jewel thought all was going well, until she saw someone leaning against the wall leading to the dining room. *Oh no, that looks like Mr. Angelis. Celia will kill me if she sees that.* Jewel quickly crossed the room to where he was standing.

"Good evening. Mr. Angelis, isn't it?"

"Yes."

"My name is Jewel, and I work with Kenneth Celia's husband, and I have been given strict orders by Celia to make sure no one is leaning against the walls, hiding in corners or behind potted plants."

"Seems like quite a job, but technically, I think this is a doorjamb," replied Angelis.

"Yes, you're right, but I'm sure doorjambs were also covered. Is your drink not to your satisfaction?"

"I'm afraid I'm not much for martinis or any of the usual cocktails."

Jewel thought quickly. "Then your drink of choice would be…?"

"Beer. Surprisingly enough, the men in our family come from a long line of beer drinkers, except for my great-grandfather, who preferred wine," replied Angelis.

"Then please let me take that." Jewel gently lifted the glass from his hand and said, "Follow me." Jewel led Angelis through the dining room and into the kitchen. She could hear Celia now. "You took the man of the hour into the kitchen!" But she just pushed the thought away and continued leading him to the kitchen. She stopped at the sink and emptied the glass and put it into the sink. She reached a rather-large refrigerator and opened the left-side door. "We have Budweiser, Coors, some kind of Chinese beer, and Heineken. What would you like?"

"I'll take a Heineken, thank you," answered Angelis.

Jewel handed him his beer and motioned for him to follow her. "Welcome to the inside-out room," she said.

"Odd name for a glass room," replied Angelis.

"That's the name Celia's boys gave it when it was put up a few years ago. I think the boys were only five at that time, and they just loved it, and one day they said they wanted to go outside so they could be inside. It was just so cute, and since then it has been called the inside-out room. The boys would come out here when it was raining or snowing and pretend they could catch raindrops or snowflakes on their tongues. Celia tried to make them stop, but Kenneth said he would rather have them believe they could do the impossible than to believe they couldn't. Celia, of course, was not amused. She is hopelessly grounded in reality. Poor soul."

"Good for Kenneth." Angelis laughed.

"So, Mr. Angelis," started Jewel.

"Please call me Justin," he said.

"Very well, Justin." Suddenly, she was feeling rather bold. "What sort of name is Angelis, anyway? Sounds just a little made-up."

"In a way, it is," said Justin. "My grandfather worked for the Italian government in the finance department when he decided to come to America. He had some background in the law and wanted to become a lawyer in this country. On his way over by ship, he met a few men traveling with their wives. Grandfather was a very charismatic gentleman and soon began to join them for dinners and the like. They discussed the businesses they were in, and Grandfather told them of his plans. Trying not to offend him, they politely told him that he should consider changing his name because a very ethnic-sounding name would make it hard for him to get into law school or the banking business. Grandfather said thank you for the advice and gave it a great deal of thought. He agreed it could be a barrier to his plans. You see, his name was Vincenzo Angelisaro. So when he arrived in the United States, he had it changed to Vincent Angelis. Grandfather did all he planned. He went to law school, passed the bar, and had a very lucrative career in banking. My father had a very bad experience growing up in Connecticut. The children would call him Vinny, which he hated, so when I came along, he wanted an American-sounding name for me and chose Justin. And there you have it. So I guess you could say it was really made-up."

"What a great story. I hope I didn't offend you by being so bold," said Jewel.

"Not at all," said Justin, "and now turnabout is fair play, I think."

"Nothing as exciting for me. Mother was Italian, but a very simple name, Sabia. Father was English, hence the name Lansby, and when the nurse brought me to my mother for the first time, she handed me over and said, 'She's a prefect jewel,' and so I was named."

"Well, I think it fits," said Justin with a small laugh.

"Thank you," replied Jewel.

"So tell me what you do when you are not patrolling the walls and corners," said Justin.

"I work for Kenneth. I design some, sew some, make patterns, and try to make myself an absolute nuisance to everyone in the shop. But they love me, at least I think they do. I hope they do. It's a fun place to work. It can be very stressful at times, but Kenneth is great in making sure we laugh at least once a day, especially when we all make mistakes."

"And what do you do when you're not at work?" asked Justin.

"Sadly, not a great deal. I spend time with Celia, Kenneth, and the boys. Take long walks with Rocky and spend the rest of my time at the Metropolitan Museum of Art."

"Is Rocky your husband?"

"No, Rocky's my dog. No husband, no boyfriend, just work," said Jewel.

"What is at the museum that compels you to spend all your free time there?" asked Justin.

"I go there to see the world's best artwork. I go to the costume department, hoping to be inspired and get some ideas for designing new apparel. But mainly I go because it's quiet. I don't get a lot of quiet where I work, and when I'm at Celia's, the boys make me crazy with all the different games they want me to play. Rocky can be a wholly terror because he doesn't like the city. So the museum is my sanctuary."

"I see," said Justin. "I have often thought of a visit to the museum to see the artwork you described, but I am ashamedly not very good when it comes to seeing the best in the paintings. I'm afraid I would need the help of a guide to walk me through them and point out the intrinsic beauty to be found in the works."

"Are you making fun of me?" said Jewel.

"Not in the slightest," replied Justin quickly. "I'm really serious about the museum. I seem to find myself in the same position you find yourself in. I work and work some more. A quiet afternoon is exactly what I need. Do you have plans to visit again in the near future?" asked Justin.

"Well, actually, I had planned to go tomorrow," said Jewel.

"I know we have just met, but I'm sure Celia would give me an honorable reference, and I would really like to spend a quiet afternoon with someone who could show me the best the museum has to offer," said Justin. "This may be just what I need to get myself ready for my business trip to Washington next week. I already know that these meetings are going to be long and tedious. So please say yes to this poor soul who so desperately needs a bit of peace and tranquility."

"Now I think you are really making fun of me, but I do recognize a soul in need of help, so yes, it would be my pleasure to guide you around the great works and show you all you have been missing by working so hard. And I know you do, because Celia is always saying that you live and breathe nothing but corporate law. It's a good thing Celia has us to make sure she remembers there are other things in her life than work. All right, if you're really serious, you can meet me outside the museum on the steps at three o'clock. I'm sure, after tonight's affair, you would like to sleep very late tomorrow morning, and then there is the matter of the newspapers. Celia said you read just about every paper printed, so that should take up most of the day. So would you say that three o'clock is a good time for you?"

"It's a perfect time. Thank you for being so considerate," said Justin.

"Excuse me, but I think people are beginning to leave now," said one of the people in the catering crew who was cleaning up in the kitchen.

"Thank you," said Jewel. She quickly wrote her number down and handed it to him and told him it was just in case he needed to cancel.

Justin followed and wrote down his number, handed it to her, and said, "Just in case you need to cancel."

"Before you go, Justin, may I ask a small favor?"

"Of course."

"Celia really wanted this night to be special for you, and she's worked hard to make sure everyone had a good time, and since you didn't bring a date with you, I would like to ask you to take Celia to the dinner with you. I know it's a lot to ask, but it would be a really nice thing to do," said Jewel.

"And you like people who do nice things."

"Yes, I do," said Jewel.

"Consider it done, with Kenneth's permission, of course," he said.

"Kenneth will gladly give his permission, just to get her out of our hair. She's been wound so tight she's been making us crazy all day."

Justin laughed and held the door open for her. He was given his coat, and as he was saying good night, he turned to Kenneth and asked if he would allow him to escort Celia to the dinner as his guest. Kenneth smiled and said nothing would give him more pleasure than for Celia to go to the dinner with Justin. Celia just stood there, not knowing what to say.

"Celia," said Jewel, "get your wrap. It's chilly outside."

Celia, in an obvious daze, continued to stand in place. Kenneth grabbed Celia's cloak from the closet and put it around her shoulders, kissed her cheek, and pushed her in Justin's direction. As Celia and Justin were almost out the door, Justin looked back at Jewel and said, "I'll see you tomorrow." Kenneth closed the door behind them and began to clap.

"You did this, Jewel. How in the devil did you arrange this?" said Kenneth, still clapping lightly. "And what did he mean he'll see you tomorrow?"

Jewel hesitated, then told him about the conversation she had with Justin in the inside-out room, where she took him after getting him a beer because he hated liquor, and that she agreed to meet him at the museum tomorrow to explain some of the art to him.

"Jewel, I hate to state the obvious, but the man is well educated and comes from a wealthy family. Don't you think he knows a little something about art?" "Of course he does. I'm not that naive. But it was so easy talking to him. He just isn't the man Celia described. He made me laugh, and I found him to be quite charming, actually. You don't think Celia will hit the roof when she finds out, do you?"

"Well, I wouldn't mention it unless she brings it up. That means Angelis would have told her, and I don't think she would voice her objection about it to him. So just wait and see if she says anything at breakfast. Speaking of food, I'm starving. Aren't you? Let's call the boys and see if they want anything," said Kenneth as he walked to the door to the family room, which was in the basement.

"Hey, guys, it's safe to come up. Everyone's gone thank heaven, even Mom." The boys ran up the stairs, following Rocky, who obviously needed to go out.

"Where did Mom go?" said Michael.

"What's to eat?" said Jonathon.

Out of the twin boys, Michael was the mama's boy. Celia couldn't go anywhere without telling Michael first. Jonathon was much more independent and more focused on what she would bring back for them. Kenneth insisted when they were young that they not be dressed alike. He felt they would have a better time developing their own individual styles if they didn't always look alike, plus it was easier to tell them apart. When they were babies, it was difficult to tell them apart, even for Kenneth, but as they got a little older, it was easier, mostly because Jonathon was the holy terror and Michael was quiet. Jonathon would eat anything you gave him, but Michael was a finicky eater, and now that they were eight, it remained the same. Michael wouldn't eat anything green or things that were really soft, like pudding or mashed potatoes. With both Celia and Kenneth working and not having a cook, just a lady that cleaned the house and stayed until either Celia or Kenneth got home from work, trying to plan a meal that everyone would eat could be stressful because of Michael and his eating habits. Whenever Jewel watched them, it was peanut butter and jelly sandwiches or pizza. The two things Michael would eat with no problem.

"Mom went to the special dinner they were having for the lawyers. You know, the people Mom works with," said Kenneth to Michael. Jonathon wasn't interested in anything except seeing what there was to eat. Before they left, the caterers made fried chicken and french fries, the two items both boys liked and, as a special treat, a chocolate layer cake. Celia didn't let the boys have many sweet desserts, so this was wonderful. Seeing it all even made Michael stop whining about when his mom would be home.

Jewel got paper dishes and napkins, Kenneth grabbed the glasses and silverware, and they all headed into the inside-out room.

"It's too bad we can't see any stars," said Jewel. That was one of the things she missed about living upstate—the stars seemed so close and were so plentiful.

"I don't care if we can't see the stars. We can't see them most of the time, anyway," said Jonathon.

"I like the stars," said Michael. "I never knew there were so many until Jewel took us to the planetarium. That was really cool. Can we go again sometime, Jewel?"

"Yes, Michael, we can go again. Now, eat up before I eat all the cake."

"No, you can't. It's too big," chimed in Jonathon.

"All right, you two, start eating, or neither of you will have any cake," said Kenneth.

The boys quickly ate their meals, and Kenneth gave both boys huge slices of cake.

"You better hope Celia doesn't come home soon and see these guys in a sugar high," said Jewel.

"That's okay. I'll just tell her you gave it to them." Kenneth laughed.

"Oh, nice, and after I got rid of her for the evening so you could relax, you'd throw me right in," replied Jewel.

"For arranging for her to attend that dinner tonight, she will forgive you anything," said Kenneth.

"Can we go finish our game?" said Jonathon, having wolfed down his piece of cake before Michael was even halfway through.

"No, wait for me," said Michael and scooped up a forkful into his mouth. "It's no fair. You eat faster than me," he whined.

"No one is going anywhere until you clean up your places, silverware, and glasses in the dishwasher and plates in the bin." The bin was what they called the trash compactor, because Celia thought the word *trash* just sounded awful, so she decided it be called the bin. With everything cleaned up, Jewel told Kenneth to go and relax before Celia got home and kept him up till the wee hours, telling him everything about the dinner. When Celia got on a roll, nothing could stop her. Kenneth even resorted to putting his hand over her mouth one time, trying to get her to stop. Jewel told

Kenneth she would make sure the boys got to bed after they read another chapter of *Moby-Dick*, and then she would also retire.

"Please don't mention anything about my meeting with Justin tomorrow unless she brings it up," Jewel reminded Kenneth.

"Don't worry, I won't," replied Kenneth. "I just hope Angelis hasn't told her anything, or she will be waking you up to find out what's going on."

"Oh, please. Tell her it can wait till morning. I'm so tired. She can be like a drill sergeant, and I'm much too tired to be interrogated. See you in the morning," said Jewel as she climbed the stairs to where the boys' bedrooms were.

"Okay, monsters, one chapter and then to sleep," said Jewel as both boys jumped onto Michael's bed. They had to scrunch together so Jewel could get on the bed. Jewel read them the next chapter, then put the book away, while Jonathon got into his own bed. Jewel gave them each a kiss good night, turned off the light, and shut the door. Jewel waited outside the door for a moment, then opened it quickly and said, "Gotcha! Now go to sleep." The boys giggled and said, "All right," pulled their blankets up around their shoulders, and closed their eyes. Jewel closed the door again and quietly went down the stairs to the family room.

Sometime ago, Celia and Kenneth had a double-size Murphy bed installed on the back wall of the family room. When it was up and the doors closed, it looked like a very large closet. Rocky was already on the bed. Kenneth had opened the doors and pulled down the bed earlier for her. She brushed her teeth, washed her face, and put her nightclothes on. She always wore pj's when she stayed over, because the boys would sometimes sneak down to wake her.

It didn't take long before she fell asleep, with Rocky snuggled against her back.

CHAPTER 2

Jewel drifted off to sleep with her dreams leading her to Chris and how unusual and a typical their first meeting had been, but then everything about Chris was atypical. Jewel had left the hustle and bustle of New York City and given up her job as designer with one of the most upcoming firms, Kenneth Dolan. She left New York after the man she thought she loved betrayed her and stole the designs that she was completing for Kenneth for his new show. Fortunately, she had duplicates of the designs and patterns, and Kenneth managed to hold his show before the firm that Lawrence worked for, leaving Lawrence and his firm looking like they stole Kenneth's design, which was like committing suicide in the fashion world. While all ended well for Kenneth, Jewel felt she needed a break and left the city to stay for a while upstate, where she grew up. She opened a small quilt shop designing quilts for the manufacturers of the fabrics she used in the quilts. The quilts would be used in the advertisements for the fabric. Her life was quiet and peaceful, just the way she wanted it. It was just her and Rocky, a dog she adopted from the local shelter. She hadn't been on a date since she arrived, but meeting Chris was to change all that.

"Excuse me, lady, excuse me."

Jewel turned to see who was addressing her. "Are you speaking to me?" she said as her eyes looked into the bluest, most hypnotic eyes she had ever seen.

"Yes," he answered. "I'm afraid I need to ask a tremendous favor. I just ordered some dinner since I've been living on sandwiches for the last two days, and the girl told me there wasn't a seat to be had anywhere, but she thought that you were here alone and that maybe you would let me sit at your table while I gulped down my food. I promise I wouldn't talk or anything, and I'll even pay for your dinner."

"That won't be necessary," said Jewel. "I guess it will be okay. I'd hate to see you standing in the corner somewhere, trying to eat your dinner."

"Thank you ever so much. I'm extremely grateful. My name is Chris, just in case you're interested. I'm the local vet here, and I just hope I can eat this nice, hot dinner before I get called out." Unfortunately, that was not to be. As soon as he had a few mouthfuls of his dinner, his pager went off.

"Damn, I'm sorry, I just thought I'd have a little more time. Well, duty calls. Thank you again for sharing the table. You enjoy your dinner now." He stood up, threw some money on the table, grabbed one more mouthful of the hot mashed potatoes with gravy, and left. The waitress brought out Jewel's dinner, which coincidently was the same as his, except she had carrots and he had string beans. The waitress asked if Chris had to leave, and Jewel said his pager went off and he bolted out of there. She said, "Poor Chris. He rarely, if ever, gets to sit down and finish his dinner." And that he only lived half a mile up the road, but the minute he came in and ordered, he was running out again. Jewel asked if his practice was up by the Weller farm. The waitress said that it was and that he was Chris Weller. He owned the practice and the farm. Jewel told the waitress to wrap up Chris's dinner and that she lived near there and she would drop it off. The waitress asked if she wanted the pie too; Chris always ate the apple pie. Jewel said, "Sure." Whatever she thought Chris would like, just wrap it to go.

Jewel ate her meat loaf, mashed potatoes with gravy, and carrots. This little diner had the best food around, and the meat loaf was the best. It was funny that it was the choice that Chris made also. She finished her dinner and paid for her own, leaving the waitress a tip. She used the money he had thrown on the table and paid for his, also leaving the waitress a nice tip. She put on her coat, picked up his dinner, and got into her car. The drive really was only about a half-mile from the diner. She pulled into the driveway, and seeing no lights on in the clinic, she drove closer to the barn. The door was opened, and the lights were on. She left the dinner on the seat and went into the barn. There was Chris with his arm up to his elbow inside a cow. She quietly watched him. She knew from the short time that she had lived on her grandfather's farm that sometimes a calf could be turned the wrong way or have a leg bent back, and the only thing to do was to try to get things straight for a normal delivery. It took him another five minutes, but finally the calf was coming out in the correct position. It plopped to the floor with Chris and another man carefully cleaning out its mouth and nose and pulling back some of the bloody sack around the calf. They dried it with a towel and dragged it around to its mother, who took over cleaning the rest of it. The other man went about cleaning up the blood-soaked straw and putting down clean, while Chris went over to a large sink to wash up. He scrubbed himself clean with a brush and towel-dried his arms. That was when he noticed Jewel in the doorway.

"That was quite a job you just did," said Jewel.

"Was nothing, really. Little guy had his head twisted back. Not good for delivery," he answered. "Was there something you needed?"

"No, we met briefly at the diner, and I just wanted to drop off your dinner since you didn't have time to finish it. I thought you could pop it in the microwave when you had time," said Jewel.

"Well, that was real nice of you. Hey, Manny, this lady brought my dinner home."

"So go eat. I've got things covered here," he said.

"All right," answered Chris. "Put enough dry straw around so he can get his footing when he tries to stand, and then go home to that beautiful wife of yours before she yells at me again for keeping you out late. Leave the lights on, 'cause I'll come back down to make sure he's on the teat." Manny said okay and waved Chris on.

Jewel followed Chris out of the barn to her car. She handed him the container and said good night. Chris asked her what her name was, and when she told him, he said he hated eating dinner alone, and since she brought his dinner to him, the least he could do was offer her a cup of coffee. Jewel's first thought was to refuse, but standing in that cold barn, she was so cold, and a hot cup of coffee sounded so good right then. She accepted his invitation and followed him up to the house, an enormous colonial with a wraparound porch. They went in by a side door that was a mudroom, where he took off his boots and layers of sweaters and hung up Jewel's coat. The mudroom led directly into the kitchen, a large kitchen, not fancy, but warm and friendly. Chris put the coffee maker on and told Jewel where to find the mugs.

"Do you always have the pot prepped and ready to go?" asked Jewel.

"Yes," he answered. "You never know around here. Something's always going on, and it's best to have this fella ready at all times. The boys and I can be here anytime day or night, and you don't always have the time to get it ready. Soon as the pot's done, we set it up for the next time. Just like the Boy Scouts." He got the sugar and cream out and placed it on the table. He unwrapped the dinner and saw the pie and had to laugh.

"I can't believe that girl remembered my pie," he said. "Well, she certainly gave me a slice that was meant to be shared." Jewel said she didn't want any, but Chris insisted and got down a small dish and cut the pie in half and put it in front of her. As Jewel warmed her hands around the coffee mug, he asked her if she lived nearby. Jewel told him that she bought the house across the street. "Oh, the old Miller place," he remarked.

"Yes, that's me," she said, "up the country lane and back in the woods."

Chris remarked that Mrs. Miller was a swell lady, and he was sad when she died suddenly like that. Mr. Miller was never the same after that. It didn't surprise anyone when the son put the house up for sale and took his dad up to live with him. Last news we had was that Mr. Miller had Alzheimer's and was in a nursing home. Chris went on to say that when he was young, Mr. Miller raised chickens for the eggs and gave his mom eggs every week, and when his daddy butchered, he always gave the Millers a fair share for payment for the eggs. Jewel remarked that they sounded like a nice couple, and Chris said that they really were.

"How long have you been living there?" asked Chris.

"In August, it will be three years," answered Jewel.

"You always lived in the area?" he asked.

Jewel told him that she grew up here and then went off to college in New York City, worked there for a few years, got tired of the rat race, and thought she needed some time off. He asked what she did, and she told him she was a designer but now she made quilts, and she had to explain that they were not made for beds, that they were for fabric companies to advertise their fabrics with the quilts she designed. He said that sounded interesting and would like to see some of her designs sometime, especially that long-arm machine she mentioned that did the quilting. He said he remembered his gran sewing them by hand.

"Speaking of a long arm, you didn't seem to freak when you saw me with my arm up the cow's butt end," he said. Jewel explained that she lived with her grandfather for a few years and had seen birthing before, even difficult ones, but the vet had been there for those.

"Yeah, it got pretty scary tonight. Few more minutes and it could have ended badly," he replied. Chris got up and put his dishes in the sink and asked Jewel if she would like more coffee, but she told him no that Rocky would be waiting for her. He asked if that was her husband, and Jewel laughed and told him that Rocky was her dog and that he didn't like being left alone too long. Chris got her coat and walked her to her car since he was going to the barn. As she was getting into her car, Chris asked her if she would like to go out tomorrow night, but Jewel replied that she and Rocky had a ritual of sorts. They got a pizza and watched really bad sci-fi movies. She told him how their Saturday nights started, and Chris laughed and said he understood, and maybe some other time. Jewel thanked him for the coffee and pie and said good night.

He watched her turn around and cross the road and wondered how it was that this beautiful thing lived across the road from him for three years and he had never seen her before now. "Boy, Chris," he said to himself, "beautiful thing like that and you missed it. You must be getting old."

Saturday evening, there was a knock on the door, and Rocky was the first to get there, barking a warning. Jewel looked out to see who it was and opened the door.

"Pizza delivery," Chris said as he stood there, balancing the pizza.

"Don't have enough to do. Now you deliver pizza," answered Jewel.

"Can I please come in? This pie is burning my hands," said Chris.

Jewel let him in, and he set the pizza on the kitchen table. He got down to pet Rocky, who already was salivating over the smell of the pizza.

"Now, would you please tell me what you're doing here?" asked Jewel.

"You ordered a pizza, and I thought I would deliver it and hope you would let me stay to watch a bad sci-fi movie," he said. "Nothin's doing over at the barn, and here I am with nothing to do on a Saturday night," he answered.

"That's what you thought, isn't it?" replied Jewel.

"Yes. I stand here humbly begging for a slice of pizza, maybe a beer, and some company to watch a movie with," he answered.

Jewel tried not to laugh, but there he was, one side of his mouth slightly smiling so it showed off the dimple in his cheek, and his blue eyes so full of mischief she had to laugh. "Well, I guess Rocky and I can take pity on you this once and share our pizza. I'm not sure about the movie, though. That depends on how well you behave," she replied.

"Scout's honor, I'll be on my best behavior." Jewel got down some paper plates and took out some beer from the fridge. She got Rocky's plate and cut up a slice of pizza for him, then poured a few tablespoons of beer in a saucer and put them on the floor.

"Now that my best bud is taken care of, here's your plate and your beer. Help yourself," she said.

"Well, I thank you, kind lady. With all the royal treatment, I can see why he doesn't like to be left alone," said Chris.

"When I got here, I wasn't in a good place mentally and emotionally. I didn't have a clue what I was going to do. I only knew I needed time away from the city. And after I bought this house, it was so quiet here, especially after the noise in the city, that I found myself at the shelter, looking for someone to keep me company. I found Rocky, and he has saved me from many a long lonely night. So if he gets the royal treatment, it's because he deserves it," said Jewel.

"I fully understand. I'm all alone in that big house now that my mom and dad have gone to North Carolina to live, and sometimes I think about maybe getting another dog. My girl had to be put down last year after a long fight with cancer. She lived to fourteen, which is a lot for a Lab, but I just don't think I'd ever find another like her, so I haven't looked for one to take her place," he replied.

"I'm sorry. It must be hard to lose a dog that you were so close to. I try not to think of the day I may have to make that decision," said Jewel.

"Can we change the subject? It still hurts talking about it," said Chris. "How about showing me some of those quilts you make?"

"Sure," said Jewel. She put on the lights as she walked to the workroom.

She tried to explain about the design process and the sewing and quilting part. She could see that he was impressed. He remarked that the quilts were like a painting and should be hung on a wall. Jewel told him that wall quilts were becoming very popular and people were doing just that. After the tour, they went into the living room to watch the movie. I was one of Rocky's favorite. For some reason, he liked the old original *Godzilla* movies, and Chris got such a kick out of watching him bark at Godzilla. When the movie was over, Chris left and thanked Jewel for the great evening and hoped he would be welcomed back for another fun Saturday night. Jewel wasn't sure if he was being sarcastic or not but told him he was welcomed any time.

Sunday, the phone rang at seven o'clock. Jewel wondered who could be calling her at this hour. When she answered the phone, it was Chris begging her to come give him a hand. He had all his people coming at ten thirty for breakfast, and he had been up half the night, trying to patch up a dog that had been hit by a car, and he had fallen way behind on his preparations for the breakfast. Jewel agreed to come right over. As soon as she walked in the door, Chris took her coat and told her what he needed done. Set up the dining room, tablecloth on the table, set up the lowboy with the dishes, silverware, and glasses. Fill the pitchers with OJ and milk for the kids, set the mugs near the gigantic coffeepot with the sugar and cream. He had the bacon and sausages in the oven and was whisking batter for the pancakes. Her next task was to crack a dozen eggs, add a little vanilla and cream, and whisk it for the French toast. Chris stood in front of a commercial-type stove, one with six burners and a huge grill. He started making the pancakes and put them in the other oven to keep warm.

His guests began to arrive an hour early, some taking some coffee, others OJ, and then going into the dining room to sit and talk. As they came in, Chris introduced Jewel to his people. Two of the men worked with him with the cattle, and the rest worked in the vet clinic. Chris told her their names, but she knew she would not remember them all. When a sufficient number of pancakes and French toast were done, Jewel carried the platters to the dining room, while Chris brought the meat. Everyone started to eat while Chris went in to make the rest of the food. Jewel tried to speak to some of his guests, Manny and Fred, with their wives, Elaina and Diane. Manny and his wife had two children, a boy and a girl. The only other children there were with their mother who worked in the clinic. Their father was in the service and was stationed abroad. Jewel met Chris's partner in the practice, Chase Cunningham, a friend who had gone to Cornell with him. Everyone made themselves at home; apparently, Chris had been throwing these kinds of breakfasts for some time. It was his way of thanking them for all they did.

Breakfast was over around one, with guests starting to leave at a slow, steady pace. When everyone was gone and the dishes and things were packed into the dishwasher, Chris went to lock both the front door and the side door. Jewel wondered why he did that; she doubted if anyone would be back for more to eat. He asked her if she wanted to eat before or after. Before or after what? she asked him, but before she could say anything else, Chris had her in his arms, kissing her. She was completely surprised by his actions but didn't try to pull away. He kissed her hard, his hands roaming her body. She knew where this was leading. She wanted to say no, but it had been three years since someone held her and kissed her, and it felt good. Chris grabbed her hand and led her upstairs to his bedroom. She didn't complain when he started to unbutton her blouse. *Oh hell*, she thought, *I could use a good screw*. They were both out of their clothes and into the bed in no time. The only words that passed between them was when Jewel asked if he had a condom. He did.

Chris was all over her. His lovemaking was like nothing she'd ever had before. Lawrence was the only man she had ever been with, and there were many times she was left unfulfilled. She knew she wouldn't be with Chris. He knew all the right places to excite her. Making love with Chris was so physical that when it was over, she felt like she had just run a marathon. Chris asked if it was good for her, and she told him that since she hadn't had any in three years, yes, indeed, it was good. Chris was like a machine—fifteen minutes and he was ready to go again. The two of them lay in bed all afternoon, talking for a while and making love again. Finally, Chris jumped up and said he was starving; making love always gave him an appetite. Jewel was relieved. She didn't think she could handle any more sex with Chris. She could feel the soreness from the friction of their bodies rubbing together. Before he changed his mind, Jewel also jumped up and put her clothes on.

They went down to the kitchen, and Chris made some fresh pancakes and bacon while Jewel hit the button on the small coffee maker. They ate, they talked, and they laughed. It was an incredible day for Jewel. Normally a little shy, she couldn't believe that she had just spent the last four hours in bed, making love to a man she barely knew.

Monday morning, Chris knocked on her door. He stood there with a bouquet of flowers and was surprised when the person who opened the door was not Jewel. It was Maria Hoffman, the woman who helped Jewel sew the quilts together. Chris asked for Jewel but was told that she had gone to New York City early this morning to deliver a quilt. Maria could see what Jewel had told them about Chris. God, he was gorgeous. If she weren't a married woman, she might jump his bones. Maria sighed and called Betty. She was the long-arm operator. Maria wanted her to see the hunk Jewel had told them about. Betty sighed too. They told Chris that Jewel would be back Thursday, and felt so bad for him. He seemed like a little boy who lost his favorite toy, and from what Jewel told them about their lovemaking, a *toy* seemed to fit. Chris handed the flowers to Maria, said thanks, and left. Later that afternoon, when Jewel called—she always called every day when she left for New York, to check on things—Maria told her about their visitor. She said that Jewel must have made some impression on him because he even brought her flowers. Jewel was embarrassed, but she had never gotten flowers before and was sorry she missed being there for that.

Thursday morning, Chris appeared again; this time he had a large pot and carried a bag. Maria let him in. He put the pot on the stove and took out a large loaf of Italian bread and a bottle of wine. He said it was his gram's favorite stew. He said his plan was to pick up Jewel at the station and bring her home to a nice, hot dinner. He never questioned if he was doing the right thing; he just knew what he wanted. Maria and Betty were a little astonished about all he had done and didn't know what to say. He asked what time she was coming in, and Betty told him. Chris said he would be back to get Rocky. He wanted to take him along so Jewel could see his happy face. By this time, Maria and Betty felt like they were melting. This guy oozed so much charm all they could do was say yes to whatever he asked. It was no wonder Jewel jumped in the sack with him.

The train was on time, and Jewel got off, looking for Betty, who usually picked her up. She didn't see her and wondered if she had forgotten. Then she spotted Chris with Rocky. Her first thought was that something was wrong with Betty, but by the mischievous gleam in Chris's eyes, she knew that wasn't the case. Rocky pulled against the leash when he saw Jewel, pulling Chris with him. This time, Chris held a bouquet of yellow roses, which was Jewel's favorite. Betty told him that earlier that morning.

"Hi, guys. What are you doing here?" she said.

"Just thought we'd give the other driver the night off," said Chris as he handed her the roses.

"Well, this is a great surprise. Thank you." Jewel took the flowers and held them to her nose. "How did you know these were my favorites?" she asked.

"We have our ways, don't we, Rocky boy?" said Chris. "This way, my lady. Your coach awaits." Of course, the coach was his truck, but you can't have everything.

On the ride home, Chris asked her why she never told him that she was going to New York. Jewel felt a little uncomfortable but said it was a last-minute decision. She didn't know why she was feeling guilty; after all, she had only known him for a few days and didn't feel it necessary to give him an itinerary of her comings and goings. They rode along in silence; Jewel could feel that Chris was feeling hurt. When they arrived at her house, Chris grabbed her bag and followed her in. The girls had done a great job. The table was all set with candles and an empty vase for the flowers. The smell of the stew wafted through the air, as well as the bread in the oven. Betty and Maria warmed everything up and shut the stove so it would be ready for when they came in. Chris thought to himself that he owed the girls big-time.

"Did you do this?" Jewel asked.

"I made the stew and brought the bread and wine, but the girls set everything up," he answered.

"Oh, Chris, this is wonderful! But you didn't have to go through all this trouble," said Jewel.

"I just wanted to say thanks for coming to my rescue Sunday morning. After all, I did wake you at seven," he said.

"More like a quarter of, but this definitely makes up for it," said Jewel.

Chris opened the wine while Jewel put the flowers in the vase. She got out Rocky's food and put it down for him. Chris pulled out her chair, and she sat down. He poured her some wine, took the bread out of the oven, sliced it and put into a breadbasket, and ladled some stew into their dishes, then sat down himself.

"Chris, this is so good. I'm impressed! First, pancakes and French toast, and now this marvelous stew. You're going to make someone a very good wife." She laughed. "Oh, but do you do windows?"

"Yes, I do windows. I know how to wash clothes, and I even iron," he said, "and I have even picked up a dustcloth or two."

"Well, now I really am impressed," said Jewel.

"You can thank my gram. She was always teaching me something, telling me that someday I might find myself alone and I had better know how to sew a button on, and she was right. After Gram passed, and now with Mom and Dad in North Carolina, I have had to do it all, so it's a good thing she taught me. This is her stew," he said.

"Well, thank you, Gram. It really is good."

After eating, Chris helped her with the dishes and they took their wine and went into the living room. Chris asked about her trip and where she stayed when she was there. Jewel told him she always stayed with the man Kenneth Dolan and his wife and kids. Kenneth was whom she worked for when she got out of college and whom she worked for the last few years before she came up here. They were such a wonderful family, and she just loved the boys, Michael and Jonathon. They talked for another hour, until Jewel told him they should call it a night, that she had to be up early and she still needed to take a shower. Chris offered to wash her back, but she told him "Another time" and thanked him again for dinner.

Chris grabbed her and kissed her and said that she really didn't mean that he had to leave. Jewel felt herself giving in but suddenly found the strength to tell him that she did mean for him to leave. Chris looked surprised. Jewel concluded that Chris had never had women say no to him before, but she stuck with it and went to open the door for him to leave. He kissed her good night and tried to nibble her ear in an attempt for her to change her mind. But she didn't.

Chris called her when he got home and asked if she changed her mind. When she said no again, he asked if she would like to take a ride with him on Saturday; he had to deliver a bull calf to a man in Vermont. He promised they would be back in plenty of time for her night with Rocky. She gave it some thought and decided it might be fun to ride to Vermont. If she stayed home, she would only find more work to do. So she told him yes. He asked if she could walk or drive over because he would have the trailer on and it would be too difficult to turn around at her house. She asked the time and said she'd be there.

The day turned out to be more fun than she thought. When Chris talked about his breeding program, he was very much the professional. His goal was to produce a bull calf that had extreme endurance, well-built body, but not too heavy, and a more gentle nature than most. He started the project when he was in high school, when he convinced his father to stop being a dairy farmer and turn instead to raising cattle for meat. A good bull could mean the difference between quality cattle and inferior ones. So far, he was happy with the results he'd achieved, and the farmers that purchased his bulls were very happy with them.

They dropped off the bull and drove to a small restaurant for lunch. On the way back, he started asking her questions about her life in the county before she went to college. Most of the things she told him were pretty general, except about the time she lived with her grandfather. That was the happiest time of her childhood. She would never tell him about the abuse she suffered as a child. She knew she would never love or trust anyone enough to tell them all that she had been through.

The drive back seemed to go quickly, and before she knew it, they were back at the farmhouse. Chris asked if she would like a cup of coffee, and they went inside. Jewel drank her coffee and said she needed to go home to take a shower. Chris said they had a shower upstairs and they could both take one. Jewel became annoyed and felt she had to get something off her chest.

"Is sex all you can think about?" she said.

"Wow, where did that come from?" he replied.

"I don't know, but it seems anytime we have a few minutes, you want to jump in the sack. There are other things, you know," she answered.

"I know. Didn't we have some pleasant conversation on the drive up and back? Did I bring up sex even once? No, I didn't. It's just that I work hard so much of the day, either in the clinic or with the cattle. I have people that work for me, that depend on me for their livelihood, and that can cause quite a bit of stress. So when I have free time that's all mine, I like to have fun, I like to laugh, I like to be with a beautiful woman, and I like to have sex. Is that so wrong? I don't do married women or women I know that have boyfriends. I always practice safe sex and try to make it as pleasurable for them as for myself. If you think I'm only seeing you because of the sex, then maybe we need to take a step back," he said.

Jewel was surprised. She thought about what he said and realized he was right.

"I'm sorry. You're absolutely right. I have my own business where people depend on me, and I know how stressful it can be, but my answer up until now is to just find more work for myself instead of having some fun. I can't remember the last time I laughed and made love, and I don't regret it one bit. I need to take a look at myself and ask the question, Am I having fun? I haven't been until I met you, so what are we waiting for? I hear a shower calling our name."

Chris cocked his head and smiled slightly, just enough to make that dimple appear. He was so handsome, so spontaneous and unpredictable, and just what Jewel needed for a while. She knew a relationship with him would never last because emotionally he was stuck around the age of eighteen, but for now, what the hell?

Making love with Chris always left her exhausted and sweaty so that she needed another shower. By the time they were dressed, it was almost seven o'clock. Chris told her to go home and he would run down and get the pizza, unless she had enough of him for one day. She smacked him on the head and laughingly told him she could take more than he could and went running out the door.

The rest of the summer was spent in much the same way: They took trips together, sometimes bringing Rocky with them. She asked him to go with her to the cape for a long weekend. She told him she always went the week after the holiday, when most of the people were gone and it was quiet. She told him she had asked the woman who operated the small bed-and-breakfast that she always stayed in if she would mind if she brought him. Since her place would be empty except for them, she didn't mind. Chris got a vet to cover his days so his partner wouldn't have to work four days straight. They spent the time walking the beaches and talking. Jewel always looked for sea glass to collect, and Rocky liked to chase the birds. Dinners were quiet and peaceful, and the two liked to spend time lying in the hammock that was strung up on the back porch. They tried to keep their lovemaking as quiet as they could, but sometimes they knew they were a little loud, especially when they received smiles from the owner while she prepared their breakfast. Soon it would be over and they would be back home.

Chris was so excited when he told Jewel that his mom and dad were coming up for the holidays. They planned to be there two weeks before Thanksgiving. All Chris could talk about was his mom's cooking. No one was as good as Gram, but Mom came close, he would say a million times over, and he couldn't wait until they met her. Jewel and the girls were talking one morning before they began sewing for the day, and Betty said that it sounded to her that Chris was pretty serious about their relationship. Maria had to agree, and they were right.

November 1, Chris took Jewel out to dinner, and after coffee and desert, he pulled out a small box containing the ring he proposed to her with. Jewel wasn't totally surprised but thought she had more time to decide on what to do. She spoke to Betty and Maria about it, and their suggestion was to accept the ring, enjoy a great holiday, and after Chris's parents went back to North Carolina, tell Chris that she thought it over and she just wasn't ready for marriage. It sounded like the best way out; Chris would get to enjoy his family, and once the holidays were past, she would give him back the ring. That was the plan. So when Chris proposed, she accepted. Chris was elated and couldn't wait to tell the world. Being the character he was, he stood up at their table and, in an extremely loud voice, proclaimed to all the people in the restaurant that she had accepted and they were engaged. The people clapped as Jewel's face turned a million shades of red. The night ended in the usual way, making love.

Chris's parents, Martin and Lorraine, arrived, and Jewel took to them immediately as they did to her. Chris's mother was originally from North Carolina, so she still had a little Southern accent. Chris's father was a big man, taller than Chris—and Chris was six foot. But his dad was laid-back and enjoyed peace and quiet. Jewel wondered how their marriage lasted so long, because his wife always found something to talk about. When she and Chris got together, it was a nonstop conversation. Jewel and Marty, as he insisted she call him, could never get a word in edgewise if they wanted to, but that was fine with them. They would put on a heavy coat and hat and sit in a rocker on the front porch, rock for a while, saying nothing, and when it finally got too cold for him, Marty would say to her, "How about we get us some coffee?" Jewel just shook her head, and the two of them would go into the kitchen, pour themselves some coffee, sit at the kitchen table, and listen to the conversation between Chris and his mom, the conversation that they started long before Jewel and Marty had gone outside.

The Tuesday before Thanksgiving, Chris said he had to deliver a bull on Saturday but he decided to do it today so he would have a nice long weekend. He asked his father to go with him, but his mom said he couldn't because she didn't drive and he had to drive her to the stores to get what she needed to cook their Thanksgiving dinner. His dad told him to wait until Saturday and he would love to take a ride, but Chris didn't want to wait. He asked Jewel next, but she had already told him that she needed to get the quilt they were working on finished and in the mail Wednesday morning. Chris walked off a little angry, but there was nothing she could do; the quilt had to go out. Manny was home sick with the flu he probably picked up from his kids, who were also sick, and Fred had to take his wife to visit her dad, who just had a stroke that morning. No one was available to go with him, but being as stubborn as he was, he decided to go by himself. His mom and dad tried to talk him out of it because the weather forecast was not all that good, but they couldn't change his mind. So about eleven o'clock, Chris took off, trailer in tow, and said he should be back around six, in time for dinner.

Six o'clock came and went, and still no Chris. They waited until six thirty, when Marty finally said he was hungry and that they should have dinner and Chris could eat whenever he got home. By eight o'clock, they were all worried. Chris wasn't home yet, and the weather report said a severe storm was moving through. First, there was sleet, then it turned to snow. Lorraine was beside herself, wringing her hands and pacing about, until Marty told her to light somewhere, that she was making him crazy. By ten, Marty started pacing. They were all silent, each one afraid to say what they were both thinking.

At eleven o'clock, the doorbell rang. They all looked at each other, hoping they were wrong in what they were thinking. But they weren't. A state trooper asked if they were Chris Weller's family. When Marty said they were, the trooper told them that Chris was involved in a traffic accident and he was taken to the Albany Medical Hospital. He didn't know his condition, but he was alive and talking. As far as they could tell, the trailer he was towing slid and turned over, pulling the truck over with it. He advised them not to attempt to go to the hospital now; all roads were closed because of the heavy snow. They would just have to wait until the storm passed and the plows could clear the roads.

The storm stalled right over them, and they weren't able to go to the hospital until Thursday, Thanksgiving Day. The roads still were not completely cleared, but with the four-wheel-drive vehicle Marty had, they were able to get through. Parking at the hospital was another story, but they finally found a spot and rushed in to find out where Chris was. They were told that he was in intensive care. Now their minds were spinning out of control. Just how bad was he?

They finally reached Chris, and luckily, the doctor that was attending to Chris was still in the unit. He was paged and came to see them. He told them that Chris had suffered only minor injuries to his body but he had sustained a concussion and was in a coma. The doctor explained that all the tests, CT scan, MRI, and x-rays were all normal and they didn't know why he was in a coma. Lorraine, never at a loss for words, yelled out loud that they better damn well find out why he was in the coma. Marty tried to calm his wife down, but she was having none of it. She barked at any nurse or doctor who came near Chris's room. They stayed all day, with Lorraine holding her son's hand and talking to him. By six o'clock, Marty said they should get started home. No telling how the roads would be. Lorraine refused, but Marty grabbed her by the arm and marched her out of the room and into the elevator and didn't let go until she was in the car. The ride home was treacherous. Most of the roads were just solid ice. Lorraine started to cry, and Marty, who was trying so hard to keep the car on the road, yelled at her to shut the hell up. Jewel stayed and had a sandwich with them and left.

Rocky greeted her at the door. She had installed a doggie door for him last summer and knew he could get out if he needed to, but the snow made it impossible for him to open the door, so Jewel got a shovel and cleared him a path. She fed him, then took a shower and got ready for bed. She was exhausted and didn't know what tomorrow would be like.

Tomorrow was like the next day and the next day and the next. There was no change in Chris's condition. The doctors were all in agreement; all tests were normal, yet Chris remained in a coma. They began to take turns going up to the hospital. Jewel still had quilts that needed to get done, so Marty and Lorraine went up during the day and Jewel would go up around four and stay until ten, still having another hour to drive home. This schedule seemed to go on forever, until two days before Christmas, when the hospital called and said Chris had died. Their reaction was one of disbelief. No one spoke a word on the drive to the hospital. Because they knew the family was on their way, they left Chris in his bed but closed the curtains around him. Lorraine had already started to cry the minute they got off the elevator. After seeing his son, Marty broke down, leaving Jewel the only one standing in the room that hadn't shed a tear. The drive home was once again in silence, interrupted only by Lorraine's sobs. Once in the house, Jewel made coffee and gave each of them a cup. Jewel remembered the first time Chris made her coffee, and she had to turn away. She walked to the sink and could feel herself falling apart. Part of it was grief, and part of it was guilt. Marty saw Jewel walk away and followed her. When she felt his arm around her, she turned and cried into his chest. He held her and told her to let it all out; that was all they could do now.

They buried Chris two days after Christmas, and that was when Jewel decided that as soon as the last quilt was finished, she needed to get away; back to the city for a while was her only option.

CHAPTER 3

Jewel awoke with tears in her eyes and tried hard to erase the past year and go back to sleep. Celia was still going on about the dinner when Jewel finally got up and went into the kitchen. She said good morning, poured herself some coffee, and joined Kenneth in the inside-out room. "Has she said anything?" whispered Jewel to Kenneth.

"She has been talking since she got in just after twelve, but nothing about you meeting Angelis. I guess he had the good sense not to mention it."

Celia took a step in the room and asked Jewel if she wanted eggs or pancakes.

"Nothing for me, thanks. I think I'll just have a roll," replied Jewel.

"You sure? I'm making eggs for Kenneth, so it's no trouble to make one more," said Celia.

"No, really, Celia, a roll is just fine," Jewel answered.

"All right," said Celia. "I swear a bird eats more than you."

"I ate a lot last night. The chicken was really good. I even had some cake, and that was a wonderful surprise, especially for the boys."

"You didn't let them eat too much cake, did you, Kenneth?"

"Yes, they ate the whole thing," said Kenneth, picking his head up from the paper.

"Kenneth, you didn't!" cried Celia.

"Of course not," replied Kenneth. "I don't think I could take them all day having a sugar high."

Celia brought Kenneth his eggs and sat down with a cup of coffee.

"So how was the dinner?" said Jewel reluctantly.

"Oh, it was grand!" replied an obviously very happy Celia. "But there is one thing I need to clarify," she went on. "Which one of you said something to Justin about taking me to the dinner?"

Surprised, Jewel and Kenneth looked at each other, both of them trying very hard to look innocent, praying Celia didn't press the issue. When after a few seconds it looked like she wasn't going to let it go, Jewel spoke up.

"I guess I have to own up," said Jewel. "Kenneth didn't know anything about it. I asked Justin."

"Justin—you call him Justin," snapped Celia.

"That's what he told me to call him," answered Jewel, surprised at the ferocity in Celia's tone.

"Fine, and just when did you ask him to drag me along?" asked Celia.

"I didn't ask him to drag you along. He said you did a very nice thing hosting the cocktail party for him, and I just said I thought it would be wonderful if you could have gone to the dinner. That's all I said. He just took it from there. Look, you're the one who told me to make sure he was taken care of. The man hates liquor, so I took him to the kitchen and got him a beer. That's what he likes to drink."

"You took him in the kitchen to drink beer!"

Jumping to Jewel's aid, Kenneth asked if Celia thought Justin seemed angry or upset when they left for the dinner.

"No," replied Celia. "He was cheerful. He actually seemed genuinely happy. In all these months of working with him, I've never seen him like that."

"Well, doesn't that tell you something right there?" said Kenneth. "If the man were angry, wouldn't you have heard about it? You yourself said he never held back when he was in a bad mood," continued Kenneth.

"Yes, he's notorious for yelling at the top of his lungs if the slightest thing isn't right, and get this, he actually commented on my attire and, mind you, told me that he had a most enjoyable evening. Can you believe that?" said Celia. "But, Jewel, did you have to take him into the kitchen? God, it must have been a mess in there,"

"Actually, it wasn't that bad in there, and besides, we went into the inside-out room to drink our beers."

"You drank a beer with him? God, this just gets better and better." Celia got up and poured herself another cup of coffee and plopped herself into her chair, shaking her head. "I can't believe you drank a beer with him," said Celia, still visibly shaken.

"What did you want me to do? He was really miserable out there with all the old cronies, and the man wanted a beer. Did you want me to just leave him out there alone or stay, have a beer with him, and make him feel relatively at ease? The whole purpose of the shindig was to keep this guy happy, and guess what? He was."

Celia could see that Jewel was getting annoyed, and quickly said to her, "I'm sorry, you're quite right. I asked a lot of you, and you did an admirable job. I have to say that everyone seemed to be in a festive mood. Why, even Mr. Wilson told me what a lovely conversation he had with you, and asked if we were sisters. He had forgotten that you told him you worked for Kenneth. He said he told you all about Marjorie and how he misses her. He usually doesn't talk much. I'm surprised he told you so much about her. Well, again, I'm sorry. I guess, under the circumstances, you did the right thing. I'm just glad the place was clean. It was clean, wasn't it?"

"Yes, Celia, it was clean," answered Jewel.

"If you don't mind my asking, what did the two of you find to talk about?"

"Ah, let's see. I asked him about his name."

"You did what?" Celia was out of her chair, standing over Jewel, scowling. This time, it was Kenneth's turn to say something.

"Celia, sit down and give Jewel a chance to tell you what was said. You asked the question, now give her a chance to answer before you jump down her throat again. And stop being so damn dramatic."

"I'm sorry, I'm a little tired. I didn't get much sleep," said Celia apologetically. "We're all tired," said Kenneth.

Celia sat down again and motioned for Jewel to continue.

"He was very easy to talk to, Celia. He told me about his grandfather coming over from Italy and about how he changed his name."

"Changed his name? Changed it from what?" asked Celia excitedly.

"His grandfather's name was originally Vincenzo Angelisaro, and since he was told it sounded too ethnic, he changed it to Vincent Angelis. When Justin came along, his father wanted him to have an American-sounding name and chose Justin. He told me about his home in Connecticut. We talked about what did for Kenneth, and that's about it. One of the catering people told us that people were leaving, so we came in, and the rest, as they say, is history." Having said all that, Jewel got up and said, if there was nothing else, that she was leaving. She was meeting Shelby to look at some apartments. She looked at Kenneth, but he had his face buried in the paper again. She looked at Celia, but she said nothing.

"We may have dinner out, but I won't be late. What time is your luncheon tomorrow?" She was trying to change the subject and get out without being grilled any further.

Kenneth picked up his head and said it was not until one thirty. Kenneth was meeting with a new fabric company from France. Celia was going along, not just because she was Kenneth's wife, but because she spoke fluent French. The representatives from the company surely spoke English, but having Celia there in case they didn't speak very well was definitely a plus.

Jewel quickly caught a cab and went down to the apartment. She took a shower and changed her clothes, opting for dress slacks, sweater, and comfortable flat shoes. Jewel was always more practical than trendy when it came to her clothes. If you know you are going to be on your feet for the next few hours, walking around a museum, why would you choose to wear high heels and not a more fitting shoe? That kind of stupid reasoning was unfortunately what many women would wear all in the name of dressing fashionably, especially when you go to meet a man. That kind of lopsided reasoning was totally lost on Jewel. She grabbed a light coat. When the sun went down in the city, it could get rather chilly, so it was always best to be ready for it and not have to stand around with your teeth chattering.

Jewel was just about to lock the door but took a glance up toward the corner. That person was there again, blue hooded, zip-up sweatshirt. He always had the hood up, so Jewel could never see his face. He was looking in another direction, and Jewel hoped she could get the door locked and get her cab. She got into the habit of calling on the phone for one after she told Kenneth about the man. He suggested she do it just in case the man was some crazy lunatic. There were so many homeless people in the city, but they were more of a nuisance than dangerous. Her cab drew up, and Jewel quickly hopped in just as the man saw her and started to walk in her direction. She told the driver where she wanted to go. She turned around to look out the back window, and she could see him pulling on the door handle of the building with one hand and shaking his other in the air. Jewel began to tremble. Who was this man, and what did he want from her? He was taunting her, but why? She tried very hard to settle down and put the obvious nutcase out of her mind, but if he continued to harass her, she was definitely going to the police to report him.

Jewel arrived at the Metropolitan Museum of Art at a quarter to three. She positioned herself on the top landing so she had a clear view. He didn't call her to cancel, which she clearly expected him to do. Why would a well-educated man need someone to walk him around the museum, explaining art to him? Jewel said to herself. Jewel was beautiful, tall, and slender. Her hair, while cut short, was the color of brilliant copper and a mass of curls. Her eyes were not really blue or green, but a color somewhere in between. Some days they appeared bluer, and on others, more green. While her beauty was obvious to others, it was not to Jewel. She was always surprised when some man she just met showed interest in her or asked her out. Her best friend, Shelby, had a habit of poking her in the ribs whenever they saw a man walking their way. Shelby would kid her and say, "Oh no, another poor creature is about to fall hopelessly in love, mesmerized by her beauty and charm." Jewel begged her to stop, but Shelby always had to end it by feigning a swoon. Jewel was one of those rare people who never dismissed a person because of their looks but rather waited until she could determine whether the person was honest and truthful. She always believed this was a better way to judge a person rather than by their looks alone. Of course, she bore the brunt of many jokes by her friends, but she usually remained true to the things she felt were important to her.

Jewel saw him walking up the street toward the museum. She thought it odd that he was wearing a three-piece suit, seemed rather formal for a walk around a museum, but maybe this was one of the eccentricities Celia had spoken about. His stride was slow, but confident, his dark hair slightly windblown. She remembered his eyes were brown. Justin was what you would call ruggedly handsome, not handsome like Robert Redford or Paul Newman, more like a Gregory Peck or Gary Cooper, but there was something else. Something intangible. He had a sort of presence. It was something that caused you to look at him as he passed, and when you were close to him, you had the feeling of being with someone of great importance. He immediately made eye contact and kept his eyes on you, making you feel like you were very special to him. Celia mentioned that fact many times in their conversations about him. She said it was as though he made you feel like you were the only person in the room when he spoke to you. Many people described a meeting with him as being very intense and that once he singled in on you, you were trapped like a rabbit by an eagle. Jewel remembered feeling just the opposite; she felt as though this person really was giving her all his attention, and she felt relaxed and safe with him. She didn't tell Celia how she felt with him, though. Celia would have laughed and said, "He eats mere mortals like you and me for breakfast. I've never felt relaxed with him, and I've been working with him over six months." Jewel never took Celia's word about anyone; rather, she preferred to find out a person's character on her own. Celia could easily dismiss someone if their hair color was not to her liking. She was not liked by many of the employees that worked for Kenneth. They thought her to be standoffish and somewhat of a snob. Jewel had gotten used to Celia's ways, and the more she got to know her, the more she realized Celia was insecure. If things were not directly under her control, she would go off in a tizzy. Letting Celia think she was running the whole show was the way she and Kenneth managed to stay sane.

Justin was making his way up the stairs and directly toward her.

"Hi," she said, trying not to act nervous. "I see you made it. I thought you might have given it second thoughts."

"What made you think I would have reconsidered?" he replied.

"To be perfectly honest, I'm not sure just what you expect out of this mini tour. You're a lawyer, educated both here and abroad, come from an affluent family, and I find it difficult to understand just what you think you may learn from me. I'm sure, at some point in time, you must have had a class studying art, especially the great masters. It wouldn't even surprise me if there wasn't some well-known artist's work hanging in your family home."

"Well, blunt and to the point. I like it. Most people would have skirted around the issue or would never have brought it up. But I see you are definitely not most people," replied Justin, still looking a bit surprised.

"I'm just wondering why you chose to join me this afternoon," answered Jewel.

"I can assure you, my intentions are honorable." Justin laughed. "I had such a relaxing conversation with you last evening, albeit for a few moments, that I needed to see if I would feel that way again. I know how this may sound, but you see, I'm not very relaxed and comfortable with people, and to find someone who can make me feel so as ease and can get me to speak about anything except the law is both surprising and unexpected. Maybe I shouldn't tell you this, but I watched you last night at Celia's party. Actually, it was hard not to. You went about the room as if you owned it, not at all impressed by the fact that the people in the room were probably some of the best lawyers in the country and that their wives were always the highlight of the society pages. You spoke to them as if they were family and had known them for a long time, and you were able to get Mr. Wilson to speak about his wife when he hasn't done so since she died."

"Were you following me?" interrupted Jewel.

"No. It may seem like it, but I just happened to be somewhat near you when you were speaking to Wilson. The rest, I observed from my resting post, the doorjamb."

"I'm sorry, I didn't mean to jump down your throat. It is just a little unsettling to find out you're being watched," said Jewel.

"Now, I'm sorry," replied Justin.

"No, it's just me. I've been more jumpy than usual. I think I have a stalker. Someone has been following me or watching me when

I go out or come home, and it's making me a little unnerved. I apologize for raising my voice," said Jewel.

"You didn't, but now I'm unnerved. Have you spoken to the authorities about this?" asked Justin.

"No. I'm not sure if it's true or not. I could be imagining the whole thing. It's probably just a homeless person trying to get some money from me. It's just that the part of town where Kenneth's apartment is so dark and deserted it could put a scare into anyone, I guess. So let's forget it and everything else and have a wonderful time looking at the world's greatest art treasures," said Jewel.

"Very good," said Justin. "For the next few hours, let us gaze upon timeless treasures and bathe in their glorious beauty."

So for the next few hours, Justin and Jewel quietly looked at some of the pictures in the exhibit. Jewel knew they would not have time to see the entire exhibit, so she directed him toward the section that included the impressionist and postimpressionist painters. These painters were Jewel's favorites. Monet, Renoir, Degas, and Cézanne were some from the impressionist period. This style of painting is characterized by the use of unmixed primary colors and small strokes to simulate actual reflected light. The postimpressionist period came after the impressionist, and these painters aspired to find more depth in the roles of color and form and to portray emotion and intellect in addition to imagery. The greatest of these were Seurat, Gauguin, van Gogh, and Toulouse-Lautrec. Van Gogh's *Starry Night* and *Sunflowers* were Jewels favorites, and she couldn't help giving Justin a brief summary about each one as they gazed upon them. Justin had asked her to describe what she saw in some of the paintings, while he barely said anything at all. Later, when they left the floor where the exhibit was held and headed outside, Jewel asked Justin why he asked her to describe what she saw, while he offered no comment of his own.

"When I see a picture, even those as famous as the ones we were just viewing, I see a picture, some I understand and some I don't, and that's it. You look at the same painting and see a hundred different colors, colors that flow from one to the other, highlights and shadows, the brushstrokes. You feel the emotion the painter must have had while painting. You bring the paintings to life. I must admit having seen many of these before. I've been to the Museum of London and the Louvre in France, and I never got excited viewing them. You made me see all that I have been missing in these masterpieces. Somehow I knew it would be like this, and I want to thank you for allowing me to accompany you this afternoon."

"You have nothing to thank me for. Actually, I should thank you for listening to me ramble. My girlfriend Shelby usually leaves me after the fifth or sixth painting. She says I give her a headache when I get so caught up and there's no way to silence me."

"You didn't ramble, as you called it, all the time. There seemed to be many moments when you were quiet, when you seemed preoccupied, and sad even," said Justin. By now they had made their way outside and were standing near the place they met two hours before.

"I mentioned to you before that in my profession, I am rather good at reading people, and I think there is something weighing heavily on your mind," continued Justin.

"I'm so sorry, I didn't mean to make you feel neglected. If I did, I apologize," said Jewel.

"No, you didn't, but there is obviously something troubling you. I realize we barely know each other, but if you would like to unburden yourself, I am a great listener and perhaps can offer an unbiased solution. Have you spoken to a friend? Maybe they can help."

"No, my friends have been through enough with me, and right now I really don't need more unsolicited advice. They all mean well, but..." Jewel paused and stopped.

"I think I understand. Sometimes you just need someone to listen, and that can be difficult for some people, especially when it comes to someone they care about. Offering them advice may seem like the thing to do, but it is difficult to remain unbiased when a friend is obviously suffering," said Justin.

"I'm so sorry. These last few years are like nightmares I keep dreaming over and over. Lawrence, Chris's death, Celia's constant nagging to put everything behind me and get on with my life. I can't put it all behind me, not while there are unresolved issues."

She could feel her body start to tremble. She couldn't stop the tears that began to run down her cheeks. She tried to turn away so he wouldn't see them, but he turned her face toward him, took out a handkerchief, and gently wiped the tears away. More quickly followed, and he just continued to wipe them away.

After a few moments passed and Jewel looked like she was calming down, Justin gave her a big smile and said, "You know what we need, don't you?"

Jewel forced herself to look up at him. She wished she could bury her face against his massive chest and cry for the next hundred years. She pulled herself together and smiled back at him.

"And what do we need?" asked Jewel, her eyes still wet with tears.

"Soup."

"Soup? You think we need soup?" exclaimed Jewel.

"Most definitely. My mother always said there wasn't any problem that couldn't be solved over a nice bowl of soup."

Jewel started to laugh.

"Don't laugh," answered Justin. "I have it on the best authority that this is the cure for all things."

"I can't believe you just said that. My grandfather used to say the exact thing," said Jewel. "Soup calms you and clears the head so you can think through your problems. I've had soup in one form or another my entire life. So yes, I think you're right. I need soup, a very, very big bowl of soup, and if it doesn't clear my head, then maybe I can just drown in it."

"There will be no drowning on my watch," said Justin. "Come on, I know just the place, the best soup in the city. It's just a few blocks from here. Would you like to walk, or shall I hail us a cab?"

"Oh, walk, please," answered Jewel. The air was crisp, and there was a soft breeze that felt good on her face.

Jewel's mind was racing. *What am I doing?* she thought to herself. *I'm about to tell a perfect stranger things I couldn't talk to Shelby or Kenneth and Celia about, but somewhere inside a voice is telling me to trust this man.* She found throughout her life that the little voice inside her was usually right, and the times she chose to ignore it were the times she had made her worst mistakes. Trust this man, the voice said.

They made their way down several blocks and crossed Fifth Avenue. Justin turned left and, a few doors down, stopped in front of a small restaurant called Josephina's. He held the door open for her, and as he walked through, a waiter crossed the room toward them.

"Oh, Mr. Justin, how good to see you. You would like a table, yes?"

"Good evening, Dante," said Justin. "No, I'm sorry, we can't stay. We just stopped by to pick up some soup. What has Josephina made today?" Everything in Josephina's was made fresh daily, and she especially prided herself on her soup. Before Justin had started eating there regularly, he always watched people coming out of the small restaurant carrying varying sizes of containers. He later found out that people would make special trips to get her soup.

"Today," the waiter said, "Mama has your favorite, minestrone, and the other one is the wedding soup."

"Does she make it with spinach, acini di pepe, and tiny meatballs?" Jewel asked quickly.

"You've heard of it?" asked Justin.

"If she makes it with those ingredients, I have. My grandfather always made it for me. It was one of my favorites," answered Jewel.

"Yes, yes, Mama makes it justa like this," said Dante.

"All right, then, we will take a quart of each to go, please," said Justin.

Dante turned and went into the kitchen. The kitchen door opened, and a man appeared and came straight to them.

"Justin, my friend, good to see you. Dante tells me you not stay for dinner. Please stay. You worka too hard, I tell you this all the time, eh, and such a beauty you bring to me," he said as he turned to Jewel and took her hand.

"Jewel, this is Guido. He and Josephina own this restaurant," said Justin. "Jewel, what a beautiful name! Such a beautiful name for so beautiful a woman. You stay, have a nice dinner, some wine, a little espresso maybe."

"I'm sorry, Guido, but not this time. Unfortunately, we have some unfinished work," replied Justin.

"Work, work, work, so much work. Sometime you need to sit down, relax, have a little vino or coffee. All this work make you in the grave before you time."

Jewel spoke softly to Guido. "We do have some work to do, but I promise, I'll be back, and it would give me great pleasure to stay and have dinner and a glass of wine with you and Josephina. I'll bet she makes some great desserts, maybe some tiramisu."

"Mama makes the best in town. You gonna love it!" Guido made a gesture, bringing his fingers to his lips and making a loud smacking sound. They all laughed.

Dante returned with the soup, and Justin told him to put it on his account.

"No, no, no," said Guido to Justin. "This is ona da house. Justa promise me you bringa this lovely thing back with you."

"Guido, you're too kind, my friend, and I will certainly try. Thank you."

"Yes, thank you," said Jewel to Guido.

"I think you made another conquest," said Justin teasingly as they walked out of the restaurant. Jewel could feel herself blushing. Out on the street they continued down Fifth Avenue. Reaching the corner, they turned left again and continued on until they reached an apartment house.

"Well, this is where I live," said Justin.

"Oh." Jewel looked at the building in front of her.

"You didn't think we would have the soup in the street, did you?" asked Justin.

"I'm afraid I wasn't really thinking that far ahead," she replied.

"I promise to be on my best behavior." Justin laughed as he climbed the steps. He pushed the elevator button for 3. A few people were also waiting for the elevator. Everyone said hello to Justin, and he replied to each one. They exited the elevator, and Justin opened the door to the apartment.

"This is very handsome," said Jewel. "It really reflects the person that lives here, simply done but stylish."

"Please make yourself comfortable. Look around if you like. Just let me put this soup down and I'll give you the grand tour, so to speak." Justin put the soup on the counter and removed his coat, asking Jewel for hers. He hung them in a small closet near the door.

"Who did your decorating? They are very good. The room has a wonderfully warm yet slightly masculine feel to it," said Jewel.

"I have some friends that own a small gallery in SoHo. Margret is also a decorator. It took her a while, but she finally got it. Then of course Mother came along and added what she thought was missing. Nothing was really missing, but I guess she needed to contribute something to her son's domicile. I think all mothers have that need to stamp everything with their own bit of style. I'm sure they think we are not capable of doing things ourselves. No matter how old I get, Mother still always finds a way to make me feel six years old again. She comes into the city once or twice a month to attend a show with friends or shop, and she stays here when she is in town. I've relinquished the master bedroom to her because it has its own bath. Mother can soak in the tub for hours. She calls it luxury time, and the older you get, the more you feel the need for more."

"The room is lovely. Obviously, she has added much more. This room has a very feminine touch to it. I love the color," said Jewel.

"Yes. At that time, Margret assumed this would be my suite. We had a difference of opinion about her color choice, however. I thought the color to be too feminine, but when she was finished, it was quite attractive, so when it became Mother's room, very little had to be changed. Mother put up new draperies and bed coverings, and I think she changed the lamps, a few vases of flowers, and it was done."

"It really is quite lovely," replied Jewel.

"The best part is out here," said Justin as he led her out the rear door. "Mother can make a garden wherever she goes."

"Oh, this is wonderful! I can't believe it. It's wonderful. What a treat for bleary city eyes! All the greenery, she did a fantastic job on this. Table and chairs, chaise lounge—oh, look, an herb garden! Does she cook when she's here?"

"Hardly," replied Justin. "She likes to give the impression that she does, but we usually dine out. She doesn't cook home either. We have a woman who has been with us for over thirty years, and she does most of the cooking and some light housework. For the heavier work, Mother has a team come in so they can be finished in a day. Mother entertains quite frequently. The Orchid Club is her main focus right now, but she still has her hand in other things and stays extremely busy."

"Thank you for the tour. I love the rooftop garden," Jewel said as she followed Justin back inside.

"Well, let us see if our soup is still hot, or we shall have to heat it. There are two things I insist on having piping hot, my coffee and my soup." Justin retrieved the containers from the bag and opened them. "Warm, but not hot, so I shall nuke mine. How do you like yours?" he said to Jewel as he took some soup bowls from a cabinet.

"It seems that I enjoy the same two things the same way you do. Coffee and soup must be hot. So you can nuke mine also."

The soup was every bit as good as Justin said it would be. Jewel made Justin try some of her "wedding" soup. He said it was very good indeed but his favorite was still the minestrone. Jewel started to pick up the dishes, but Justin took her hands in his. "The dishes can wait. Are you feeling a little better?"

"Yes, thank you, and thank you for all your kindness. Celia was totally wrong about you, or was she right and the man she works with is not the same man here with me now?"

"And the lady is perceptive too! We are here to talk about you, but just a brief explanation and you will understand all. I needed to create that other Justin because, as you have guessed, this one is rather shy and not very good in confrontational settings, and any lawyer worth his salt must, on occasion, be rather ruthless. I created my alter ego after working for three years in a small but very well-known firm. I was doing fine work and making them a fair share of money but was not being recognized for it. I put the word out that I was looking to work for a much larger firm. My work record was unsurpassed for creating and finalizing contracts with clients and, of course, bringing in more money for the firm, which is how one is rated in these times, unfortunately. I was approached by Deacon, Halron, and Deacon and knew they were not only a much larger law firm but they had a large, broad-based clientele as well, mostly Fortune 500 companies. I knew I would have to be pretty sharp to land a position with them, and I also knew I had never worked personally with anyone from the firm, which gave me a distinct advantage. The senior partner I had been working with for the past few years was the one who actually created the character of Justin Angelis, Esq. He knew the work I had been doing and told me that

I would be much more effective if I could just be a character people would remember. He said to stomp my foot occasionally or throw something now and then, yell at a typist for a typing error, anything to get noticed. He didn't want me to be cruel or obnoxious, but be different. I took his words to heart and knew he was right. New firm, richer clients, I would have to be different. And so I gave birth to another Justin Angelis. Eccentric, vociferous, more intense. Even my physical appearance needed to be changed for this character to work convincingly. A rumpled shirt, tie askew, hair standing on end—it was all in the plan to make me be someone everyone remembered. And it worked. Sometimes, I think, a little too well. People have a way of trying to avoid annoying people, so I had very few real friendships in the office. I did, however, bring another partner into my confidence just so I could take a break from the pompous ass I was forced to play. We had many a good laugh over some of the stunts I pulled, but he knew the character worked, so he told no one. And if I may ask, how and when did you figure it out?" he asked.

"Friday evening," she said. "A man who was having a special dinner given in his honor, accolades for a job well done by his peers, that kind of man would certainly want to be up and front and enjoy all the pomp and circumstance, but the man who spent half an hour quietly drinking a beer away from all the others led me to believe it was all a charade. No one was looking for you, which told me you were not well-liked, although tolerated. The silence that you didn't seem to mind. Most people can't stand silence when they're talking. They always feel as if they have to fill up those places with unnecessary superfluous chatter. Few people find the silence soothing, and someone like your alter ego would have hated it." Jewel, as was her fashion, looked directly at him as she did when speaking to anyone. She knew instantly she had gotten it right. She could see it in his eyes. These were the eyes of a gentle man, a trustworthy man, a man who was truthful and honorable, a man she very much liked, and right now she didn't like too many people.

"I don't know what to say. I'm quite at a loss for words. What mysterious powers do you possess that allow you to see into a person's heart and soul?" Justin was completely awestruck.

"It isn't a secret. I've just learned to read people too. As for poor Mr. Wilson, everyone was so busy giving him their condolences they never gave the man a chance to talk about the one thing he needed to talk about, Marjorie, his wife. You know, they were married for fifty-two years. Quite an accomplishment, don't you think?" said Jewel.

"Yes, it certainly is, and you're right. It never occurred to me to ask about his dead wife. I always thought it would be too painful to talk about her," replied Justin.

"That's what most people think, and for those who haven't gone through the entire grieving process, it would be too soon, but for most, they love to talk about the one they lost. Does your mother talk about your father much?"

"My mother will talk to anyone who will listen. I'm surprised she hasn't had a granite stone figure of him placed in the living room so everyone could see and ask about him. It does get quite embarrassing at times. I've lived through it, and yet to this day she still finds things to tell me about him," said Justin. "I guess you are right about that too. Explain how one so young has the wisdom of a sage."

"A sage—I don't think so. Just survival skills," answered Jewel.

"There, there is that look again. The one I saw at the museum. The one that makes you look like something terrible has happened," said Justin.

"Sorry, just remembering things from the past."

"If I remember correctly, that is why we came here and had this soup. I don't want to pressure you, but I think you'll feel better if you divest yourself of these things that are causing you pain," said Justin.

Jewel looked up at Justin and could feel the tears start to well up in her eyes again. She looked up at the ceiling to stop them. She had read somewhere that you could stop tears by just looking up at the ceiling. She would try anything; she hated to cry and had learned at an early age to hold her emotions in check, but this time was different. She knew she would be safe if she let her guard down.

"Yes, that was the reason you had to eat soup instead of a leisurely full-course meal, so I guess I do owe you some explanation," said Jewel.

"Nonsense!" said Justin. "You owe me nothing."

"Thank you, but you're right. I need to talk to someone. I just feel so confused and guilty and quite numb, really. I thought all this would be over, but it isn't. I have to deal with it all again, and I don't want to." Justin could see Jewel begin to tremble and tears fill her eyes.

"Jewel, please talk to me, and maybe I can help you somehow, or maybe I can't, but at least you will have exposed it, and that is usually a good thing to do." Justin felt alarmed but wanted to remain calm and assured for her. This was no time for him to show too much emotion. She needed someone reachable but unemotional right now.

"It's the damn letter, the letter from Chris's parents telling me I have to meet them upstate and to go through all this sadness again." Jewel looked at Justin and could tell he was confused. How could he not be when he didn't have all the information that he would need to process it all?

"Are you sure you want to do this?" asked Jewel.

"If it will help, I'm quite certain," replied Justin.

"If I just tell you about Chris, you won't have the whole story, so I think I need to go back to my last semester of school. I'll try not to make it too long and drawn out. In my last semester at FIT, I met a man. His name was Lawrence, Lawrence Miller. He was not into fashion design, but sales and merchandising. We dated, became very close, and I fell in love. We fell in love, or so I thought. After we graduated, he asked me to move in with him. It was a really big step for me because I had never been in love or been with a man before. So I did, and everything was wonderful. I got a job with Kenneth, and Lawrence went to work for another design house, Francious LaNeve. They were an old house, very big in the sixties and seventies, but their designer was old and their clothes were just not up-to-date. Lawrence was having a difficult time selling their work, but other than that, things were great. We were together almost a year.

"One day during lunch hour, Kenneth walked by and stopped to see what I was doing. I rarely ate lunch. I usually worked on one of my own designs. I would design something on my own time, buy the fabric, make my patterns, and always work on my time so no one could say anything. I explained to him what I was doing, and he asked to see some of my work. I had a few sketches I was working on and gave them to him. I thought I would be fired or something—I was so nervous. He handed them back to me and asked if I had seen his lineup for the fall show. As a patternmaker, I had. He said to bring him six or seven new designs that would fit in with his collection and he wanted to see them in three weeks, and he left. I could not believe he even stopped and spoke to me. I was stunned. So for the next three weeks, I worked every minute, staying up late, getting up early. I was so tired, but I got them done and even made the patterns for them just in case he actually liked one of them. I also made a copy of each drawing, making sure they were dated, and mailed them to Kenneth. They called it a cheap copywrite.

"About this time, things were going really bad for Lawrence. Everything he tried to do failed. He became moody and depressed. I couldn't say a word to him without him biting my head off. Sometimes I really thought he hated me, and I didn't know what to do. On the day I was to bring in my designs, I got up early and Lawrence was already gone. As I headed out the door, I went to get my portfolio. I couldn't find it anywhere. There was just a note on the door that read, 'I need these more than you do. Sorry.' Lawrence had taken my designs. I couldn't believe it. He had stolen my designs. I didn't know what to do. I just stood there looking at the door. Now what? Now what do I do? I went to work and asked to speak to Kenneth and told him what happened. He asked if I had mailed the duplicates, and I had. He called down to receiving and asked them to bring up the box. He went over the designs. The look on his face was so stern I could only imagine he hated them and I was fired. He tossed one on the floor. Then he made some changes to two of them, and the other four he put up on the wall with his collection, and here I was, standing with my mouth open. I was terrified, but I managed to blurt out that I had also made the patterns for all of them. I remember he turned and smiled. He grabbed me by the shoulders and asked me what my name was. I said Jewel, and he said I certainly was, and just laughed. He asked me to bring the patterns to his assistant and stay with her. I didn't know what I was supposed to do, so I got the patterns, and she gave them to Kenneth's personal sewers. They just had to wait until Kenneth decided what fabrics he was going to use.

"Meanwhile, they made the changes to the other two patterns. He chose the fabrics, and everyone started working like little worker bees to get them finished. I packed up my things and moved out of the apartment and in with my friend Shelby. I never saw Lawrence again. Kenneth had his own replica of a runway so he could dress the models, have them walk the runway, and see if something needed to be changed. He had a great eye for detail, and everything had to be perfect. The clothes looked incredible. I couldn't believe they were my designs. It felt unreal. I asked his assistant if I should be doing something, and she just said to watch and learn. Kenneth came out of his office periodically to check on things. Sometimes he made changes to the garment or the accessories. When everything was completed, he had them do a practice walk down the runway. Then they did it again and again. Kenneth said something was wrong but he couldn't quite put his finger on it and asked his assistant. She said it looked fine to her, but it wasn't. I knew of two things that were wrong, but I didn't know if I should say anything or not. So I figured why not? All he can do is fire me. So I said aloud, 'Mr. Dolan, I can see two things that don't work.' He turned and walked over to where I was standing with kill in his eyes, but I decided, in for a penny, in for a pound, so when he was looming over me, I stood up straight, looked him directly in the eye, and waited for the roof to come falling down on me.

"Jewel, isn't it?' he said.

"Yes, sir," I replied.

"All right, tell me what you see that the rest of us don't."

"I explained the best I could what I thought was wrong and how everything would work better with these simple changes. He thanked me for my suggestions and told me I could leave, go back downstairs, and sew or do something. Well, I guess I'm not fired, I said to myself. That's a good thing. I didn't talk to anyone upstairs again until the day of the show. His assistant called down for me. I went upstairs and was told that Kenneth wanted me backstage to help get the models ready for the runway. I told her I didn't have any experience doing that, but she said it was what Kenneth wanted and the boss always got what he wanted.

"At this time, I had no idea what had transpired the previous month. Apparently, Lawrence's actions stirred up something deep inside Kenneth. He found out when LaNeve was to have their show, where it would be, and even who was catering. I guess he called in a few favors and booked our show two weeks before theirs. He got it in the same place and with the same caterers. He changed a few things, like the seating arrangements and a few things on the menu. Other than that, the two shows were going to look the same. Well, we had our show. I really don't know how I got through it, but somehow the show went off beautifully, and the changes I had suggested to him the month before, he did them. He actually changed the designs. I couldn't believe it, and no one told me he changed anything. All the reviews in the papers the next day were positive. 'Best original show in ages,' 'Youthful yet stylish,' and on and on. It was a dream come true for me. To be a part of a show like this was…well, I can't describe what it was like. It was like your birthday and Christmas and everything rolled together. When I think back, it still seems like a dream, but the best part was the next day.

"Kenneth gathered his staff and me and told them what a fabulous job everyone did. He was so proud of them, how he owed it to them for all their hard work. Then he told them to take Monday and Tuesday off and get some rest before they started working on the fall collection. You know, we're always planning six months ahead of the season. Well, anyway, before they left, he asked me to come up next to him, and he told them my name and said that I had saved the show. My ideas about the changes were right on the money, and it made the difference between an okay show and the razzle-dazzle show we presented. He said that I would be moving upstairs, and he wanted everyone to welcome me. I just stood there like a limp rag. It was a good thing he didn't ask me to say anything. I know I would have been speechless and tongue-tied. 'This is our own shining jewel,' he said. 'Let's see how bright she can shine. All right, everybody, go home. See you back here on Wednesday'

"When we got back, Kenneth explained the theme he had chosen for the spring lineup. He would like to see any and all ideas. It was pretty quiet the next two weeks, then the house of LaNeve had their show. It was a complete disaster. It was obvious they were our designs—well, mine, anyway—but they had altered a few things. It really didn't matter, because the next day's reviews said it all. 'Obvious knockoffs of the Kenneth Dolan line,' 'Couldn't even be original enough to hold their show in a different location or hire a different caterer.' It was really bad. They were ruined, and I heard that Lawrence was fired and blackballed. He would never be hired by anyone in the fashion business, and I never knew what happened to him. I tried so hard to hate him for what he did. He could have asked me for help, and I would have designed a few things for him, but he chose his path and I tried not to look back.

"I asked Kenneth if I could go down to the second floor and sew. Most places farm out the sewing of the garments to other companies, but Kenneth had his own factory of sewers. He liked to keep an eye on the quality they were producing. I think he could tell I was hurting and needed to stay busy. I just couldn't put my pencil to paper and make anything come out that remotely looked like a garment rather than a bunch of squiggle lines. So I went down to the second floor and started sewing. I would start early and stay late. Shelby had her boyfriend move in with us, and it was too awkward to stay there. They tried to include me in whatever they did, but I just couldn't manage even a smile. All I wanted to do was to bury myself in a pile of fabric and sew till my fingers were numb, just like the rest of my body. I sewed for months. I even managed to work out a few designs and make the pattern.

"One day, the workers came in and found me slumped over my machine. They called an ambulance, and I woke up in the hospital, suffering from dehydration and exhaustion. I spent a few days there and back to work. When Kenneth saw me, he almost didn't recognize me. I had lost about fifteen pounds and looked like the walking dead. He said he was worried about me and that I needed some time off. Was there any place that I could go to get some rest? I said I could go upstate. I had a cousin and an aunt and some friends there. So I threw some things in a case, took the train, and went upstate. I checked in to the local hotel and never left the room for two days. I just slept and cried. By the third day, I realized I had better get out and get something to eat or they would be finding my body in bed. I guess my will to survive finally kicked in.

"The next few days, I walked around the city of Hudson and ate four, sometimes five, meals a day. I gained back the weight I lost and my strength and was beginning to look like myself again. I visited with my relatives and friends, even went out with them a few times, barhopping. Barhopping was not my thing, and I soon realized my friends were still living out their high school years. I grew bored and needed to find something that would interest me. They begged me to go to the county fair on Saturday night, but I told them no. They really didn't need me to get drunk with. They could do it on their own. The fair, however, sounded like something I would like to see. When we were young, we looked forward to the fair all year. We filled our faces with cotton candy, jelly apples, hot dogs, and whatever else we could find. Then we would play the games until our money ran out. So I got up early Saturday and went to the fair. None of the rides or games started early, but the judging of the animals for the 4H kids did start early. With my map in hand, I went into every barn and watched the judging. There were cows, goats, sheep, pigs, and then the smaller animals. The chickens, pigeons, rabbits, and whatever else they had. I marked off my map methodically to make sure I would hit every exhibit. The only one left was the quilt exhibit.

"I looked at the quilts and was surprised at the beautiful handwork in some of them. I thought they were really too nice to just lie on a bed, but that was what they were made for. I studied them for a time, then went into another room, and I could feel my heart stop. There, adorning the walls, were smaller quilts, but not just squares and triangles, but pictures. Pictures made entirely of fabric and made to be hung on the wall as you would an oil painting. They were incredible. I had never seen anything like them. I asked a million questions of anyone who would talk to me about how one got started making these wall quilts. The ladies were so patient and tried to explain and, in the end, told me that if I were serious, I should buy some books and magazines about wall quilts, plus there was a quilt guild that meets every week at the local school where I could get more information. I felt new, like I just awoke from a long sleep. I knew what I wanted to do for the first time in months.

"I went to the bookstore and bought some books and magazines on wall quilts and read everything twice. When I looked at the advertisements for the lines of cotton fabric that the fabric companies had in the magazines, I noticed that in most of them, they showed a quilt made of some of the fabric they were selling. The more I studied them, the more I realized that I could do a much better job showing off the fabric to their best advantage. I was really positive that this was what I should be doing. I loved designing, I loved fabric, and I loved sewing. I went back to the hotel and made a plan, and then I called Kenneth and told him about it. He was so understanding about everything. He really wanted me back, but if this was what I thought I needed to do, then that was what I should do, and if he could help in any way, to just call him. He gave me the names of some people to contact, and the rest I got from the magazine ads. I sent out detailed letters of what I could do for them. I crossed my fingers and mailed the letters, praying I was doing the right thing.

"The next day, I went out and bought a used car. I remembered all the money I had in the bank. Lawrence never let me spend a dime toward our living arrangements, so my paychecks went directly into the bank, and when I left the city, Kenneth gave me a check, an enormous check. He said it was to buy the designs he used. I couldn't believe the amount on the check and told him he must have made a mistake, but he said, with the orders coming in, this was nothing and that any designs I submitted to him that he liked and wanted to use, he would pay me for them as well.

"I spent the next few days riding around the county, looking for a place to start my business. I found a few houses I wanted to look at and contacted the realtor. The last place I wanted to see, she told me it probably wouldn't do because it needed a great deal of cosmetic work. The house itself was sound, but nothing had been done to the interior in years. I wanted to see it anyway. You couldn't see the house from the road. It had this long driveway, and the house sat behind a row of trees. Secluded and quiet. I liked it already. It was small, and she was right about the inside, but with a new paint job and some furniture, it would be fine. She told me that the wife died a year ago and the son, who was a dentist in Syracuse, was taking his father back with him to put in a nursing home. He had Alzheimer's and could not live alone anymore. The son was very anxious to sell and had a lawyer there with his power of attorney to handle the closing. The price was low for a quick sale. I offered him a little less than the asking price and was surprised when he agreed. So in a few days, I owned a house and a car."

"May I just stop you a moment?" said Justin, hating to stop her obvious need to get it all out at one time.

"Of course. Was I going too fast?" replied Jewel.

"No, I just thought you could use a cup of tea or coffee or something. Your voice is beginning to sound a bit hoarse," said Justin.

"Oh, thank you. Yes, I would like a cup of tea very much. Thank you for being so thoughtful."

Justin got off the sofa and headed to the kitchen, with Jewel right behind him.

"You should not have gotten up," he said. "I may not be able to prepare a full-course meal, but tea, I can do, and even a proper tea."

"What's the difference between tea and proper tea?" asked Jewel.

"A proper tea is when you heat water and pour it into your teapot to get the inside hot, then when you have more heated water, you dump the teapot, add your loose tea, the new water, and let it steep for three minutes."

"Don't you just have a teabag?" Jewel laughed.

"As a matter of fact, I do have a few boxes of assorted teas. They are convenient when you don't have the time or inclination to brew a proper cup," said Justin.

"Well, since I don't own a teapot, a tea bag will do very nicely for me, thank you," replied Jewel.

"Very well, then, tea bags all round. I'll just put the kettle on." Justin open a cabinet door and said to Jewel, "Which tea would you prefer?"

"Anything mild. I don't like really strong tea, and no Earl Grey, please. Now that tea is like drinking some awful witch's brew."

Jewel laughed and grabbed her throat with her hands, as if she were gagging.

"I know what you mean. It is really fowl, but we have it in the house because it is one of Mother's favorites. Actually, I think she brought all these teas in. If not for her, there would be just one box of tea bags, something mild to sip when you return home after being out in a damp, dismal, rainy day. You never seem to be able to warm up unless you have some hot tea," he said.

"Oh, I know what you mean, and I like honey in mine. When I was young and we lived with my grandfather, his famous drink for whatever ailed you, especially a cold, was one part tea, one part lemon juice, one part honey, and one part whiskey. I remember asking Gramps what the tea was for, and he said it was there to warm everything up and take the chill away. It took a while to get used to, but I rarely had a cold," said Jewel.

"I sometimes think, if we kept some of these old-fashioned home remedies instead of the chemicals we ingest when we are not feeling well, we would be better off," said Justin.

Jewel quickly did up the dishes as Justin made the tea. Picking up their hot cups, they headed back into the living room. Taking their same places on the couch that they had before, they said nothing, instead just sipped their hot tea. After a few minutes, Jewel said, "This is just what the doctor ordered. How did you know?"

"It was just a guess, really," said Justin. "I know that when I'm involved in long contract debates, my throat gets so parched and water doesn't do the trick. I usually have someone fetch me a pot of tea. That alter ego of mine has been known for holding up negotiations until he gets his tea." Justin couldn't help but laugh. "I could never get away with something like that, but he could, and he does."

After a while, Justin asked Jewel if she was feeling better and if she would like to continue or save the rest for another time.

"I'm fine now, thanks to you, and I really would like to continue, if you don't mind. I'm not sure I would be able to start this all over again. It's hard enough this time," she replied. She finished her tea and placed the cup in the coffee table.

"I don't remember where I ended. Oh, yes, I do. I just bought the house. I spent the next week from dawn till dusk cleaning and painting. I bought myself a bed and checked out of the hotel. I went to the department store and bought the essentials, a coffeepot, bread, and peanut butter and jelly. The first few nights were a bit scary. I had forgotten how quiet it was in the country. Every time I heard some leaves or a bush rustle, I thought it was a bear or something equally frightening. I only had a radio and kept it on all night, just so I wouldn't hear the outside noises. I worked so hard each day, but it felt really, really good. I was so happy I never gave a thought to the events that led me to this place. I was a girl on a mission.

"Saturday and Sunday, I decided to give myself a much-needed break. I was going to drive around and check out some yard sales. Everyone had yard sales upstate. I got some very nice end tables, lamps, and odds and ends. Some places had furniture, but I decided to buy my couch and chair new. I wasn't taking any chances—you never know how long they had been hanging around or where. I also bought a TV and finally got the cable guy to install it the following week. Sunday, I was going to check out the yard sale that the Humane Society was having. I picked up a few pretty vases and a wall clock. I put the things in the car and decided to look at the animals in the shelter. I hadn't given any thought to adopting. I just wanted to see what they had. I'm not a cat person, so I breezed through that area. The dogs were kept in another building. I walked in, and the noise was ear breaking—dogs were jumping up and down, spinning in circles, barking, and howling. I walked the length of the kennels, and on my way, while all the other dogs were going nuts, this one little dog was just sitting there as nice as you please. It never got up or barked or anything, but I could feel its eyes on me as I walked by. I went to the end and turned back to go out. I passed the little dog who was still sitting so quietly, and I swear I heard a voice that said, 'If you take me home, I'll be the best friend you will ever have.' I took a step back and looked at it, and it was wagging its tail. I started to laugh—I mean, *really* laugh. I had tears running down my face. All I could think of was that I had finally lost it. I had become a nutcase.

"I went to the desk and told the lady, who was looking at me strangely, as if she knew I had lost it. I tried to stop laughing long enough to tell her that I just lost my heart to the little dog named Rocketman. She began to laugh to and said, 'I know just what you're feeling. Sometimes it's just love at first sight.' I filled out all the papers, and she told me he was under a year old, was housebroken, and had all his shots. The lady who had him had fallen and broken her hip and just couldn't keep him. He was such a sweet dog and really deserved a good home with someone to love him. She brought him out for us to get acquainted, and it felt as if we had been together forever. It was the strangest thing. He got into the car without my having to say a word to him. He was already wearing a halter, so I just had to slip the seat belt through and fasten it. He sat as nice as could be, looking out the window, and, once in a while, gave me a quick look to see if I was watching him. On the way home, I stopped and got a pizza. When we got home, I unfastened him. He jumped out of the car, ran to the bushes, and found his spot. He didn't lift his leg like most male dogs. He just did this funny little squat and peed, then walked to the front door and waited for me. He went in, walked all through the house, then came back and sat down. I put a dish down with some water, and he drank some of it. I realized I hadn't gotten any food to feed him with, and except for peanut butter and jelly, there wasn't anything else. I put the TV on and put a few slices of pizza on a dish, grabbed a beer, and went into the living room. He just sat there, looking up at me. I asked him if he liked pizza, because that was all we had. He was so funny, cocking his head from side to side, listening to what I was saying. I put a slice of pizza on a dish and cut it up, and then I put a few teaspoons full of beer in another saucer.

"If they find out at the shelter that the first meal I feed you was pizza and beer, I'd probable wind up in jail, so don't tell,' I told him. He looked up at me again, and I swear that dog can smile. He ate the pizza, drank the beer, and jumped on the couch next to me. I had planned to watch the Saturday science-fiction movie. They're usually pretty dumb, but for two hours, I could be transported to another place and not have to think about anything. Rocky—that's what I decided to call him—just snuggled up and went to sleep, probably drunk from the beer. That was the most pleasant evening I had had in quite a while, so Rocky and I decided this was the way we would spend our Saturday nights, and except for a few that we make up on Sunday, this is how it has been for over three years.

"I was thrilled when I received my first package of fabric and quickly went to work. I sent it out, and the next day, I received a call from the man at the top congratulating me on a job well done. He said the quilt was everything they hoped for and more. Never before had they received work that really captured the taste of the fabric. This was what they were trying to relate through their ads. The rest is history, or so they say. I had to hire two women to help me, one to piece and one to do the quilting, which was done on a machine called a long-arm. It sews the three layers of the quilt together, sometimes using a very specific design, and I had to have the wall knocked down in the larger bedroom, where we worked, and have an addition put on to accommodate the long-arm machine. We had so much work. I can't tell you how happy I was. Less than three years, and the business that I thought would never get off the ground was supporting two people and making me a considerable profit. We had so much fun together. The girls I hired had so much experience working with quilts that they were, in many ways, teaching me. Getting up in the morning, having coffee with the girls, then going to work was like a dream come true.

"It was in at the end of March that I met Chris. He happened to live directly across the road from me. He was a vet, and I saw his building every time I went out, but Rocky used a different vet, so I never paid much attention to his place. There was also a red barn and a very large white colonial. The kind with shutters on all the windows, a wraparound porch with wicker furniture. It was really beautiful. The barn was even nice.

"Chris was a great guy, wonderful sense of humor, considerate, and kind, the kind of guy that would do anything for anyone. He had two farmhands and a partner in the vet practice, and every few months, he would invite them with their families to a pancake breakfast. Everyone loved him. He was never serious, always making jokes out of whatever problem came along. He was fun and just what I needed for a while. Chris's main passion besides the practice was breeding Black Angus bulls. He had a very complicated breeding system and produced some of the finest bulls on the East Coast. He delivered the bulls all over to large cattle farms, and sometimes if the trip was fairly short, like to Vermont or Massachusetts, then I would go along. We would deliver the bull, then stop someplace for dinner on the way home. We got very close, and around the beginning of November, when he told me his parents were coming up from North Carolina to spend the holidays, he presented me with an engagement ring. I loved Chris, it was hard not to, but I wasn't in love with him. He never took anything seriously, and that was the problem. It was really annoying at times. I hated to disappoint him, especially with his parents coming up, and I knew I would never marry him, but I thought I would just accept the ring, and then after the holidays, when his parents left, I would tell him I couldn't marry him. Looking back, I never should have taken the ring. It was a silly thing to do.

"The week of Thanksgiving was so busy. I remember it was Tuesday, and I was racing to get the last quilt done and mailed so I could let the girls have the rest of the week off, and I would be free to visit with Chris and his parents. Chris came in and asked me to take a ride with him to Vermont to deliver a bull. The bull didn't have to be delivered till Friday, but I guess he had the same idea I had, get the work out of the way and then be able to relax and enjoy Thanksgiving. I told him that I couldn't go because this quilt had to be in the mail by three. He asked his dad to go, but he had to stay near his wife, who was baking and cooking, and he would have to run her to the store if she needed something that she had forgotten to buy on their last trip. She never learned to drive, and someone would always have to take her. Manny, one of his farmhands, was in the hospital with a ruptured appendix, and Fred, the other farmhand, had to stay and take care of the new calves and the pregnant moms. If the weather got too cold and the temperature dropped too low, they put all the cattle in the barn. So there wasn't anyone to go with him. We tried to talk him out of going, but he said he knew what he was doing and he would be fine. Even after his dad told him that we might be getting some bad weather and he should stay home, he insisted he was going. There was nothing we could say to make him change his mind. His mom was furious with him, but in the end, he went anyway.

"By six o'clock, we started to get some freezing rain and Chris was not back yet. He should have been back by four thirty at the latest. His dad was worried that he hit some bad weather on the trip home. We waited and waited, and with each hour that went by, we all started to think the worse, and we were right. It was a quarter past eight. The doorbell rang, and his dad went to the door. A state trooper was there and asked if we were the Wellers. His dad said yes and asked if there was an accident. He just knew something was wrong. The trooper told us that Chris had an accident about ten miles from home. It looked like he hit some freezing rain and lost control of the trailer, and when it flipped, it pulled the truck with it. Both vehicles were on their sides when they found them. Chris was taken to Albany Medical Center. But the trooper told us we couldn't go to the hospital that night because of the severe storm. The roads were not drivable, they were just a sheet of ice. His mom and dad wanted to go, but the trooper warned them again that all traffic was to remain off the roads. We were all so worried. We tried to call the hospital, but even the lines were down and we couldn't get through. By now, of course, we were all thinking the worse.

"Chris's mother made a fresh pot of coffee, and I think we stayed up half the night, drinking it. We all finally fell asleep in the chairs we were sitting in. The next day, the roads had been plowed and sanded, and we finally were able to get to the hospital and find him. The doctor said that he had a broken arm and wrist. Other than that, nothing else was broken. There was, however, something else that they couldn't find the reason for. Chris was in a coma. They did all the tests they could and found no reason for it. His mom just collapsed. We were at a loss. What do we do now? We stayed until just before dark, and Chris's father said we should leave before the roads froze up again. We went up every day, staying almost all day. Thanksgiving Day, we ate in silence. All the cooking and baking his mom did, and none of us could eat anything. On Monday, we decided that they would go up in the morning and stay until four, and then I would go up and stay until nine or ten. I had quilts to work on, and going up there every night was getting harder and harder. The longer Chris was in the coma, the worse his mom got, and they finally had to give her something. It went like this until two days before Christmas.

"The hospital called at three in the morning and said Chris was dead. I had been staying there at the house, trying to help Chris's dad take care of his mom. A few days after Christmas, we buried Chris. The hospital said there was a blood clot they couldn't see and it went to his heart and that was the cause of death. It didn't make it any easier knowing the cause. He was still dead. You can't imagine what we were going through. The sadness, the guilt we all felt because none of us had gone with him. His mom just cried and cried. I don't know where she got the tears, because I was cried out. I was just numb. I did manage to send out letters to my accounts and said I had a death in the family and that I would be taking some time off and therefore was not accepting any new commissions but would inform them when I was ready to start again. I even got some sympathy cards from a few companies I had made quilts for. I thought that was really a nice gesture.

"The funeral was simple—that would have been the way Chris would have wanted it, and that was the first time I met his sister. It was a hell of a way to meet someone, standing over a grave. She was pleasant, blond like Chris, but she didn't have Chris's charm. She was a financial adviser or something, married to probably the second richest man in Massachusetts. They had one son, who was away at boarding school. Apparently, the death of an uncle wasn't important enough to take him out of school for a few days. But everyone else was there. All the people he worked with, friends from school, plus so many others, people whose pets he worked on, even some of the people who now owned one of his bulls. It was unbelievable. Everyone brought food to the house and stayed to make sure we all had something. They even cleaned up everything. All I remember was drinking about a hundred cups of coffee. Many of the employees didn't go home until nine or ten o'clock. Everyone had a story to tell about Chris, and I think somehow it helped his mom and dad get through a very sad day. Although they had spoken to Chris every day, especially his mom, they hadn't seen him in over six months. So I guess hearing about the crazy things Chris did somehow made it seem like they were closer to him. I went home, over their objection, but I really wanted to be alone, and I thought they needed some time alone too.

"A few days later, Chris's parents asked me to go to the lawyers with them. I couldn't imagine why. I thought it was just so I could be there in case Chris's mom collapsed again. The lawyer had the will that Chris amended in the beginning of November after he had given me the ring.

"The house and farm were always to be kept in the Weller family. If we married and had children, it would go to them. If we married but had no children, I could live there as long as I liked, but I didn't own the house. I couldn't see why they found it necessary for me to be there, until the end. Chris left half of the vet practice to me. He said he knew the way I loved animals after helping him at three o'clock in the morning when he needed an extra hand."

Justin could see that Jewel was becoming very excited and tried to calm her, but it didn't work. She became hysterical. She started to cry, and all she could say over and over was, "Why me? Why me? I certainly didn't deserve it, not after what I did, letting him think I was going to marry him. I told the lawyer I didn't want it, that it should go to his parents. His parents were unbelievable. They said if that was the way Chris wanted it, then that was the way it would be. I tried not to cry, but the guilt was just too much. I'm sure his parents thought I was crying because Chris was dead, and in a way I was, but most of it was guilt, deep, gut-wrenching guilt. The kind of guilt that just leads you to the blackness, then swallows you whole. I tried to keep it together for their sakes, but I couldn't wait until I was away from them. I remember going home, throwing some things in a bag, and telling the girls that I just had to get away for a few days. I told them they could stay and use the machines if they wanted. I told them I was going to the city and they had the number if they needed to reach me. I went over to the Wellers' and told them some story about how Kenneth called and although it was a bad time, but he could really use my help developing the new line of clothes. They said they understood, and wished me a safe trip."

Jewel was on her feet by now, pacing back and forth and sobbing so hard she could barely speak. Justin remained seated and quiet;

somehow, he knew that Jewel needed to go through this, although it was torture for him to watch her. He wanted so much to grab her, hold her close, and tell her all would be well, but he didn't.

"Where do people like that come from? All they had ever been was kind, and here I am, running out on them the moment it gets too much to deal with. I just couldn't look them in the face anymore, knowing the lie I was keeping from them. I didn't deserve their kindness. I felt like I betrayed them."

Jewel was beginning to calm down and talking slower, but she couldn't stop crying.

"I ran. I just left them to their pain, and I ran away. It seems that when the going gets tough, I just run away. I took Rocky, and we drove to the city. I really don't even remember driving. The next thing I remember is crying on Kenneth's shoulder. He took me into the apartment and made me lie down and said I could stay as long as I needed to, and that's where I've been since, sewing all day, most nights, and weekends. I drove back upstate one weekend to drop off the car. I certainly didn't need it in the city. The girls thought I was coming back to work, but I told them I needed more time. How could I work there? Every time I would have to go out the driveway, I would have to see his practice and the house. I didn't even stop to see his parents. I just had Fran drive me to the train, and I came back here. Kenneth and Celia were lifesavers. They insisted I start coming to dinner on Monday nights. I don't know how I would have gotten through without them, especially the boys. I played games and read stories to them when they went to bed, and not just some silly kiddie story for these boys—they were into the classics. Right now we're reading *Moby-Dick*, and that's how it has been these past two months.

"The party last night was the first time I have been in a social gathering since Chris's death. I was actually looking forward to the party. Celia was right. It was time to put everything behind me. Then Friday morning, I received a letter from Mitch, Chris's partner in the veterinary practice. He said he had found someone who would like to buy my share of the practice. The Wellers were driving up from North Carolina because he wanted to talk to them about the breeding program of Chris's. He was interested in continuing what Chris had started. Apparently, he had studied genetics in college and was anxious to do the same work. After Mitch told him that they would never sell the house, he wanted to see if they would consider renting it to him. The house had been in the Weller family for a hundred years.

"So here we go again. I knew at some point I was going to have to see the Wellers. They asked the girls for my address and sent me a note to see how I was doing and said they would contact me when they got the stone for Chris's grave. They would like to have a small graveside service, just the family, and since I was almost family, they would like me to be there.

"As if the first go-round wasn't enough, now I was going to receive money for half the vet practice, which shouldn't have been mine in the first place. It's like the world has gone mad. I don't have a clue how I got through the party last night. If it hadn't been for you, I don't think I would have made it."

"You give me too much credit. You're stronger than you think," replied Justin, happy to see that she was feeling more in control.

"What do I do now? I haven't the foggiest idea how much a veterinary practice is worth, and then what do I do with the money? God, I just keep thinking this is all some crazy nightmare and I will wake up soon," said Jewel.

"First, let me say how sorry I am that you have had to endure such sadness these past few years, and if you don't mind my making a few observations, Lawrence betrayed you. To profess his love for you, then steal from you, that is not a scoundrel you should ever feel sorry for or have any sympathy for. As for your engagement to Chris, you shouldn't consider it a betrayal. He was happy, you made him happy, and the small white lie you told was going to be rectified as soon as the holidays were over, so you really couldn't call it a betrayal on your part. As far as feeling guilty, it is natural to feel some guilt when someone we love dies, and you're refusing to go with him that day to deliver the bull should not make you feel guilty. He knew the bull didn't need to be delivered until Friday, and even after his father told him you were in for bad weather, he chose to go. He made the choice to go. He was showing the world that he could do what he wanted when he wanted and took nothing seriously. The exact issue that made it impossible for you to think you could ever marry him. So there should be no guilt felt there. As for the veterinary practice, I'm sure this fellow Mitch must have made the accounting books available to the prospective buyer, and I'm sure your lawyer would also be privy to the same. You do have a lawyer and an accountant up there, don't you?" he asked.

"Yes, I do, and I trust both men equally," replied Jewel.

"Well, then, you should have them look at the books and determine a fair price for said practice. I then see four options for you regarding the money from the sale," he said.

"Four options? I haven't even been able to think of one," said Jewel.

By now Jewel had stopped crying and pacing and had taken a seat next to Justin, on the couch. His heart hurt for her; to see her in such a tortured state was almost more than he could bear, but he knew she needed him to be strong, realistic, and maybe just a little analytical. She was acting strictly on emotion, and one of them needed to be clearheaded enough to see possible solutions to her problems.

"As I see it," continued Justin, "the four options are these: One, you offer the money to the Wellers, but we know they will refuse it. Two, you can keep the money to use any way you see fit, perhaps expanding your quilting business." "No, no way will I keep that money!" snapped Jewel.

"Please calm yourself, Jewel. Knowing you, I know with complete confidence that you would never keep the money, so please let me continue. Three, you could give it away to some charity, and four, which I think will be the one you will choose, you can put it back into the veterinary practice by buying them some medical equipment. I'm sure they could use something, a better x-ray or an ultrasound machine, a better-equipped surgery room, and you could put Chris's name on the wall, like the Chris Weller Surgical Room. What do you think of number 4?"

"Justin, you're incredible, a genius! No, better than a genius. It's perfect, absolutely perfect! I can't believe I didn't think of it. Chris was always going on and on about how much they could use better equipment. The x-ray machine was purchased used, as was much of the rest of the equipment. I even heard Mitch saying that they needed better diagnostic equipment and they could use a vet tech trained to handle the harder surgeries. It's brilliant! I have no idea what the practice is worth, but what better way to use the money? Wow, you can't believe how I feel right now. For the first time in what seems like forever, I'm out of the darkness and into the light. I probably sound ridiculous, but that's how I feel right now. You... you have taken this weight off my shoulders, and I can't think of a single word to thank you."

As they looked into each other's eyes, Jewel took Justin's face in her hands and very gently kissed him on the lips, then whispered, "Thank you." Justin said nothing.

Jewel knew she had to break this emotional mood or fall hopelessly into his arms. She looked at her watch and exclaimed that it was near ten.

"Oh gosh, I must go. I told Celia I would be home early. They have that luncheon tomorrow, and I'm watching the boys. I have my own key, but I don't like using it if I know they are home. Could we leave now, please?" pressed Jewel.

"Yes, of course. I'll call for a car. It should only take them a few minutes. Excuse me," said Justin.

Justin was equally glad that Jewel recognized the direction the evening was going. An emotional moment like this could have changed the whole dynamitic of their relationship, and Justin didn't want to rush into anything that could quite possibly hurt the chances of this developing into something he really wanted.

The car arrived in ten minutes, and as they sat beside each other on the way to Celia's house, Jewel wanted—no, needed—to thank him for listening to her. She knew deep down that he recognized the need she had to speak to someone and knew now why she felt it easier to talk to a virtual stranger. He didn't feel that way; he felt as if he had known her for as long as he could remember. But speaking to her close friends would have been a mistake; they were too emotionally involved and, wanting only the best for her, might not have given her the best advice. He hoped he had given her the information she needed to get through this upcoming tough time. He walked her to the door and asked her what time she expected Kenneth and Celia home tomorrow.

"They promised the boys they would be home by four. Kenneth promised them they would take them to the ice cream parlor if they had behaved for me, and they had to have their homework for Monday finished and their rooms picked up," answered Jewel.

"Well, then, could I pick you up, say, at five o'clock and make sure you get back to the apartment safely?" asked Justin.

"That's really not necessary. I would think by now you would be well rid of me. I was awfully intense this evening—not my usual style," answered Jewel.

"Please, there is no apology necessary for being human. The events of the past few years in your life would cause anyone to become a little emotional. I'm just grateful you felt confident enough in our newly found friendship that you could confide in me, and as for ridding myself of you, that is the last thing I want to do. In fact, I am more enchanted with you now. So please let me call for you, just to see you safely home. I'm afraid I won't be staying long. I will be flying to Washington tomorrow evening to attend contract negations early Monday morning," stated Justin.

"All right, then, thank you. I bet you never expected a stroll through the museum to lead to a night like this." Jewel laughed.

"No. You could say this was a first for me, but I am in no way sorry it has ended like this. Thank you for letting me share things so personal." The car arrived and took them to Kenneth's house.

"Please don't mention any of this day to Celia or Kenneth. I would prefer to tell them myself. I don't like holding anything back from them. But as far as Celia is concerned, I'm not sure she will take my spending this day with you lightly," said Jewel.

"I'll see you at five tomorrow," answered Justin and quickly turned to get back into the car. The urge to kiss her was too strong, and he needed to remove himself from the temptation.

"Good evening, all. Sorry I'm late. We stopped for a bite after the museum," Jewel said with ease. She knew it best to be perfectly honest now and tell Celia about her day with Justin. Jewel hated lying about anything, and if she had learned anything these many years dealing with Celia, it was that it was always best to be perfectly honest from the beginning with her or she would never let you forget how hurtful you were to her by not confiding in her the way good friends always did, and the fact that they thought of her as family made it all the worse. If Celia's reaction was going to be bad, she would rather it be over with before she told her that she planned to see him again.

"I thought you and Shelby were going to look at apartments today?" questioned Celia.

"That is what I told you because I didn't know how you would react if you knew what I was really planning to do, and since I didn't want a scene, especially with the boys within earshot, I thought it better to wait until we were alone, and I really wanted to see what this day was going to be like. Positive or negative," answered Jewel.

"Well," said Celia, "it's nice to know we are still included in your circle. So where were you, then?"

"I had sort of a date with your mentor, Justin Angelis," said Jewel.

"You what?" said Celia. "Kenneth, did you know anything about this?"

"What difference does it make if I did or didn't? Jewel wants to tell you now, so please give her the courtesy and listen," snapped Kenneth.

"Fine, go ahead, but I want the two of you to know right now that I'm deeply hurt. It seems I'm always the last to know anything around here." Celia quivered as she sat back down.

"Last evening at the party," started Jewel, "when I had taken Justin to the inside-out room after speaking with him for a few minutes and sensing his discomfort with being in there with all his business associates, we talked about many different things. What I did for Kenneth, how long I had known you both, that kind of thing. I, in return, asked about his work and why he went into law. He went on at great length and told me about his family, his grandfather, who came from Italy, and how he was the one responsible for changing the family name."

"He changed his name from what? I never heard about that. Why did he tell you about that?" asked Celia, raising her voice.

"I don't know why he went into such detail about it. Maybe he was just feeling a little more relaxed being away from everyone. Do you want to hear this or not?" answered Jewel.

"Yes, go on," said Celia, obviously agitated.

"Like I said, he told me a lot about his family, his home in Connecticut, where he went to school, even some of the things he got into while away from his mom and dad. He has quite a sense of humor."

"Are we still talking about the same man I work with? 'Cause I've got to tell you, I have worked with this man closely for six months, and I can't even remember him smiling, let alone saying something at all funny," quipped Celia.

"Well, as I said, he seemed totally relaxed, and maybe at the office, he is all work and doesn't like to clown around and tell jokes," said Jewel. "Anyway, we somehow got around to what we did in our leisure time, and I told him, if I wasn't at work or playing with Rocky or being here with you and the boys, then I usually could be found at the Metropolitan Museum. I told him how I studied the paintings, especially the clothes in the paintings, and got a lot of ideas for new designs, like using a collar or rows of buttons, things like that."

"And he found this interesting?" asked Celia.

"I guess so, because he asked me when I had planned to go again and if I would act as his guide and explain what I saw as I was looking at the artwork," answered Jewel.

"Now, why would an extremely educated man such as he need to be guided through the museum to look at artwork that they probably have hanging right in their home in Connecticut? And you fell for that? Really, Jewel?"

Jewel didn't like the condescending tone coming from Celia, but she knew that this had to be very hard on her, especially since she had worked with him for so long and never got even a smile out of him. But Jewel tried to overlook Celia's obvious jealousy and continued.

"I told him I was planning to go on Saturday because they had changed the exhibit and I wanted to see what they had added. I was so surprised and caught off guard when he asked me if I would mind if he would come along. Like I said, it caught me so off guard that the only thing I could think of to say was okay. He smiled and asked me what time he should be there. I told him at three and to meet me on the front steps, and just at that time, one of the catering people stuck their heads in and told us that most of the guests were leaving. I don't know where I got the courage, but I asked him for a favor."

"You did what?" exclaimed Celia. "What favor? And how could you! You just meet the man!"

"Celia!" shouted Kenneth. "Will you shut up long enough for Jewel to tell you? I know you will be grateful for what she had the courage to do and will be owing her a thank-you. Now please, let's let her continue. Go ahead, Jewel. The next time she opens her mouth, I'm going to tape it shut."

"Kenneth, you wouldn't!" cried Celia.

"Oh, just try me," said Kenneth as he winked at Jewel.

"I told him how hard you worked to throw this party for him and how grateful you were that he had been good enough to act as your mentor. That you had learned so much in the past six months and that I hoped he wouldn't take my request as being too forward since I barely knew him. I said that I knew he was here alone and that it would be extremely kind of him if he would escort you to the dinner as his guest. I know, Celia, that if you knew, you would have chopped my head off, or worse, but I just wanted to see you get some kind of recognition for all you did in hosting this party. Then he did the most surprising thing: he took my hand in his and said for you to instill such loyalty in a friend, you must be a worthy person, indeed, and it would be his honor to escort you to the dinner as his guest, but be prepared for the gossip in the office come Monday. I told him you could handle it, and he laughed. So when he was saying his good nights, that was when he asked Kenneth if he could escort you to the dinner. Kenneth looked at me, and I gave him a quick wink. He knew what it meant and gave the appropriate answer, and you were off to the ball," concluded Jewel.

"I can't believe you did that!" Celia tried to stop the tears gathering in her eyes as she went to give Jewel a hug. "Thank you," she said. "It was a wonderful night, a truly wonderful night. I'm so grateful to you, my darling, for doing what you did, and I must admit that Justin Angelis did seem to be enjoying himself at the dinner, or maybe you just cast some kind of spell on him. It really doesn't matter. Either way, I had the best time, and yes, I do owe you a very warm, from-the-bottom-of-my-heart thank-you. But we're not done yet, my lovely. Now, I want to hear about today. Did he meet you? What did you do? What did he say? Did he take you out to dinner? Where? Come on, tell all. I must know, please, Jewel. I can't stand the suspense any longer. Oh god, I need a drink. Would anyone else like one? Kenneth?"

"No, thank you, Celia, but I will have some coffee. I think this is going to take a while. How about you, Jewel? Up for coffee?" asked Kenneth.

"Yes, please, Kenneth. Shall I come?"

"No, you stay with Celia. I'll get it. I have to hit the head, anyway," said Kenneth.

"Kenneth, you know I don't like you using that crude language. What if the boys were to start using it?" scolded Celia.

"Sorry. What was I thinking?" he said to his wife with a quick wink to Jewel. "Don't go on without me," he said quickly as he was leaving the room. "I have got to hear this."

Kenneth came back into the room, juggling two large mugs of coffee; he knew Jewel preferred these to those dainty little things Celia called coffee cups. He could never get his finger in the handle to raise his cup. No sissy cups for him, he had once said to Celia. He demanded a good old mug, something he could get his hand around. Celia thought it funny one day when she came home with the four mugs, thinking she had gone too far, but she couldn't have been more surprised when Kenneth gave her a kiss and yelled, "Hooray! Finally, I can have a real cup of Joe! Thank you, my love." He said that as he sat back with a big smile and warmed his hands around the mug. The very next time Jewel came for dinner, Kenneth took out two of the new mugs and proudly proclaimed that Celia had finally taken pity on them and bought them these fine, new mugs. Jewel, like Kenneth, preferred her coffee in a mug; there was just something better, more comforting drinking coffee this way.

"Now, if you two are finished, may we continue and listen to the rest of the story? Thank you," said Celia.

"When I left here and returned to the apartment, I had a little work I wanted to finish. I played with Rocky, showered, and changed, then caught a cab up-town and waited on the top landing of the museum. I wanted to see if he was really going to show. I had given him my phone number in case he needed or wanted to cancel, and I wanted to see if I could judge his mood by his walk. Sure enough, five after three, he bounded up the stairs and asked me if I had been waiting long. I told him I had just arrived myself. We went into the museum, and I asked him if he had a preference as to what he would like to see. He said no and to just go wherever it was that I would if I had been alone, so we went to the third floor, where the new impressionist exhibit was. We walked slowly by the paintings and stopped at a few. He kept asking me what I saw so appealing in the paintings. I explained the best I could. I pointed out some of the clothing the figures were wearing and how that could be used in today's apparel. He said I had a very good eye for detail, and most of the time, he never even saw the clothes, just the colors and what seemed to him to be an endless sea of brushstrokes. I laughed at him and told him to confess. Having been educated as he was and that he had studied abroad, he must have had seen these paintings or some like them. He admitted he had in the London Museum, as well as the Louvre in Paris. I called him a scoundrel and asked if he was deliberately trying to make me seem foolish. He apologized and said he wanted to see the paintings through my eyes. He said my eyes would just shine each time I looked at a new painting and it was as though he were seeing them for the first time. He seemed so sincere. I actually felt a little sorry for him. To have been to London and France and to have seen all these and more and had felt nothing was so sad.

"We walked around the museum until five, when I asked him if he had had enough for one afternoon and that I didn't want him to overload on all the colors. He laughed so hard he had tears in his eyes, and then I had to laugh at him laughing. It was too funny. We left the museum, and he said he hadn't had an enjoyable afternoon like that in such a long time and asked me when we could do it again. Well, I was so surprised that before I had time to think, I just blurted out, 'The next time you need a color fix, just call me,' and we both laughed again. It was so surprising to me that this was the same man I had heard so much about from you, Celia, because this most definitely was not the same guy. This guy was laughing with tears in his eyes, making jokes. He was so warm and friendly and down-to-earth I was beginning to think he must have a twin, one who went to work and the other for social occasions. I'm telling you, it was really strange."

"Did he ask you to dinner?" asked Celia.

"She just told you all about the most interesting thing yet that I have ever heard about your holy mentor, and all you can ask is if he asked her to dinner? Celia, have you been listening to any of this? Because quite frankly, I seem to be more puzzled than you seem to be over his bizarre behavior," said Kenneth.

"Oh, don't worry, Kenneth, when this conversation is concluded, I shall go over every bit of information given here tonight and try to make heads or tails of it. Bizarre behavior indeed," answered Celia.

"He did ask me if I would like to get something and if I had a preference. I laughed and said, 'Believe it or not, I could go for a great big deli sandwich, maybe corned beef, yes, definitely a Reuben.'"

"Jewel, you didn't?" said Celia.

"Why? What's wrong with a Rueben?" asked Kenneth.

"Oh, you two, honestly? A man like Justin asks you out to eat and all you can think of is a big greasy sandwich, not to mention the way you eat, like there were three of you, and all of them starving?" said Celia.

"Funny you should say that, Celia, because I told him exactly that. How you tease me all the time because I have an appetite of a truck driver, and he said that it was refreshing to be with someone who could be themselves, especially when eating. He said it provoked him to no end the amount of money he had spent on dinners only for his date to take three bites and say she was so full and had to watch her waistline. Seeing me in action would restore his faith in the opposite sex, and I told him to remember that as he watched me put away my sandwich and the pickle. We had such fun. He actually pulled some of my corned beef from my sandwich to see if he liked the corned beef or the pastrami better, then he licked his fingers and said that I had made the better choice. I told him I was willing to share, but he had to give me his pickle, and he did. I think we sat there talking for a few hours, then I suggested we go out and walk for a while. He had a car service, and he just had them follow us. I don't even remember how long we walked, but when I saw the time, I said I had to come home. I told him that I was watching the boys tomorrow while you had a luncheon to go to. He asked what time I would be free and said he would like to make sure I got home safe and sound because of the neighborhood the apartment was in. I told him it wasn't necessary, but he insisted, saying it was on his way. He had to fly to Washington and could drop me along the way. I thanked him for a wonderful day, and so the end. I hope I have entertained you this evening and haven't upset you too much, Celia, especially when I tell you that I enjoyed his company so much that when he comes back on Thursday, we will be having dinner, and not just a sandwich. I would like him to see that I do have a little class, much of what you taught me. And now if you will excuse me, I am going to bed. Good night."

Obviously at a loss for words, Celia said good night. Kenneth couldn't let this night go; he stood up, clapped his hands, and said, "Nicely done, kiddo, nicely done. Good night." He then turned to his wife and asked if she was coming to bed.

"Not just yet, darling. You go on and warm the bed for me. I'll be up in just a few moments."

Celia knew there was no way she would get any sleep tonight trying to process all the information she was handed quite out of the blue. She doubted if she would ever sleep again. What would she do at work? How would she face him? Would he behave differently toward her? Would she behave differently toward him? Oh, life was so simpler before she threw that party. There was nothing to be done about any of it now; she would just let it play out and see where it went. And then in typical Celia moment, she said to herself, "Should I kill her now or wait?"

CHAPTER 4

Justin rang the doorbell at precisely five o'clock. Jonathon ran to the door, with Michael well behind. As he was taught to never open the door until he asked who it was, and with Celia now standing next to him, he asked in his most sober voice, "Who is it, please?"

"Justin Angelis," he answered.

Celia opened the door and invited him in.

"Please excuse our rather rambunctious boys. We have been trying to teach them not to open the door to strangers. They must call one of us to verify who it is before they may open it. Please, please come in. This is Jonathon, and this is Michael. Children, please say hello to Mr. Angelis. Mr. Angelis and I work together."

"Is my mommy your boss?" asked Jonathon.

"Jonathon, I am definitely not Mr. Angelis's boss. He is mine. Now please go upstairs and finish getting ready while we visit with Mr. Angelis." Celia was blushing with anger. "I'm so sorry. You never know what will come out of their darling little mouths when you least expect it," apologized Celia.

"Justin," said Kenneth, "I thought I heard a small racket going on. Don't tell me you have just met the terrible duo."

"I have, indeed. Handsome young men, and very polite," said Justin.

"Are we talking about my boys?" Kenneth laughed. "You have my wife to thank for that. If left to me, they would still be swinging from trees."

"Kenneth, what a perfectly awful thing to say about your children!" Celia was already feeling uncomfortable, and Justin hadn't been in the room but for five minutes.

"Kenneth, would you be a dear and tell Jewel Justin is here? She might not have heard the bell, and we don't want Justin to be missing his flight." Celia hoped she didn't sound like she was in a rush to get rid of him, but she was at a loss as to what to say.

"Jewel told us all about your day at the museum and letting her take you to a deli for sandwiches, of all things," said Celia, trying to sound calm and collected.

"I had a most enjoyable day," answered Justin. "It was really more than I expected. Jewel is a very knowledgeable tour guide."

"She should be. Since she has been back, that's where she spends most of her time. If she isn't there, she's working. I keep trying to tell—"

"You keep trying to tell who, Celia? Is she complaining about how little time I spend away from work or the museum? Lies, all of it. She doesn't know about my secret life as a spy or how I dress up as a hooker at night, looking for love." Jewel tried so hard not to smile as she was saying all that, but she couldn't. She saw the look of horror on Celia's face and had to laugh. Kenneth couldn't help it either, and both of them waited for Justin to jump in, but taking one look at poor Celia, he decided not to go along and openly laugh in front of her. But it was really hard not to. Celia fought hard against it but could see them all staring at her and decided it was better to laugh at the joke than be one.

"Do you have everything, dear?" Celia asked.

"Just waiting for my main man, Rocky. That is, if your boys will give him up. Poor guy, he is going to sleep for a week after the day he's had," said Jewel. Jewel called Rocky, and before long, he came running down the stairs to her.

"There's my little man. Ready to go home? Come on!" Jewel snapped his leash on and kissed Celia and Kenneth good night and headed toward the door.

"Dinner tomorrow, Jewel," reminded Celia.

"Yes, Celia. See you then, and thanks," said Jewel.

"When do you think you will be back in the office, Justin?" asked Celia.

"I'm hoping to be back on Thursday. I should have a rough draft of the merger on paper, so we should go over it as soon as possible. I don't want this to take too much time. I don't want anyone to change their minds after these lengthy negotiations. If I have to make one more trip to Washington for these fools, I'm liable to wring their necks myself. I'll call if there are any changes in my plans," said Justin to Celia.

"All right, see you then," replied Celia.

Jewel got in the car with Rocky at her heels; he was standing on Jewel's lap when Justin got in the car. As Justin seated himself, Rocky walked over Jewel and sat on Justin's lap. Without thinking, Justin put his arm around Rocky and began to pet him. Rocky seemed quite content.

"Oh my god," said Jewel softly, "Rocky's on your lap, and he's letting you pet him." Jewel was rather excited.

"Indeed, he is. It is all right, isn't it?" asked Justin.

"That's just it, the only people he lets pet him are me or the boys. Celia and Kenneth can't even pet him, let alone have him sit on their laps. He's never been this close to anyone since Chris. I guess he knows you're one of the good guys and he trusts you, like I do," said Jewel.

"Well, then, I think it's a fine start," answered Justin.

The ride back to the apartment was quiet, but before they reached the turn down to the street, the factory was on. Justin asked Clay to pull over.

"Right here, Clay. I'll just be a moment," he said and got out of the car. "Where's he going?" asked Jewel.

"Small errand," answered Clay.

Justin reappeared with a box and got in the car.

"You got a pizza?" queried Jewel.

"Yes," stated Justin. "It occurred to me that Rocky never got his pizza and movie night."

"Justin, I can't believe you did this."

"I do have my moments," joked Justin.

After they had gotten out of the car, Jewel was startled when she saw the man in the blue hood coming toward them.

"Oh no, here he comes, the man I told you about," cried Jewel.

Justin quickly motioned for Clay to get out of the car. As Jewel fumbled with the keys, she watched as Clay walked toward the man.

"Justin, what's Clay doing? We don't know if the man is dangerous or not. He could get hurt. Please call him back," cried Jewel.

"Please don't worry. Clay knows what he's doing. He is not just a driver but also acts on occasion as a bodyguard," answered Justin.

"Bodyguard—you need a bodyguard?" asked Jewel.

"He's not for me. He's for you," replied Justin as he watched what was taking place on the street.

Jewel finally got the huge door opened and waited to see what Clay was going to do. She held the door opened in case they had to get inside quickly. Clay approached the man and stopped about twenty feet from him. She could see the man hesitate and then turn and walk quickly back to the corner. Clay didn't move until the man had made it to the corner and turned and walked away. Clay then turned and walked back to Justin and Jewel.

"I think you're right, Mr. A. I think she has a definite stalker," said Clay.

"Can we please go inside?" said Jewel, holding the big door open with her body. Justin held the door as she went in and followed, leaving Clay to come in last. Jewel locked the door and threw the dead bolt. She quickly typed in the code to turn the alarm system off, then threw the switches for some of the overhead lights.

"Now, would someone tell me what that was all about?" Jewel said, trying not to quiver.

"Mr. A here told me about the man you thought was stalking you, and I needed to see for myself if I thought there was a legitimate threat," said Clay. "And...?" asked Jewel, not really sure she was ready to hear the answer. "And," continued Clay, "I'm afraid you have a right to be concerned. I think this character, whoever he is, means you harm."

It was Justin who asked the next question. "On what do you base your hypothesis?" he asked.

"First, the fact that he is going to so much trouble to hide his face, and when I approached him, he tried to give me the impression that he had something in his pocket, either a gun or knife, and he didn't back away quickly," said Clay. "I'm afraid I had to open my coat to show him that I was also armed. Seeing that I would not be intimidated, that was when he turned and walked off."

"You have a gun?" asked Jewel. By now she was really shaking. "I don't understand. What's going on, Justin? Please tell me what's going on, and please don't treat me like a child."

"Jewel, please calm down. I'll explain everything in due time. Now please show Clay the security system here in the factory," said Justin.

"But..." was all she could get out before he asked her again. She thought it over and figured she might as well go along, and then she would find out just what Justin and Clay were doing. She knew that Justin was worried about her; she could feel it. So she decided to play along, to see just how much danger they thought she was in.

Jewel explained the various components of the security system that Kenneth had installed when he turned the empty building into his factory and design center. They walked around the ground floor, then took the elevator to the second floor, and Clay examined the windows and any other place he suspected someone might be able to get in. Satisfied with the second floor, they rode up to the third floor. Again, Jewel explained the setup and answered Clay's questions. Finally, they got to the apartment. The only way into the apartment was through Kenneth's office. The apartment had a door lock that opened with a key. Once inside, you had to quickly turn off the alarm for the apartment. Then you had to set the alarm for the factory part of the building. The alarm was divided into sections, one for the apartment and one for the factory. Jewel said that she usually left the apartment alarm off until she was ready for bed and had to let Rocky out for the last time.

"As you can see," she told them, "the windows in the bedroom are just glass blocks that are built in and can't be opened, and the windows in the living room as well as the door have bars on them that are so close together that even I can't squeeze through. I lock the outside door and the inside door and set the alarm. Kenneth spent a lot of time with the security system people to be sure he was safe when he built the apartment and started staying overnight," said Jewel.

"It looks pretty secure, but I want to go out on the roof to see where the fire escapes are located. Excuse me a minute," said Clay.

While Clay went to look at the roof, Jewel looked at Justin.

"What the hell is going on, Justin? You and Clay have me scared out of my wits here. This place is a bloody fortress, and suddenly I'm not feeling so secure. What gives?" she said.

"I'm sorry, I didn't mean to frighten you, but we just wanted to make sure the building had all the safety precautions. Clay is the best in what he does, and if he feels there is a need to worry, then we must take that very seriously indeed," answered Justin.

Clay came back and told Justin about the fire escapes. "There is one on each end of the building and two in the rear," he said. "Anyone with the right motivation could easily find a way up here, but the bars are close, and with the double doors and the alarm system, I don't think anyone could pick the lock on the bar door and open it before the alarm was triggered, so I'd say this is a pretty tight system."

"All right, Clay, you're the expert," said Justin.

"Jewel," started Justin.

"What? I don't think I'm going to like this, am I?" said Jewel.

"No, I don't think you are. It is purely for your own protection, until we can get you away from here. Clay agrees with my assessment that you are in some danger, and this should not be taken lightly," continued Justin.

"Don't worry, I don't take danger lightly," replied Jewel, "especially when it's me who's in danger."

"For this reason, I have asked Clay to look over the security here in the building. While I'm in Washington, Clay is going to be watching over you. Anytime you go out, you will use the car service. Clay will be on standby, so the minute you know where and when you are going, you call him. He has put himself on a light schedule, so he should be there when you call. This card has the number for the car service, and on the back is Clay's cell. Call him first, directly," Justin said.

"Are you sure this is all necessary?" asked Jewel.

"Jewel, please humor me and make sure Clay is with you whenever you go out, please," said Justin.

"Monday, I go to Celia's for dinner, but I leave with Kenneth when he leaves, so I just need a ride back," said Jewel.

"What time would you like me to pick you up?" asked Clay.

"Around nine," stated Jewel, uncomfortable with the whole arrangement.

"Nine it is," said Clay. Clay looked at his watch and said to Justin, "Twenty minutes, Mr. A."

"All right, Clay, be right with you," answered Justin.

"Clay," said Jewel, "take a slice of pizza. Heaven knows Rocky and I can't eat the whole thing."

"Thank you, but I'll pass. Don't like to eat in the car," he said.

"You either," said Jewel, turning to Justin.

"Sorry. I make it a point not to eat before I fly," answered Justin.

"I'll meet you downstairs, Mr. A," said Clay to Justin, figuring he needed a few more minutes with Jewel in private.

"Yes, I'll be right there, Clay. And thank you for looking around. I feel better now that you've seen the security measures in this place," said Justin. Clay turned and headed for the elevator.

Justin looked at Jewel and said, "You will look out for yourself?"

"Just as I have always done. Remember, I have lived in this city for some time," stated Jewel. "I may be from the country, but I'm not careless or reckless," she added.

"I know your aren't careless, but you have never had a stalker before," reminded Justin.

"Point taken," answered Jewel. "Come on, we wouldn't want you to miss your flight."

Jewel turned and walked to the elevator. Inside she could feel herself getting angry. She knew she shouldn't be directing the anger at Justin—he was, after all, trying to look after her best interest—but why did she feel like he was treating her like a child? They didn't talk to each other as they rode down in the elevator. Once they reached the ground floor, Clay was waiting. Jewel opened the door, and Clay went through. She looked up at Justin and told him to have a safe trip. Justin thought to himself that this was one obstinate woman, but he liked her spirit and was thankful she didn't prove to be one of those poor, wretched creatures who would crumble in the face of any danger. No, this one hit things straight on and didn't back down. He couldn't help but smile as he looked at her.

"I shall miss you," he said and bent to kiss her forehead, then turned and went out the door. He made sure he didn't look back to remind her to lock the door as he wanted to, because at this point he wasn't sure she wouldn't pick up something and throw it at him. Maybe he did come on sounding a little overprotective, but she had awakened something in him, something primal, something he thought was gone, and the need to know that she would be there when he returned was too great to take lightly.

Jewel watched him get in the car, then closed and locked the door. She went back up to the third floor and into the apartment and set the alarm for the factory. Suddenly, she felt so alone, and for the first time since she had been living in the apartment, she felt frightened. She shook her head. "Damn dummy," she said aloud. "Rocky, guess what we've got? Drum roll, please." And as she opened the pizza box, she yelled out a "Ta-da!" She got down two dishes and placed a slice on each. Then she cut one of the slices up into small pieces.

"Here you go, Rock. No beer tonight, though. Those guys have me too upset to be drinking, so bon appétit. Rocky, we have our movie-pizza-night, thanks to Justin." She thought a minute about the kiss on the forehead and, for a second, gave in to the fear that Justin didn't see her in a romantic way, not in the way she was beginning to feel about him. His kiss was something you would give a child when you left. She felt totally confused, but not for long. Jewel had learned from the past few years not to prejudge anything, play along, and see where things would take you, and if you didn't like it, change it if you think it'd be worthwhile. If not, then get out.

At ten thirty, Jewel decided she was tired, and since she was always up early, she decided to call it a night. She turned off the TV, did the dishes, and put the pizza in the fridge. "Come on, Rocky, wake up. It's time to go to bed." Funny, she thought, he had already been sleeping for two hours while she was watching the movie. Not one of Rocky's favorites. Rocky loved the old Japanese Godzilla movies; there was something about the voice of Godzilla that kept him looking at the TV screen. It really was funny to anyone who saw him. She remembered the first time Chris saw Rocky watch a Godzilla movie, how he laughed and laughed, saying it was the funniest thing he had ever seen. Yep, the Rock was one in a million. She never regretted that day she decided to go to the yard sale the local shelter had to raise money. Her friends laughed when she told them that she heard the little dog talk to her as she walked by, but she knew she did, and if no one believed her, it was fine with her. She and Rocky knew the truth.

"Come on, sleepyhead, time to go pee."

Rocky waited for her to put the lights on and unlock the door, then out he went to his favorite patch of green on the roof. She watched him sniff around and squat, as was his preferred method. Jewel was always happy he went like that; dogs that lifted their legs, whizzing all over everything, seemed dirty somehow. Rocky's little puddle was neat, like a little puppy, and so less offensive, even to Celia. She gazed out the glass again but didn't see the little dog. Where had he gone? There wasn't much out there to interest him. She opened the door and called his name, but nothing. She called again and thought she saw him by the bush behind the chaise lounge. Jewel called again, but again the dog did not appear. Jewel had all the outside lights on and looked very carefully around the roof. She didn't see anything, so she went out to find Rocky. She found him sniffing wildly all around the bush and around some of the branches that were lying on the floor. *What in the world?* she thought to herself as she looked at all the broken and discarded branches. The back of the bush was nearly broken in half. She bent down to look at some of the broken branches. What could have caused these branches to be broken like this? She picked up two that seemed crushed.

As she examined the bush further for damage, she noticed one branch in the middle of many broken ones, as if everything was deliberately broken so you would notice that particular branch. There appeared to be a piece of paper impaled on the branch. Jewel could feel the hair on the back of her neck stiffen. She needed to get the paper and Rocky and get back into the apartment quickly. She did both with amazing speed.

Once in the apartment, she locked both doors and quickly set the alarm. She drew the drapes closed but left all the lights on.

Now she focused on the piece of paper in her hand. It was folded into quarters. She was about to open it, then suddenly stopped. *I should call the police,* she thought. *And what? Tell them I found a piece of paper on the roof?* The first thing they would want to know was what the letter said, and she wouldn't know that unless she opened it. Taking great care not to mangle the paper, she carefully opened it, first one side, then the other. The words printed on the paper made her blood run cold. Written in a childlike fashion were the words "I'm always watching you." Jewel began to tremble. She couldn't think; she felt frozen, like a rabbit caught in the headlights of an oncoming car. Was this meant for her? Who did this? Why? She thought about calling Justin. *Why would I want to call him? Besides, he is in Washington.* After the way she acted when he was asking her to take things seriously, she doubted he would want to hear from her anyway, and she certainly didn't expect him to drop everything and come running home just because she found a small piece of paper. *Clay, I should call Clay, he said day or night.*

"Jewel," she said to herself out loud, "get a grip. There's no need to call anyone. You're safe here, and this is nothing more than a prank, probably some kids playing around on the roof. Clay said someone could get up the fire escape if they really wanted to, and kids can climb anything. Everything is locked, all alarms are on now, so just go to bed and deal with it tomorrow."

But sleep did not come this night.

Jewel hated Mondays at the shop—everyone complaining about how fast the weekend went, how much they had to do that never seemed to get done, and how it seemed to take everyone so long to get back in the smooth rhythm of work. Jewel was already working on a pattern when most of Kenneth's personal staff came in.

"How long have you been up and working?" inquired one of them. "Don't you ever sleep? Here, have a doughnut."

"Oh, sure, give the Energizer Bunny more sugar. That's just what she needs." Another laughed.

"Well, just for that, I will have a doughnut and lots of highly caffeinated coffee with it." Jewel laughed as well.

CHAPTER 5

This group of people Kenneth assembled as his personal assistants was a close-knit group; they all got along so well and were always there to help out one another no matter what. Putting on a show was one of the most stressful events a designer could have, but Kenneth's crew were the best, and they all worked together to make sure it always went off without a hitch. They did this because Kenneth always treated them with respect and listened to their ideas. Plus, when a show was a hit and the clothes were selling well, Kenneth gave them each a card thanking them for their hard work and giving them a small bonus. It was never the idea of the bonus that made these people work so hard for Kenneth, however; they would all tell you that it was knowing you were appreciated and your ideas, however small, were listened to.

Jewel took a doughnut and refilled her coffee mug. She had made the pot when she came out of the apartment instead of leaving it to someone else. No one was in charge of making the coffee. There was just one rule: whoever drained the last cup made the next pot, and with this crew, there was never an empty pot. Jewel decided to wait until everyone had their coffee and doughnuts and was working on their assigned project for the day before she went to Kenneth with the paper, but after working a while, she decided against it. He didn't need any further distractions, and besides, there was nothing he could do. No, she would wait until Clay picked her up tonight, and she would tell him. Until then she would put it out of her mind.

Clay was there precisely at nine. Celia was surprised when Jewel told them she was using the car service at the insistence of her boss. It was Kenneth who asked if there was something going on that they felt she needed the car. Jewel didn't want to go into the whole thing at that time, so she just said she would explain everything to him at work tomorrow and not to worry, that she was fine. She hated putting them off like that, but she needed to tell Clay the events of last evening first. As he pulled the car up close to the curb, Jewel told him she needed to show him something and asked if he could come upstairs. Clay turned off the motor and followed Jewel inside. She turned off the alarm but threw the deadbolt on the door. Riding up to the third floor, she began to tell him what took place after they left her. She disabled the apartment alarm and unlocked the doors leading to the roof. She took Clay over to the mangled bush. Clay examined everything, the broken branches, the ones that looked like they were crushed underfoot, and the one branch where the paper was impaled.

"This branch was sharpened to a point with a knife. The rest were just broken around it. But you can see that someone has been standing here, and for some time too. Let me take a quick look around, and we'll go inside. I want to see this letter before we decide what to do," said Clay. Clay walked around the roof, checking the fire escapes, then came back and told Jewel to go inside.

"Let's see the paper that was on the branch," said Clay. Jewel went to hand Clay the paper, but before he would take it, he put on rubber gloves.

"I didn't do that. I just opened it," said Jewel.

"You reacted the way anyone would, but the fewer prints on this paper, the better. They may be able to get some prints off it other than yours," said Clay. He carefully took the letter and read it.

"Have you told anyone about this?" he asked Jewel.

"No. I wanted to wait until I spoke to you," answered Jewel.

"Good, but now I think we need to get the police involved. Whoever this is, they are getting more daring, and that is never a good thing. I still have some friends at the department. I'll give them a call."

Jewel paced around the apartment and finally decided to put a pot of coffee on. She had a feeling this was going to be a long night. When Clay got off the phone, Jewel asked him if she should call Kenneth. He told her she should, because they would need his fingerprints so they could rule his out. Jewel took a long sigh and picked up the phone. She tried to remain calm, but Kenneth was getting excited, and she could hear Celia in the background trying to ask him questions. She heard her say something about a sitter and going with him, but she heard him say positively not and told Jewel he would be right down. At this time of evening, there wouldn't be too much traffic after Forty-Second Street. The garment district was completely closed at night; all the business closed around six, so with the exception of a few small eateries, the area was desolate.

Clay took the cup of coffee Jewel offered him and sat down in the kitchen. He was not a very talkative person, rather sober actually, which she supposed was a good thing when you were in the kind of business Clay was in. No useless chatter to distract you. Clay jumped up as soon as he heard the bell and took the elevator down. When he returned, he was with two other men that Clay introduced as two friends of his, Detective Jason Leeds and Detective Warren Beach.

"Sorry I didn't call you yesterday," said Clay, "but Ms. Lansby just told me about it tonight when I brought her home." The detectives followed Clay out onto the roof and examined the bush where the paper was found, then all three marched around the perimeter of the roof, occasionally bending down to pick something up or to turn something over. When they were satisfied that they had seen everything, they came back into the apartment. Clay walked them through the security systems for the factory and the apartment. As they were returning from the lower floor, Kenneth was with them. He was the first to reach Jewel.

"Jewel, what the blazes is going on? Are you all right? You're not hurt, are you?"

"Kenneth, I'm fine. Please calm down. I'm really all right."

"How long have the police been here? Did you call them? When did this start? Why didn't you tell me this was going on?"

"I'm sorry, Kenneth. I was going to tell you yesterday, but we got so busy and I didn't want to tell you at dinner. If you or Celia raised your voice, the boys might have heard, and I couldn't take that chance. I thought it best to wait and tell Clay. He would know best what to do," said Jewel, almost on the verge of tears. She quickly turned away so he wouldn't see that she was so frightened.

The detectives talked to Kenneth a while and told him they would need him to go down to the lab tomorrow and be fingerprinted, but Kenneth told them his prints were already on file. He had to have them taken for the pistol permit he got a few years ago. He kept the gun in the safe in his office and showed it to them. When they were finished looking over the place and talking to Kenneth, they asked Jewel for the piece of paper and to described in as much detail as she could when she thought she realized someone was watching her. Jewel went as far back as the end of January. She described the man she kept seeing in the blue hooded jacket and how he would walk toward her from the corner when she came home at night. She told them that she had even begun to ask the cab- drivers if they could wait until she got the door opened.

"Yeah," snickered Detective Beach. "I bet that went over big, any of them actually wait."

"Yes, a few," answered Jewel. Not as many as she would have liked, but her faith in the people who drove the cabs was not jaded because of those who did not wait. She looked directly at Detective Beach and immediately could see that this man had faith in no one. He was older than his partner, possibly close to retirement age, and had no doubt seen his share of the worse the city had to offer.

They continued to question her until well after midnight. Kenneth asked if he needed to stay and left by eleven, eager to get home knowing that Celia would be waiting for him and would want a detailed account of these evenings' events. Celia could be relentless if she felt even the slightest that she was not being kept in the loop, but when it came to her close family and friends, Celia was unyielding, and despite their occasional differences of opinion, Celia regarded Jewel as the younger sister she never had. Although Jewel was not as socially aware or as sophisticated as Celia, the two often went shopping together and, on occasion, enjoyed a day at the spa. Celia loved to see the boys interact with Jewel, and when she left and decided to stay in the country and start her quilt business, she made it a point to come into the city and spend the day with them and try to explain why she was leaving for a while, constantly telling them how much she loved them and that she would come back for visits all the time. And she did. When she returned to the city in January, it was as though she had never left. She loved them, and they loved her, and she always put them first. Celia loved her for that. Despite the fact that she worked long hours and sometimes questioned her decision to become a lawyer, knowing it would take her away from them for much of the time, Celia believed in her heart that her greatest achievement would always be Jonathon and Michael.

Kenneth told Celia what had transpired at the apartment.

"Why didn't Jewel say something before now? She could have been killed going back down there at night. Didn't she say anything to you about this, this stalker?" asked Celia.

"She did mention some weeks ago that she thought someone was watching her, but I remember we joked about it. I think I said something stupid, like, 'Hang on to your portfolio' or some such thing. I really wasn't thinking until I saw the look on her face. But you know Jewel. She just laughed, and I guess I thought that was that. She never mentioned it again," said Kenneth.

"Why the hell would she if she didn't think you were taking her seriously?" answered Celia. "That poor thing, sending her home every Monday night alone. God knows what could have happened to her. I know the factory is a fortress, but even with all the security, you still have to get inside in one piece," said Celia. "And why do you think she was using the car service? Do you think Justin knows and that's why she has it? Why would she tell him and not us?"

"Celia, all questions will be answered in due time. Right now all I want to do is take a shower and go to bed," answered Kenneth.

Jewel was exhausted by the time the police finished with her, and as she followed them to the main door to lock it, she made it a point to ask Clay to please not tell Justin anything if he spoke to him.

"He's not going to like being kept in the dark about this. This has been exactly what he was worried about, that things could escalate. That's why he brought me in," said Clay.

"I know he was worried. I felt it when he left Sunday evening. But there is nothing he can do, and you're here, doing exactly what you're supposed to. So what's the point of telling him? He'll be back Thursday, and we can tell him everything then, okay?" replied Jewel.

"All right, but if we uncover anything or if anything else happens, I'm calling him. Understood?" said Clay.

"Understood," replied Jewel.

"All right, get the locks and alarms set. You know I would really feel better if you had someplace else to stay for a while," said Clay.

"I'll be fine," said Jewel. "Don't worry." *Don't worry,* thought Jewel. *I'll be worrying enough for the both of us.*

Jewel let Rocky out while Clay and the police were still there, so she wouldn't have to open the roof doors again. "Looks like another sleepless night, Rocky."

Tuesday proved to be an interesting day. What had started out like so many others ended in Jewel getting a new apartment. Kenneth came out of his office around one o'clock and gave Jewel a phone message he had just taken for her. A man named Eugene Oshanski called and had an apartment for rent and wanted her to be there at four thirty if she was interested. Please call the number to verify if she was coming to see it.

"Kenneth, what do you think? Did he sound legit or like a psycho?" said Jewel.

"He actually sounded quite professional, but how can you tell on the phone?" answered Kenneth. "But if you're planning to go, I'd take someone with you. What about that car driver who was here last night?"

"That is who I'm going to call right now. I hope he's free."

Jewel called Clay's direct number and told him about the phone call about the apartment. Jewel thought it odd that Clay didn't seem at all surprised. He said he would pick her up in and around three thirty and would stay until she decided what she wanted to do.

The next few hours seemed to be moving in slow motion. Jewel kept looking at the clock and was relieved when three thirty arrived. She told Kenneth she was leaving. He told her to let one of the men check outside before she went out, but that really didn't feel right to her. Putting someone else in danger that was meant for her wasn't something she could do. When Jewel arrived on the ground floor, there were two of the men who worked in shipping, waiting for her.

"Mr. Dolan called down and told us not to let you out of the building until we know who's out there. We know about the goings-on here last night, and we mean to keep you safe as can be."

"What would we do down here without our little jewel?" said one of the men. "Yeah, nobody bakes us real cookies like you do, or gives us a hand when we get in those big shipments of specialty fabrics from France. You're one of ours, and we don't let family get hurt."

"Now you just stay put till I tell you it's okay," said Ned. He unlocked the door and looked up and down the street. It looked all right, but he wouldn't let her out until the car came.

"You know, I love you guys, but you're making me feel like some weak debutant, and you know I can kick ass if I have to," said Jewel.

"We know you can, Jewel. I remember when you took that sissy boy Greg down in arm wrestling, nearly had the little bugger crying, but the boss said you don't go out till the car comes, so live with it," said Ned. "Here's the car now."

Jewel thanked the guys and told them she owed them cookies.

"We like them peanut butter ones," said Joe.

"Yeah, the peanut butters are the best," added Ned.

"You got it, guys, first chance I get," replied Jewel as she climbed into the car.

Clay had the door opened for her, and she could feel her face getting hot. God, this is so embarrassing. *I don't know why I just couldn't ride up front instead of back here.* Just grin and bear it, she thought to herself again. Clay had asked for the address when she called him, so he knew where they were going. Jewel tried to think of something to say to him, but she couldn't. She could usually find something to say to just about anyone, but Clay was just a little intimidating, but not in a way that frightened her, because she felt just as safe with him as she did with Justin; there was just something about him. She thought it strange that all her life she trusted no one, and now she had two men she felt safe with.

They rode up town in silence. She never gave any thought to the address when she told him, but when he stopped and parked, she was surprised and had to look at the telephone note she had written the address on. This was the place. Why didn't she recognize it? The address was just two buildings down from where Justin took her to his apartment.

"Clay, doesn't Justin live right there?" she said, pointing to the building on her left.

"Yes, he does," replied Clay. And that was all he would say.

Jewel instinctually knew that asking him anything further would be futile. She opened the car door and started up the stairs; there were only four, and she quickly arrived at the front door. As she was looking for a bell to ring, the door opened.

"Ms. Lansby?" inquired the man.

"Yes. You must be Mr. Oshanski," replied Jewel.

"Please come in. It's good to see someone who takes punctuality seriously. Nothing irritates me more than people who are late," said Mr. Oshanski as he turned and told Jewel to follow him. He went to a door on the left side of a very large foyer. He opened the door and motioned for Jewel to go in.

"Please don't let the condition of some parts of the apartment worry you. The apartment is getting a complete renovation. New thermal windows, a completely new kitchen. As you can see, most of the old ones have already been removed. This sliding glass door is being replaced as well with a new, energy-efficient model. We are also putting in a completely new bath. The carpeting in all the rooms are being taken out and replaced, and of course, the entire apartment will be painted. Feel free to look around, Ms. Lansby," he said.

Jewel walked through the apartment and tried to envision what it would look like with all the improvements they were doing to it. It was wonderful. The rooms were good size, but not so large that they would take forever to clean. Cleaning was not one of Jewel's favorite things to do, especially when there was much more things to do with her time. Her goal in life was to make enough money so that she could hire a cleaning lady to come in every week and do it. She went back into the kitchen and looked at the new cabinets that were on the floor, ready to be installed. Nice finish, she thought to herself. *Not white, which shows every spot, especially when Rocky comes in after being in the rain and stands in front of the lightest thing in the place, which usually is the kitchen cabinets, and shakes himself free of the water.* She knew all too well how that went because of the cabinets in her house upstate. She was always wiping them off.

"Mr. Oshanski, may I go out to the yard?" she asked.

"Sure. Here, let me get that door for you," he said and opened the sliding door.

"Mr. Oshanski, I should tell you that I have a small dog, and I know many places don't like to have animals in their rentals," continued Jewel.

"Thank you for being so honest. Be surprised with the people that say they don't have animals, then after they move in, you find out they have more than one," Mr. Oshanski replied. "A small dog is fine, as long as he ain't a barker. I have some cops renting here, and they do shift work. Can't be having a barker."

"Oh, I promise you, he isn't a barker, and I take him to work with me every day, so no problem there. Is it all right for him to come out in the yard?" asked Jewel.

"He can come out, all right. If you look here, you'll see that there's a wall all round that separates it from the main yard. So if you let him out, he can't go anywhere. Some of the other tenants have dogs, and they get together now, and then in the big yard. They had a birthday party a week or two ago for one of their dogs, cake and all, a whole lot of money spent on a dog party. Silliest thing I ever heard of," said Mr. Oshanski.

Jewel followed the man back inside and was about to ask the question that she dreaded. Great apartment, great neighborhood, and sounded like great tenants—it was all too good to be true. She gathered up all her courage and prepared herself for the big letdown.

"What is the rent on this apartment?" she asked. Jewel couldn't believe her ears. No, this must be a mistake. She repeated the amount aloud and asked him if she heard it correctly. He said she had, but with all the renovations, surely it must be more.

"Mr. Oshanski, if you're absolutely sure that's the monthly rent, then I'll take it, and I hope I don't wake up and find out this has been a dream," she said quickly.

"It's no dream, I guarantee that. I expect to have everything finished in about two weeks. I'll give you all the lease agreements to read over and fill out. If you could get them to me as soon as possible, I will of course be doing a background check, so if you have anything to say that might disqualify you from taking this apartment, tell me now so neither of us wastes each other's time," said Mr. Oshanski. "And make sure you put down the telephone numbers of the people you use as references."

"No problem. I'll get them back to you tomorrow. What time can I meet you?" asked Jewel.

"You don't have to make a special trip. Just drop them in the mail. Here's my card. Send them to this address. If you can get them in the mail tomorrow, that will be fine," he said.

"Thank you so much, Mr. Oshanski. I promise I'll be your best tenant," said Jewel.

"Don't have to be the best, just a good one," answered Mr. Oshanski. "I'll be talking to you soon. Goodbye, Ms. Lansby." Jewel turned and floated out the door. When she reached Clay leaning on the car, she couldn't contain herself any longer.

"I have an apartment, Clay, I have an apartment. I can move in two weeks. I can't believe it! It's being completely renovated, new everything—can you believe it? It's one bedroom, perfect for me. And get this, Rocky will have his own little yard! How cool is that? When I saw where we were, I knew better than to get my hopes up, but when he told me the rent, I couldn't believe it. I even asked him twice if he was sure, and he said he was, and it hit me, I just got an apartment. I just hope he doesn't call me tomorrow and say he made a mistake. Oh, please cross your fingers, Clay. In two weeks, I could be out of that downtown hellhole, and the best part, no more stalker, Clay, no more stalker! This absolutely calls for a celebration. What do you want to do, let me buy you dinner?"

"No, thank you," replied Clay.

"Come on. Nothing fancy. We can go to the deli. You have to eat sometime, I have to eat sometime, so why not?" said Jewel. He could refuse all he wanted, but nothing was going to bring her down; she just got an early Christmas present, and if he didn't want to celebrate with her, then she would find someone who would even if she had to ask every person at work.

Clay hated to spoil her good mood, but as long as he was entrusted with her care by Mr. A, he felt it was his obligation to make sure she remained safe, and even something as innocent as sitting down and having a meal could distract him, so he knew he had to refuse.

"I know you're flying high right now, and I really don't mean to rain on your parade," he started.

"Then don't," snapped Jewel.

"I'm sorry, but we still need to take certain precautions. We don't know how serious this joker really is. You can tell your friends that you found an apartment, but don't give out the address, not to any one, especially at work. Just say down near Little Italy. We don't yet know if anyone on the inside could be giving him information about your comings and goings," he continued. "Of course you can tell Mr. Dolan, but no one else for now."

"I know you're just doing your job, Clay, and I really appreciate all you've done for me thus far, but you sure know how to end a party," said Jewel.

"I am sorry, Ms. Lansby, but—"

"Can you at least lighten up and call me Jewel? I hate Ms. Lansby!" cried Jewel.

"I'm afraid that wouldn't be professional, Ms. Lansby," replied Clay, looking very serious. "And I need to keep our relationship strictly business. If I start to think of you as a friend. It could comprise my objectivity, and I would lose my effectiveness. I'm really sorry, but that's the way it has to be."

"I'm sorry, Clay. I guess I'm behaving like a child. I do understand what's at stake here. Believe me, I do. It was just fun for a while not to have to think of it," said Jewel.

"I know this has to be hard for you, but you need to stay focused. Be aware of your surrounding at all times and try to take note of anyone who looks suspicious. Let that voice inside alert you to possible danger. It has been my experience that most women have some kind of built-in radar that tells them if something doesn't feel right. Tap into it, let it work for you. As long as we can stay on the offence, we should be able to wrap this up in no time, and you can get back to your normal life," said Clay.

"I hope I remember what my normal life was like after this." Jewel laughed. "Okay, if you won't have dinner with me, then I guess you can just take me home. Rocky and I will split a can of chicken soup."

"Your dog eats chicken soup?" asked Clay as he opened the car door for her.

"Yep. If it's good enough for me, then Rocky will usually eat it. He does have a few things he won't eat, like mushrooms or peas and broccoli, but other than that, I've got the best dog in the world," answered Jewel. "My little guy is the best dog ever." Jewel rode back to the apartment in silence. Only when they pulled in to park did Clay speak.

"Remain in the car, please, Ms. Lansby, until I open the door," said Clay very formally. Jewel did as she was told. Clay finally opened the door and told her she could get out.

"Please unlock the door, turn off the alarm, and wait for me," said Clay.

Jewel watched Clay carefully look in all directions. When he was satisfied there was no one around, he followed her into the building. Jewel didn't know what to do next; she was already accustomed to waiting for him to give her her next order. God, she hated this, she thought to herself. Clay finally appeared and told her to bolt the door, which she did.

"Are there any small rooms on this floor that can be locked from the inside?" he asked her. Jewel had to think. Her mind was racing. Now, what was going on?

"I think there is a maintenance room on this level, and I think it can be locked from the inside. I know whenever Ned is fixing some broken equipment and doesn't want to be disturbed, he locks the door. It's right over here." Jewel led Clay past the elevator and to the maintenance room; she opened the door and put on the light. There was a wooden counter and a chair. Above the counter were hooks that held an assortment of different-size wire, containers of nails and screws, and neatly labeled tools. Clay looked inside and examined the door. There was a hook and latch and a keyed door lock. Clay was satisfied that it was constructed well enough for an emergency; it even had a phone on the wall, which was a plus. It just needed a few simple touches.

"I want you to get a small flashlight, a throwaway cell phone, a candy bar of your choice, and a bottle of water. Put them in a bag. I want you to put the bag in the closet, on the floor, or in back of something, so it won't be easily detected. This is just an extra backup plan. Now, listen carefully. If someone was to breach the apartment door with the bars, then the first alarm will go off. You are not to look, not to do anything, but run down to this level, hit the factory alarm so it goes off, and go directly to this room. It might be a good idea to get a key made for this lock, just in case someone accidentally locks it. You can hide it somewhere near here. You go into the room, throw the latch, and put a screwdriver through it. Leave the light off. That's what the flashlight is for. And if you have to be in there for a while, you have the candy bar and water. They shouldn't be necessary, because the alarms will get fire and police here in no time. Under no circumstances will you leave this room until you hear the sirens and vehicles outside. Then run and open the door. If the power is cut and the alarms don't go off and you think someone is trying to get in through the roof doors, Rocky should pick that up before you. Follow the same procedure and use the cell phone to call 911. Any questions?"

"No, Clay, I think you've made it pretty clear. You have scared me to death, but I think I've got the message," answered Jewel. "Where's James Bond when you need him?" Clay gave her a serious look, trying to decide whether or not she was taking him seriously, but he knew instinctively that she was strong and would follow his plan.

"Are we good here?" said Clay.

"We're good," replied Jewel. "I will get that stuff together tomorrow and put it in here, but how am I going to get a key to the lock?"

"First, ask Mr. Dolan. You will have to explain what all this is for, but remind him to tell no one. If he doesn't have a spare key, ask him to see if Ned has a spare. If not, he will have to take Ned's and have a duplicate made. I doubt a worker will question the boss. Anything else?" asked Clay.

"No, I think we're good," said Jewel.

"All right, let's go up. I want to take a look around," said Clay.

They got into the elevator and went through Kenneth's office, opened the door, and quickly turned off the apartment's alarm. Clay asked her to unlock both doors, and he walked around the perimeter of the roof. He stopped to look at the greenery, and when he found nothing, he asked her to lock up and escort him out of the building. He didn't say anything further to her except good night. Jewel was surprised she got that. After all the alarms were on and she and Rocky were eating their soup, she thought again of the apartment. Taking the apartment meant that she had made up her mind to stay in the city and not to go back to the country even though she was much happier there. She let her mind take her back to the country, the place that really felt like home. She endured some horrific things growing up there. As a child, the awful happenings with the man she had to call uncle, and then later, when her mother married and she had to endure much of the same and prayed daily for school to end and summer be over so she could go away to college. It didn't even matter that she had to live with her aunt; all she wanted was to be away from there. It wasn't all bad, though, and those were the memories she chose to remember; the rest she just put out of her mind. Jewel was a survivor.

Wednesday, Jewel took care of the things Clay told her to do. She had explained to Kenneth what Clay wanted her to do in case of an emergency, and luckily, he did have a spare key to the maintenance room. Kenneth expressed his deep concern for her, but Jewel told him not to worry, that she would be in her new apartment in two weeks, and hopefully this nightmare would be over. Kenneth suggested she stay at his house until her apartment was ready, but Jewel refused. She didn't want to throw the balance of their lives off, especially the boys. Celia had everything running like a well-oiled machine, and Jewel didn't want to upset it. Staying overnight once in a while was one thing, but to move in for a few weeks, maybe longer, was not something she wanted to do.

Thursday, Justin called and asked if she was free for the evening. She told him she was, and he said he would like to take her to Josephina's for dinner. Was she up for Italian? Again, she said she was. He told her Clay would pick her up at six thirty and promptly hung up. How strange, thought Jewel. He acted so impersonal, so businesslike. What had changed?

CHAPTER 6

Clay was as punctual as ever, and they drove silently uptown. Clay parked, opened the door for her, and told her that Justin would like to see her in his apartment. Did she remember where it was? She told him she did. She took the elevator up to his apartment and knocked on the door. Justin opened the door and stepped back, allowing her to go in. He closed the door, and when Jewel turned around to look at him, he stepped closer, cradled her head in his hands, and kissed her. Time was suddenly standing still.

Jewel opened her eyes and said, "Again, please."

Justin laughed and repeated the kiss. "I missed you so," he said.

"I wondered if you missed me at all, the way you spoke to me on the phone," said Jewel.

"I'm sorry. I knew if I spoke to you for any length of time, I would never be able to hang up. I missed hearing your voice, but I needed to get some business out of the way so that I could see you tonight, and so I needed to be curt," he answered.

"I may forgive you if you tell me the reason you kissed me on the forehead Sunday evening when you left and not like you just did," replied Jewel.

"Again, I must argue, the same applies had I kissed you the way I have wanted to for such a long time."

"How long?" said Jewel.

"Since the first night," said Justin, "you must have felt it. It has been the hardest thing I've ever had to do, trying to restrain myself. All I've been able to think of is to hold you in my arms and kiss you."

"Then you're forgiven. Just promise. No more kisses on the forehead. It makes me feel like a child being scolded and forgiven," said Jewel.

"I promise, no more kisses on the forehead—unless you're ill, of course. A kiss on the forehead is perfectly acceptable when one is ill. Especially when the other doesn't want to catch the same thing." Justin laughed.

"All right, then, funny man, only when I'm sick." Jewel had to laugh with him and wanted to tell him that she would kiss him no matter what, but she didn't.

"I'll let you kiss me again, and then you can tell me about your trip," said Jewel. Justin took her in his arms and kissed her, longer this time and with more passion. Time stood still again. Jewel opened her eyes slowly and smiled.

"I will tell you about my trip at dinner," he said. "There is something of importance I need to discuss with you now."

"Oh, please," begged Jewel, "don't get all serious on me. I have endured nothing, but with Clay, I swear the man is made of stone."

"I'm sorry, but this is important. I have known from the beginning that you put honesty and trust above all in a relationship, and I am of the same mind. So this needs to be said and heard, and please try to refrain from bombarding me with a million questions until I have concluded. Now please sit down. About five years ago, my accountant told me I needed some write-offs because I was making a great deal of money and thus needed the deductions. He suggested real estate, so I bought this building. Over the past few years, as other buildings became available, I bought them too. Not knowing anything about running an apartment building or having any interest in doing so, I hired a building manager. He would be responsible for whatever it took to keep these building running smoothly. I only met with this man twice a year with my accountant to review and approve or disapprove the way he was handling the buildings. The collected monies from the rentals are deposited in an account set up by my accountant. So to sum it all up, I own buildings but have nothing whatsoever to do with them except to take advantage of the deductions my accountant gets for me come tax time. Do you understand so far?"

"Yes, it's pretty clear. Kenneth does similar things to save money come tax time," answered Jewel. Jewel suddenly jumped to her feet. "You own my building! The building that has the apartment I just rented, are you telling me you own it?"

"Yes," said Justin, remaining quiet.

"Did you call and arrange for me to get that apartment? You did, didn't you?" said Jewel excitedly.

"No. All I did was ask the manager if any apartments were available. I gave him your name and number and asked him to give you first refusal. As I told you, I have nothing whatsoever to do with the running of the buildings. I have no idea what the rents are, and I certainly wouldn't know if you could afford one or not. All I did was make an inquiry. The rest was up to him."

Justin was now on his feet, facing Jewel. Jewel looked at him, then turned and walked away. She looked out the window to the street below. Justin was reluctant to say anything to her until he could determine how angry she really was. Jewel remained silent for a few more minutes, then turned and walked back to him. Justin couldn't tell what she was thinking and therefore remained quiet and observant. Jewel knew she had him but couldn't resist the temptation to let him squirm a little longer. She stood directly in front of him now.

"Kiss me," she said.

Justin was completely surprised by her sudden request, but not knowing what to expect and expecting the worst, he did as she asked. Suddenly, Jewel bubbled over with emotion.

"Justin, you're home. I'm so glad!" squealed Jewel. "I've got the best news: I got an apartment. And you'll never guess where it is— just two doors down from yours! Isn't that wonderful?" Jewel could not control herself any longer and just started laughing.

The look on Justin's face was priceless. It took him a minute to realize what she had just done to him. He flopped down into the chair, looking like he was just hit by a train, and then started to laugh too.

"I can't believe I got you," she said. "That's for the kiss on the forehead."

"You're an evil woman, Ms. Lansby, an evil woman, indeed. Does this mean you are keeping the apartment?"

"Of course I'm keeping the apartment, silly. I may be many things, even a little devilish when necessary, but I am definitely not stupid," answered Jewel.

Justin breathed a very long sigh of relief.

"I can't tell you how much this apartment means to me. I told Shelby about it because she is going to help me decorate, but I didn't tell her where it was. Clay told me not to tell anyone the address except Kenneth, but Shelby doesn't work with me, so I don't see why I can't tell her. Can you talk to him and get him to lighten up a little? I know he takes his work very seriously, but does he have to frighten me? He's got me seeing men in blue hoodies behind every bush and lamppost," said Jewel.

"Well, if what he told me about the incident Sunday evening is true, then I think you had better stay frightened. At least then we know that you are watching what's going on around you. Face it, Jewel, since this all started, things have been escalating, and both Clay and I think the worse might not be over yet. We have some concerns about your safety and can't stress enough how important it is for you to be vigilant. Clay's purpose is not to frighten you but to make you aware of what is going on around you," said Justin.

"I know, and I promise I will stay alert. Now can we please talk about something else? Better yet, food. I'm melting away, and I need food," said Jewel, holding her stomach.

"You are incorrigible," replied Justin, "but if food is what m'lady desires, then food it shall be."

Justin told Clay that they wouldn't need him to take them to dinner since it was just a short walk around the corner, and he told him he would call when they were finished. As they walked, Jewel put her arm around his and waited to see his reaction. It was pleasing and felt so normal the way he placed his other hand over hers. Thinking back on it, since the beginning of their relationship, which was really less than a week, except for the kiss on the forehead Sunday evening when he left for Washington and discounting the kisses tonight, they had never touched. Jewel knew their relationship had just changed to a more intimate one, and she felt happier than she had in so long. Such an unlikely pair, she could hear Celia say now.

As they stood inside Josephina's, waiting to be taken to their table, Jewel had a moment to look around. The restaurant was nicely proportioned, large enough so you weren't within listening range of the next table, yet small enough to have a warm, cozy feel to it. The colors were a refreshing change from the usual red, green, and white that most Italian places were decorated in. The colors here were warm greens and golds with just a few accents of deep burgundy. Very nicely done, thought Jewel. The table covers alternated between green and gold, with the napkins all in burgundy. Cut crystal glasses sparkled from the mauve-colored candles in the center of the tables. Jewel had just finished taking it all in when a man came rushing toward them. Jewel thought she remembered his face from the night they stopped in for the soup. *Was it only last Saturday?* she thought to herself. *Somehow it seemed so much longer than that.* No, that was all it was. They met Friday night at Celia's party, then went to the museum on Saturday, and that was when they stopped in for the soup and went back to Justin's apartment, where she shared with him the problem she had with Lawrence, her leaving the city, the quilt shop, and finally, her involvement with Chris. They had shared so much in such a short time together.

"Mr. Angelis, so good to see you tonight?" he said. "Are we dining in tonight or just here for more soup? Yes, I remember, two soup to go. Was good no?"

"It was splendid, just the thing. We will be dining in tonight. Thank you, Dante," said Justin.

"Very good. Please to follow me," said Dante as he led them to a table in the back corner. "Your favorite table, yes. Mama's gonna be so happy to see you tonight, and you bring us such a beautiful woman." He then held the chair for Jewel.

"Thank you," said Jewel as she sat down.

"I give you a moment, and I bring the menus, yes." Dante turned walked away, signaling another waiter to fill the water glasses.

"This is a lovely place, Justin. I love the color combinations, so warm, not overly done, like so many Italian restaurants who seem to think the only colors should be the same as the Italian flag. I don't think I've ever seen one pull it off with those colors and create the subtle ambience this place has," said Jewel.

"And if anyone would know about color combinations, that would be you," replied Justin.

"No, I don't claim to be an expert, but I know when something works and something doesn't, and this works beautifully. Burgundy is a very strong color, but by using it sparingly, they have created a rich feel to the dining room. I wonder if I can create a garment using these colors, and if I can capture the feeling they have here, I just might be able to pull it off. Kenneth doesn't always like my designs, but he almost always likes my color choices," she said.

Dante returned with the menus and a wine list and asked if they cared for something to drink.

"Mr. Angelis, you would like your usual, yes?" asked Dante.

"Yes, Dante," he answered.

"And for you, lovely lady, we have many fine wines to choose from," he said.

"I think I'll just go for your house red, thank you," said Jewel.

"Very good choice. Our house red is very superior. I will bring your order at once while you take your time and you look at our dinner menu," said Dante. Dante returned a short time later with a glass of house red for Jewel and a beer for Justin. He poured the beer into his glass and stood back, giving them a minute to taste their drinks.

"Is okay?" said Dante.

"Yes, it's fine," said Jewel. Dante smiled back at her. He didn't bother to look at Justin, because no matter what he ordered for his dinner, he always ordered a beer to go with it. Jewel had gazed over the menu and knew immediately what she wanted.

"You would like to hear the specials for tonight, yes, or you prefer something from the menu?" said Dante, still directing his gaze toward Jewel.

"I would like to order from the menu, please," said Jewel. "I would like the Calamari Fra Diavolo, hot, tossed greens, with your house dressing and coffee, and tiramisu for dessert." Dante didn't write anything that Jewel just told him down; he just stood there, looking at her, then he looked at Justin as if looking at him for conformation. Justin just smiled at Dante and gave him a small nod, and Dante quickly put pen to paper. Justin gave his order, which Dante quickly wrote down, smiled, and turned and walked quickly to the kitchen. Within a few moments, a gentleman with a large white apron tied about his waist emerged from the kitchen and approached their table, smiling from ear to ear.

"Justin, my good friend, so good to see you." And with the greeting, Justin rose from his chair and the two men embraced. "Mama was justa saying to me the other day that she no see you in such a long time. She say maybe you find someplace else and no come anymore," gushed the man.

"You tell Mama that would never happen. You and Mama are like family to me, and no one can cook like Mama," said Justin. The man's face beamed with delight, then he turned his attention toward Jewel.

"Jewel, I would like you to meet Guido. Guido, this is Jewel." Jewel extended her hand toward Guido, which he quickly took, and placed his other hand on top and shook them gently.

"I think we met briefly when you come to get the soup, yes. It is my great pleasure. A friend of Justin's is always welcome here by me and Mama. You maybe meet Mama later, yes. She would like to see how you like her food," said the man, looking every bit as startled as Dante when she had given him her order.

"Justa so I make sure Dante got your order correct," said Guido. "You would like your calamari hot, yes, and you wanna order your dessert before you eat, yes?"

Justin couldn't help but grinning and watching Guido. Poor man was so shaken he could barely speak.

Jewel looked directly at Guido and told him that Dante had indeed gotten her order correct, and yes, she did order dessert.

"Very good, then I go tell Mama. Scusa," said Guido as he bowed his head slightly toward Jewel, then put a bent finger in his mouth, bit down on it gently, and looked at Justin, then hurried off to the kitchen.

"Have I said or done something wrong?" she said to Justin.

"No. What makes you say that?" he answered.

"Haven't you noticed how oddly people are acting? Come on, you must admit that little episode with Guido was just a little weird, and what's with the finger biting? I know in my family someone does that, and it usually has a message attached," she said.

"I think he was just surprised to see you with me. I haven't brought a woman here to dinner in well over a year, possibly longer," answered Justin.

"No, that isn't it. It's something else. I can just feel it. Clay has made me so conscious of everything around me, especially people, that I just sense it's something else."

"Forget it. It's nothing," he said.

"All right, if you say so, but this isn't over. So tell me about your trip. Everything go, okay?" said Jewel.

"Yes, all is well, finally. Dealing with one corporation's CEO and board members is hard enough, but dealing with two can make your life hell. You know what everyone wants and expects, you put it in a contract for them to see, and suddenly it's as if they are really seeing it for the first time. Someone wants this changed, another doesn't like the language, and so on and so on. Something seems to happen to intelligent men and women when they see things in black- and-white, even when they are getting exactly what they want. However, we were able to prevail, and thus another happy ending to a long and tedious negation."

"That's great. So why don't you seem happy about it?" asked Jewel.

"Oh, I'm content the parties involved were quite satisfied with the outcome. I myself have a feeling of disenchantment. I'm not really sure why," he answered.

"Maybe you need a break. When was the last time you took a vacation?" Jewel asked.

"Well, let's see. I can't seem to remember when-no, wait, I think I took a few days off on my last trip to England. Yes, I remember. I hired a car and took a quick tour through Scotland. There were some castles I thought would be interesting to see, and if memory serves, it rained the entire time. Dreadful place, always raining, or about to, and damp. It felt forever damp. I remember it was so damp I felt chilled the entire time I was there. I couldn't wait till I got back to England. However, the weather there is not much better," said Justin.

"When were you there?" asked Jewel.

"I believe it was two years ago. No, maybe three," answered Justin.

"Well, there you go. Sounds like you need to get away to some warm tropical island for a few weeks, kick back under some big umbrella, one of those fancy drinks with rum and fruit juice in your hand, and nothing to do except watch the waves come in and the dolphins jump in the beautiful turquoise water, or maybe you'd prefer watching all the bikini-clad babes walking up and down the white sands. Sound good. Just what the doctor ordered. Work can make you crazy if you don't get away from it occasionally. Believe me, I know," said Jewel.

"And just where is your tropical island?" said Justin.

"I can't afford tropical, but every September, after the official season is over, Rocky and I go to a little bed-and-breakfast on Martha's Vineyard and just chill out for a long weekend. The woman who owns it usually closes at the end of the season, but she stays open for the Rock and me. She even cooks dinner for us some days. When her girl leaves, she's the only one there, and it's nice having a quiet dinner with her and listening to her stories about the people who have stayed with her over the years. The first year we went, it was hard to relax, but it gets easier every year. You really need to try it," said Jewel.

"Perhaps you're right. I'll have to give it some thought. Speaking about getting away, do you think Kenneth would let you play hooky tomorrow?" he asked.

"I'm sure he would. Why?"

"I thought we could go to Connecticut. I'd like you to meet Mother. We would stay overnight and drive back Saturday, getting back in time for pizza-and-scary-movie night. I think a day or two out of the city would do us both good. Mother loves showing someone new her orchid collection, and you would get to see where I grew up. And if you're really good, I'll tell you about all the times I got into trouble, all the things no one else knows." Justin laughed.

"Something no one else knows, huh? That sounds just too good to refuse. You realize, of course, I will have to tell Kenneth should he ask why I want the day off," said Jewel.

"I see no problem with that," he replied.

"Oh, it isn't Kenneth I was thinking about. It's Celia. When Kenneth tells her where I'm going, and he will, she will turn into a green-eyed monster. I can hear her now. She will confront me on every minute detail of the trip. Dinner on Monday will be just awful!" exclaimed Jewel. "I don't know how I'm going to handle her."

"I see the solution clearly," replied Justin. "Get me an invitation to dinner on Monday, and we shall handle her together."

"Brilliant!" Jewel said, laughing. "Together, Celia will be going down. Yes, I love it! Getting an invitation to dinner will be no problem. She will practically beg me to ask you. This is going to be such fun."

"Now that we have that sorted out, can we talk about something else, something infinitely more interesting?"

"All right, tell me what things that you did as a child to get you into trouble, because frankly, I can't imagine you in trouble," answered Jewel.

"I will tell all, I promise. The ride to Connecticut is about two hours, plenty of time to hear about my childhood antics," said Justin.

"Fine. What would you like to talk about?"

Just at that moment, Dante came out with their dinner. They each had the look of surprise on their faces when they realized that they had talked their way through the salad course and weren't even aware that the salad plates had been removed. Dante was careful to place the food onto the table. He asked if they would like something more to drink and quickly filled Jewel's glass with more red wine. He placed another beer before Justin and left just as quietly as he arrived. Jewel couldn't believe how absolutely wonderful her dinner choice looked and couldn't wait to try it.

"This is incredible! It looks and smells so good. I did tell you once that I could consume half a pound of spaghetti, didn't I?" asked Jewel.

"Yes, you did. Why?" replied Justin.

"Because I didn't want to embarrass you when I devour this." Jewel laughed. "A hearty appetite is nothing to feel embarrassed about. Quite the opposite, actually. A good cook like Josephina will find it rewarding to know her food is appreciated, but in the event someone does look at you strangely, I will just tell them this is the first meal you've had since being rescued from the island. How's that?"

"Excellent!" said Jewel, winding the first strands of pasta in her spoon, then ever so carefully into her mouth. She could see that the pasta was hot, and didn't want to burn her tongue, but the temptation to have a quick taste was too great.

"Oh, this is pure heaven!" Jewel sighed, spearing some of the calamari rings. "Here, try some," she added.

"Thank you, but no, thank you," answered Justin. "You enjoy your whatever it is and I will enjoy mine."

"Haven't you ever tried calamari? This is the best way to eat it. Some people like it fried, but I think all you taste is breading and oil. How many times have you eaten that chicken parmesan? What kind of Italian are you?" teased Jewel. "Half, same as you, but after my grandfather passed, my father didn't feel the need to embrace our Italian heritage, so dinners in our house were purely American foods. Many of the dishes prepared were taken from mother's Pennsylvania Dutch roots. As a child, I never had the opportunity to try the exotic pleasures of the Italian culture, and now that I am an adult, I can say no to anyone who offers me things with long tentacles. I appreciate the offer, but it gives me infinite pleasure watching you enjoy every succulent morsel," answered Justin.

"Woos!" teased Jewel. "Even Rocky eats calamari."

"I knew there was something strange about that dog." Justin laughed. They bantered back and forth, and in the end, she gave up trying to get him to try the smallest piece. Jewel consumed all the calamari and left a few strands of linguini in her dish. She sat back and proclaimed that she was full.

"Too full for tiramisu?" Justin asked.

"Never!" Jewel laughed. "I'm just letting things settle a bit."

Justin left most of his pasta on the dish but ate the chicken. As Dante removed the dishes, he gave another wide-eyed look at Justin, then said he would give them time to relax before he brought the dessert and coffee.

"Thank you, Dante," said Jewel. "I really could use an extra few minutes before dessert. I can't believe I ate the whole thing, but it was so good."

Again, Dante looked at Justin, then left, taking the empty dishes with him.

"All right," said Jewel, "now I know I didn't imagine that look Dante gave you. Come on, Justin, what's going on?"

"Jewel, if I tell you, you will only think I made the story up, because it doesn't sound plausible, at least it won't to you. I will tell you if you insist, but when you question the truth in it, I will have to get Guido and Josephina to verify that the story is indeed the truth."

"I still want to hear it," said Jewel. "I know you wouldn't lie to me."

"All right, if you insist," Justin said. "When I first moved into my apartment, I knew nothing about the neighborhood. One evening, I found myself without work to do, and I thought it would be a good opportunity to see what stores were in the area, especially any that delivered. I also hoped there were a few decent places to eat. I never remember to stop on the way home to get something, and if it weren't for Mother coming into the city each month and filling my fridge with bread, deli meat, and cheese, I would probably starve. Anyway, I walked around and collected a few take-out menus when I came upon Josephina's. I hadn't had dinner yet, and even though it was Italian, I decided to go in. The food and service were always excellent, and I found myself eating there two or three times a week. I knew all the waiters by name and eventually met the owners, Guido and Josephina. I dined here so often that on a few occasions, when it was late or extremely slow, they would join me first for coffee, and then sometimes for dinner. We talked about so many different things, my family, their family, our travels abroad, our work. I felt very content here, which, under most circumstances, is hard for me to do. I found I enjoyed our weekly conversations and didn't mind it at all when they asked questions of a personal nature.

"One day, Guido asked me why I hadn't brought any women to dinner in a very long time. I told him I hated wasting Josephina's delicious food on someone who didn't enjoy eating. I laughingly told them I would marry the woman I brought here that ordered salad through dessert and ate it all with gusto, and of course, she would be beautiful. The entire thing was meant as a joke, but it got passed around to all the staff, so of course, whenever I brought someone to dinner, they were falling all over themselves to see what she ordered. It got to be quite funny, really. I thought, since I haven't brought anyone here in some time, that they would surely have forgotten what I said, but apparently not. I think you surprised all of them with your dinner order, especially Guido. You see how fast he came out of the kitchen. I'm sorry if they made you feel uncomfortable."

"They did a little, mostly because of the stalker business. Anyone who looks at me lately, I think, must be a mass murderer, but you're telling me the truth, aren't you?" said Jewel.

"Yes, of course. I'm not clever enough to make up a story like that," replied Justin.

"Oh, I think you're clever enough," she said, "but I don't think you would. You're too honest. And besides, I think I would know if you were lying to me."

"You think you know me that well?" asked Justin.

"I may not have known you long, but I think I know you pretty well. Maybe *know* isn't the right word. I feel that I have a sense of you, and that's more important," answered Jewel.

Dante emerged from the kitchen with their coffee and the tiramisu for Jewel. The slice was gigantic, and Jewel just stared at it, then looked at Justin and laughed.

"Do you think the slices are always this big, or do you think this is a test?" she asked. "Because if it is, they are in for a big surprise. I have been known for eating my weight in cheesecake."

Justin laughed, picked up his coffee cup, and watched Jewel begin to devour the dessert.

"Even after you've eaten your weight in pasta," he said and just continued to laugh.

Dante came over to the table to ask if everything was all right.

"Yes, Dante, everything is fine. Jewel was just surprised at the size of the dessert," he said.

"Yes, it's a kinda big, but Mama cut it and said to bring it to the lovely lady who was with Mr. Justin, so I bring. I can put it in a box to take home ifa you want, yes?" he said.

"Oh no, it's just the right size, perfect after eating a pound of pasta!" exclaimed Jewel. She took a deep breath and dug into the mammoth slice again. Dante turned away, and Jewel couldn't help but notice the little smirk on his face as he turned.

"I think war has just been declared," said Jewel and picked up her coffee for a sip. There was no need to add anything to the coffee as she usually did; she would be getting enough sugar from the dessert.

"Would you like some?" she asked Justin.

"No, thank you. I very seldom eat dessert," he replied. "There are, however, two things I am quite fond of. One is the coconut cake my mother has prepared during the holidays, and the other is Sarah's apple pie. It is by far the best pie I have ever tasted. Sarah bakes one every few months, when she knows that I am coming up for the weekend."

Jewel continued eating the rich dessert as if it was the only thing she had eaten thus far. She had to stop for a sip of coffee and to let things settle occasionally, but she continued on. She refused to lose this game. Justin watched as she ate, then finally asked her if she wouldn't prefer to have the rest put in a take-home box. He said he didn't want her to make herself ill over a silly statement made such a long time ago, and in jest at that. She assured him that she wouldn't get sick—she seldom did, so not to worry. While they continued talking, Jewel slowly managed to eat all but a small amount and knew she couldn't get one more mouthful down, but she was pleased with herself. She felt she had given it a valiant effort and that the contest was unfair to begin with, but she was satisfied that she had won this round. Justin couldn't believe she actually did it, and very softly clapped his hands to congratulate her on a job well done.

"Now, if you will excuse me, I have something important to take care of," she said, and putting her napkin on the table, she got up and started walking toward the kitchen. As she approached the kitchen door, she met Dante just coming out.

"May I help you, miss?" he said.

"No, thank you," she said, and continued into the kitchen. "Josephina?" she asked.

Josephina was at the stove, stirring a large pot of what looked like fresh tomato sauce. "Yes?" she said as she turned toward the voice. She was so surprised to see Jewel standing there, and continued to stir the pot. She quickly put the spoon down, wiped her hands on her apron, and approached the woman in her kitchen.

"Can I help you?"

"I just wanted to meet the woman who was responsible for the most incredible dinner I have ever had. The calamari was perfect, just like my grandfather made it, tender and not overcooked; the pasta, al dente; and the sauce, not overly spiced, so the flavor of the calamari came through. And the tiramisu? Well, I can only say that it was like a slice of heaven, so delicious. Thank you for an exceptional dinner." Jewel smiled, waiting for a response.

Josephina was so surprised by Jewel's statement and by the fact that she had come into the kitchen to seek her out that for a moment she couldn't utter a single word. The two women faced each other for what seemed like an eternity to Jewel, but she couldn't back down now and just smiled and stood her ground. Josephina was surprised by the courage of this woman standing before her. She finally got over the shock and approached her.

"You are the one with Mr. Justin?" she asked.

"Yes" was all Jewel answered.

"I'm so glad you like the food, miss."

"Jewel, please call me Jewel."

"Jewel, yes, it's such a pretty name. You surprised me by coming into the kitchen, but it is good to hear that you like my cooking," said Josephina, trying to untie her apron. She finally got it off and laid it on the counter. It was obvious to Jewel that she had really been caught off guard and was searching for something to say. Score 1 for Jewel, she said to herself. The woman finally was able to speak.

"Miss," she began.

"Jewel, please call me Jewel. I feel like family," she continued. "I've heard so much about you from Justin that I just had to meet you. I hope you don't mind that I came into the kitchen to find you. I didn't tell Justin what I was going to do, and I apologize for being so forward. It's a flaw I've been trying to correct without much luck," said Jewel.

"No, no, it's all right, but I would have come to your table to see you and Mr. Justin. I haven't seen him for a few weeks. He's good?" asked Josephina.

"Yes, he's very good," replied Jewel, "and I know he would love to see you if you have a moment."

"Pardon my forwardness now," said Josephina, "but are you and he seeing each other?"

Jewel noticed that Josephina had no accent when she spoke, unlike Guido. Jewel guessed that she was born here, probably the first generation born here from parents who emigrated from Italy.

"Yes, we are," said Jewel proudly. "We just started, actually, almost a week."

"Mr. Justin is a very good man," said Josephina, sounding very much like an overprotective mother. "Guido and I care about him very much."

"I'm sure you do, and so do I, and I promise you that I would never do anything to hurt him, if that is your concern," answered Jewel.

"Good, then we understand each other," said Josephina, softening from her confrontational mode of a moment ago.

"Please come out and say hello. I know he would love to see you," said Jewel, turning on all the charm she could muster. It was even hard to smile with her stomach hurting as it did from all the food she had just eaten, but it was worth it. Jewel liked a good contest.

"Yes, let's go say hello." But before she started to walk away, she gave Jewel a brief kiss on each cheek. The two women looked at each other, knowing this contest was over. Jewel had won.

On the way back to the apartment, Justin could not help but to tell Clay all that had transpired at the restaurant. All three were laughing when Clay said to Justin, "I think you've caught yourself a wild cat here, Mr. A. Better hold on tight."

"I think you're right on this one," said Justin.

Jewel unlocked the door and turned off the alarm.

"I won't be coming in," said Justin. "I have a bit of work to finish if I plan to take tomorrow off. Call me as soon as you know, whether or not Kenneth will give you the day off. I will call Mother and tell her we're coming, and I will have to get another driver if Clay doesn't want to make the trip."

"Kenneth is usually in by eight thirty, so I should be able to call you by nine at the latest," said Jewel.

"Good. If you are going, the car will be here to pick you up at ten thirty. It's about a two-hour trip, depending on who is driving, and Mother will have lunch ready for us so we won't have to stop on the way. I must warn you, Mother will be greatly surprised when I inform her I'm bringing a guest, and female at that. So prepare yourself for a barrage of questions. She won't be as subtle as Josephina. But I forget whom I'm talking to. In a few short minutes, you cast a spell on everyone at the restaurant, defeated Josephina at her own game. I believe you will do fine. Maybe it is Mother I should warn." Justin laughed.

"Maybe you should," said Jewel, laughing with him. "I had a wonderful time tonight. Thank you for taking me to Josephina's. I know that place is special to you."

"No, it is I who should be thanking you, for being who you are and giving them such a warm welcome in spite of the obvious challenge they handed you."

"Piece of cake!" Jewel laughed. "Or should I say tiramisu?"

Jewel barely got the last word out when Justin pulled her close to him. His arms fully engulfed her. The gentleness of this man was surprising. His eyes conveyed everything he was feeling at that moment. There was no need for words. Jewel found she couldn't wait for him to kiss her and found his lips first. Had a second passed, a minute? Jewel was having difficulty keeping time in perspective whenever they kissed. A smile and then he was gone.

As she went through the motions of bringing the elevator down, she thought about his kiss, his smile, and his departure. So unlike anyone she had ever been involved with. Looking back, she realized that Lawrence was cold and kissed or hugged her only when it suited him. Chris, on the other hand, never wanted to do anything like talk; all he wanted was to make out and jump into bed. Nice for a while, but the novelty wears off all too soon, leaving nothing in its place. It reminded her of the story of the three bears and Goldilocks. One was too small, one was too big, and one was just right. She had a warm feeling that Justin was going to turn out to be "just right."

The following day, the car arrived at exactly ten thirty. Clay was there to open the door for her. "Good morning," she said as she got into the back seat.

"Morning, Ms. Lansby," he replied. Jewel was never going to get used to being called Ms. Lansby; every one called her Jewel, but she had finally processed everything Clay told her and understood the need to keep things professional. Clay had explained it to her clearly enough a few times.

"Do you drive back into the city after you leave us in Connecticut?" she asked.

"Sometimes I do when I have a high-profile job, but occasionally I like to take a few days off and get out of the city like everyone else," he replied.

"Do you have friends or family you stay with or go to a motel?"

"No family or friends up there, and I don't stay in motels, if I can help it. I prefer a nice small bed-and-breakfast. I found one a few years ago when I first started driving Mr. A. It's just a few minutes from his house and closer to the water. I like to scour the beachline and collect sea glass," said Clay.

"Oh my god, that's what Rocky and I do when we go to the cape just after the season ends! We stay in a small bed-and-breakfast too. The woman who owns it closes for the season but she lets us stay for a long weekend, and one of the things I love to do is to search for sea glass," said Jewel. "What do you do with the glass you find? I have a jar full and just have them lying in a dish. Some of the colors are beautiful."

"I make mobiles, but if you tell anyone, I'll deny it," said Clay.

"Why?" asked Jewel. "What's wrong with making mobiles?"

"Oh, there's nothing wrong with making them, but in my line of work, people don't want you if they know you do artsy things in your spare time. Would you feel safe if the person who is supposed to be protecting you makes mobiles in his spare time? No. I've learned that everyone takes it for granted that I'm working out at the gym or I'm in a boxing ring, knocking someone's block off, so I would appreciate it if you kept this to yourself and we say no more about it," said Clay.

"Okay, I promise, but if I give you all my sea glass, would you make a mobile for me to hang in my new apartment?" *There I go again,* she thought after the words were out of her mouth. *I don't think I'll ever learn to keep my mouth closed.* She was totally surprised, however, when Clay said he would but he would only take them from her when they were alone. Jewel thanked him, and they rode the rest of the way up town in silence. Clay parked the car. Justin must have been waiting in the foyer and came right out before Clay could ring the bell. Clay took his bag and placed it into the trunk as he had with Jewel's, then opened the door for Justin to get in.

"Good morning," said Justin as he gave her a kiss.

"Good morning," she replied.

He looked different somehow. He wasn't wearing a three-piece suit, which was the way she had always seen him. He had on a brown turtleneck with brown slacks and a soft camel-colored jacket.

"Wow, take a three-piece suit off you and you look like any other guy. I'm impressed," she said.

"I must make a confession: I feel a bit like a duck out of water without one on, but Mother bought these clothes for me and always chides me for not wearing casual clothes more often, so here I am. Won't she be surprised!" said Justin.

"Well, I think you look wonderful. Clay, what do you think?" asked Jewel.

"Lookin' good, Mr. A," replied Clay.

"There you have it! And I'm sure you mother will be thrilled to see you dressed like this," she said to Justin.

"Yes. Well, that remains to be seen," he answered.

"Mr. A?" said Clay.

"Yes, Clay, what is it? Have they found anything yet?"

"No, I'm afraid not. There were too many prints on the fire escapes. Most of them appeared old, so they think the guy must have worn gloves. They asked around, especially on the corner, if anyone remembers a person wearing a blue hoodie. A few people did remember someone who was always begging for a smoke, but no one really got a good look at his face. The descriptions varied. Some said he was over six feet, some said around five nine or ten, one hundred sixty pounds or thereabouts. The only thing they agreed on was that he was white, maybe midthirties. No one got a good look at his face because he always pulled the hood down. The patrol car for that sector has been told to watch out for anyone fitting that description, but once he finds out the cops have been asking around, he will probably lie low for a while. Sorry, Mr. A, that's all we got," said Clay.

"Well, that's more than we had before. Thank you, Clay," replied Justin.

"Could we please try to forget him for now? I just want to enjoy these next few days," cried Jewel.

"Quite right. I'm sorry if we upset you," said Justin. "We do need to have a few days to relax without worrying what this lunatic is up to."

"Good, thank you," said Jewel.

Now that his conversation with Justin was over, Clay raised the window so they could have privacy. As soon as the window was closed, Justin pulled her closer and kissed her, and kissed her again.

"Wow," said Jewel. "Was all this passion hidden under that three-piece suit?" Justin laughed and said that no, it had always been there; he just seemed to have more restraint when he wore it.

"Well, I'm all for no more three-piece suits," said Jewel laughingly.

"How would I get any work done without it?" replied Justin.

"All right, wear one to work, but when you're through for the day, you have to come home and change," she said.

"How about I prove to you that I can be just as passionate with a three-piece suit on?" said Justin.

"That works for me!" Jewel laughed as she snuggled close to him. "This feels nice," she said.

Justin held her closer and agreed that it did feel nice. They sat snuggled together until Jewel could see that they were just leaving the city.

"Okay, tell me a story," said Jewel.

"What kind of story?" asked Justin.

"You promised to tell me some stories of when you were little and something no one else knows about you," replied Jewel.

"Good God, woman, do you remember everything?" he asked.

"No, just the important things." She laughed.

"All right, to placate your curiosity, I will tell you something. Let me see. You do know that I was a very good child. Just ask Mother and she will tell you. I rarely got into trouble, but the few times I did were very memorable. So would you like to hear about the frog in the punch or the cigar?" he said.

"Come on, it's a long ride. I think we have time for both if you stop procrastinating," she said, kidding Justin.

"Ah, where to start, where to start?" said Justin.

"Start when you were the youngest," answered Jewel.

"Then we shall start with the frog." Justin smiled. "You remember I told you that Father loved to entertain, especially on the weekends? There were always people milling about in just about every room, and Father would say, 'Stay in your room or play somewhere outside. Just stay out of trouble.' Well, in those days, children didn't have all the electronic games they could play on the television, and I certainly did not have a television in my room. The only things I remember having were a great many books. Mother started reading to me while I was just an infant, and by two, I could already read a little."

"Two, you could read at two?" said Jewel.

"Yes, two-or three-letter words. However, by three, I was reading those small simple children's books, and by six, which was the approximate age this accident took place, I read everything. I call it an accident because it was not premeditated, nor did I feel there was any malice of intent on my part. I remember it was a warm summer day and I couldn't play out on the veranda because they had set up tables and chairs out there for the guests. My room was stifling, and I became weary of reading. I left the house by a side door so I would not be detected and headed straight for the small patch of woods just beyond the stable, where my grandfather had his carriage horses. He would have them hitched to one of his fancy carriages and take guests for a ride. After Grandfather died, Father sold the horses and had the barn taken down."

"How old were you when he died?" asked Jewel.

"I was ten. I remember it was just after the other time I got into trouble. The cigar business, I remember Grandfather was there when it happened. Anyway, once I got to the woods, I headed straight for the stream that flowed through it. I removed my shoes and socks and went walking in the stream, turning over rocks and watching little things swim away. I had no idea what any of those things were. For all I knew, they could have been poisonous. But when you're six, you don't think of those things. I lost track of time and knew it had to be getting late, as the sun was nearly gone. I put my shoes and socks on, and as I headed back, a huge frog jumped in front of me. I chased that frog and finally caught it. I had intended to put the frog in a glass container of some sort, and I was sure Mother would have something appropriate.

"I was walking toward the kitchen and had to pass the table where desserts and a huge punch bowl were sitting. Just as I got to the punch bowl, the frog made an extreme effort to escape and dived headfirst into the punch bowl, which was filled with something orange. I panicked. I didn't know what to do, and people were approaching, trying to get some of the punch. The only thing I could think of was to stand in front of the bowl so no one could reach in and scoop any out. They made some rather-loud comments, and that was when Father arrived. He asked me what I was doing and that his guests would like some punch and that I was acting quite rudely. I knew I had to confess. I explained to Father what had happened and prepared for the worse. Father didn't yell or even raise his voice. He laughed and told the guests to gather around and look inside the punch bowl. He said that I had seen this frog so completely out of its element, that the first source of liquid it saw was the punch and immediately jumped into it, and that I was trying to keep everyone away. As Father had the bowl removed and another brought out, he proclaimed to everyone that I had saved the day. All the guests clapped and called me their little hero. Father asked me if I had eaten and told me to go to the kitchen and have Sarah prepare me a sandwich. After I had eaten, I was to go directly to my room. I was filled with terror. Surely, Father had some sort of punishment for me, and as the day passed into night and no one came to my room, I fell asleep on the floor with my face in a book.

"The next morning, I went down to breakfast and everyone behaved as if nothing happened. Mother and Father said good morning and continued to eat breakfast as usual. After I finished my breakfast, my father got up and came back into the room with a bucket. He said that since I liked frogs so much, I was to go outside and collect ten frogs and not to return until I had them. I told him that I was sorry about the frog that I brought home and that I wanted to put it in a container and that the frog tried to get away and jumped into the punch bowl, but he was unrelenting. 'Don't come home until ten frogs are in the bucket,' he said again and pointed to the door. I looked at Mother for help but found none. I knew she never liked the punishments Father doled out, but she never tried to intervene on my behalf. I reluctantly took the bucket and left the house, going to the woods and the stream. I searched and searched, walking down the stream then back up. By the time it started to get dark, I had only found three frogs. I stayed until it was so dark I couldn't see anything, so I went home. Father was waiting for me and took the bucket. He saw that there were only three frogs in the bucket and said that since I had not found ten frogs, I was to go to bed with no supper. In the morning, I was to have my breakfast and go out and find seven more frogs. If I returned without the seven frogs, I was to go to bed with no supper again, and it would continue that way until I had collected the ten frogs.

"Fortunately, school was out, so every morning I had breakfast and went out to find the frogs. I had to cancel my riding lessons and my sleepover with a classmate as well as the birthday party I was to attend for another classmate, the most beautiful girl in the class, the lovely Rachel, who had stolen my heart as well as those of most of the other boys in class. It took me six more days to find the frogs. Sarah felt so sorry for me that she would put a wrapped sandwich in the bucket and handed it to me as I was going out the door so Father wouldn't see it. I think I must have lost five pounds missing dinner each evening.

"When I finally found the ten frogs, Father handed me a sheet of paper. It was a list of all the guests that had attended the party when the frog was in the punch. He said that I was to write an apology to each name on the list. I missed a few more parties and sleepovers and thought I would never finish. When I did finish and gave the notes to Father, he said that I could have avoided the punishments if I had only gone to him the minute the incident happened and took responsibility for what I had done. He said he hoped I had learned from my mistake and would think twice in the future and own up to any errors in judgment I made. I told him I would remember the lesson well, and to this day, whenever something goes wrong and it is definitely my fault, all I can think about is someone sending me out for ten frogs, and I immediately own up to the mistake. And that concludes the story of the frog," said Justin.

"Well, I am pleased to hear your father was not the kind of parent who would embarrass you in front of people like so many do, but I think he was awfully ruthless to make you go without dinner for so long," stated Jewel.

"Whether you think he was right or wrong, believe me, I learned a lesson that has served me well to this day," answered Justin.

"I guess, but you were only six. If I were your mother, I don't think I could have stood by each day knowing you didn't have dinner," she said.

"I know she had concerns, and I think it was she who had Sarah put a sandwich in the bucket for me," answered Justin. "My grandfather took me aside a few days later and said he had something important he wanted to tell me and to remember. He said there were three kinds of people, those who never learned from their mistakes, those who did learn from their mistakes, and lastly those who learned from other people's mistakes. He said he was sure that I fell into the second group and had learned from my mistake and, hopefully, as I got older, I would fall into the last group and learn from other people's mistakes, because when I learned that, I would always make the best decisions. That was something else I never forgot, and I think what I learned from my father and grandfather played a large part in my success as an attorney."

"That was an excellent story. Do you think you would be like your father in doling out punishment?"

"I don't know. I don't think anyone really knows what they would do until they found themselves in that situation. I hope I would be a little more lenient in the punishment. However, I would hope a lesson had been learned," stated Justin.

"I think your child would have you wrapped around their finger and you would send them to their mother for punishment, which is just like Kenneth and Celia. He explains what they did wrong, and Celia doles out the punishment," said Jewel.

"Really?" said Justin. "How interesting."

"Oh, believe me, punishment in their house is nothing. She will send them or him to their room, and what good is that? They have TV, all the electronic toys you were speaking of before, and a computer. Some punishment. When I started watching them, they knew better than to start anything. I would make them sit at the kitchen counter, on the uncomfortable stools, with nothing to do. After doing that a few times, they learned very quickly not to mess around when I watched them. Celia and Kenneth are always amazed at how little resistance there is when I ask them to do something," said Jewel.

"I would have never guessed you had a mean bone in your body," said Justin.

"Not mean, just in control. You need to be with kids and dogs, or you'll be living in a state of continued pandemonium," she answered.

"Yes, I see your point," replied Justin. "Do you see yourself with children someday?"

"Yes," Jewel quickly answered. "Someday, when I have things the way I want them and find the right person. Do you think you would ever settle down and start a family?"

"My answer is similar to yours. My career is fine. I just need to find that certain someone, which is difficult, since I'm always working," he said.

"Well, maybe you should try to work less." Jewel laughed. "Now, tell me the cigar story."

"After all that and you haven't forgotten about the cigar?" he asked.

"Nope. Soon I will know all there is to know about Justin Angelis," Jewel answered.

Justin laughed and said she was making a good start.

CHAPTER 7

"The cigar story... let me think a second how that all started. Oh yes, I remember. Father sent me to his study for a talk about my report card. I had gotten a B in history, and nothing except As were good enough for Father. I remember I had been in there for an awfully long time. I found out later that he had received a phone call and had been on the phone all that time. I was bored with just waiting around. I sat at his desk and looked at the papers and correspondence and pretended to be him. I took a cigar from his cigar box, not knowing that they were his very expensive ones, and put it in my mouth. I walked around the room, as I had seen him do so often, pretending to talk to someone and biting on the cigar end. It soon became a wet, mangled mess, so I broke some off and put it back in my mouth.

"Just then, Father walked in. He apologized for being so late but was glad I had found a way to amuse myself with his very expensive cigars. Grandfather walked in just then, and Father asked him how he thought I looked with the cigar. 'Well, I think he looks just fine,' said my grandfather. 'I was coming in myself to get one and go out to the veranda and have a nice, relaxing smoke after that marvelous dinner.' They always went outside if the weather was good, because they knew Mother didn't like them smoking in the house. My father remarked that he thought it was a great idea and picked up a cigar for Grandfather and one for himself and said that since I already had one, I could join them on the veranda. We all went out to the veranda, and Grandfather took out a little cutter and clipped the tip. Father followed, then asked for my cigar and clipped the end of it too. They both lit up, and then Father lit the end of mine and told me what to do. He said to inhale the smoke, then blow it out. I watched each of them do it, and it didn't look too difficult, so I did it. I sucked in as hard as I could and tried to blow the smoke out, but I think I swallowed it all. Father kept saying, 'Do it like this, Justin.' I tried again and again. My head started to ache, my stomach was turning over, and I was sure I was about to lose my dinner. Father kept saying, 'Isn't it good, Justin?' and encouraged me to keep trying.

"My grandfather started to laugh because he knew what was about to happen. Very calmly he said to me, 'Remember your mother's flowers, boy, and go in the back by the bushes.' Well, I almost didn't make it. I think I hurled for an hour. When I finally stopped and walked back to where they were, Father said to my grandfather, 'I think that went well. How about you?' Grandfather agreed. They extinguished their cigars and went into the house, leaving me on the veranda. I didn't know if I dared going in the house with the way my stomach felt. Mother finally came out to find me. She asked if I was all right and if I wanted some dessert. That was all it took, and I was running for the bushes again. It took me days before I could hold something down.

"Grandfather and Father said they were proud of me for not quitting even after the first time I threw up. Father said that if I wanted to practice again, the cheap cigars were in the case by the fireplace. I remember I just gave him a big smile and nodded in acknowledgment. I knew I would never touch a cigar in my life after what I had just gone through, and I never have."

"My, you learned some powerful lessons as a child," said Jewel.

"Didn't you learn any lessons as a child?" asked Justin.

"Unfortunately, I did," replied Jewel.

"Anything you would like to share?" asked Justin.

"Maybe sometime. Not now," she answered. "Today we are focusing on you." She hoped he didn't notice how fast she changed the subject. She tried to remain as cheerful as possible; the lessons she learned, she wouldn't wish on anyone.

"Now, tell me something you did when you were in college," said Jewel.

"My, I guess you do want to know everything," answered Justin.

"Well," she said, "I figured, if that was the worst of your childhood, then we had best move on to a more interesting time, and college is usually where most people have some juicy stories—unless, of course, you were a model student there as well as being such a good child."

"Jewel, really, I can assure you that I was not always a good child. I was reprimanded many times, as Mother can attest to, should you ask her. The two stories I told you just happen to be the most memorable, but if you want to jump to my days in college, you will find I was equally as boring as I was in my childhood."

"Somehow, I find that hard to believe. I think, once you got away from home, you were just like the rest of the guys, waiting for your chance to break out and begin the road from boyhood to manhood by way of doing all the sophomoric things young men do," answered Jewel.

"Sophomoric," said Justin, raising his voice ever so slightly. "You really think I fell in with that group?"

"Oh, come on, get down off your high horse and admit the truth. When boys leave home for the first time, something takes over their minds and bodies. It's like they suddenly awaken and find Mommy and Daddy are not there to watch them, and they all start behaving like rutting animals. They can say what they like and do whatever they like, so unless you were the campus nerd, you had to be in the bad boys club. Don't be embarrassed if you were the nerd. It just means you learned your lessons from your father very well and feared serious retribution if your father found out you were goofing off like every other boy on campus. So really," continued Jewel, "what were you? The good little nerd or in the bad boys club? If I had to guess, I'd say you were somewhere in between."

"And just how did you arrive at that conclusion?" asked Justin.

"Well, you really wanted to please your parents, especially your father. He was the one you wanted respect and approval from. And you wanted to please your mother because you were an only child and you held all her hopes and dreams for a wonderful life. But I think you were a little slow developing socially, and now you had the next four years, the perfect playing field to refine the person that was to become Justin Angelis. Am I close?" she asked.

"Amazingly close. However did you become so insightful, and will there ever come a day that you don't surprise me?" he asked.

"I hope not." Jewel laughed.

"You're absolutely correct about my conflicting intentions. Yes, I wanted Father's approval above all things, and I knew Mother would love me no matter what I did, but I knew I needed to break free from the yoke I felt my father had me harnessed to and see what kind of man I was becoming. I wanted to experience all the things the others no doubt had already. I felt Father had stifled me and I was far behind the other boys of my age. Many of my friends already had sex, and here I was, a freshman in college, and still a virgin. I didn't smoke, drink, or use foul language and felt so completely out of place. I made a vow to do all the things everyone else was doing. I so desperately wanted to fit in somewhere, anywhere.

"The first year was really a blur, trying to fit in, to pledge with the best fraternity, going to all the parties, losing my virginity, which was at the top of my list, and of course trying to keep my grade average up, because I knew Father would accept nothing less than perfect. My roommate, as it turned out, was a friend from prep school and one of the boys I think you would call cool. We pledged together, and he was the one that got me drunk for the first time. He also tried to set me up with a girl who was known for being easy, so I would lose my virginity status, which seemed to be a major concern to my fraternity brothers.

"One evening, some of us were down in the central living room, not doing anything much. Some were reading, some drinking, a few telling jokes, when one of the guys started in on me, telling me it was a disgrace that I still had not been laid. By now it had stopped being funny. I needed some way to get them off my back when suddenly my roommate took center floor and told them that I was getting some almost every night. He began to laugh and said they would not believe how good sex was with a Snickers bar. Now, of course everyone was howling and wanted in on the joke. I could feel my face redden, but I knew if I folded now, I would never live it down. I rose rather regally from the table where I was studying, cleared my voice, and began what was to be the opening sentence of my rise to greatness in the eyes of my fraternity brothers.

"My brothers,' I went on to say, 'a Snickers bar is not just a mere piece of candy. No, I say it is love carefully wrapped in a brown bit of paper. As you carefully and gently tear open the paper, the aroma of what lies inside first tickles your senses, wafting up into your mouth and nose with the promise of something so wonderful you are breathless. You pull the paper down, gently exposing just a small portion, all you need to see to know that the next step will bring you closer to your reward. You put your mouth around the candy, slowly pushing it in and pulling it out.' As you can well imagine, their eyes were riveted on me, their imagination already filling with sexual desire," said Justin. "And so I continued, and I knew it had better be good. Fortunately, creative writing was a subject I rather excelled in, so this, I knew, would be easy. Not laughing as I spoke was going to be the hard part. Nevertheless, I continued. 'Now you take it into your mouth and bite off a piece that is neither too small nor too large. You want the piece to be just the right size so you can roll it around in your mouth, feeling its chocolate goodness slowly melt. When you can no longer feel and taste the chocolate, you begin on the creamy caramel. You turn the piece over so the caramel lies on your tongue, and you gently massage it. You can feel the creamy smoothness sliding down your throat, that warm, creamy goodness. When alas the caramel has gone, you now feel the firmer texture of the nougat. But what to do? Should you be rough or continue to take your time and savor the slightly vanilla morsel. The nougat does not give in to your tongue and the gentle massage that the caramel did. Now we are faced with a dilemma. We can't chew it, it's too soon. We don't want to hurt the nuts that are patiently waiting for their turn, but the nougat is not yielding to the gentle pressure of our tongue. Not to be outdone, we push the nougat with the nuts up against the roof of our mouth. The nuts hurt slightly, but soon the thought of the conquest over the nougat takes away any pain from the nuts. We must hold on as long as possible for. The end is near. Using our tongue and much more pressure, we go after it. We make small sucking noises as our tongue pulls back. We continue until we have worn away the nougat from the nuts. We turn over each piece of nut to make sure there is no nougat still holding on. Now we have only the naked nuts. Now we chew with delight, and we have once again held it till the very end. Not every man can hold it till the end. Some attack it at once, and something is lost in the taking. No, my brothers. Savor it, love it, and hold on till the end.'

"Well, as you can imagine, I was beside myself with worry, wondering if my tale of the Snickers bar was a success or not. Would they stop torturing me and find another poor soul, or was I to be forever on the top of the list when they needed entertainment?"

"Well, come on," said Jewel. "I can't stand the suspense. What did they do? I know it got me hot. Whew!"

Justin began to laugh. "It got the response I was hoping for, very much like the feeling you just had. Some were on their feet, some were too embarrassed to stand, but all agreed, if I had a Snickers bar each night, then I was definitely getting laid, and furthermore, it was decreed that Snickers bars were to be in the candy bowl at all times and that whoever finished the last one was to replenish the stock, under penalty of dismemberment, or worse. And it was also decreed that there would be no more joking about my sexual prowess, as clearly I was getting more than most. But the most curious thing that came out of it was that most of the guys were staying in more and studying. It had a most unusual effect on the girls also. They kept flocking to our house. I guess the story of the Snickers managed to get around the campus, and the girls said no way were they taking back seat to a Snickers bar. So I was not the brunt of their jokes anymore. I lost my virginity, and over the course of the next few months, I enjoyed the company of some lovely young ladies who taught me a great deal. Eventually, the novelty wore off and things returned to relative normality."

"Oh, what a great story! So you were a little rascal in college? I just knew it! No one can help but go a little crazy when you're away from home for the first time. Good for you," replied Jewel. "Wow, would I love to tell Celia that story."

"No, absolutely not! These words were for your ears only. Promise me you will not tell anyone anything of what I just imparted to you," said Justin. "Promise me, Jewel, this remains between you and me."

"I hear and obey my lord." Jewel laughed. "So what else have you got in your past that proves you started out just as wild as the rest of us?" replied Jewel.

"Never mind. I will tell you nothing more. I may wake up some morning and find my reckless days on the front page of the *Times*," he answered.

"Oh, ye of little faith, please tell me more. I promise whatever you tell me will not leave this mouth." And before she could say anything more, he held her close and kissed her.

"I can't tell you any more, because we have arrived at my house," he said. "Your house?" she asked. "I thought it was your mother's?"

"I'll explain all to you another time," answered Justin as he was getting out of the car. Clay barely had time to open it for him.

"Thank you, clay," he said as he held a hand out to Jewel. "If you would get the bags, please." Clay did as requested and placed them near the door.

"Are you staying at the usual place?" asked Justin.

"Yes, sir. Love the ocean," replied Clay. "What time would you like to leave tomorrow?"

"I think we should leave at five. That will give us plenty of time to get into the city, and we'll still be able to have tea with Mother before we leave. You know how she loves showing off her tea service," said Justin.

"Very good, then. I'll be here at five. Have a pleasant visit, Ms. Lansby. You too, Mr. A." Clay got back into the car and slowly drove away.

Suddenly, Jewel felt frightened. Clay was a familiar face, and now she was heading into untried waters. She tried not to look anxious, but Justin saw how nervous she was. He grabbed her hand, kissed her cheek, and said not to worry, that his mother would love her. She tried to smile back as he rang the bell and opened the door for her. Jewel was shocked by the enormity of the foyer. A large table stood in the middle with the most beautiful clivia on it. She had never seen one in bloom before. It was drop-dead gorgeous. She couldn't take her eyes off it and so didn't notice Justin bringing in the bags or his mother walking toward them.

"It's a lovely specimen, isn't it?" said Justin's mother.

"It's breathtaking. I have never seen a clivia in bloom before," mumbled Jewel, still looking at the plant. She suddenly realized Justin's mother was beside her. "Oh, I'm sorry, I was just so mesmerized by the plant I didn't hear you coming," said Jewel.

"That's quite all right. I'm glad you can appreciate the wonder of such a beautiful thing. I'm afraid its beauty is lost on Justin," replied Mrs. Angelis.

"Now, Mother," said Justin, bringing in the bags, "while I don't quite understand the fascination you have with all things green, it doesn't mean I can't appreciate its apparent beauty, to some extent, anyway. Now it seems there are two of you I must contend with." He smiled. "Jewel, I'd like you to meet my mother."

"I'm so pleased to meet you, Mrs. Angelis," said Jewel as she extended her hand.

"Please, my dear, call my Evelyn. Everyone does. You have to excuse me. I never could stand all the formality of an introduction. That was more Justin's father's thing."

"Thank you, Evelyn. I'm not one for much formality either. I often think the world would be a better place if it were not for all the posturing and formality our world leaders chose to use," said Jewel.

"I think you are absolutely correct on that. So much more could be accomplished if they could sit down over a nice cup of tea and be more civil to one another," answered Evelyn.

"Oh god, now there's two of you," said Justin, shaking his head.

"Never mind him, my dear. Please come in," said Evelyn to Jewel. "Justin, please take Jewel's overnight bag up to the yellow room. If you would like to follow Justin to your room and get settled in, then we can chat while Sarah prepares lunch. I'm sorry, my dear, is there anything you can't or don't like to eat? I guess I should have asked you first."

"Actually, there is," said Jewel. "I am allergic to peppers, just about any kind, but other than that, the only other thing I don't eat is liver."

"You don't have to worry about that," said Evelyn. "I won't eat it either." Justin picked up the bags and headed for the staircase. Jewel fell in behind him and gazed about the room. The furnishings were elegant, nothing gaudy, as in some homes of this size where people made the mistake of trying to fill up the space with golden cherubs or huge marble statues or adding extremely ornate frames around small painting. Jewel knew no professional designer had a hand in decorating this house; it was as elegant as Evelyn was. Justin opened the door to the room Evelyn had chosen for her and put her bag on the stand. Jewel walked in behind him and looked about the room. It had a slight French feel about it, yellow with touches of blue placed strategically about the room. It had a warm, friendly feel to it. Justin asked if she liked the room and if she needed anything.

"No, thank you. I'm just fine. I love the colors in the room, just enough blue to tone down all this yellow. Justin, I would really like to see some of the other rooms," said Jewel. "I bet they are all a different color, aren't they? Your mother did all the decorating, didn't she?"

"I'm not sure, but I think she did. The entire house has a totally different feel than when my grandfather owned it. It was more ornate, with statues and the like. After he died, Mother went to work and changed the entire decor. Father was all for the changes, as I remember, his taste ran similarly to that of mother's, more understated than gaudy, as was grandfather's taste. I think Mother did a wonderful job. A house of this size cannot be easy to decorate," he answered. "After you settle in, I will show you some of the other bedrooms."

"Will you show me yours?" she asked.

"If you like. Mine is across the hall. When you're settled, just knock on the first door," he said as he took his bag and walked away.

Jewel quickly hung up a few items and placed the rest in a drawer of the dresser. She put her toiletries in the bathroom, which she saw had another door. This bath must be shared with the bedroom on the other side. She turned the doorknob, and the door opened, revealing a bedroom approximately the same size as hers but was done in a soft sage, with cream and a very light shade of lavender for accent. "I really need to see the other rooms," she said to herself and quickly finished putting her things away. She wasn't sure what the weather would be like here or if they planned to go out at all, so Jewel packed a few extra things just in case. She was glad she paid attention when Celia was giving her the lessons on packing for an overnight weekend and what you should never be without. She finished putting her things away and put her bag in the closet and went to find Justin. She walked past the enormous staircase to the other side of the hall and knocked on the first door. Justin opened the door, and she realized he still had things lying on his bed.

"I'm sorry, you're not finished," she said.

"That's quite all right. Please come in. I just have a few things. I can't decide whether to hang them or place them in a drawer." He held up a few sweaters and asked her what she thought.

"The drawer," she said and walked in farther. Justin placed the items in the drawer, not paying attention to Jewel and her fascination with the room's decor.

"This is absolutely perfect," she said. "The maroon and cream are beautiful together, and with the soft sage accents, it looks like a page from the best decorating magazine. It is just perfect for you. It captures your masculinity yet shows your softer side. Oh, Justin, this is just perfect! Your mom could put any professional decorator to shame. I would love for Shelby to see this house. I can't wait to tell her all the color combinations."

"Well, I'm done here. Come, I'll show you a few of the others, quickly though. We don't want to hold up lunch. It wouldn't bother Mother, but it makes Sarah a bit irritable," said Justin.

"Okay, quickly, then," she said as she followed him to the next door and waited for him to open it. This room was done in shades of blue with soft lavender and mauve accents.

"Wonderful, just wonderful!" said Jewel, utterly astonished.

"Can I see the next one, please? This is the last. And you can show me some of the rest later," she said.

"How many bedrooms are there?" asked Jewel.

"Counting Mother's suite and the suite on the main floor, I believe there are eleven in total," he answered.

"Just how many rooms are there in this house?" asked Jewel.

"Too many. I promise to give you the grand tour after lunch, or maybe Mother would like to do it, then you may ask her about her color choices and the rest of the million questions I know you are dying to ask," he answered.

"Am I that obvious? I've been in some beautiful homes in the city, doing fittings for Kenneth, and some were really grand, but most were done by a professional and just don't have the character that this one has. I hope your mother won't find me annoying if I ask her questions about her choices for this house," replied Jewel.

"Oh, she won't, just as long as you mention her orchids. Throw in some questions about them, and you'll have her wrapped around your finger," answered Justin.

"Luckily for me, I do know a little about them and can easily identify some common varieties," said Jewel.

"Well, get your tour first, because you'll be spending the rest of the day in the greenhouse if you show the slightest interest in them," said Justin. "Come on, let's go down."

Just as they reached the bottom landing, his mother was coming out of another room.

"What perfect timing! Sarah has set up lunch in the breakfast room instead of the dining room. I hope you don't mind. I prefer it to the dining room. It has a friendlier atmosphere, don't you think, Justin?" she asked.

"Yes, Mother, it does, and you can put the dining room on the tour I promised Jewel, since she is so taken with the house," answered Justin.

"I hope you don't mind, but I asked Justin to show me a few of the other bedrooms. I guess working with fabric and color all day, I have learned to appreciate a wonderful color combination when I see it. I don't have a great deal of knowledge about period furniture pieces and was hoping you could assist me in identifying some of them. I have to say, though, that your color combinations for the bedrooms Justin showed me are amazing, the blue with the lavender and mauve, and Justin's room reflects his personality perfectly. I apologize if I'm babbling. I tend to do that sometimes. Justin has to put his hand over my mouth when I get too wound up," said Jewel as she looked at Justin, who had started laughing.

"Yes, I admit I've had to do it on occasion, so feel free to do it anytime she starts," said Justin, still laughing. Jewel could feel her cheeks turn red as she looked at him, her eyes pleading him to stop.

"I have been known to babble myself from time to time, so don't even give it a second thought," said Evelyn, smiling. "Except my passion is orchids, and I have been known to go on and on to anyone who will listen, haven't I, Justin?"

"Yes, Mother, you have, and I think you may just have found the perfect person to talk to about them. Jewel admitted to me that she knows a bit about them herself," said Justin.

"Really?" said Evelyn.

"I'm sorry, Justin is exaggerating. What I said was that I knew a little about the most common ones, and I'm sure your collection includes more exotic specimens," said Jewel.

"Well, whatever your knowledge, just to find someone who knows anything about them is a definite plus, so let's have lunch and a quick tour, if you like, and then on to the greenhouse. Besides, Justin will be lost in his newspapers. How many did you bring, Justin?" asked his mother.

"You both have your individual passions. Please allow me mine," he said jokingly.

"Please come this way, Jewel—lovely name, there must be a story behind it," said Evelyn.

"Thank you. It's not so unusual. When the nurse handed me to my mother for the first time, she said, 'Here is your perfect jewel,' and that's the story," answered Jewel.

"Well, I think it's a lovely name. It suits you. You have a sparkle about you, a brilliance that shines through. Doesn't she, Justin?" asked Evelyn.

"Yes, Mother. That was one of the first things I noticed when we met," he answered.

"Thank you both very much, but could we please talk about something else?" said Jewel, feeling a little flustered.

"You'll find, Mother, that Jewel doesn't know how beautiful she is, both inside and out. Just ask any of her friends," replied Justin.

By now Jewel was turning beet red; she didn't know where to look, and she just wanted to hide. She never could take a compliment about her looks. Celia tried to convince her that she had a beauty that was classic, whatever that meant, and to always keep her natural look with little makeup and her copper hair always shining and in curls. The look was perfect for her. Jewel tried experimenting with makeup and eyeliners and such, but she thought she looked like a clown, so she stayed with the way God made her and accepted it.

She followed Evelyn into the breakfast room, which did indeed create a very friendly atmosphere. Again, the colors were similar to those in her bedroom, yellow and blue, although now the blue was more predominate, and the yellow, with some added green, now took a lesser role. On one wall were large French doors with a coordinating valance above the doors. The doors themselves were bare, and Jewel quickly understood why. There was an assortment of birdfeeders out among the bushes. Jewel stopped to gaze out the windows and noted a variety of seed in the feeders.

"Someone is a bird-watcher," said Jewel.

"I must confess, it is I," replied Evelyn. "I started with one feeder, and before long, I couldn't resist putting in the variety you see there. I wanted to see how many species I could attract, and I am happy to say that I have spent a good deal of time just delighting in the various colors of these little birds. Our gardener doesn't share my interest, though. He thinks they just make a mess with all the seed scattered round. But I enjoy watching them. When I have my meals in here, it makes eating alone more enjoyable. I've even had a few put in down by the fern garden. I had a bench erected there with a sunroof, and I often take a sandwich and sit and watch them. It is so very relaxing. Sarah has had to call me many a time to remind me of the time."

"Do you have a book to identify the different birds?" asked Jewel.

"Yes. Justin bought me one for my birthday, right after we put the feeders up. It has been so interesting watching the different species. The plumage on some of the male birds is quite breathtaking. I even started a chart for the different seasons, so I know which ones to look for. Are you a bird-watcher, Jewel?" she asked.

"I am, but in the city you don't see many, unless you go to Central Park, and even then you can't see the variety you must see here. When we lived with my grandfather, I would make a list just to see how many different birds were around the farm. Grandpa put a few feeders up to keep the bug population down, so they wouldn't ruin the vegetables he planted, but I just liked to watch them," answered Jewel.

Sarah brought in their lunch and asked Jewel if she would like coffee or tea. Jewel answered that she would just have water with her meal but would love a cup of coffee after.

"I'm trying to cut back on coffee," said Jewel, "but I'm addicted. When I'm in the shop, working, I must drink about ten cups or more, and they always keep the pot full, so it's easy to drink much more than I should."

After coffee was served and everyone had time to relax and enjoy the view, Evelyn asked if Jewel would like to take that tour of the house now. It was just as she imagined, every piece chosen with care for the spot it was to be in. The colors, while all different, coordinated with one another; there was a beautiful flow from one to the other. Most of the larger rooms were papered, while most of the smaller rooms were just painted.

"I really must ask, Mrs. Angelis," said Jewel.

"Please, my dear, do call me Evelyn," she said again.

"Yes, I'll try. I know that you did the decorating in the house, and all the colors work so perfectly together, but my question is, How did you decide on the colors to use?" asked Jewel. "I've been working with fabric for years now and don't think I would have thought to put some of these color combinations together. What was your inspiration?"

"Well, if you promise to keep my secret, I'll tell you," said Evelyn. "It really was very simple. I used all the colors I found in my orchids, and some came from the garden flowers. I don't have any bearded iris in the garden, but I do have Siberian iris, so the yellow and blue combinations for the bedroom you have and the breakfast room came from them. I just varied the amount of each color for the different rooms. The maroon and cream for Justin's room came from some daylilies and geraniums. Some of the other rooms' combinations, I got from the Helleborus. I think they were the Royal Heritage strain. They come up in the most varied colors, from deep maroon to pinks, creams, even greens. Most of the plants were ordered from various catalogs, and I simply brought the book and, in some cases, the flowers themselves to the paint store. The machines they have today are wonderful in matching any color you want. It's remarkable! So you see, I'm really not so clever, after all," replied Evelyn.

"Well, I beg to differ. This house is enormous, and to have all the areas flow so smoothly from one to the other is no easy task. It takes someone with a well-trained eye to accomplish what you have," said Jewel.

"Thank you, my dear. It pleases me that you can appreciate what I have tried to achieve. Working in the garment business with all the lovely fabrics they have today, I'm sure, has given you a well-trained eye also," she replied. "Now that we have seen the house, are you ready to see my pride and joy? I think I have some of the most beautifully colored orchids you have ever seen."

As they walked back through the house, past the kitchen, and down a long hallway, Evelyn asked Jewel what she knew about orchids. She said that she knew a few and probably could recognize some of the more common varieties but she knew nothing of the more exotic or rare plants. Evelyn opened the glass door to the greenhouse, and Jewel stood there awestruck. There were rows upon rows of orchids in so many beautiful colors and shapes. Jewel just stood there, looking at the profusion of color; she didn't hear Evelyn talking to her. When she finally turned toward the voice, she looked at Evelyn and spoke softly to her.

"I'm sorry, did you say something? I'm afraid I was caught up in the moment and didn't hear you," said Jewel. "I don't know why I'm whispering, but this place makes me feel like I should. I had the most unusual feeling, that the orchids preferred it quiet. You must think I'm really losing it," said Jewel.

"Not at all, my dear," said Evelyn. "You are quite perceptive. They do prefer it quiet. How strange that you could feel it. Most people that I bring in here just talk away in their loudest voices, not giving a second thought about the comfort of these most delicate plants. I've been told that they like soft classical music played, but I'm not sure about doing it."

"I've heard of it also. A friend of mine who recently passed away used to play classical music for his cows, especially when they were near their time to give birth. I think you should try it. I know that they say to talk to your plants, and I always have, so maybe a little music would be just the thing, especially when you're not in here. If they can't feel your presence, I think the music would have a calming effect on them," replied Jewel.

"You do actually believe that plants feel our presence when we are with them?" asked Evelyn.

"I know it may sound crazy, but when we lived with my grandfather on the farm, I was more in touch with Mother Nature than ever before. My grandfather made me aware of the animals and plants and the way we could communicate with them without words. He would sit and water the plants in the garden and talk softly to them. Sometimes he would walk among them and gently stroke their leaves while thinking only positive thoughts. Grandfather made a small garden for me and told me how to get in touch with that side of myself that projected only kindness and love. Our gardens produce the most beautiful and the largest vegetables you ever saw. We had tomatoes that were well over a pound each. We always gave some of our produce to a neighboring farmer who raised cattle, and he just could not believe the size of the vegetables we gave him. Everyone always asked what kind of fertilizer we used to get such gigantic tomatoes and squash. All the crops grew like that. I thought it silly at first, but when my small garden produced the same large vegetables, I knew it was because they felt our projection of love for them. Our chickens produced more eggs than anyone thought possible, and almost always extra large. So do I believe they feel our presence? I most certainly do," answered Jewel.

"That is quite a story, and I can't help but believe you are correct, though I wouldn't share this with anyone. They would think I had finally lost it! But sometimes when I walk in here, I swear I feel something. I can't really describe it, but it is as if they do know it's me. Most women in my garden club have very beautiful orchids. We visit one another's houses to see what each of us has growing, and there have been times when the club is to meet here, and I swear my flowers put on their very best faces to show off. The girls are astonished at the profusion of flowers. I have even been accused of purchasing new orchids to replace some of the others I had in my collection. I just can't explain it," said Evelyn.

"I can. I mean, I can't explain what transpires between us and the plants, but I know it works. You believe it, too, or you wouldn't have these beautiful blooms. They sense that you love them and are kind to them. That's all that matters," answered Jewel. "Now, let's see if I can remember any of their names. These are easy," said Jewel. "Phalaenopsis, and next to them are cattleyas. How am I doing so far?"

"You're correct on both. See the colors on this phalaenopsis? The deep lavender and white. This is Vincent van Gogh. The background color of dark lavender and the spots and tessellations make this a very striking specimen. This panda is more purple with white. Now, let's see if you can name this," said Evelyn. "I'll give you a hint. It is used by florists in corsages."

"I think it is dendrobium. The flowers are just a little smaller than the cymbidium, and before you ask me about the others, the only other one I know is the vanda," answered Jewel.

"My dear, you already know more than some of the women in the orchid club. Where did you get your education in orchids?" asked Evelyn.

"Other than being able to recognize a few varieties, I really don't know much about them. Justin may have told you that I went to FIT and I had to walk through a part of the wholesale flower district. Since I walked the same way every morning, I became friends with some of the people. There was an old man very much like my grandfather, and they happened to have a few orchids, and by the time the first semester was over, he had taught me about the most popular ones that they sold. But I don't know if they grow from seed or if they like the sun or anything about raising them, but I would love to learn more about them," replied Jewel.

"Well, I think I can give you a five-minute course about them, and then we shall have to go in for tea. Sarah serves precisely at four, no matter what," said Evelyn. "Orchids belong to a diverse family of plants. There are well over three hundred thousand registered cultivars. They produce seedpods with hundreds of seeds that are released by the wind, and then they establish a symbiotic relationship with a special fungus. Many plants take over five to seven years to mature before flowering. Today, greenhouse growers sow seeds on moist, sugar-rich, sterile agar. The roots of the plants need plenty of air circulation, and many growers make their own blend. I myself have a blend of osmunda fiber, pine bark, perlite, and just a hint of peat. Now that you know a little more about them, do you think you would ever like to try cultivating some of your own?"

"I really think I would. It would appear that patience is also a crucial factor in producing beautiful flowers, and I have developed a great deal over the years, so yes, I think I would like to very much," said Jewel.

"You certainly have enough knowledge to start," said Evelyn, "and yes, while patience is a factor, the proper atmosphere is paramount for the loveliest blooms."

"Someday, when I can open my quilt studio again, I will make sure there is room for a small greenhouse. I'm really curious now to see if I have what it takes to grow anything half as beautiful as yours."

"Quilt studio—you must tell me more about that sometime. Now, though, I'm afraid we must hurry in for tea. Please go to the office and see if Justin is still there, although I'm sure he remembered and is waiting for us. He has a habit of reminding me of the fact that I lose track of time when I am with my lovelies and would miss all my meals if I wasn't called. And I'm afraid it's true," said Evelyn.

Jewel was about to go to the office when she saw Justin heading out toward them.

"I was wondering if you two would remember the time. Mother can lose a day when she is in her greenhouse," said Justin.

"I can understand why," said Jewel. "It's like another world in there, surrounded by all those magnificent flowers. Some just take your breath away with their beauty, and I never knew that they could be so fragrant."

"Please don't tell me Mother has you hooked?" said Justin.

"I just may be, and anyway, there are worse things I could get hooked on," answered Jewel.

"Justin, this girl is a natural. She already knows as much about the orchids as most of the ladies in the club," said Evelyn, coming to Jewel's defense, "and it wouldn't surprise me, if she had the right work environment, she would surpass me in producing some breathtaking, new cultivars."

"I apologize for my earlier comment, Jewel. You must indeed know something about orchids, for I have never heard Mother give anyone a compliment before."

"Justin, you're being ill-mannered," said Evelyn. She glared at her son and looked at Jewel and asked her what she would like in her tea.

Sarah had just placed the tray in front of Evelyn, and she, too, gave Justin a sour look. After they got through tea, Evelyn excused herself and told Jewel it was her custom to have a short nap before dinner. Jewel asked Justin to show her around the grounds since it was still warm out. Justin grumbled but got their coats, and together they walked outside. The grounds were so well-kept; even though it was still a little early for most of the flowers to bloom, the arrangement of the trees and bushes still created a lovely scene. Red-leaf shrubbery against green was a wonderful arrangement. Each stood out on its own, as if creating a colorful painting. Justin never really looked at the grounds the way Jewel did, and now that she pointed out various layers and different-colored foliage, he had a new appreciation for his mother's ability. They walked down to the shade garden filled with different shades of green. Almost all the plants here were Hostas, since they preferred the shade. The feeder for the birds was filled, and they watched as the birds flew in and out for the seed. Justin suggested they take the road on the other side of the garden. He said there was something he thought she would like to see. They walked on down the road, with Jewel holding on to Justin's arm, trying to get as close as she could. There was such strength in this man, and she could feel it just being near him. *If only some of it would pass to me by holding on to him,* she thought to herself. Jewel always thought she was strong, but the events of the last few weeks left her feeling weak and frightened.

"Justin, look," said Jewel, running ahead of him toward the building set back of the road and nearly covered by bushes.

CHAPTER 8

"What is this place?" she asked. "It is absolutely wonderful! It looks almost like a carousel might be housed inside. Oh, the workmanship is unbelievable! Look at the carvings. This must have taken someone hours to do all this intricate work. What was it for? Can we go inside?" Jewel was so excited she could hardly speak. She pushed through the bushes so she could walk completely around the building.

"Jewel, be careful. You'll get all scratched up. Come out of there. I think I can open it, if I can remember where the darn key is. It's been so long since I have been down here," said Justin.

Jewel made her way completely around the building while waiting for Justin to find the key. He finally remembered it was hidden behind one of the shutters. He found the key and tried to open the lock. Over the years, the elements had rusted the lock, and he was having difficulty opening it. While Justin might have been an incredible lawyer, his work kept him inside, and his skills outside work as far as doing anything manual were nil. Jewel was getting impatient waiting for him to open the lock. She finally asked him to let her try; having lived in the country and doing much of the work around her house, hammering, sawing, chopping wood, she was better suited for this job. Justin stepped back to allow her to try. Just a few quick yanks and she got the key in the lock and the lock open. It took both of them, though, to open the door all the way because of the overgrowth of some of the bushes, but now the doorway was open. Jewel was the first to go in, leaving Justin behind.

"Is there nothing you are afraid of?" asked Justin. "There could be rodents or, worse, snakes or bats." He still held back a few moments, until Jewel told him it was completely safe.

"Don't worry," she said, "if anything was living in here, it would be just as frightened as you are."

"Oh, and that is supposed to make me feel better?" answered Justin.

"Don't worry, I'll protect you." Jewel laughed.

"I'm beginning to think this was not such a good idea after all," said Justin. "You do seem to delight in taking precarious chances. Please be careful. I can't remember the last time anyone was in here. There could be loose boards or something."

"I promise I'll be careful," said Jewel as she looked in every nook and cranny. "This is a carriage for horses, isn't it? Is that what this building was for, to house carriages? Oh, it is such a splendid building, a place for a carousel or a wonderful children's playhouse. Is that what it is for?" she asked Justin again. "A carriage house?"

"Yes. Grandfather had three carriages in here. He housed the horses down the lane farther, in a barn with much the same design as this carriage house. He had a man who tended to the horses, and whenever Grandfather threw one of his grand parties, he would have the horses hitched to one of the carriages, and he delighted in taking them for a ride around the grounds. In those days, there were many paths he could take as he drove the horses. Even in the winter, he would like to take them through the snow, with all the bells jingling on their harnesses. Grandfather was very good at driving the carriages, although he really wasn't that fond of the horses. He never brought them from the barn and hitched them. His man always performed that duty. After he passed away, father sold the horses and eventually had the barn removed. This building was left standing because Mother insisted it should stay. She felt something should remain that reminded them of the fun times Grandfather made. Grandfather was a grand old man. Any occasion was a time for a party, and he certainly knew how to throw one. He even enlarged the house, adding more bedrooms so the guests that traveled a long distance could stay over. Grandfather's parties usually lasted the entire weekend, and longer if it was a holiday. He entertained some of New York's and Connecticut's finest. The house was never the same after he passed. While Father did entertain occasionally, they were never like the parties Grandfather threw. Father was more reserved. Some even called him stiff, even boring. He liked to take the men into the game room and play billiards and smoke fine cigars, but he wasn't much for conversation with mixed couples. That was more Mother's responsibility. She never complained, knowing the gatherings were necessary for Father's business, but she never really liked having to entertain all the stuffed shirts with their made-up bimbos. But she did and did it well."

"Your grandfather sounds like a hoot. Nothing was ever dull when he was around. I think I would have liked him," said Jewel.

"I know he would have loved you," said Justin. There could never be enough beautiful girls for Grandfather, and with your curly red hair, sparkling eyes, and beautiful face, he would have fallen head over heels for you, much the way I have."

Jewel, who was still looking at every part of the interior of the building, stopped and looked at Justin, not believing what she thought she just heard him saying.

"Are you surprised by what I just said?" said Justin.

"About your grandfather or about you?" answered Jewel.

"You know very well I meant about what I just said," he replied. "You must know I have been drawn to you since the first night we met. My feelings for you can't come as a complete surprise. I've never brought anyone here to my home before. There is just something about you, something that makes me want to be with you all the time. It is very difficult for me to explain what it is I feel. I know it's the reason I hate having to go to Washington on business. I just want to be near you all the time." He looked embarrassed and found it difficult to make eye contact with her.

Jewel could see how uncomfortable he was, this big, strong man reduced to a quivering mass by uttering a few short words. She couldn't just let him hang there, but was she ready to say the words she knew he wanted to hear? After all, they had only known each other a few short months, and yet it did feel as if she had known him so much longer. She had already begun to rely on him, to follow his suggestions; she knew instinctively that he was the one person she could count on even though she had known Celia and Kenneth well over six years and trusted them completely.

Without thinking, reacting solely on what she was feeling, she closed the distance between them. She placed her hands on his arms, moving them slowly up until they were on his shoulders, then around his neck. With her cheek resting against his, she softly whispered to him, "You don't have to explain anything to me. I can't explain it either. All I know is that I feel you with me every minute of every day, and I'm happy."

Justin wrapped his arms tightly around her, his face buried in her hair. She could hear him sigh. They both knew what it was they didn't say. There was no need to.

The evening passed quickly, and soon everyone retired. Jewel thought about the carriage house and smiled, then fell off to sleep. She didn't hear anyone stir the next morning, but Justin and his mother had already gone down to breakfast.

"Should we wake Jewel?" asked Evelyn.

"No," answered Justin. "I want her to get all the rest she can. These past few weeks have been difficult for her, and we don't know yet what still might come."

"That sounds very ominous, Justin," said his mother. "Is she in some danger?"

"We really don't know. That's the upsetting part," answered Justin. "We believe someone is stalking her. We have evidence to support it, and the police are now involved, but we don't know what will happen next. I have appointed Clay to take her wherever she has to go and make sure she is never alone."

"You care for her a great deal, don't you?" said his mother.

"Yes, Mother, I do. I love her," said Justin confidently.

"And does she feel the same toward you?" she asked.

"I believe she does," he answered.

"I'm so happy for you, my dear. I was afraid you had just about given up on finding someone that you could share your life with, and I like this girl, very much. I think the two of you go well together. It reminds me very much of your father and me. We brought a balance to our lives. He was so serious, and I wasn't serious enough, and together we met happily in the middle. I see that in you two. She seems much wiser for her age, and so confident. I know women three times her age and they aren't half as wise or confident. No, this is a very special girl. I felt it the minute I met her. Even Sarah, who is suspicious of everyone, couldn't get over her wanting to help her with the dishes because she saw her limping. I never noticed Sarah limping, and I've lived with her for thirty years," Evelyn said. "Remember all the girls your father had paraded through this house in hopes of finding the right one for you and how Sarah came to your rescue and nearly frightened them to death?"

"Yes, Sarah saved me quite a few times, as I recall," said Justin.

"This one, Justin, is very special. As I said before, she has great empathy for people, and I think that is why she is so well received. Yes, compassion and empathy in one so young are quite uncommon," said Evelyn.

Just as she finished her sentence, Jewel came bounding in.

"Good morning. Justin, why didn't you wake me?" asked Jewel.

"Because I wanted you to get as much rest as you could. The stress of these past few weeks have made you look a little tired, and I know you've lost weight, so I let you sleep in," he answered.

"Thank you for worrying about me, but I'll be fine. I refuse to let some crazy person get the best of me. Can you really tell I've lost weight, though?" asked Jewel.

"Yes. Even Clay said you were looking thinner. And you haven't been sleeping either. That's easy enough to tell," said Justin.

"I'll admit, last night was the first night in a long time that I felt completely safe. I guess that's why I slept so long."

"Justin has just been telling me of the dire situation you are in," said Evelyn. "Are you certain this person means you harm?"

"We really aren't certain of anything at this time, Mother," said Justin, "but his threats do seem to be escalating. At the last contact, he left a note on a plant outside the door, and written on it was the message, 'I'm always watching you.' The police think this is a serious threat and we shouldn't take it lightly."

"Could we please just have a pleasant breakfast? We'll be back in the city much too soon, and I would like to put off thinking about what could happen for as long as possible," said Jewel.

"Quite right," said Evelyn. "Now, what would you like for breakfast? Anything at all."

"Is Sarah feeling better today? Because I can just make some toast," said Jewel.

"I'm doing fine, young lady. You don't have to worry about me. And toast is not what I would call breakfast. How would you like some of my famous stuffed French toast?" said Sarah.

"That sounds decadent! I would love it," answered Jewel.

"That's better, then. I'll just be a minute. Coffee's on the table," said Sarah as she disappeared into the kitchen.

"Sarah makes the best French toast, better than any restaurant's," said Justin. "I never eat it anymore. I find the next day I always seem to weigh five pounds more. I think it may be just the right breakfast for you, though, and she always warms the syrup to make it just a little extra special too."

"Mmmm, sounds so good! How will I ever go back to a lowly piece of toast?" Jewel laughed. "Maybe it will put the five pounds I lost back on."

The French toast was beyond belief, and Jewel had all she could do to stuff the last piece down, but she did it.

"I can't believe I ate it all. It was so delicious! But I think I had better get up and move a little. I must say thank you to Sarah for the splendid breakfast. Do you have plans for this morning, Evelyn?" asked Jewel. "I would really like to take another look at some of the orchids."

"Justin and I have about a half-hour of work to do, and then I'll gladly show you more of my little darlings," said Evelyn.

Jewel, having nothing to do, decided to go up to her bedroom and packed up her things. She brought the overnight bag down and placed it by the front door. Then she just wandered through the house, looking at some of the paintings hanging on the walls. She thought she recognized a few artists from her visits to the museum. *Could these be originals?* she thought to herself. She had no doubt they were and could hardly contain herself with excitement. She couldn't ask; she would feel like a fool. *Wow, wait till I tell Celia!* Jewel wandered into the kitchen after hearing someone stirring.

"Hi, Sarah," she said. "Can I help you with anything?"

"No, my dear, just tidying up a bit," she said.

"I'd be glad to help dry the dishes for you. I'm afraid I feel like a fish out of water. I can't remember the last time I had nothing to do," said Jewel.

"Well, now, if you did the dishes, then what would I have to do?" said Sarah, looking quite serious.

"I'm sorry, I didn't mean to bother you. I guess I could go outside for a while," said Jewel.

Sarah put her hands on her hips and laughed softly. "Now it's I who should say sorry. By the look on your face, I guess you thought I was trying to shush you out of my kitchen."

"Yes, I'm afraid I did," answered Jewel. "I know I can be a bother sometimes. I just always seem to have to be busy. My friends back in New York have nick-named me the Energizer Bunny because I just keep going and going. I don't know why I can't sit still."

"Well, then, I guess we better put you to work. The drying towel is there. You can just place the dishes on the counter, and I'll put them away, and while you're doing that, I'll make us a nice, fresh pot of coffee. Or would you prefer some tea?" asked Sarah.

"Coffee for me, please," she said as she began to dry the dishes. "How long have you been here with the Angelis family? I'm only asking because I wanted to know what Justin was like as a child. Was he much like he is today, all quiet and reserved?"

"I have been here going on thirty-two years. My husband and I both worked here. We were hired by Justin's grandfather. Oh, there was a grand man, always the life of the party, even when there was no party. When there was a party, though, he never stopped laughing from the time his guests arrived until they had all gone. Always found the good in people even when things were difficult, and as for Justin, yes, he was a very quiet little boy. His father was hard on him and always made sure the boy had plenty of schoolwork to do even on vacations. When other children were off enjoying the holiday, that one was in his room, working on his lessons, and nothing short of perfection was tolerated either. His grandfather would make up excuses why he needed Justin's help and would whisk him off to town for an ice cream or just a stroll around the park, then they would come home with some books, and his grandfather would say he thought the boy was lacking in reading some of the classics, but everyone knew that wasn't true. Justin had been reading from the age of two and had read just about every book in the library, but they let the old man have his fun. Justin loved his gramps. He took it particularly hard when the old man passed. Wouldn't come out of his room for days, just stayed up there and re-read all the books his grandfather had ever given him.

"I don't want to give you the wrong impression. Justin had his days, and when he decided to cut up a bit, he did it with pure delight. I remember many a day when his mother and I were sitting here in this very kitchen, laughing so hard our very sides would ache."

"Justin told me about the frogs in the punch and the cigar he got caught smoking," said Jewel.

"I remember those times. His mother and I had all we could do to stop from laughing every time we thought of it. There was other mischief he got into occasionally, but for the most part, he was a very good lad. We were all so proud of him, even his father, though he tried not to show it. He believed by being hard on the boy, it would better prepare him for life as an adult." Sarah took out two cups and poured the coffee while she spoke, then motioned for Jewel to have a seat. She had finished the dishes long ago but still stood against the counter, listening to Sarah talk about Justin. They had just started drinking their coffee when Justin and Evelyn came into the room.

"What's going on here?" said Justin.

"I was just getting the lowdown on what you were like as a child. Pretty interesting stuff too." Jewel laughed.

"Mother, would you like a cup of coffee?" he said to her after motioning for Sarah to stay seated.

"Yes, please, dear. Books and figures always give me such a headache. Thank the heaven I never had to do it for a living," she replied. "Thankfully, I have

Justin to make heads or tails out of this stuff," she continued as she took the cup from Justin.

"Now," she said to Jewel, "what did I miss?"

"I was just curious about Justin when he was young," replied Jewel, "and Sarah was kind enough to tell me a little about him."

"I had to do something. The girl dried all my dishes for me, leaving me with nothing to do, so I put on a fresh pot of coffee and told her some of what I remembered. Don't worry, child," she said to Justin, "it was all good."

"Then why does Jewel have that gleeful look on her face?" said Justin.

"Why, she does, indeed," said his mother. "Sarah, did you tell her about the time he—"

"Oh, yes," said Sarah.

"And how about the time he—"

"And that too," continued Sarah, trying ever so hard to hold back a smile.

"All right, the three of you, I know when I'm outdone." Justin laughed. "I hope you left me with some dignity intact."

"You know we're just havin' a bit of fun, my dear," said Sarah.

"Yes, I know, Sarah, love. I'm just teasing. Besides, Jewel will find out all of it sooner or later," he said.

"And sooner is better, then I will have that much longer to remind you of what a naughty boy you were," said Jewel.

"Mother, weren't you going to take this wench into the greenhouse? You best do it soon, or I'll have her over my knee," said Justin.

"You'd have to catch me first." Jewel laughed defiantly.

"All right, you two, I shall have you both over my knee in a minute," said Evelyn. "Come along, Jewel, there is one plant I remembered I specifically wanted to show you before you left."

"I'll be right there, Evelyn. I just need to get a glass of water."

Jewel waited until Evelyn had left the kitchen and said to Justin, "Do you have a piece of paper and a pen? I want to write down a few of the names of the plants your mother has. I have some friends in the flower district, and maybe we can find something she doesn't have in her collection."

"I have one right here, my dear," said Sarah. "I keep it handy if I need to remember something I need from the grocer. Here you are."

Jewel took the paper and pen and ran after Evelyn, who was almost to the greenhouse.

"Did you get your drink?" she asked.

"I did, and I also got some paper and a pen. I thought I would write down some of the names of the orchids I particularly liked and look them up on the computer when we get back. That way, I'll be able to learn more about them," answered Jewel.

"How very thoughtful. I'm glad that you are taking such an interest in these wonderful plants. Once you get proficient at remembering their names and identifying the subtle differences in each species, you may like to join me the next time the orchid club meets at the home of one of the other members," said Evelyn.

"Oh, I'd love to, but I think it will be a while before I can tell one from the other," answered Jewel.

"Nonsense!" she said. "You already know most of the more common species, and if you study some of the others on the computer, I'm sure you will have no difficulty conversing with the other members. We will have to wait a while, though. The member who has a collection almost equal to my own will be away until the latter part of May. She and her husband spend most of the winter in Spain. Her husband is Spanish, and they maintain a home there."

"Who takes care of her plants when she's away?" asked Jewel. "I can't imagine she would just leave their care to just anyone."

"Oh, she wouldn't. They're her pride and joy. No, the local florist has a great deal of knowledge about orchids, as she herself has a small collection and has a modicum of success propagating a few of her plants. She comes in twice a week to tend to them, and she and Murial are on the phone weekly. Her housekeeper has strict instructions. No one may enter the greenhouse except Mrs. May. She's a bit dramatic, but she does have a beautiful collection," said Evelyn.

Jewel and Evelyn spent nearly two hours in the greenhouse, with Jewel writing down as much information as she could about the species Evelyn had in her collection.

"I think you two have given these flowers as much attention as they need for one day," said Justin, making his way toward them. "Sarah sent me to ask if you wanted her to fix a complete lunch, or would you prefer just a little soup and crackers?"

"I would prefer just some soup, dear. Jewel, is there something special you would like for lunch?" said Evelyn.

"No," she answered. "Soup will be fine, thank you."

"All right, I'll go and tell Sarah myself," said Evelyn. "I think my son is getting jealous of our time together, dear," she whispered to Jewel. "I don't blame him. I think he may be right. I just lose myself in these beauties and love to show them off."

"He'll survive. I've loved this time with you here in the greenhouse. I am just so overwhelmed by the splendor of these orchids. I can understand why you lose track of time in here. Each time I look at them, I see something different. I guess that's why they're so interesting," said Jewel.

"There aren't many men who can really appreciate the wonder each flower holds," said Evelyn as she gave a disappointed look at Justin when she passed him in the doorway.

"I think your mother is a bit annoyed with you," said Jewel.

"Yes, but as you said, I'll survive," he answered as he walked deeper into the room where Jewel was standing. He took her in his arms and kissed her. "I'm feeling terribly neglected," he said.

"Oh, you poor baby, what was I thinking to leave you alone in this big empty house for so long? What's wrong? Have you run out of papers to read?" she said laughingly.

"No, I have not. I just missed you," he said.

"Justin, we only have a few hours, and then we'll be leaving and you'll have me all night. I think we can spend a little more time with your mother. She only has you, and she loves you so, and I know she misses you," said Jewel.

"All night," replied Justin with a large grin on his face.

"All night, if you want it," answered Jewel, matching his grin.

"I most definitely want all night," he answered. "But for now, I think we had better move out of here, before I forget where we are and I have my way with you."

"You're right. I think it's a little dangerous for us to be here alone. Come on," said Jewel as she led them out of the room.

The remainder of the afternoon went by quickly as they sat and spoke with Evelyn. They had just finished the four o'clock tea when the doorbell rang.

"That must be clay," said Justin as he got up and went to the door. Justin opened the door and invited Clay inside.

"Afternoon," said Clay. "It's five o'clock. Are you ready to leave, or would you like me to wait?"

"Good afternoon, Clay," said Justin. "No, we are almost ready. Do come in and say hello to Mother."

"Good afternoon, Clay," said Evelyn. "It has been a while since we've seen you. How have you been? You're looking well."

"Thank you, Mrs. Angelis. It has been a while, and you look as beautiful as ever. Haven't seen you in the city lately. Folks in Connecticut keeping you busy, or is it those orchids?" Clay replied.

"Clay, folks may try to occupy my time with nonsense, but when it comes to my orchids, well, let's just say that they take preference over some silly card games. That is, of course, unless they are playing poker. You know how I love to take their money," said Evelyn.

"Yes, I do, Mrs. A. Don't ever play poker with her, Ms. Lansby. She will clean you out. She has incredible luck," said Clay.

"Luck, you say?" replied Evelyn. "Some would say it was skill. Just like the song, you have to know when to hold them and know when to fold them, and that, my boy, is skill, not luck."

"If you say so, Mrs. A," said Clay. "Are these all the bags, Mr. A?"

"Yes, Clay," said Justin. "We'll be just a minute, to say our goodbyes."

Clay picked up the bags and left the house and placed them in the trunk, then waited for his passengers.

"Well, Mother," said Justin, "thank you for another enjoyable weekend."

"Weekend, a very short one," she said. "I do wish you could stay a little longer. You know how I love your company. Jewel, please promise me you will convince Justin to make your next visit a much longer one."

"Thank you for everything, Evelyn, and I promise our next visit will be longer," said Jewel. "Goodbye, Sarah."

"Goodbye, my dear," answered Sarah, "and, Justin, mind what I told you, and we'll see you soon."

Justin gave his mother a kiss on the cheek, and also one on Sarah's.

"Oh, I just hate to see you go," said Evelyn, giving Jewel a hug and kiss on the cheek too. "Do come back soon." Evelyn finally let go of Jewel and followed them out to the car. She and Sarah waved as they pulled out of the driveway.

Jewel resisted the urge to look back; she was overcome with emotion and thought she might cry if she looked at Evelyn's face. She couldn't help but feel the loneliness in her manner and voice. She turned to Justin and told him how affected she was by his mother hugging and kissing her. Justin said he was just as surprised by what she did and said he had never seen her act so emotional. Sarah either. Usually she just said goodbye to him from the kitchen.

"I hope there's nothing wrong," said Jewel.

"I'm sure they're fine," replied Justin. "I think they were just thinking about how quiet it will be now that you're gone. They both really enjoyed having you here. Sarah told me it was good to have someone who could make Mother loosen up a bit. She also said that you were special and that I should do all I could to make sure you didn't get away."

"Did she really, or are you just making that up?" asked Jewel.

"God's honest truth, that's exactly what she said," answered Justin.

"That's really nice," said jewel as she moved closer to Justin. She snuggled in as close as she could, and Justin held her tight.

The ride back into the city was slow; there was a lot more traffic than expected. Jewel began to get restless.

"Do you mind if I do some sketching while we are stuck here in traffic?" she asked Justin.

"No, of course not," he answered. "Do you have your art supplies?"

"Yes. I always keep them close. I never know when I might get an idea, and I have a few ideas for some evening wear. I want to get them down on paper before I forget them."

"If you can make an evening dress that comes anywhere near resembling one of mother's orchids, I know she would just have to have it," replied Justin.

"We often make one-of-a-kind evening wear for large benefits, like the hospitals," said Jewel. "They auction them off to raise money."

"Well, let's see what you can do," said Justin.

Jewel picked up her bag, removed her pad and pencils, and began to sketch. Somehow, Jewel managed to drown out the noise around her and immerse herself in her drawings. She sketched quickly, first the figure, then the outfit. She didn't waste time refining the sketches; it was more important to get the different ideas down, and then she could go back and refine them. Her fingers flew across the paper. After a few minutes, what looked like a pad full of unrelated lines soon gave way to a woman's figure with a rendition of a gown with a startling resemblance to an orchid. Slender body with a series of what looked very much like the overlapping petals of an orchid. Jewel continued to draw until she realized they were almost in the city. She put her drawing things away and looked at Justin, who had fallen asleep. He looked so much like a man in peace. She hated to awaken him; she moved closer and put her arm around his waist.

"If you're planning to get fresh with me, I'll pretend I'm still asleep," he said. "Well, now, you'll never know." She laughed as she slid her arm around him further and reached up to kiss him. He pulled her even closer, and with this kiss, she could feel the excitement and longing he felt for her. Not surprisingly, she felt it too. He held her close a moment longer, then slowly pushed her away and told her when they stopped for Rocky, which would be in just a few minutes; she would have to get him. Jewel looked at him seriously, then realized the situation he was trying to communicate to her and buried her head in his chest and laughed.

"Go ahead, laugh. It's entirely your fault, you know," he said.

"I'm sorry," she said. "No, I'm not, and if it happens again, maybe we should do something about it."

"Yes, maybe we should. We most definitely should. Now, stay away from me," he said.

"Oh, do you really want me to stay away? You don't want me to do this, or this?" said Jewel as she nibbled on his ear and put her hand inside his shirt.

Justin was blushing; she had never seen him blush.

"Justin, you're blushing," she said to him.

"No, I'm not. It is just suddenly very hot in here," he answered. "Very hot, indeed, and you keep your distance or you'll force me to sit up front with Clay."

"And how are you going to explain it to Clay? Let's see, 'Clay, Jewel is giving me a hard-on, so I have to sit up front with you.'

I can hear Clay now. He'll have to pull the car over to the curb because he'll be laughing so hard. Shall I knock on the window for you and tell him?"

Now they both were laughing so hard that Clay was on the speaker, asking if everything was all right and that they were just pulling up to the Dolan house. Justin answered that all was well, just a little joke Jewel told him. They both tried to stop laughing but were finding it difficult. Suddenly, the door opened, and Clay was standing there, holding the door.

"It's better if I go in alone, Justin. Otherwise, Celia will keep us talking all night," she said to him.

Justin was greatly relieved that she didn't expect him to go with her. Under the circumstances, it would prove a little difficult. Jewel was out within minutes, which surprised both Justin and Clay. Rocky jumped into the car, followed by Jewel, and Rocky took up his place, again sitting on Justin's lap.

"That didn't take long. How in the world did you get away from Celia that fast?" asked Justin.

"Celia wasn't there. Kenneth said she went to a shower for one of her friends who is having a baby, so I got Rocky and told Kenneth I'd see him at work Monday. Thankfully, Kenneth is a man of few words, especially when the boys are occupied and he has a chance to watch a movie on TV," she answered.

"Any other stops, Mr. A?" asked Clay.

"No, Clay, just downtown to the apartment, thank you," he replied.

He and Jewel each took turns playing with Rocky, but Rocky would not leave Justin's lap, even when Jewel tried to coax him onto hers.

"Looks like you have a new best friend," said Jewel.

"It appears so," said Justin, smiling. He had never really had a dog of his own; they always had a dog around the house that he could remember, but they were his grandfather's, not his. It pleased him greatly having this little ten-pound ball of fur preferring to sit on his lap rather than his owner's.

They arrived at the apartment in a relatively short time; there never was much traffic in this part of New York when the clothing factories were closed. Except for a few small mom-and-pop eateries and grocers, everything else closed at five, when the factories got out. Clay opened the door for them and asked Justin if he would need him any more this evening. Jewel quickly told Clay that they would not need him at all the rest of the night. Clay couldn't help but smile and gave Justin a quick wink, letting him know that he understood that this would be the night.

Jewel opened the door and cut off the alarm. After going through Kenneth's office to the apartment, she cut off that alarm as well. She turned on the lights on the roof and gave a quick check before opening the doors to let Rocky out. He sniffed around a bit, relieved himself, and came running back inside. Jewel locked both doors and pulled the drapes closed. Justin dropped the bags on the floor and was about to get comfortable on the sofa when Jewel asked him if he was tired. He answered that he wasn't but the trip home from Connecticut seemed to get longer each time.

"Is there something you'd like me to do?" he asked.

"No," said Jewel. "There's something we need to finish. I, for one, could use a nice, long warm shower, and I thought you might like to join me." She was saying this all while she was unbuttoning his shirt.

"That sounds like an interesting proposition. You do know I don't have any other clothes?" he said.

"You won't need them once you're in bed, will you?" replied Jewel. She had all the buttons undone and was gently pulling his shirt out of his pants, then his T-shirt. As she started to undo his belt buckle, she could feel his body quivering. Justin grabbed the bottom of her sweater and was about to pull it over her head when the door buzzer went off.

"Who can that be?" she said. "That better not be the pizza delivery. I ordered it for after nine."

"I'll go down and see who it is," said Justin.

"No, I'll go. If it is the pizza, I know the boy who delivers, and I can tell him to tell his boss I asked for a later delivery. I'll be right back. Besides, you would have to button up, and I would just have to unbutton everything all over again," she said to him, smiling. He pulled her close and said he wouldn't mind that at all.

"Just hold that thought," she said and slipped out the door.

She took the elevator down to the ground floor, thinking of the tongue-lashing she was about to give the pizza-delivery boy. She knew she wouldn't have to unlock and open the door, because there was a slot made just for the purpose of accepting pizza boxes. When Kenneth designed the door, he thought of all the best ways to accept deliveries, if he and his team stayed late, without having to open the door fully.

Jewel opened the small window. She looked out but didn't recognize the man.

"Can I help you?" she said.

"Are you Jewel?" he asked.

"Yes," she answered, and before she could say anything else, something wet hit her face.

"There you are, bitch!" said the man.

CHAPTER 9

Jewel quickly closed the small door and took a few steps backward until she felt the wall behind her. Her eyes were searing with pain, her face burning. She could feel her eyelids swell so quickly that her eyes were almost swollen shut. The pain was unbearable. She fought the temptation to rub them; her instinct kicked in, and she knew it would be the worst thing she could do. She slid down to the floor and screamed. She held her head and realized she needed help fast, but Justin was on the third floor. He would never hear her. Somehow she would have to find the elevator and get upstairs.

She got up, steadying herself against the wall, and began to feel her way toward the elevator. Was she going the right way? she asked herself. She tried to remain calm, but the pain was making it impossible. Her eyes were on fire. She kept stopping and started up again, thinking that if she got to water, she could put her face in it and the pain would stop, but each time she started to cry, the pain intensified. She realized that water was not the answer. *What if I'm blind? What if I can't see to draw or sew?* A thousand questions and a thousand answers before she finally felt the steel cage of the elevator. She continued to feel around for the strap that brought the doors together. *Think, Jewel,* she silently said to herself angrily. *You've taken this elevator every day for years. Where is the strap?* But the pain was affecting her coordination.

Finally, she found it and pulled the door of the cage together, then searched for the elevator buttons. *There, they must be over there,* she thought as she moved more to the right. Finally, she found the buttons and counted up for the button that would take her to the third floor. She pounded on it. Somehow, in her pain, she thought it would move faster. It felt like hours since something was sprayed into her face. She thought then that she would not be able to stand the pain because the pain grew worse with every minute.

The elevator finally reached the third floor, and Jewel opened the doors. She screamed for Justin, but she had no way of knowing that he had put the TV on for Rocky. He and Rocky sat on the couch, looking through the channels for something Rocky would like. When there was no response to her calling Justin, she knew he probably couldn't hear her because she was so far from the apartment. There was half of the design floor and then Kenneth's office to navigate through before she felt he would hear her. She started to walk out onto the floor with arms out in front, trying to feel what might be in front of her. She tried hard to remember where the machines were, and she knew there were some large boxes on the floor. But where? She tried to walk in a straight line but knew this was dangerous, as some of the machines were staggered. After a few steps, she hit her knee on one of the wooden machine tables; she swore to herself but continued on, only to trip and fall over a small box with her next step. Now sitting on the ground with skinned elbows and knees, she began to cry again, but the salty tears felt like they were ripping her eyes to shreds. She called Justin's name.

In the apartment, Rocky got off Justin's lap and stood on the edge of the sofa.

"Is she finally coming with your pizza, boy?" he said to the little dog, but Rocky just stood still, listening for something that only he could here.

Jewel finally realized that Justin probably couldn't hear her, but maybe Rocky could, so she called his name as loud as she could. Inside the apartment, Rocky turned his head this way and that, trying to pick up the sound better. He knew something was wrong and started to bark. He ran to the door, barking and scratching on it. Justin got up immediately and went to see what the dog was doing. Rocky rarely barked—Justin remembered Jewel telling him that when he first met the little dog—so there had to be a reason for his behavior.

Rocky continued to scratch furiously at the door. Justin realized he had better open the door and find out what had Rocky so upset. Rocky squeezed through the door before Justin could open it all the way. Well, whatever it was, it must be serious, thought Justin. He tried to follow Rocky as best as he could, but the dog was small in comparison to the large sewing tables and was easily missed; only his constant barking kept Justin on the right track.

Rocky reached Jewel and began to lick her face but stopped when the substance began to burn his tongue. Justin finally caught up with Rocky and saw the reason for his excitement; Jewel was on the floor, with Rocky standing over her. Through her tears Jewel told Rocky to get Justin.

"I'm here, Jewel, I'm here. What's wrong? What's happened?" he asked.

Jewel lifted her face toward him, and Justin was stunned by what he was seeing.

"My god, Jewel, what happened to you?" He tried to help her up, but she just screamed in pain. He asked her again what had happened but realized she was nearly unconscious. He looked for something to put under her head and saw a bundle of fabric on one of the boxes. He grabbed a handful and placed it under her head.

"Jewel, please, if you can, tell me what happened," he asked.

"I opened the window and the man sprayed something in my face. It burns, Justin! I feel like my face is on fire." And then she just went limp. He called her name, but there was little response. He knew he had to act quickly.

He told her not to move, that he had to go back to the apartment to phone 911. He didn't know if she understood him or not, but he had to get to the phone. He grabbed his cell and went running back to Jewel, calling as he ran. He told them as much as he knew and pleaded for them to hurry. Not knowing what else to do, he called Clay. Clay answered, and Justin told him what had transpired. Clay said he would be there in five minutes, that he was just up the street, having dinner. Whenever possible, Clay preferred to eat in the small mom-and-pop diners; large restaurants made him uncomfortable.

It was something that started when he came home from the war. He didn't like open spaces anymore. That was where the worst of the worst took place. Clay needed to be in an area where he felt he had control, and he always sat facing the door, just another thing he brought home from the war.

After Justin spoke to Clay, he called Kenneth and explained all he knew and asked him to get downtown as quickly as he could because he didn't know how to lock up and set the alarm for the factory and he needed to get to the hospital with Jewel. Kenneth promised to be there as fast as he could.

The buzzer rang, and Justin knew it had to be the ambulance. He ran to the elevator and closed the doors, pushing the button for the ground floor; he jumped out and opened the door for the EMTS. As they rode up in the elevator, he told them everything he knew, which wasn't much. Justin led them to where Jewel lay, with Rocky lying beside her. Rocky, not knowing that these people were there to help Jewel, growled when they tried to approach her. Justin picked Rocky up as naturally as if he had done it a hundred times before.

"I'm sorry, he is quite attached to her, as you can see," he told the men, who were now down on their knees, administering to Jewel. They asked him if he knew what was sprayed on her. Justin explained again just what he knew, that she went down because she thought it was the pizza delivery and after a while Rocky started going crazy and led Justin to where she was on the floor. He said he asked her what happened, but all she was able to say was that someone sprayed her in the face and she was in excruciating pain, then seemed to pass out.

Justin stood by helplessly while they attended to Jewel.

One of the men asked Jewel her name and age, but Jewel's face was so swollen she could barely speak.

"Can you tell me her name and age, please?" asked one of the medics.

"Her name is Jewel Lansby, and she is twenty-six," answered Justin.

"Any history of illness or any allergies? Any medication she takes?" he asked again.

Justin tried to think clearly, but the vision of Jewel so swollen and red and in such pain made it difficult. *Think,* he said to himself. *They need this information to save her.*

"No history of any illness. She doesn't take any medication except an occasional valium for muscle spasms or Tylenol for headaches, and the only thing she is allergic to is peppers," he replied. He hoped he remembered everything correctly.

Justin continued to watch as they placed the pads on to run an EEG to check her heart. One of the men said to call it in to report her current condition. He gave the hospital her vitals and waited for a reply. Her blood pressure was extremely high, and the reaction from the sprayed solution was causing a very dangerous hive reaction. While they were putting an IV in her arm, they were told to administer epinephrine for the swelling and morphine for the pain and to transport immediately. She was already on the gurney; they wrapped her with a sheet and told Justin to get the elevator for them.

"Where will you be taking her?" he asked.

"New York Presbyterian. They have one of the best ophthalmologist there, and he'll be waiting for us in the ER." They quickly wheeled Jewel to the elevator and then into the ambulance.

Justin wanted desperately to go with her but knew he couldn't; besides, he had to wait for Kenneth to arrive to lock the door and set the alarm. Plus, there was Rocky. There was no way he would leave that little guy alone. He had a new respect for that dog, for without him Justin might not have found Jewel in time. Justin waited for what seemed like an eternity. He stood inside the building with the door locked, just in case this nefarious person was still lurking around. Justin paced back and forth, hands in his pockets and head hung low. He looked at his watch, then looked at it again. The time seemed to be standing still. He cursed at the watch for not moving the time.

Then he finally heard something outside. The bell rang, and Clay was yelling to Justin, who quickly opened the door.

"What the hell's going on, Justin? Where's Jewel?" Clay yelled. He grabbed Justin by the shoulders and shook him; he knew that Justin was in shock, and he needed him to think clearly.

"Justin, come on, man, tell me what's going on." He could see Justin tearing up, but he couldn't let him fall apart and shook him again.

"Clay, oh my god, Clay, it was horrible! I thought she was dead. Her face was so swollen, her eyes swollen shut. She couldn't speak. I thought I'd lost her. I can't believe this. What should I do?" Justin was so distraught he could barely talk.

"Justin, you have to calm down. This won't do Jewel any good. Justin, do you hear me? I said calm down and tell me what happened."

Justin finally began to calm down and looked at Clay. He caught his breath and told Clay the events as he knew them.

"Where did they take her?" Clay asked.

"New York Presbyterian. They said they had the best ophthalmologist there," said Justin, settling down at last.

"Good, that's good. Did she say anything? Anything at all?" asked Clay.

"When we first found her, she said she opened the window and a man sprayed something in her face and said, 'This is for you, bitch,' then she passed out from the intense pain. I called 911. They came and took her away just a few minutes ago. They said I couldn't go with them. I couldn't, anyway. I have to wait for Kenneth to lock up the building. He said he would be here as quickly as possible," answered Justin.

"All right, we'll wait here together. Kenneth should be here soon," said Clay, trying to reassure his friend and, at the same time, quell his anger.

Clay had grown extremely fond of Jewel. She was different from most of the women he knew. She didn't try to fill in the quiet moments with conversation. She always said what was on her mind instead of making you guess. There was no game playing with her, and on occasion, he caught himself thinking about her as more than just the girl that belonged to his best friend. If anything would happen to her, he was worried that if he caught this creep before the police, he wasn't sure what he would do to him. He counted Justin as one of his few friends, and to see him in this pain was something he wouldn't soon forget.

Time passed slowly, but Kenneth finally arrived, looking just as perplexed as both Justin and Clay did. Justin told Kenneth everything and said that he must get to the hospital, but before he left, he told Kenneth to please take care of Rocky, for if it hadn't been for him, they might not have found Jewel in time. Kenneth told Justin not to worry; he would take Rocky home with him, and he asked to please call when they found out about Jewel's condition. Clay and Justin left Kenneth to get Rocky and to lock up the building and headed to the hospital.

They arrived at the hospital and immediately went to the emergency room. Justin asked at the desk about Jewel. The nurse behind the desk asked him all kinds of questions. He told her he was her fiancé as well as her attorney and asked to see her. She said he would have to wait, that the doctor was looking at her now and he would talk to him when he finished his exam, and pointed to the room they could wait in to see the doctor. Justin couldn't sit; he just paced back and forth. Clay finally had to tell him to pull himself together, that he was not helping things. Jewel needed him to be strong right now.

Hearing her name brought Justin back from the edge of panic.

"Thank you, clay," said Justin. "I guess I was losing it there for a while, but I'm all right now. I just need to know how she is."

"I know, Mr. A. It's okay. I'm sure they're doing everything they can. They'll be out as soon as they can. How 'bout I go get us some coffee? I know you haven't had anything to eat. I'll be right back, okay?" said Clay as he walked away. He hated to leave his friend alone, but he knew he needed a little space right now; he didn't want Justin to see just how angry and concerned he was.

Justin never replied and was surprised when Clay returned with coffee for the two of them.

"Here you go, Mr. A, nice and hot," said Clay.

Justin took the cup and thanked Clay for it, but he was not in the mood to be here drinking coffee when he didn't know what was happening to Jewel. Finally, though, he succumbed and surrendered to the aroma of the coffee in his hand. It was a pleasant diversion, if only for a moment. They both finished their coffee and waited.

The doctor finally came out and asked which one of them was her fiancé. Justin jumped up at once and told the doctor he was and told him his name. The doctor told them that they were very lucky to have gotten her to the hospital when they did. Because of the severe allergic reaction, they concluded that she must have been sprayed with pepper spray. Not only were her eyes swollen shut, but her airways were also swelling at an alarming rate. They had to insert a breathing tube and were giving her drugs to get the swelling down, but they were also keeping her heavily sedated because of the intense pain. They put ointment in her eyes to help with the pain and dryness but wouldn't know the damage, if any, to her eyes until the swelling went down. They had planned to move her up to the ICU so they could monitor her closely, and advised them to go home. Justin insisted that he wanted to see her, but the doctor said she wouldn't be responsive and it would be better to see her tomorrow.

"Come on, Mr. A. Doctor's right. She needs them more than us right now. We'll come back first thing in the morning," said Clay.

Justin looked at Clay and back at the doctor; it was obvious he didn't want to leave, but Clay was right. There was nothing they could do but wait. Justin thanked the doctor and allowed Clay to gently escort him out of the hospital.

Once in the car, Justin called Kenneth. He told them to come up to the house. He needed to know what the hell had happened. He told Justin that he wanted Clay to come in with him. Clay, at first, refused. He found Celia both shallow and annoying, but it was Jewel he was thinking of, so he gave in. On the ride uptown to Kenneth's house, Clay put in a call to his friend Detective Warren Beach and told him what just went down. Beach told him he would check out the neighborhood and see them at the hospital in the morning. Clay relayed to Justin what Beach just told him.

When they arrived at Kenneth's house, Clay asked Justin if he was sure he wanted him to come up. Justin said he wanted him there. He wasn't just a driver to him; he was his friend, and Jewel's too, and he needed him. He looked at the time and told Clay that before it got too late, he wanted to call his mother and tell her of tonight's events. His mother took the news well, as he knew she would. His mother was always the strong one in the family and, in any critical situation, was the one that reviewed the options with any sort of clarity. He told her he would call tomorrow after he spoke to the doctor. Then he and Clay went upstairs to talk to Kenneth and Celia, something he was not looking forward to.

Working with Celia was one thing, but now having to know her on a more personal level, especially as she and Jewel were so close, was uncomfortable for him. He knew he would be grilled, and he couldn't tell her anything more than he knew an hour ago. He was glad Clay was with him, though.

Celia welcomed them in and told them Kenneth was in the inside-out room. They followed her back and accepted the coffee she was already pouring for them.

"I'm sorry. Would the two of you care for something stronger?"

Justin and Clay both told her that the coffee was just fine. She took her place beside Kenneth and waited for someone to say something. The boys were upstairs in bed, so they didn't have to worry about them overhearing what happened to Jewel. Celia couldn't stand the silence any longer.

"Would someone please tell us, for Christ's sake, what's going on? Justin, please!" she cried.

Justin told them every detail he could remember and then conveyed to them what the doctor had told them at the hospital. He tried to remain stoic but found he could not keep up the behavior of his alter ego he used at the office. He looked at Celia with tears in his eyes.

"If she weren't so damn stubborn, she would have let me go get the pizza. At least then it wouldn't be her in the hospital, going through this. It would be me."

"Knowing Jewel, do you really think she would want you to be the injured party?" asked Celia.

"No, I suppose not," answered Justin as he took out his handkerchief to wipe his eyes, not caring at all if everyone saw him.

Celia placed her hand on his, trying to comfort him as best as she could, knowing in her heart that nothing could comfort him. She could see that Justin was deeply in love with Jewel.

After an hour or so, Clay stood up and said he would like to get Justin home so he could get some sleep. Justin looked up at his friend and agreed that he would like to go home and get some rest. Later, in the car, Justin thanked Clay for getting them out of there and told him he didn't know what he would do without him.

"You're like the brother I never had, Clay. You mean a great deal to me," said Justin.

Clay couldn't answer; he realized that in these past few years driving Justin just about everywhere, and even accompanying him on the occasional trip out of town, he felt just as close to him. He hoped Justin knew how he felt. Clay could not put the words together easily to describe what he felt for Justin.

He parked outside Justin's building and asked him what time he should pick him up, then watched as Justin went inside. When he was sure Justin was inside and safe, he drove away, back downtown, to ride around the area, in hopes of seeing the man in the blue hoodie. Clay knew if he found him, he'd be dead.

They arrived at the hospital before nine and went straight to the ICU. Detective Beach was waiting for them. Beach wanted to hear the entire story from Justin, but he said it would have to wait until he saw Jewel. Justin stopped at the desk and announced who he was and whom he needed to see. The nurse said that the doctor was with her now and he would have to wait until the exam was over.

"Bloody hell I will," said Justin and went to find Jewel's room. He stood inside the room, watching the doctor as he tried to look into Jewel's eyes, but the swelling proved to be too much for him to get a good look at the cornea. He turned when he heard a small rustle behind him and saw Justin.

"Are you the fiancé?" he asked.

"Yes, Justin Angelis," he said. "How is she doing?"

"Well, as you can see, she still has a great deal of swelling, which is making it very difficult to examine her eyes fully. I don't want to force them open. I'd rather wait until more of the swelling goes down on its own. We've given her something to facilitate the process, but she must have a very extreme allergy to peppers for the swelling to last so long. We also have her on some pain medication, but she claims she doesn't want too much. She'd rather deal with it herself. We removed the tube. As you can see, she seems to be breathing well enough on her own. Besides, she keeps trying to talk."

"That's our Jewel, one hell of a fighter," said Justin.

"Justin, is that you?" she whispered.

"Yes, I'm here, Jewel. Please don't try to get up. The doctor needs to finish his exam," answered Justin.

"Actually," said the doctor, "I'm done for now. As I said before, we need to let the swelling go down to get a better look at her eyes. I'll leave you alone now. Don't let her try to talk too much, if you can, and please don't stay too long. She needs her rest."

"Yes, I understand. I won't stay long."

The doctor left the room, and Justin went to Jewel. He sat on the edge of the bed and took her hand and kissed it.

"Justin, I'm so glad you're here. They won't tell me anything. I hear them making comments, but they won't say anything directly to me. How bad is it? I must look horrible. I can feel my face is swollen, and I can't open my eyes. What happened to me?" she said in a raspy voice, occasionally holding her throat with her hand.

"Don't you remember anything from last night?" he asked her.

"I remember we got home, and I think I went down to get our pizza. After that, everything is a blur," she answered. "Please tell me, Justin. Please, I need to know." Justin could see that she was getting very excited, and she needed to remain calm.

"I'll tell you on one condition," said Justin. "Promise me you won't try to talk and will stay calm. The doctor emphasized your need for rest because of the medications you were given. Now, promise me, Jewel."

She promised him she would try to remain calm, so he told her what had transpired the night before and realized that she remembered very little.

"Why can't I remember?" she said.

"You promised you would not try to talk, and as for remembering, it will come back to you. It was such a traumatic event, and you were suffering extreme pain. Sometimes the brain has to shut down to protect the body. I'm just guessing here, but I'm sure you will remember it slowly when you're ready. Do you remember anything of the man who did this? Detective Beach is outside with Clay, and he wants as much information as he can get to try to find this guy. I know it's hard, but do you remember anything, anything at all? Height, color, anything. I have a pad and pencil so you can write down what you remember."

"I'm sorry, Justin, I can't."

"No talking, write."

Jewel picked up the pad and started to write. "No taller than the window. I was looking into his eyes, and they were brown. Yes, they were brown. Hood pulled over his face, but I could still see his eyes. Must be as tall as me, five nine or ten, not much taller. I'm sorry, I don't remember much after that."

"Well, that's enough for now. I'll tell Detective Beach. It's a start, anyway. Did I tell you how much I love that little dog of yours and that I will never shoo him off the furniture again? He can have his pick of wherever he would like to sleep. He is just as special as you are, Jewel. No wonder you two found each other."

"He's all right, though, isn't he?" she whispered.

"The little guy is, at this moment, enjoying the royal treatment at the Dolan residence, and yes, to answer your question, he is fine. And now, my love, you need to rest. I'll be back in a few hours. I'm afraid the guards at the desk won't let me come sooner or stay too long. Do your lips hurt?"

"No, not really. The pain meds are pretty strong. So please kiss me. I miss you so, Justin."

Justin leaned down and kissed her lips lightly, fearing causing her any discomfort.

"Again. I barely felt it," said Jewel.

Justin kissed her again. "I'll be back soon," he told her and quietly left the room.

The three men went down to the coffee shop, got a cup of coffee and some muffins. Detective Beach asked Justin if Jewel remembered anything. He told Beach what she said about his height and eye color but that she had no memory of the rest of the night.

"Too bad," said Beach. "Not much to go on, but under the circumstances, I'm surprised she even remembered that. This guy must be one crazy son of a bitch."

"He just better hope that I don't get my hands on him first," said Clay.

"You stay out of this," said Beach to Clay. "My boys will find him. I don't want to be hauling your ass in for being stupid. You just better stay close to Angelis here, in case this nutjob goes after him next. I don't need two people in the hospital."

"Don't worry, I've got him covered," said Clay.

"I really don't think he would come after me. Jewel is the one he seems obsessed with," replied Justin.

"Yeah, but you can never tell with nutjobs, right, Clay?" said Beach.

The three men drank the rest of their coffee. As they were leaving the coffee shop, Beach's partner, Detective Leeds, showed up.

"You guys learn anything from the girl?" asked Leeds.

"The girl has a name," said Justin, showing his anger.

"I'm sorry, Mr. Angelis, I didn't mean anything. Sometimes we have so many working cases that I forget it's real people were working for and not just a number. Sorry if I offended you," said Leeds.

"The dummy here is still a rookie, Angelis. He didn't mean anything."

"I'm sorry, I didn't mean to jump down your neck. It's just that this is so personal for me. I've never had to deal with anyone close to me being in this kind of situation. I don't know how you deal with this kind of thing every day. Again, my apologies," said Justin.

"No sweat," said Leeds. "I canvassed all around the area, but of course no one saw anything. One guy thought he saw someone running down the street, but his back was to him, so he couldn't give me any kind of description. You get anything here?"

"Afraid not. Ms. Lansby doesn't remember anything after the attack. She did, however, remember that our perp was five nine or ten and had brown eyes, but that's all. She can't remember anything else. Lots of people don't remember anything after a situation like this, but sometimes they eventually start to remember bits and pieces. Maybe we'll get lucky."

"You don't know Ms. Lansby," said Clay. "I can guarantee she's up there right now, trying to remember, and she will. She's as tough as they come. Right, Mr. A?"

"Stubborn, willful, and tough—I would say that describes the woman I love perfectly," replied Justin.

"Got yourself a tiger, then," said Beach.

"Yup, and then some," answered Justin.

The detectives said they would stay in touch if they found out anything else, but didn't sound too optimistic. Justin wanted to go back upstairs to see Jewel, but Clay told him he should let her rest. Clay took Justin back to his apartment and told him to get some rest, that he would be back at five to take him to the hospital. Justin asked him if he would like to come up, but Clay said he had some errands to do before he came back. That was a lie; Clay planned to go back to the scene of the crime and see if he could find anything the cops missed.

He drove back downtown and parked the car by the factory. He walked up and down the block, talked to a few people hanging around the corner, but found out nothing more. He was pissed. He decided to stop and get something to eat. Even on Sunday, some of the little local shops were open. He ordered some eggs and coffee. At the end of the counter was a man wearing a blue hooded sweatshirt. He looked familiar. Was this the same man Clay faced down on the street when he was bringing Jewel home a few weeks ago? Clay tried to get a look at the man's face, but the man noticed Clay's interest in him and pulled the hood down to further cover his face, then he put some money on the counter and left. Clay got up and followed him out the door.

"Hey, you!" he called to the man, but the man had already started running around the corner. Clay ran after him but lost him when the man got to the alley. *Shit,* thought Clay to himself, *that could have been the bastard.* He walked back to the coffee shop and said he still wanted his eggs, as the cook hadn't begun to cook them when he saw Clay running out the door.

"Do you know that guy that just left, the one with the blue jacket?" asked Clay.

The cook said that he came in a few times a week but he didn't know his name or anything. He said that he came in a few times with another guy, a little taller and clean-cut, not grubby like this one. The nicer-looking one was always friendly and paid the tab all the time. The shorter guy was a mean son of a bitch, always giving his waitress a hard time.

"I warned him more than once to knock it off or he'd have to find another place to get his coffee," said the cook.

Clay ate his eggs, paid the check, and thanked the cook. Clay decided to go back to his place and kill some time before picking up Justin. His mind was working overtime, putting together all the times he saw this guy in the neighborhood. *There must be some connection,* he thought to himself, *and if there is, I'll find it.*

The doctor told Justin he would feel better if they could keep Jewel overnight again, just as a precautionary measure. He assured him that she was coming along fine. All her vitals were back to normal, and almost all the redness from the hives were gone, but she still had some swelling, especially around the eyes, that prevented him from doing a complete exam of the cornea. If he couldn't perform the exam in the morning, she could go home, but he wanted to see her on Tuesday.

Justin went to his office and tried to get some work done. Fortunately, there were no pressing matters at this time. Celia was doing everything she could to keep matters moving smoothly. He made a call to his mother to keep her up-to-date, then called Celia's house to give them an update.

Celia answered the phone and was glad to hear from Justin. She had called the hospital several times, but they wouldn't give her any information. She asked Justin where he was, and he told her he was at the office. She asked if he still had his driver. Justin said he did, because he didn't know how long he had planned to stay in the office. Celia told him to come to their house so he could tell them about Jewel and she could give him an up-to-date on the legal matters they were working on. At first, he thought he was just too tired to talk to anyone but then decided he should go because Celia might need advice on certain matters. He knew she was extremely competent, but he liked to stay abreast of what she was doing. He told Celia he would be there in about forty-five minutes.

He gathered up his papers and went down to where Clay was waiting. He told him he needed to go up to the Dolan residence. Justin already told Clay about Jewel when they were at the hospital, so Clay knew he was going to inform them about the doctor's decision to keep her over another night. Justin was quiet on the drive uptown. Clay thought about telling him the bit of information he learned at the diner but decided to keep it to himself for a while. He had enough to deal with already.

Celia insisted Justin have something to eat, then asked if he thought Clay might like something as well. Justin informed her that when Clay was on duty, there was nothing you could do to get him to come inside for a bite. He had been driving Justin around for years, and he never even accepted invitation to come inside by his mother in Connecticut, so there was no point in trying. Justin told them all he knew at this time about Jewel, and Celia was taking it very hard. At one point, Kenneth had to hold her while she cried into his shoulder. When she finally stopped crying, she became extremely angry.

"This has gone on far too long. Where are the police? What are they doing? They haven't done anything yet, as far as I can tell." Celia was near hysteria.

"I'm sure they are doing everything they can, Celia," said Kenneth.

"Well, obviously, it's not enough," she said.

Justin and Kenneth let Celia rant and rave a while longer while they drank their coffee. Then Justin asked Celia if there was anything going on at work that he should know about. They went over a few details in one of the mergers they were handling, but for the rest, Celia was doing a fine job. Justin just had to tell her a few things to remember when dealing with some of the clients, and he expressed his delight in the way Celia was handling the business. That was one less thing he had to think about. Justin thanked them for the coffee and said he wanted to get home to relax a while; he was going in the morning to bring Jewel home, and he wanted to freshen up the room for her. He was letting her stay in the room his mother always used when she came into town, because it had its own bath. He didn't know what condition she would be in, and he didn't think she should stay alone, at least for the next day or two. Celia told him that Jewel could stay with them, but he told her that Jewel didn't want the boys knowing too much of what was going on, and in the end, both Celia and Kenneth agreed. The boys were extremely close to Jewel and would be upset to learn she was injured. Justin bade them a good night and motioned for Clay to remain seated. He certainly could open the car door himself. Clay drove him to his apartment, asked what time he wanted to be picked up tomorrow, and waited until Justin was inside before driving away.

He circled the block just to be sure no one was following him, and he didn't see anyone on the street that looked suspicious. Clay was always careful.

Justin and Clay brought Jewel home by ten after they received instructions about the drops for her eyes. Both of Jewel's eyes were covered completely. The doctor explained that the coverings would help keep the eyes from moving too much, and since there was still a great deal of irritation there, it would be better with the patches on. Of course Jewel objected, but she soon gave up when both Justin and Clay agreed with the doctor and said they would make sure that the patches would remain on until he saw her on Tuesday. They helped her into the car, and she remained quiet during the ride. Justin told her that she would be staying at his place for the next few days, until the doctor said she could be on her own again. She balked, but Justin just ignored her. He knew there would be those times when she couldn't have her way, and this was one of them.

Jewel tried to familiarize herself with the layout of the apartment and of the room she would be occupying for the next few days. Justin knew better than to try to help her. He asked if there was anything she needed, and she asked for a large cup of coffee and two Tylenol. Her head was pounding, and this was her proven method for getting rid of the headache. The pain in her eyes was helped by the drops the doctor had given her, but they were only to be used twice a day, and the pain came back well before it was time for more. Justin made the coffee and got her the Tylenol. He conveyed Celia and Kenneth's regards and that they would wait to see her until she was feeling better, but if she wanted to talk, they were there for her. Jewel finished her coffee and told Justin she was going to lie down for a while, and if he needed to go to the office or anywhere, she would be fine alone. He quickly stated that he wasn't going anywhere.

Justin checked on her after a while and saw that she was sleeping. He was glad she was being cooperative; he really expected more of a fight from her. He could only imagine that the pain emanating from her eyes was keeping her docile, at least for the time being. Justin used the time to get caught up on the daily papers. He always read the *New York Times* and the *Wall Street Journal*, and sometimes the lesser-known publications. He had picked up a copy of *Women's Wear Daily* a few days ago just to see if Kenneth was mentioned. He was getting to be one of the major designers in the city, and he hoped he was getting good reviews. Justin read the papers quietly, and when he finished, he took a look at Jewel and saw that she was still sleeping. He made a few phone calls, then lay on the couch and soon drifted off to sleep.

It was dark when he woke up, and he immediately went to check on Jewel. With the patches over her eyes, he couldn't tell if she was sleeping or awake. He went in and sat on the bed and softly said her name.

"You don't have to be so quiet, Justin. I'm not sleeping," she said.

"In case you were, I didn't want to awaken you," he answered. "Would you like to have something to eat? You haven't had anything all day."

"I suppose I should," she said, "even though I'm not hungry and my throat still feels like it is on fire."

"How would you like some soup from Josephina's? It would just take me a few minutes. Or maybe something more substantial, like pasta," he said, trying so hard to think of something that would make her feel like eating. He didn't like it when she was so quiet; this just wasn't the Jewel he had come to know. But going through what she had, anyone would behave differently. He just wanted to see that adorable smile and incredible, warm, happy glow she always had.

Jewel said she would like the soup from Josephina's; any kind would be fine. Justin asked her if she would like to come and sit in the living room and maybe listen to some music. Justin put on the music she requested and left to walk to the restaurant. He never noticed the car parked a few doors down or the man inside, nor did he notice the other car parked a few cars behind the first. Clay was in the second car. Ever since they brought Jewel home, Clay had stayed close to the house, waiting and watching for anything out of the ordinary. He knew at some point Justin might want to go out, so he stayed close. He would circle the block a few times, then find a parking place and wait. He was watching a car that had circled the block several times then parked a few car lengths in front of him. He couldn't get a good look at the man behind the wheel but suspected this might be the man they were looking for. He debated about whether to get out of the car and walk behind Justin or just wait to see if the other man made a move. He didn't.

Justin returned and went into the building carrying a bag. Clay guessed he had gone to Josephina's for food. Shortly after Justin entered the building, the man who was watching him drove away. Clay wanted to follow him but thought it better if he stayed at his post; if he followed him, he could lose him and he might double back, so Clay decided to sit tight. *Patience,* thought Clay to himself. *Sooner or later they all screw up, and when he does–Clay smiled–he's mine.*

Jewel and Justin ate their soup, and Justin cleaned up the dishes.

"Are you feeling better?" he asked.

"Yes," she answered. "The soup hit the spot." It was so unlike Jewel to be quiet and withdrawn. Justin didn't know if he should try to keep up a conversation or to just let her be.

"I spoke to Mother today, and she asked me to send you her love," said Justin.

"Thank her for me when you speak to her again," she said.

"Jewel, is everything all right? I know you must be terribly worried about your eyes, and they must be awfully painful, but I'm sensing something else."

"You're very astute," she replied. "Actually, there is something on my mind, and now may be the best time to talk about it, since my eyes are bandaged and I won't be able to see your face when I tell you."

"Jewel, I don't think I like where this is going," said Justin, sounding anxious.

"I'm sorry. I have given this a great deal of thought over the past few days, and I need to tell you. You know everything about me from college on, but you don't know anything about the years before college, and that's what I want to tell you about. You had such a great childhood, mother and father who loved you, wealth, private schools, all the things that made you as wonderful as you are, and you are wonderful, the most wonderful man I've ever known or loved. I like to think I turned out pretty well. I'm a survivor. I think my past made me as strong as I am. Anyway, to begin, I was born in Brooklyn. My mother met a man who was in the Army. It was during wartime, so they really didn't have a lot of time to get to know each other, but they married anyway. He shipped out shortly after. My mother went to the base to see about support and was told that she could not get anything because he was already married to someone in Texas. My mother was shattered. She loved him, and now she was pregnant with me. Everyone told her to give me away, but she wouldn't. It was all she had left of him. She was still living at home with her mother, father, three sisters, and a brother.

"Her mother and father had a small grocery store. My grandmother died suddenly of a stroke when I was just three months old. My grandfather never really liked the city and sold the store, moved upstate, and bought a small farm.

"My uncle was in the service, and my mother's sister Josie married a man nearly twenty years older than she was, and they, too, moved upstate, where they bought a small restaurant and bar. That left my mother and her two sisters still living in the city. Julia was a few years older than my mother, and Gloria was just ten years older than me. Aunt Gloria went to school and watched me when she got home, and my mother and Aunt Julia dropped me off at my grandfather's sister's house before they went to work in a factory that wove sheets. Neither of them had finished high school. They took a few trips upstate to visit, and my aunt Julia met a man and decided to marry him. The town where my uncle had his restaurant had many mills, from paper to cloth, and his restaurant business was doing very well, so well, in fact, that he asked my mother to move there to help out with the business. With just the three of us still in Brooklyn, it seemed the thing to do, so we moved. I was just about four years old when we moved. It was exciting for me being in the country.

CHAPTER 10

"I remember when we got there, the first thing I was told was not to go near the dog my uncle had. He was some kind of hunting dog. He was so pretty, with long white hair and a few black spots. I always knew I had some kind of connection with animals and rarely feared them, so of course the first thing I did was to go to the dog and wrap my arms around his neck while my mother almost had a heart attack. Everyone else I remember were too shocked to come after me. I heard my uncle yell out the name Duke. I think he expected the dog to go to him and away from me, but he didn't move away from me. I hugged him and buried my face in his fur, and he, in turn, licked my face. It was wonderful. I had never had a dog, and from that day on, my uncle told everyone that Duke was considered mine. It was such a happy time for a while.

"My uncle built a rabbit cage for me and bought me three rabbits. He was also raising two pigs, which he had planned to butcher, but as I was only four, I didn't know what that really meant. It was great living in the big house. The restaurant and bar were on the first level, the family living space was on the second level, and on the third level were some bedrooms. The place was originally an inn for the mill workers, but my uncle shut the top floor and only used it when friends came up from the city. The family living space was kept up by a black woman my cousin and I called Aunt Grace. She would cook and clean and watch us as best as she could. As I said, friends of the family would come up at different times of the year, either to hunt or for holidays or just to get out of the city for a week or two. For the most part, it was lots of fun.

"One of the men who came up was a friend of my uncle's, called Steve. We had to call him Uncle Steve. My cousin and I didn't like him. He smelled bad. I always got up early to go out with Duke because he wasn't allowed in the house, and we would feed the rabbits and lie in the grass or roll down the hill. He would chase me, and at the end, he would plop down beside me as if he were checking to make sure I was all right. Aunt Grace watched from the window and used to laugh at us.

"One morning, when I went out, Steve was waiting for me. He grabbed me by the wrist and told me not to yell or he would hurt me, so I didn't. He pulled me into a corner that was shaded and that couldn't be seen from the kitchen. He pulled down my panties and felt me with his hands. I tried to pull away from him, but he twisted my wrist. When he was done, he told me not to tell anyone or he would do something to my rabbits. I was so frightened I didn't know what to do. The next few mornings, he did the same thing, but this time he put his finger inside me. I wanted to scream and told him I was going to tell my mother, so he took me over to where my rabbits were, took one out, and cut its throat with a knife he had in his pocket. It was the most terrifying thing I had ever seen. All the blood...it was awful. But I tried not to cry. After that, I did pretty much what he wanted, because he said that he would do the same to my mother and me.

"After a few more days, he would pull his zipper down on his pants and take out his penis and make me hold it and rub it until he came. One day, I just said no, and I started to scream. Duke came running and grabbed him on the leg. He tried to cut him with his knife to make him let go, but Aunt Grace heard all the barking and was looking out the window, and she came running with her broom, hitting him, all the while Duke was biting him. Aunt Grace was yelling so loud that my uncle, mother, and aunt came out to see what was going on. Aunt Grace told my uncle what she saw, and my uncle asked me if he did anything to me. I told him that he said he would cut my mother's throat like he did my bunnies if I told. My uncle promised me no one would hurt my mother or my bunnies and just to tell him what Steve did to me. I was crying so hard, but I told him everything that he made me do. My mother was screaming and holding me so tight I couldn't breathe. My uncle hit Steve with his fists and then took Aunt Grace's broom and hit him with the long stick side. He told him to go away and never come back. Steve wanted his things, but my uncle told him he would never set foot in his house again and to go as fast as he could or my uncle would call the police.

"I remember they took me to the doctors, but he said everything was all right. I had nightmares for a while, but I had Duke, and he was allowed to sleep in my bedroom with me, but otherwise he wasn't allowed in any other part of the house. As I got older, I understood it was some kind of health department thing because it was a restaurant. We lived there until I was almost nine. The mills had started to shut down, and business was getting bad, so my uncle closed the restaurant and just kept the bar opened. My grandfather, who was living on his little farm, was getting older and had emphysema, and since my uncle didn't need my mother's help anymore, we went to live with my grandfather."

"Let me stop you right there," said Justin. "Would you like some coffee or anything?"

"I would like some water, please," she replied.

Justin got her a glass of water and poured himself a cup of coffee. He handed her the water, and after she drank some of it, he asked if she wanted him to place it on the table where she could reach it.

"Thank you, but I would probably just knock it over trying to find it." She laughed.

"How silly of me," he said. "I didn't think of that."

"Yeah, not so easy taking care of a blind woman, is it?" she answered.

"Stop that. You're not blind. This is just a temporary situation, that's all. Once the bandages are off, you will see fine," he said, but she could hear the fear in his voice.

If I can't see when they take off these bandages, she thought to herself, *I will have to say goodbye to this man I love. Maybe I'm telling him all this for nothing, maybe I should have waited...*

But she decided to go on.

"You're right, I'll be fine," she said, "and now back to the story of my less-than-perfect childhood. Where were we? Oh yes, we had just moved to the farm. The years on the farm were my absolute favorite. My grandfather was wonderful, filled with knowledge of the animals and with growing things, and he tried to teach me everything he knew. Even though I was only nine, I was the one who would do most of the things that needed to be done on the farm. My mother got a job in town as a bookkeeper in a department store. Mom was always good with numbers. She even kept the books at the restaurant.

My aunt Gloria never finished high school, but she got a job at the factory that made ladies' handbags and became very close to the woman who ran the department.

"She was much older than my aunt, but my grandmother died when my aunt was only ten, and this woman was like a mother to her, so everything worked out well, except I missed Duke so much. I couldn't take him with me because my uncle wanted him as a watchdog for the bar.

My grandfather showed me how to take care of the chickens, to feed and water them, and to collect the eggs. He even showed me how to check to see if they were good or not using a big candle. He started to teach me to make cheese from the goat's milk he got every day. Milking the goats and the cow was to be my next big lesson. I think my mom and aunt were so proud of the way I was helping my grandfather that one day, when they came home from work, they brought me a puppy. They knew how much I missed Duke, and my nightmares had returned, not every night, but when I had one, it was usually pretty bad. I saw everyone I loved with their throats cut and blood everywhere. They were pretty awful. So here I am, with the largest ball of fur I had ever seen. I didn't know what he was, and I couldn't have cared less. He was mine to love and to love me, and something I could hold on to when the bad dreams came. In a year, he was the most majestic and beautiful dog you ever saw, an Alaskan Husky. As he got older and had such a heavy coat, he preferred to spend his nights outside, but somehow he knew when I would need him, and on those nights, he would bark until they let him in and he would lie on the bed next to me. Grandpa had a little dog named Spotty, a mixed something or other, but he and Lucky—that's what I named him, because that was how I felt when I received him—he and Lucky, they were best of friends.

"When spring came, Gramps had the garden tilled, and we planted everything. Gramps always planted and harvested by the cycles of the moon. Sounds pretty silly, but that was how he did everything. Once the garden was planted, they surprised me again and bought me a horse. Her name was Sparkle, because she was born late on the Fourth of July. We had an extension put on the shed so she would have plenty of room when she couldn't go out. By this time, I was really good at milking the cow and the goats, cleaning out stalls, taking care of the chickens and eggs, plus working in the garden. I got up so early to get things done before I went to school, but when school let out for the summer, it was easier. Gramps and I made cheese, and we gave eggs, cheese, and a great deal of fresh garden vegetables to the farmer up the road. He raised cattle, and in the fall, when he butchered, we got half a side of beef for everything we gave him all year. The rest of the veggies, we canned for ourselves for the winter, and we put away potatoes and winter squash in the root cellar. It didn't leave me much time to ride, but I always got in a few hours.

"Lucky would follow us through the fields and down into the forest. I was always bringing home a new flower I found growing, and Mom and I would try to look it up in the library if she had the time. Sometimes I would bring home a frog or something just to scare her. When I think back on my childhood, these were my magical years. Then when I was almost fourteen, it all ended. My aunt moved out to go live with her friend from the factory, and my mother said she was getting married. Gramps and I didn't like him at all, but they got married. In the spring, they informed me and Gramps that they bought a house closer to where he worked. He was a driver of those big trucks. The house was surprisingly close to the bar my uncle owned, which was good, but it meant we had to move from the farm. They sold my horse, gave my dog and Gramps's dog away, gave the chickens to the farmer we traded with, and closed down the house. My aunt who had moved out was building a new house with her friend, and when it was finished, my grandfather went to live with her because he hated my mother's new husband. And so did I.

"The only thing good about the move was that I was close to my friends from school and my cousin. We all got together after school, and on weekends, we went fishing and took long walks everywhere through the woods. We used to sneak up the hill and steal apples from the farmer's orchard. I still have a scar on the back of my leg from when his dog chased us. We all got sprayed by a skunk once when we passed it on the road. I thought the smell would never leave us, even after we got tomato juice poured on us. Those were the good things, and then the bad things started.

"My mother wanted to make her new husband happy and tried to get pregnant. She would get pregnant and then miscarry, then get pregnant again, and miscarry again. This went on and on, until the doctor told her to stop trying. No sex until she was stronger. But that didn't stop the creep. Our walls were not very thick, and I could hear them every night, my mom saying they weren't supposed to have sex or that he was hurting her. She pleaded and cried, but that didn't stop him. The next time she got pregnant and miscarried, she had a stroke, not terribly severe, but she had weakness in her right arm and leg and her face sagged a bit on the right side. She had to stay in bed until she was stronger, then she could start therapy. When he couldn't make her life miserable any longer, he turned his attention toward me.

"Whenever I went into the bathroom, I'd catch him peeking through the keyhole, so I had to put something over the knob. Then I would hear noises in the pantry, which was just on the other side of the bathroom, or I would hear him go down to the cellar whenever I went into the bathroom. One day, when he took her to therapy, I put the light on in the bathroom and went into the pantry. He had made holes in the wall so he could look into the bathroom when I was in there. I also went down into the cellar and made my way toward the bathroom and found small holes in the floor around the sink and toilet. He had been watching me all the times I went in to shower and get dressed. I remember throwing up in the cellar, and I just stood there, trembling. Now that I knew they were there, I always brought extra towels with me to cover all the holes. When he couldn't watch me anymore, he started to expose himself to me and massage his penis, moaning. I started having nightmares again, and finally I decided to go down to my uncle's and tell him what he was doing. My mother was still recovering from the stroke, but I couldn't take it anymore.

"My uncle was outraged. He never liked him either. He brought me up to our house and, in front of my mother, told him that he knew what was going on and that he was going to the police. At first, he tried to deny it, but then he admitted everything and started to cry. My mother was horrified and said she and I were leaving. That was when he turned to my mother and pleaded with her to stay, that he would kill himself if she left, and he promised he would never do anything to me again. My uncle didn't believe him and still wanted to go to the police, but my mother caved in and said she believed him and didn't want the police involved.

"Things were pretty good for a few weeks, and then he started again. I told my mother, but she said I must be mistaken, because he promised he wouldn't do it anymore. That was when I lost respect and love for her, and that's why we haven't been close in years. I stayed out of the house as much as possible, bathed in the dark, locked my bedroom door, and started wearing headphones to bed, so I wouldn't have to hear them.

"The summer between my junior and senior years, I got a job at the motor vehicle office, so between work and my friends, I was never home. I was rarely there for dinner, and my mother never even asked why. She knew but did nothing. Halfway into my senior year, my best friend's parents were moving out of our school district, which meant Gail wouldn't be able to graduate with us. I begged my mother to let her live with us for the last few months so we could graduate together, and she agreed. The first thing I did was to get face-to-face with my stepfather, and I told him that Gail knew every perverted thing he did, and if he tried anything to me or her, she would go to the police as fast as she could and that with both our statements as well as my uncle's, he would be going to jail. Of course I was bluffing. I never told anyone except my uncle about what the creep did. But he believed me. After Gail moved in, he avoided us like the plague. On weekends, I went with her to her parents' house. We graduated, and I left early for New York to get settled in, because I was sharing an apartment with three other girls, and the creep had to pay for the whole thing. He took so much away from me I had no guilt about taking as much money from him as I could get. Whenever there was a weekend trip, like the dude ranch or the winter ski trip, I just called home and told my mother I needed extra money, and it was there the next day."

Jewel was shaking. "So now you've heard the worst of my past. My present with this crazy stalker isn't so great either, and my future is doubtful, as I could be dead anytime soon. So tomorrow morning, you can drop me off at the factory, and I don't want to see you again. The less you're around me, the better off you'll be."

"Now, look here," said Justin. "You can't drop this on me just like that."

"I can, and I just did," answered Jewel.

"If this is the way you want it, fine, but I shall be the one to take you to the doctors tomorrow, and there will be no discussion about that," replied Justin, trying very hard to hold back his anger. He knew deep inside that Jewel was only doing what she thought was the best thing for him. Her stories were horrifying, and he was sure she felt as if she somehow attracted all the evil that plagued her past and was still plaguing her now. He knew better than to argue with her while she was in this fragile state, for he could see that she was, especially after telling him the horrific story of her childhood. And right now she didn't need any more stress.

"Do we agree that I will be escorting you to the doctors tomorrow?" he said.

"Yes," she replied, "and now if you'll excuse me, I'm going to my room."

Justin tried hard not to get up to help her, but knowing Jewel as he did, it would only infuriate her. He watched as she felt all around the couch till she reached the back, then walked in a straight line to the bedroom. He guessed that she must have counted out the steps when he went to get their dinner.

"Please give me a little extra time to get dressed tomorrow morning," she said, then "Good night," and closed the bedroom door. Justin sat there with his head in his hands and thought back to the time when she referred to herself as a survivor. *Indeed she was, indeed she was,* he thought to himself.

The following morning, Justin knocked on Jewel's bedroom door. She answered that she was up and would be out momentarily. Justin had made coffee, and he wanted to make sure she had a little breakfast before they left for the doctors. Jewel came out with her jacket and her overnight bag. He watched as she walked the straight line to the end of the couch and placed her bag on the floor.

"I've made coffee. Would you like some toast with it?" he asked. She replied that she just wanted the coffee and asked him to help her to the table. He did as she asked, and when she was seated, he poured her coffee.

"Your cup is directly in front of you, and the cream is to you're right." He knew she didn't take sugar, so he didn't mention it. He asked if she needed assistance but knew she would want to do it herself, and he was right. She poured a little cream in the cup, holding the index finger of her left hand down into the cup so she could feel the amount in it. Justin was surprised by her ability to make and drink her coffee without spilling a drop, but then she always surprised him.

The phone rang, and it was Clay, telling him that he was downstairs and ready to go anytime. Clay was always a little early; he knew Justin would need time to make sure Jewel was ready. She finished her coffee and stood up.

"I'm afraid I may knock something over if I try to find my way back to the door," she said. "Would you please help me?" Justin guided Jewel toward the door and helped her get her jacket on. He picked up her bag and opened the door for her. He helped her onto the elevator and then to the car.

"Morning, Ms. Lansby, Mr. A," said Clay.

They both said good morning at the same time, although Jewel said it so softly Clay barely heard it. Justin just shrugged his shoulders and followed her into the car. Nothing was said for the entire trip.

The doctor removed Jewel's bandages and was pleased that the swelling was all gone. He put some drops in her eyes and proceeded with the exam. When he finished, he told her that she was very lucky that there was no permanent damage to her eyes. The drops would make things a little cloudy, but they should clear up in an hour or two and she would be able to see just fine. She could see. She looked slowly around the room, letting her eyes adjust to the light. *Thank you,* she silently said to herself, *thank you, thank you, thank you.* She did not look directly at Justin. She got off the table, put on her jacket, thanked the doctor, who told her he would like to see her in two weeks, and left the office.

When they arrived at the factory, she thanked Clay and Justin and disappeared inside.

"What was all that about?" asked Clay.

"Apparently, she has decided she doesn't want to see me anymore. I'm out of her life," replied Justin.

"What are you talking about? She loves you! What happened?"

"I have no idea. She told me last night that she was afraid she may end up dead by the hands of this lunatic and didn't want me anywhere around her. I think she's afraid I may also be injured," said Justin.

"But that's crazy," said Clay. "She knows we're watching you."

"She must believe it's not enough," answered Justin. "Hopefully, she will come to her senses." Justin said no more and got in the car and told Clay to take him to his office. Clay thought about telling Justin about the man he watched outside his building, but in the mood Justin was in, he decided to wait.

As they were driving away, Justin called Kenneth and told him to try to talk some sense into Jewel about staying in the apartment. Kenneth said he already tried but she insisted she would be all right. Shelby was going to stay with her at night, and Jewel's apartment would be ready Sunday, so it was only for a few days more. Jewel was adamant about staying alone. Kenneth agreed with Justin that sometimes Jewel was just too stubborn for her own good.

Jewel changed her clothes and went out on the floor to see what everyone was working on. Although her eyesight was still blurry, she wanted to get back to work. Kenneth tried to make her take the day off because she had just had all the bandages removed and her eyes were blurred. He tried to explain to her that she would be putting too much strain on them. She said that she just couldn't sit around, doing nothing. What would everyone else think? She didn't want any preferential treatment.

"Damn it, Jewel, I'm the boss here, and if I say you need more time, then you damn well better listen. Now go to your room and keep those eyes closed for the rest of the day, and I don't want to see you out here again."

Jewel had never heard Kenneth talk to her like that before; she could tell he was really angry and serious, so she did as she was told. She drew the drapes because the light was hurting her eyes, and she lay on the couch. She lay there for some time, thinking about Justin. *I did the right thing in sending him away,* she thought to herself. But she missed him so much.

Jewel slept for most of the afternoon and didn't awaken until Shelby came in.

"Hey, girl, you gonna sleep all day?" she said.

"No. I had no idea it was so late. Have you been here long?" asked Jewel.

"No, but I wanted to get here before Kenneth left, so he could set the alarms. I've even brought dinner, Chinese. You hungry?" said Shelby.

"Not really," answered Jewel, "but I had better eat something. All I had so far today was a cup of coffee. Justin tried to make me have some toast, but I just couldn't get it down. I guess all this nonsense is getting to me."

"Well, the last thing you need is to get weak from not eating. How are you gonna kick ass if you're too weak?" Shelby laughed as she got down some plates and forks.

"How are the peepers feeling?" asked Shelby.

"Really good now. I guess resting them after the exam was the best thing I could do, especially since it was the only thing I could do after Kenneth yelled at me."

"Get out! Boss man actually raised his voice?" said Shelby. "I'm sorry I missed that."

"Well, he did, and I guess he was right. Let's talk about something else, though. How's the apartment coming? I'm dying to see it," said Jewel.

"Remember our deal? No lookie until finished. You're going to love it. I man- aged to get everything we talked about in the design, and if I do say so myself, it's one of my best yet. Sunday you will be all moved in and have your very own palace of solitude."

"God, I can't wait. I'm so tired of living in other people's apartments. I don't mean you, of course, but you know what I mean."

"Yeah, I know. It's been rough on you these past few months. Hell, the last few years. It's time for you to start having fun again."

"Yep, as soon as they catch this deranged person, I'll be out and about and making this town my own."

"Wooo!" said Shelby. "I'll drink to that."

Both girls had a bottle of beer and clicked bottles and took a drink. Jewel told Shelby that she was so sick of the last few months that she really considered going back to her house upstate.

"You hang in there, baby girl. It will get better. After all, you have that hunk protecting you. Why would you want to leave that?"

"Are we talking about Justin or Clay?" asked Jewel.

"Either one." Shelby laughed. "I'm not proud. I'll take your leftovers."

"Shelby, you are so bad. What happened to...what's his name?"

"Gone. He was a loser. Thought he could lie around and let me support him, but he soon found out how it was going to be. I work, you work, there's no other way. So he left. There's lots more where he came from. So tell me about this guy Clay. A girl always has to have a backup."

"Shelby, I love you," said Jewel.

"Yeah, well, don't be getting any ideas. I only swing one way, and you ain't it. Just kiddin'. You know I'd do anything for you, girl. You were the best roommate, and you've been the best friend I ever had. I worry about you, girl. We all do. So cut Kenneth a little slack. Now shut up and eat."

They finished dinner and cleaned up and settled back on the couch. Shelby asked Jewel if she was scared. Jewel knew what Shelby was referring to without coming right out and saying it.

"I am, Shelby. For the first time since I was a child, I'm really scared," she answered. Not much was said after that; the girls took their showers and got ready for bed. They both had work tomorrow.

Wednesday, Jewel was happy that Kenneth gave her something to do, make a pattern for a new design. Jewel got right to work with the muslin, draping and folding it so it resembled his sketch, but no matter how hard she tried, she just could not get the skirt to drape the way Kenneth drew it. She pinned it up over and over, then had to take it apart again—it just wouldn't work. She finally decided to try draping it on the bias; that worked much better, but she knew the fabric Kenneth chose for the dress would not work on the bias. Gathering her courage, she approached Kenneth and told him of the problem, and he told her rather curtly to go find something that would work. "Three floors and bolts of fabric everywhere," she muttered to herself. "Where do I start?" She began her hunt on the third floor, because that was where some of the newer fabric was. No luck. None on the second either.

She moved down to the ground floor, where the shipping and receiving departments were located, but there was also a very large storage room with huge bolts of fabric on metal racks, so that was where she headed. The room was open, with large fans overhead to keep the air circulating. The heavy smell of formaldehyde that was used in fabric to keep insects away could really give you a headache without the fans moving the air. Jewel turned on the overhead lights and was slightly overwhelmed by the amount of fabric they still had in stock. Kenneth was usually pretty good about keeping inventory down, but Jewel guessed he forgot about this room. With Kenneth's drawing in hand, she started looking for fabric that could be used for this garment. She was determined to find something and lost complete track of time.

She heard a noise behind her and realized someone had closed the door on her. She ran to the door to reopen it, but it wouldn't open. She banged on the door, hoping someone would hear her. She glanced at her watch. *God, it's five o'clock. Everyone would have left for the day.* She began to panic. She banged on the door as hard as she could, but no one came. She looked at her watch again: five fifteen. *Where is everyone? Why can't anyone hear me?*

Upstairs, Kenneth was gathering his things and getting ready to go home when Shelby arrived.

"I don't think Jewel is in the apartment," he said. "I haven't seen her all afternoon."

Shelby looked in the apartment. "You're right, she isn't in there. Where do you suppose she is? She knew I'd be here at five," replied Shelby. "And she certainly wouldn't leave without telling you, would she?"

"No, she wouldn't. The last time I saw her, she was going to look for some fabric that would work for one of the dresses. I think we better check all the floors." Kenneth and Shelby fanned out and checked each floor. When they finally got to the ground floor, they were really worried.

"Where the hell is she?" said Shelby. "I don't like this."

"Neither do I," replied Kenneth.

Both of them began to search frantically.

The two of them met in the middle of the shipping department, and Kenneth told Shelby to be quiet; he thought he had heard something. Shelby heard it too. Some kind of banging noise was coming from the room farther back in the department. When they arrived at the place they thought they heard the noise emanating from, they stood quietly and listened. There it was again; it was definitely coming from inside that room. Kenneth checked the lock on the door; it was closed, but not locked. He opened the lock and removed it. Shelby almost ran over him, trying to get the door opened. There was Jewel, holding a large metal rod that she had removed from the rack holding the bolts of fabric. She had been using it to bang on the door, hoping someone would hear her. Her hands were dirty, and blisters were beginning to form from her striking the door so hard.

"Jesus Christ," said Kenneth. "Are you all right? Who the hell locked the damn door?"

"I don't know," sobbed Jewel. "I came in to look for fabric. A lot of people saw me go in there. I don't know why anyone would close the door and then lock it. Christ, I thought I was going to have to spend the night in there, and the fumes from the formaldehyde were making it hard to breathe. Can we please get out of here? I need some water."

They went up to the apartment, and Jewel got herself a glass of water. She was trembling so hard she could barely hold her glass still.

"Do you think it was an accident?" asked Shelby.

"I doubt it," replied Kenneth. "That room is never closed, let alone locked. Someone did this on purpose, and believe me, when I find the person who did it, they better have a damn good explanation for this."

"Kenneth, go home, I'm fine," said Jewel. "We can figure it out tomorrow. Go home. The boys will be waiting."

"The boys have Rocky. I'm more concerned about you. Do you think we should have you checked out at the hospital? That formaldehyde can be dangerous if you breathe in enough of it."

"No, I'm fine. Go home, please, Kenneth. I'm really okay."

Kenneth was hesitant about leaving, but with Shelby there, he decided Jewel was right; there was nothing they could do tonight. He made sure they were in the apartment, had something for dinner, then set the alarms and left.

On the ride to his home, he phoned Justin to tell him what happened and that maybe they should alert the two detectives Clay had working the case and maybe get fingerprints off the lock; it was a long shot, but maybe they would get lucky. Kenneth assured Justin that Jewel was okay, or he wouldn't have left her, and Shelby was with her, staying the night.

Justin immediately phoned Clay to tell him of the latest developments. He asked Clay for his honest opinion. Did he think it could have been an accident, someone locking the door with Jewel inside? Clay, always direct, said no. Someone did it on purpose. He told him he would get back to him.

Detectives Beach and Leeds were waiting out front of the factory for the first person to arrive that had a key to the door. Some mornings it was Benny Cahill, shipping and receiving manager, or Marcie Stillman, the office manager. The only other people who had keys were Jewel and Kenneth. This morning, it was Kenneth who arrived first. He was glad to see the detectives and another man carrying a large case that Kenneth surmised was for taking fingerprints. He greeted them and unlocked the door and turned off the alarm. They asked Kenneth to take them to the room where they found Ms. Lansby. Kenneth walked them through the ground floor to the back of the building and showed them the room.

The other man, only introduced to Kenneth as Ben, put his case on the floor and grabbed a large odd-shaped brush and a jar of some kind of powder. As he worked, Beach asked Kenneth the same questions he did last night on the phone after Clay called him to relate the latest development. After a short time, Ben told Detective Beach that he had some prints and would need prints from Kenneth, Shelby, and Jewel. Kenneth escorted them up to his office and knocked on the apartment door. Jewel opened it and was surprised to see Kenneth. Kenneth told her that she and Shelby needed to be fingerprinted so they would have their prints on file to match against any others that they found. As soon as they were done getting their fingerprints taken, Ben said he had what he needed and would get back to them as soon as he could.

Beach told him to put a rush on it.

Shelby and Jewel went to the bathroom to wash their hands. When they came out, Jewel put a pot of coffee on. Detective Beach told Shelby that he wanted to hear her story. Jewel poured each of them a cup of coffee and sat down, listening to Shelby's accounting of what took place. It was the same as she told Jewel last night. After asking Kenneth and Shelby a few more questions and asking for another cup of coffee, Detective Beach asked Jewel to tell him everything she could remember, every move she made after she left the third floor. Detective Leeds was writing down as much as he could, with Beach asking him a million times, "Did you get that?" Leeds just kept writing, saying "I got it, I got it." After they got as much information as they needed, Beach thanked them for the coffee and said he would get back to them if they found out anything.

"In the meantime, Ms. Lansby, I would try not to go anywhere alone."

Kenneth spoke up and said she wouldn't be going off the floor. Jewel didn't sleep at all the night before and was extremely tired, or she would have challenged both Kenneth and Beach about where she could or would go, but she just let it go. As soon as they left, she cleaned up the kitchen, while Shelby finished getting ready for work.

"Bye, kiddo. I'll see you later. You want chicken or fish for dinner?" she said.

"Surprise me," she said, then quickly replied, "Wait, I've had enough surprises for one day. I'll have chicken. Wait, let me get you some money."

"I'll collect when I get back," answered Shelby as she was walking toward the elevator.

"I'm so sorry, Kenneth," said Jewel. "I've been nothing but trouble since I've come back. I think I should go back upstate. I feel like I'm putting you all through hell."

"You don't hear us complaining, do you?" said Kenneth.

"No, but that doesn't make it right. I'm afraid to go to your house in case I'm followed, and I miss Celia and the boys so much. Rocky won't even remember me if this goes on any longer. I even told Justin I couldn't see him anymore because I'm afraid for his safety. Oh, Kenneth, when is this nightmare going to be over? I can't sleep, I can't concentrate, and I feel like I'm losing my mind!"

"I know," said Kenneth, "but you have to hang in there. They'll get this guy, and when they do, things will get back to normal. I promise."

"I hope it's soon, I really do," she said. "Poor Shelby, I may be putting her in danger every time she goes out."

"I wasn't supposed to tell you this, but I think you need to know. Justin has hired a car to take Shelby wherever she needs to go, so she'll be fine."

"I can't believe he did that," answered Jewel.

"Why not?" said Kenneth. "The man would do anything to make sure you're okay, and if that means protecting everyone you love, he'll do it."

"I don't know what to say. I've been so difficult, and here he is, doing this." "Hopefully it will all be over soon. Now, can we please get some work done?" replied Kenneth. "And no looking for fabric. Start a pattern for another piece. We will figure something out for the one you've been working on. Do we have an understanding that you will not leave this floor?"

Jewel laughed and promised she would always be within hearing range. Kenneth gave her another workboard, and by the end of the afternoon, it was completed. Kenneth looked it over and told her to bring it to his select sewing group. They were the only ones that got to work with the new pattern in the fabric of Kenneth's choice.

When it was completely sewn, Kenneth would see it for the first time and accept it or make changes. It would go on this way until Kenneth was totally satisfied with the design. The finished product was carefully wrapped and hung in Kenneth's office, so no one saw it until the show.

Jewel began to put her things away when she saw people heading for the elevator. The afternoon had passed so quickly. She always kept her area as neat and clean as possible. Her pins and needles, as well as her scissors, were always sharp. One of her instructors at school made everyone get in the habit of doing things like that, and it was surprising how easy a project would go if you just kept things neat. A place for everything and everything in its place, she would say. Jewel remembered her Greek accent and how well she liked her. Her commonsense approach to even the smallest task made all the difference in how much Jewel learned.

Shelby arrived just as Kenneth was leaving.

"Be good tonight, girls. No porn on the TV, or I'll have to get that channel blocked." He laughed as he left.

"Oh, Dad," said Shelby. "Now you're just being mean."

"Good night, girls."

"Good night, Kenneth. Kiss the boys for me," said Jewel.

"I always do," he said.

Tears welled up in Jewel's eyes, and she turned away so he couldn't see. Shelby put her arm around her shoulders and tried to assure her things would get back to normal soon.

The following morning, Detectives Beach and Leeds arrived at Kenneth's office around ten. They told Kenneth they had some news and needed to talk to him. Kenneth asked if it was about the incident the other day, and they said it was. Detective Beach was the first to speak.

"We got a hit on the prints we got off the lock and door and needed to speak to you," said Beach. "We identified two sets of prints, yours and another set, and since you already told us you touched the lock, we could rule you out. Do you have an employee named Elena Mendez?"

"The name sounds familiar," said Kenneth, "but I don't know everyone personally. Hold on one moment." Kenneth buzzed the outer office, and when his office manager answered, Kenneth asked her if they had an employee named Elena Mendez. She answered that they did, that she worked down on the ground floor, in shipping. Kenneth asked her to bring in her file and not to say anything about it. Marcie brought in the file Kenneth asked for and asked if there would be anything else. Kenneth handed the file to Beach and asked him if he had any questions for Marcie.

"No, I think I have what I need right here, but I would like Marcie to accompany Detective Leeds down to shipping to get this Elena Mendez and bring her up here." Marcie agreed, and she and Leeds left the room.

"Is it her fingerprints you found on the lock?" asked Kenneth.

"Yes," said Beach, "and I see by her file she has only worked for you a little over four months. You do any kind of background checks on the people you hire?"

"I really don't, except when I'm looking for an expert sewer or fitter. The rest, especially in the shipping and receiving department, come and go faster than I can learn their name. In a company this large, I really only know the top-level people. I leave the rest to the managers of their departments. Marcie would know a name because she does payroll."

Detective Leeds, Marcie, and Elena arrived at Kenneth's office.

"Thank you, Marcie. You may resume your duties," Kenneth told her. Marcie left Kenneth's office. Detective Leeds closed the office door and then positioned himself in front of it.

"Is your name Elena Mendez?" asked Beach.

"That's what people call me," she answered.

Beach told her to take a seat, but she said she would rather remain standing. "Suit yourself," he said. He took his time reading over her file, which was beginning to make Elena nervous.

"Look, if you got something you need to ask me, then ask it. Otherwise, I got work to do," she said defiantly.

"Miss—is it miss?" asked Beach.

"Yeah, it's miss," she answered.

"Ms. Mendez, did you hear about someone being locked in the storage room near your area last night?" Beach asked.

"I might have heard something," she answered.

"Did you have anything to do with it?" asked Beach.

"No. You think I got nothing better to do than lock the princess in the room?" she said angrily.

"And who would that be, this person you just called the princess?" asked Beach, trying to remain as calm as he could and never looking directly at her. Elena kept shifting her weight from one foot to the other. Obviously, Beach was getting to her, and that was his plan. Usually, when subjects became anxious and started getting restless, it was when they slipped up, and that was what Beach was waiting for.

"So you say you had nothing to do with locking the storage room door," he said.

"Look, I already told you, I had nothing to do with it. I was working, and then I left, end of story," she said.

"Then how would you explain your fingerprints on the lock and door?" asked Beach.

"How do I know? I work there. I must have closed or locked that door sometime in the last few months. Other than that, I don't know."

"Ms. Mendez," said Beach, "are you sure you wouldn't like to sit down?" "I told you already I'd rather stand. Can I go now?" she said, her face beginning to show anger.

"I'm afraid not," said Detective Beach. "I'm not convinced about when your prints got on that lock. I've spoken to the rest of the people in your department, and they said that the storage room door is never closed or locked. How do you explain that, Ms. Mendez?"

"Look, I don't know. Maybe they forgot or something," she answered.

"You think it's possible that everyone is wrong here, Ms. Mendez?" replied Beach.

"Look, like I said, I don't know how the door got closed with the little princess in it. Maybe she did it herself," she said.

"Yes, maybe she could have accidentally closed the door behind her. But how would she have gotten the lock through the latch? And who did you say was in the room, Ms. Mendez?"

"Are we playing some kinda game here? I don't know how Lansby got locked in that room, but I bet the little princess soiled her diapers when she found out she would have to spend the night in there." Elena laughed. "You got no proof I did it, so I'm out of here."

"You're right, Elena," said Kenneth. "You are out of here. Get your things and get out of my building. You're fired!"

"Shit, you can fire me, but it ain't over. You'll see. It ain't over," she said as she pushed her way past Leeds, opened the door, and left.

"Well, she's right about one thing: we don't have any proof it was her, and she could have gotten her prints on the lock just as she said, but I'm willing to bet she knows who's behind all this. We'll keep an eye on her to see what she does. Maybe she will lead us to this person. In the meantime, remind Ms. Lansby to stay alert. I'll be talking to you, Mr. Dolan."

CHAPTER 11

The detectives left Kenneth, and he immediately went down to the ground floor to make sure Elena was gone. He spoke to his shipping and receiving manager, Benny Cahill, and asked him if she left and if she said anything when she left. Benny said she just gave him the finger and walked out. Kenneth told him that under no circumstances was she allowed on the premises. If she came to meet one of the girls for lunch or something, she had to wait outside, no exceptions. Benny wanted to ask what she had done but knew better, but he surmised it had something to do with Jewel being locked in the storage room. It wouldn't surprise him in the least that she did it, the way she always had something to say about her. She always referred to her as the little princess. Benny asked her once if she knew Jewel and why she called her the little princess. She just laughed a laugh so evil sounding it gave him chills. He never spoke to her about it again.

Kenneth wasn't sure whether he should tell Jewel that they knew who it was that locked her in the storage room. He decided against it and instead called Justin and told him about Elena. Justin asked if the cops knew whom she was involved with, but Kenneth told him they didn't yet but they had plans to keep their eye on her. Justin agreed with Kenneth not to tell Jewel or Shelby until they found out more.

Justin relayed all the information that Kenneth just told him to Clay. He knew Clay had people everywhere, and wouldn't be surprised at all if there was someone watching the building. Clay was a strange duck. He didn't make friends easily, but when he considered you his friend, there wasn't anything he wouldn't do to make sure your life was good. The things he did to protect the people he cared for were never known or spoken of. That was the way he did things, and Justin respected it.

Shelby arrived before Kenneth left, and as usual, he secured the building and reminded them to stay in. Shelby held up the bag with Kentucky Fried Chicken printed on it and told Kenneth not to worry, that they were not going anywhere. It seemed to Shelby that all this craziness was taking a toll on Kenneth as well as Jewel. He looked like he hadn't been sleeping very well, and the dark circles under his eyes certainly verified that. She wondered if Jewel noticed it as well; she was sure she did. Jewel was always so good at reading people's faces and knowing what they were feeling. Shelby gave a yell to Jewel, who was still tiding up her workplace.

"Hey, that can wait. We have chicken here. Get it while it's hot," she said.

"One minute," answered Jewel. "I'm almost finished."

Shelby went into the apartment and got down some paper plates. She knew Jewel would have a fit, but Shelby didn't feel like washing dishes tonight. When they finally sat down to eat, Shelby was surprised when Jewel didn't mention the paper plates.

"What's up, kiddo?" she asked.

"Oh, I don't know. A little bit of everything, I guess. I miss Rocky. I miss Justin and Celia and the boys. I feel so guilty about taking up your evenings. You should be out on a date or something instead of babysitting me, and I know that Kenneth fired someone after the cops were here, and I'm guessing it had something to do with me being in that storage room."

"He didn't tell you?" she asked.

"No, and that makes me feel like some little kid who has to be spared the truth because he thinks I couldn't handle it. Shelby, I'm disrupting so many people's lives. Have you seen the way Kenneth looks? I bet he hasn't gotten a decent night's sleep since this whole thing started. I really think I'm going to leave."

"But what about your new apartment? I've been working so hard so you could move in," said Shelby.

"I know, but this may not stop just because I move uptown. And look how close I'll be to Justin. I could really be putting him in harm's way. I just don't know what to do," said Jewel.

"Well, I don't think you should do anything until you hear from the cops, or call Clay and ask him if he thinks you should go. At least he sees things realistically," answered Shelby.

The girls started cleaning up when Shelby thought she heard a noise. They both stopped what they were doing to listen. There it was again. It sounded like it came from the living room. Both girls crept quietly into the living room. The drapes on the windows were still open because it hadn't gotten dark out yet. Shelby said she felt like a fish in a well-lit bowl when it was dark out and the drapes were opened. She made sure they were closed as soon as it began to get dark. The noise was definitely coming from somewhere outside. Jewel approached the drapes, but Shelby caught her and told her to close them and to disregard the noise. Jewel said it sounded like a cat scratching at the window, but Shelby was adamant about not going near the drapes. Jewel assured her she would close them; she just wanted a peek, and reminded her that there were bars in front of the windows. Shelby cautioned her again but relented when she remembered the bars.

Jewel moved close to the drape on the left side of the door and started to pull the edge. Suddenly, it sounded like they were in the middle of a war zone. The glass window that Jewel was standing in front of exploded. Something came through and hit her on the shoulder. Fortunately, Jewel had started to turn away when she heard the crash, or she would have been hit by the flying glass shards. The object that Shelby now identified as a brick would also have hit her in the face. Shelby acted quickly and ran over to Jewel and pushed her down on the floor. They both covered their heads as more bricks reigned in on them. Shelby told Jewel to keep her head down as they crawled to the couch, where Shelby had left her handbag and cell phone. She dialed 911 and told the operator what was happening and the address. Shelby knew she would have to get Jewel to turn off the alarm to the factory so they could go downstairs to let in the police.

Shelby quickly dialed Justin to tell him what was happening. He told Shelby to get Jewel downstairs and turn on the alarm for the apartment as they were leaving, then wait until they heard the police outside, check the window carefully to make sure it was the police, turn off the alarm, and only then open the door. He would be right down. Justin called Clay first thing, and as usual, he said he was nearby. Justin was convinced Clay had been watching his house but would never mention it to him. After everything that had been going on, Justin felt more secured knowing Clay was there. His next call was to Kenneth, who took the news badly. Justin could hear the fear in Kenneth's voice. Celia got on the phone and asked Justin exactly what was going on because Kenneth didn't tell her anything; he just bolted out the door. Justin apologized for disturbing them yet again and explained the events as Shelby had relayed them to him.

"Justin, I'm so worried about Kenneth. He isn't sleeping, and he barely eats anything. Please don't keep him there any longer than is necessary," she said.

"Don't worry, Celia," answered Justin. "I promise to get him home as soon as I can. I'll have Clay run him up as soon as the police say he can go."

"Thank you, Justin. Please give my love to Jewel. Take care of her for us, Justin, please. I know you will. Keep in touch, will you? I'm so worried."

"Don't worry, Celia. I'll talk to you soon. Bye." Justin hung up the phone and went downstairs to wait for Clay. Clay was just pulling up to the curb. Justin quickly opened the door and got in.

"Have you heard anything?" asked Clay.

"Not really. I just got off the phone with Celia, who said Kenneth bolted out the door and didn't even stop to tell her what was going on. I told her what Shelby said and that I would get back to her as soon as I could. She is quite worried about Kenneth. She said he hasn't been sleeping or eating, just worrying about this insane business with Jewel. To them, she is every bit a family, and this business is hurting them all. She is especially worried about the boys. They keep asking when they will be able to see her, and they don't know what to tell them. Thankfully, they are being amused by Rocky's presence. Have you heard anything on your end?" asked Justin.

"No. The cops are en route. They also sent out the emergency squad, just in case. That's all I know. I've had someone watching the building, but with all the possible entry points to the roof, he can't cover them all," said Clay."

Justin had no more to say. He began to blame himself. If he had just thought about it, he would have hired people to cover all entry points, but he knew that was not really practical; they could be there for a day or a year. Besides, he had no idea how to conduct such an operation. That was why he left such things to Clay, and Clay never failed him. The ride downtown was slow going, but Clay knew all the back streets and alleys that they arrived the same time as Kenneth was pulling up. They all headed for the door, asking each other if they had any further news. No one did. A cop was posted at the door and asked who they were and why they were there. He let them in, and they quickly headed for the elevator. There was another cop posted by the elevator, and again they were asked for identification. Racing to Kenneth's office, they saw it was overflowing with the police and EMTs. Detectives Beach and Leeds were also there. Clay called them as soon as he heard the news. Justin and Kenneth were frantic, looking for Jewel. The police had the drapes drawn back, and you could see the broken windows as well as many bricks scattered about the floor. Some of the police were walking around the roof. Clay caught Beach's eye, and he immediately made his way toward them.

"Few seconds more and we may have gotten the bastard," said Beach.

Justin spoke hastily and asked if the girls were all right. Beach told them that the EMTs had them in the bedroom, checking them out.

Kenneth and Justin ran into the bedroom and saw Shelby pacing by the bed. Jewel was on her stomach, lying on the bed, with a medic checking her back.

Justin called to Shelby, who quickly turned and ran into his arms, crying. Justin tried to be supportive but was slightly uncomfortable and wasn't sure what to say to comfort her.

He held her tight and let her cry until he thought she was able to speak.

"It's all right, Shelby, you're quite safe now," he said as he held her. Her grip on him became stronger, and at one point, he thought she might faint as he began to feel her go limp. He held her up, and she began to regain her strength. Through her tears she tried to tell him what happened.

"Oh my god, it was terrifying, Justin!" she said. "Glass was flying everywhere, and the bricks...oh my god, it was awful! I didn't know what to do. I was so scared." She kept repeating how scared she was and the glass flying everywhere, sobbing all the while she tried to speak. Justin desperately wanted to go to Jewel, but he held Shelby tight, for if it hadn't been for her quick thinking, things might have been worse. Jewel was lying on the bed but heard Justin's voice and bounded off the bed despite the objection made to her by the medic. Justin saw her getting up and asked Kenneth to hold Shelby. Shelby was still crying hysterically and didn't even realize she was now being held by Kenneth, but Justin had to get to Jewel, who was now just inches away. She threw herself into his arms, crying and saying his name over and over.

"You're here. Oh god, you're here! I'm so sorry! You must hate me. I'm sorry, I didn't mean what I said. Please, please don't leave me," she cried, holding on to him with her right arm only. Justin saw that her left arm was dangling at her side, and she was uncovered on that side. He tried to calm her, but she clung to him even harder.

"Jewel, you have to lie down so the medic can take a look at your shoulder," he told her. He didn't want her to become too excited until they could evaluate how badly she was injured. "I'm right here, and I promise I'll never leave your side. Now please, for me, let the man take a look at your shoulder," he said as he walked her back to the bed. He told her to lie down, but she refused to let go. He could feel every ounce of her trembling.

"Please, Jewel," said Justin, "please let them take a look at you. I'll be right here, holding your hand the entire time, please."

"Justin, I was so frightened. If it weren't for Shelby..."

"I know, Jewel, I know. But it's over now, and I'm here, so please hold still." Jewel finally did as Justin asked and held still for the rest of the exam. The medic pulled some glass shards out of her neck and shoulder. He ran a light over her again, hoping to see anything glisten, because that would most likely be another shard. He found none. Her shoulder was starting to swell, and he opened an ice pack and placed it on her shoulder. He took her blood pressure again and called into the hospital with the information. He stated that her scapula might have damage he couldn't see, and recommended an x-ray. After conferring with the hospital, he told Jewel they were taking her in. She became hysterical at this point, and both the medic and Justin tried to settle her down. The medic got back on the phone and told them of her response and was given the okay to sedate her. Even after the shot of valium, she still couldn't settle down.

"Justin, please come with me, please." She was crying again, and the medic said if it would keep her quiet, he could ride with her in the ambulance.

"Yes, Jewel," said Justin, "I'll be with you. Now please try to settle down. You may have injured your shoulder, and you could be making it worse."

Kenneth and Shelby came into the bedroom to see how Jewel was. They were told that she was being taken to the hospital to get her shoulder checked out. Justin insisted that Shelby be brought to the hospital also, but she said she was fine, just shaken. Justin insisted and asked Kenneth to find Clay so he could bring her. He knew Kenneth would have to stay until the police were finished. He told Kenneth to call Celia to let her know he was all right and what was going on and that he would call them from the hospital as soon as he could.

At the hospital, they x-rayed Jewel's shoulder, did a thorough check for any glass shards, and concluded their exam by saying nothing was broken, but her scapula was severely bruised. There was no treatment for it other than to rest her left arm, keeping it in a sling so she wouldn't move the scapula, and to use cold packs for two days to keep the swelling down, then apply moist heat. They gave her a prescription for pain and one for a muscle relaxer, and she was free to go. Shelby checked out fine; she wasn't close enough to the window to get hit by any flying glass fragments. Justin asked Shelby if she wanted to go home with them, but she declined and said she would rather just go back to her apartment.

Justin asked again, reminding her that she would be alone, but she said she would be fine and would really prefer to go home to her apartment. Justin asked Clay if he had someone available that could take Shelby home and watch her place through the night. Clay said he had to make a phone call and it would be done. By the time the girls were discharged, one of Clay's men was there to take Shelby home. She was told that the man would be outside her building all night and was given his number. Clay told her to call his number if she felt anything was wrong. Shelby thanked Justin and Clay for their prompt action and for the overnight protection, then she hugged Jewel gently, and they both began to cry.

"Shelby," said Jewel, "I'm so sorry I got you mixed up in this mess. How can I ever thank you for being there with me?"

"Oh, kiddo," she said as she hugged Jewel, "I'd do it again in a heartbeat, but just wait till you get your bill." Both girls laughed and held each other close.

"No more talk about moving upstate either," said Shelby. "Or you will have a problem."

"Okay, I promise, I'll stay and make you all miserable," replied Jewel.

"Better miserable with you than without you, right, Justin?" answered Shelby as she pushed Jewel into Justin's arms.

"I couldn't have said it better myself," said Justin. "Now, let this good man take you home so you can get some rest."

"Amen to that. Good night, all. I'll talk to you tomorrow, Jewel," said Shelby as she was being escorted out of the hospital.

Justin walked Jewel out of the hospital, having to hold her up. Between the painkillers and muscle relaxers, she was pretty well out of it. Clay got the car and helped Justin get Jewel into the back seat. Justin held her close, mindful of her left shoulder. Jewel was asleep as soon as the car started moving. When they got to the apartment, Justin was going to carry her up, but Clay said he was a better choice to carry her. Justin didn't argue with him; he knew Clay worked out every day and could probably pick him up if he had to. Justin opened the door and told Clay to bring her to the back bedroom. He ran ahead to turn on a small lamp on the nightstand and pulled down the bed coverings and closed the blinds. Clay put

Jewel down gently, and Justin removed her shoes. They decided to let her stay dressed the way she was so as not to wake her. Justin pulled up the sheet and blanket and kissed her forehead.

"This is getting outrageous," said Justin as he walked to the bar and poured himself a shot of scotch. He motioned to Clay to offer him one, but he refused. "I can't remember the last time I had a drink, but I bloody well need one tonight," said Justin, plopping onto the sofa.

"What do we do now? How the hell can we protect her, if we can at all? Besides locking her in her room, what else can we do?"

"That's something I'd like to see," said Clay, "locking her in her room." Clay started to laugh, forcing Justin to relax and chuckle himself.

Justin leaned back on the sofa and gazed at the ceiling. "I know she's strong, Clay, but how much more of this do you think she can take? How much more of this can any of us take? Did you see Kenneth? The man looks like he hasn't slept in a month! No wonder Celia is worried about him. Speaking of Kenneth, I better call and see if he is still at the factory."

Justin called Kenneth, and he was still at the factory. The cops had just about finished up, and his shipping manager, Benny, was bringing another man with him to cover the windows with plywood. Kenneth sounded exhausted and couldn't wait to go home. He asked about Jewel and Shelby and was glad to hear that they were all right. Justin told him to go home and that they would talk more tomorrow.

Jewel woke up around three thirty in the morning and, at first, wasn't sure where she was. She went to the bathroom, then found her way into the living room. She still felt drugged, and her shoulder hurt like hell. She saw Justin asleep on the sofa. She hated to wake him; he had been through so much with her, and she couldn't help thinking that another man would have dumped her long ago. But Justin was still here.

"Justin," she called softly as she touched his shoulder.

"Yes?" said Justin. "Jewel, are you all right? Do you need something? Are you in pain." He sat up quickly to see how she was and if she needed something. He made her sit down and tell him how she was doing.

She told him her shoulder hurt and she would like one of the pain pills, but she thought she had better put something in her stomach before she took it. Justin agreed and told her to stay put, that he would make her some toast, or did she prefer something else? Toast and maybe some tea would be fine, she said as she lay down on the sofa. Her head was spinning and aching at the same time, and she felt slightly nauseous. She remembered that she hadn't eaten her dinner last night but was a little foggy about the rest. She must have fallen asleep while Justin was making the tea and toast. He called her name and told her he had her toast and the pain pill. After she ate her toast and had some tea, she took the pill. She asked him if he had something she could wear because the heavy sweater she was wearing was uncomfortable to sleep in. He suggested one of his pajama tops, but before he could get up to get her one, she wanted to know exactly what happened last night. She told him she only remembered bits and pieces and needed to hear it all. Justin told her everything, the parts he witnessed himself and the parts that Shelby conveyed to him after he got there. Was Shelby all right? she asked. And where was she? Remembering the whole thing now was getting her very excited, and she needed to know where Shelby was and if Kenneth was all right. Justin assured her that Shelby was fine. The doctor at the hospital said she sustained no injuries, and he told her that Clay had one of his men take her back to her own apartment and would be outside her building all night, and if she needed to go anywhere, he would always be with her. Kenneth left the factory around midnight after he and some of his men boarded up the windows. "So you see, everyone is fine. Now I'll go get the pajamas, and we should get you back to bed."

When he came back, Jewel began to cry.

"What's wrong? Are you in pain?" he asked her.

"No. I was just thinking about all the things you've done for me and my friends, people you didn't even know until a few months ago, and I've been such a bitch."

"Everything I've done, however great or small, has been for you. I love you. You must know that. Yes, you have been trying at times, because you insist on being so damn independent, but a bitch? No, not that. I know you tried to push me away because you were worried I might meet with some danger, and if it made you feel a little better, I went along with it. I knew once this nonsense ended, we would be together. I never doubted that for a moment," he said.

Jewel lay against him and told him she would never be able to go on if anything happened to him, and he reassured her that nothing would. He had Clay. He held her a while longer, until he could feel her body relax. He followed her to the bedroom and removed the sling and helped her off with the sweater. He didn't ask her if she wanted to remove her bra; he just put his pajama top on her. She said she would like to remove her slacks, so he unbuttoned them and slid them down so she could just step out of them, then he quickly got her into bed. He felt so guilty. Here she was, arm in a sling, pain in her shoulder, and he wanted her so badly.

The doorbell rang at ten o'clock the next morning, and Justin figured it was the police but was surprised to find Celia standing there.

"Oh god, tell me I didn't wake you? I'm so sorry."

"It's all right, Celia," said Justin. "I was just lying on the sofa. I managed to get a few hours in after I got Jewel back to bed."

"Is she all right? Is it awful, her injuries? Kenneth was so exhausted when he got home he couldn't tell me anything, and I've just been so worried." Justin let Celia babble on until she calmed down. He was getting used to her mild hysteria when it involved her friends and family.

"Please sit down, Celia. I was just about to put some coffee on in case Jewel got up. She awoke about three, was in some discomfort, but she had some tea and toast, then took a pain pill and went back to bed. She has her left arm in a sling, but that is just precautionary, so she doesn't move her shoulder too much. Nothing is broken, just a nasty bruise on her shoulder blade. They did remove a few pieces of glass from the side of her face and neck, but you can't even see where they were. She was incredibly lucky. If Shelby hadn't had the clarity to grab her and pull her to the floor, she might have incurred additional injuries. Shelby is fine. She didn't receive any injuries."

Justin replayed last evening's events to Celia as he made the coffee. He got out the cups and silverware, the sugar and cream, and poured the coffee in a warmed carafe and placed it all on a silver tray. His mother trained him well, thought Celia as she watched him move. He moved rather gracefully for a large man, she thought.

"What's all the noise out here, and where can I get a cup of that delicious-smelling coffee?" said Jewel.

Celia nearly jumped out of her skin when she heard a voice, as her back was to the bedrooms and she didn't see Jewel coming in.

"Oh, my darling, how are you? Here, come sit down," said Celia. "I'm so sorry I came so early, but I was just so impatient to see that you were all right. After Kenneth told me about how all the windows were shattered, I just had to see for myself how you were. It appears Justin is taking good care of you," she said as she gazed at what Jewel was wearing.

Justin caught the look and immediately went to his room to retrieve a robe. "Here you are, my dear," he said as he helped her on with it. She put the right arm through, and Justin carefully covered up the left shoulder and affixed the tie around her waist.

"We don't want you to catch a chill on top of everything else, do we?" he said. "And here is your coffee. What else would you like? I think I may have some cereal, or I'm afraid it's just toast again."

"The coffee's fine. That's all I want for now," she replied. "Celia, shouldn't you be at work?"

"Yes, I should. I'm hoping I have a very forgiving boss," she said, looking at Justin, who gave her a nod. "I just needed to see you and to tell you, if you need anything, anything at all, just call, all right? And the boys and Rocky send their love. All right, then, I'm off," she said as she swallowed her last bit of coffee. "Justin, anything I need to take care off in the office?"

"At the moment, Celia, I can't seem to think of anything, but I do have a few calls to make, so I may contact you later," answered Justin.

"All right, then," she said and put her coat on, kissed Jewel on the cheek, and left.

"Have you been up long?" Jewel asked.

"No. Actually, I was still sleeping on the sofa when I heard the bell. I thought it was the police. I'm certain they will be calling on us sometime today with more questions about last night. Did you sleep all right after we got you back into bed?"

"I did, actually. Do I have you to thank for undressing me?" she asked, blushing.

"I only did what was necessary to make sure you slept comfortably," he said, also blushing slightly.

"Thank you, and did I tell you I love you this morning?" said Jewel.

"No, actually, you did not," he answered.

"Well, come give us a kiss and I'll tell you." Justin reached over the table to kiss her. "I love you. I very much love you," she said to him softly. "And if this damn shoulder didn't hurt so much, I'd make love to you right here, right now."

Justin pulled back, surprised, looked at the devil in her eyes, and smiled. "If I weren't a gentleman and you weren't drugged, I would have had you last night, smart-ass," he replied.

"Oh, sir, I do believe you are toying with me," said Jewel as she pretended to fan herself. Just as she was about to say more, the doorbell rang.

"Perfect timing, and I'm guessing this is the police?" said Justin as he got up to answer the door.

The police asked Jewel to go over her story again. She remained calm and told them everything she could, explaining to them that there were some gaps in her memory either from being frightened to death or from the bump on the head she received when Shelby pushed her to the floor.

"Jewel," said Justin, "why didn't you say anything about your head at the hospital?"

"Because I didn't remember it until this morning, when I went to the bathroom and felt this egg on my forehead," she replied.

Justin moved over to her and pushed the hair off her forehead, and there was a very nasty bump already turning a deep shade of blue. "Jewel, we need to have this looked at promptly. You may have a concussion. Did you notice it when you were up at three?" he asked.

"No. I guess my shoulder hurt more than my head at that point, and then after I took the pain pill, I fell asleep. But it is certainly making its presence known now."

Justin asked if they needed anything more and if it could wait until after he took her to the hospital to have her head checked.

They seemed pretty satisfied with what they had and said they would be in touch. Justin immediately called Clay and told him he needed to take Jewel to the hospital. As usual, Clay said he would be there promptly.

Justin helped Jewel get back into her slacks. He told her to stay the way she was in his pajama top and robe because they would only make her change at the hospital and it was too difficult getting the sweater back on. She managed to slip into her shoes and told Justin that they would have to stop at the apartment in the factory so she could pick up some clothes. She'd like to get there before Kenneth left for the day. Justin told her he would call Kenneth and relay her request, but right now, she was going to the hospital.

The x-rays were taken, and Justin was proven correct; Jewel did have a slight concussion. The fact that she didn't remember hitting the floor so hard was not surprising, said the doctor, but he assured them that he had no concerns for her recovery. He suggested she abstain from taking too many pain pills and to come back if the pain in her head worsened or she felt nauseous or started to vomit or couldn't stay awake. They left the hospital with Justin feeling vindicated for insisting that she was going if he had to have Clay carry her again.

"What do you mean again?" she asked.

Justin told her how Clay had carried her from the car to the apartment after she had fallen asleep on the ride home, and before she asked why he didn't carry her, Clay chimed in by saying Justin had all he could do to get himself upstairs. Clay laughed and said he thought he might have to come back down and carry Justin up. They all had a good laugh, and Jewel, while still laughing, had to tell them to stop making her laugh because her head hurt.

"I think I'd rather have a good hangover than a concussion," she said, holding her head.

As they arrived at the factory, Clay noticed the unmarked car. He knew it must be Beach and Leeds, back for more info. When Jewel and Justin got out, Clay, who usually just remained in the car, said that he would like to go up with them. He thought he recognized Beach's car. As they walked into Kenneth's office, Clay had been right; both Beach and Leeds were there, as well as another person he didn't know. A rather plain-looking woman he guessed to be about thirty-something.

"Clay, you have impeccable timing," said Beach. "It's scary, like you could read my mind. Who told you we were here?"

"No one. We stopped because Ms. Lansby needed to pick up a few things," stated Clay.

"How are you feeling, Ms. Lansby?" asked Detective Beach as he offered her his chair.

"We just came from the hospital," said Justin. "Seems, along with a bruised shoulder, she has a slight concussion."

"Jewel, is this true? How did that happen?" asked Kenneth.

"I didn't feel anything until this morning, and last night, it wasn't blue. The only explanation I have is that when Shelby pulled me away from the window and pushed me to the floor, I struck my head. I guess I was just too frightened to notice it last night. Anyway, it's no big deal. What's going on here? Hi, Donna," said Jewel to woman sitting next to Kenneth. "Everything all right?" Donna just replied with a little wave.

"Ms. Weidner here," said Beach, "was just going to give us some information she thought pertinent to this case."

"What?" said Jewel. "Donna, do you know who's doing this?"

"I'm not 100 percent sure, but I think so," she answered.

"Now, let's not get ahead of ourselves," said Beach. "Ms. Weidner, please continue."

CHAPTER 12

"Well, as I started to say, I bumped into Lawrence—that would be Jewel's old boyfriend in the Laundromat over on Seventh Avenue. It had been over three years since I last saw him, but I recognized him from when he used to come in with Jewel. I said hello to him and told him how I knew who he was. We talked while our things were getting dried, and then he asked me out for coffee. I usually go right home, but I thought, What the heck? He seemed really nice. So we went to the little diner around the corner and ordered coffee. We talked about a lot of things, but then he asked me how Jewel was. I told him that she left a few weeks after Kenneth's show and was living in Upstate New York for the past few years but that she just moved back in January and was back to work for Kenneth. He said he was such a fool back then, he just wanted so badly to make it big and he ended up screwing up his whole life. That all the things he loved, he ended up losing. He didn't blame Jewel for any of it. It was all on him. He said at first he blamed her, but later he realized she had the talent and he didn't. Anyways, he asked if he could see me again, and I said yes, and we have been dating for about five months. He's so smart and real charming, and he never once tried to get fresh, if you know what I mean."

"Please go on, Ms. Weidner. Okay, so you dated and he was nice, then what happened?" said Detective Beach, obviously trying to speed things along so they didn't have to sit and hear her life story.

"Yes, as I said, he was such a gentleman. He couldn't get a job anywhere in the fashion business, not after he was exposed for stealing the designs from Jewel. He did a lot of things to make ends meet but finally landed a job as manager in a little hotel over on Seventh, just down from the Laundromat, which is just near where I have my apartment. Small world, isn't it? Anyway, he had a room at the motel, and when his brother got out of jail in February—"

"His brother? What brother?" asked Jewel. "I never knew he had a brother."

"He didn't like anyone to know because he was in jail for eight years for robbery and assault upstate someplace. He really didn't like to talk about him, but when he got out and looked Lawrence up, he expected Lawrence to be living in a grand apartment and be doing real good, and he thought he could live with him until he got his own place. But Lawrence said that his brother was so mad when he found out what his brother was doing. He wanted to know about all the big important things and all the money he was making that was in the letters he had been receiving. Lawrence explained that when he started writing about all the important things he was doing, he was too ashamed to tell him about what he had done to lose it all. He thought he would have gotten a better job by the time his brother got out of jail, but his brother got out early for being good or something. Willy, that's his name, Willard Russell. Willy was drinking a lot and wanted to know all about what Lawrence did to make him end up in a dive like the one they were living in. It really wasn't such a bad room. Lawrence brought me up once, and he kept it real nice, but I guess it wasn't good enough for Willard. You'd think that a guy who just spent the last eight years in prison would be less critical of where he lived, wouldn't you?"

"Yes, you would think that," said Beach, again trying to keep Donna on track.

"Lawrence said that Willy knocked him around a few times and kept asking him all kinds of questions about Kenneth and Jewel and the show and all. Lawrence kept telling him that it wasn't anyone's fault but his own, but it seemed like Willy needed someone else to blame. He told Lawrence not to worry, that he would square things up for him. Lawrence said that he told Willy to let things be, but Willy didn't listen. He started talking to some of the men here at the factory that worked on the ground floor when they had the door open and found out that Jewel was living in the apartment upstairs. He came home one night and told Lawrence how he scared the s-h-i-t"—she carefully spelled out the word instead of saying it—"out of the girl. Lawrence told him to leave her alone, and Willy told him that he was just having a bit of fun.

"Then another time, he said he left her a nice little note on a bush outside her door. Then when Jewel got sprayed in the face that time, Lawrence said he asked his brother if he did it and he said no. Why would he do a thing like that? he asked. Lawrence said he wanted to believe him, but he was worried Willy was getting out of control with the drinking and all, and now Lawrence thought he was doing drugs. He kept finding money missing from the cashbox at the hotel. He thought about turning Willy in because he was breaking his parole, but he was his brother, and he couldn't. But he told him he wanted him out. He couldn't live with him anymore, that he was a slob and a thief. Willy left, but before he did, he trashed the place. So when I called Lawrence and told him about the latest thing to happen to Jewel, he told me to go to Kenneth and tell him about Willy. He said he knew that they would want to talk to him, but he didn't want them to go to the hotel to see him, in case Willy saw them. He said he was really afraid of his brother and felt he would kill him if he turned him in. He told me to get your number and he would call you and tell you where he would meet you. He really is trying to help, but he's afraid of Willy, and believe me, this brother of his is real scary. Anyway, that's what he told me to tell you. I'm real sorry, Jewel. Lawrence didn't mean for any of this to happen to you. He feels real bad about it."

"Good God," said Jewel. "It wasn't enough that Lawrence almost ruined my life. Now I have to deal with a maniacal brother." Jewel got up from her seat and went to Justin, who carefully put his arm around her. "I need to get some things from the apartment, and then I'd like to get out of here. I've had enough for one day." She left Justin's side and went into the apartment. Justin asked if she needed any help, and she said she might once she got her bag packed.

The five men in Kenneth's office just looked at one another, no one saying a word. Finally, Kenneth asked Detective Beach if he needed anything else from Donna. Beach said he did not and handed her his card. He told her that she could tell Lawrence to call him and they could meet anywhere he felt he would be comfortable. Kenneth thanked Donna and told her she could get back to her duties.

"You mean I'm not fired?" she said.

"Of course not, Donna. Why would you think you would be fired?" replied Kenneth.

"I thought because I was seeing Lawrence and it might be his brother who has been doing all this stuff to Jewel," she answered.

"Nothing you've done has, in any way, been your fault. You have actually done a very good thing in telling us what you have, right, Detective Beach?" said Kenneth.

"Absolutely, Ms. Weidner. You did a good thing here," he answered.

"Thank you, Mr. Dolan. I'm so relieved. Thank you so much."

Kenneth got up and escorted Donna out of the office; he figured it was the only way they were going to get her to leave.

"Shit, some goddamn little psycho. I'm telling you, if I find him first, I'm gonna cut his balls off," said Clay. All the other men had a similar look on their faces, pure revulsion.

Jewel returned in a few minutes, trying to carry a small bag. both Justin and Clay went to help her. Clay grabbed for the bag and told Justin to take care of Jewel. She asked if they were needed any longer, and after being told they could go, Jewel said she would like to see Shelby. After they got into the car, Justin called to make sure she was home. She said she was so glad they were coming; she very much wanted to see Jewel.

When Shelby opened the door and saw Jewel, she immediately began to cry. Jewel tried to hug her, but it was difficult with one arm. Shelby put her arms gently around her.

"Oh, kiddo," said Shelby, "you sure know how to throw one hell of a party. Here, let me look at you." She held Jewel at arm's length. "What's with the noggin? You have a blue egg on your forehead. Did you get hit by another brick? My god, that looks awful! Does it hurt?"

"It looks worse than it is. How are you? You were whisked away so fast last night I didn't have a chance to see you. You're okay, aren't you? Plus, I wanted to thank you for...for everything. I don't know what I would have done if you hadn't been there."

"Oh, please, just another day in the life of a superhero," said Shelby, trying so hard to pretend she was all right.

"Justin, Clay, both of you here is making me a little nervous. Are you sure everything is all right, boys?" It was Justin who spoke and told Shelby he wanted to thank her for being there and that they may have a very strong lead thanks to a girlfriend of Lawrence Russell's. He didn't mention the concussion that Jewel sustained when Shelby pulled her to the floor; Jewel had given them all orders that they were not to mention how she got it. She was so thankful to Shelby that she didn't want her to feel in any way guilty over making her hit her head.

"*The* Lawrence Russell?" said Shelby.

"Yes, that Lawrence Russell," replied Jewel. "It seems he has a girlfriend who works for Kenneth."

"Get out!" said Shelby. "Who in their right mind would date that creep? They all know what he did back then. Do you know her, this girlfriend?" she asked Jewel.

"It so happens I do," she answered. "A mousy little thing that works in the accounts receivable department. Her name is Donna. I doubt if you know her. She's always hidden behind a stack of ledgers."

"Well, what do you know? I don't believe it, but you're not telling me that Lawrence is behind this, are you?"

Justin spoke up and explained what happened just an hour ago as they listened to the story she told to the police. Lawrence wasn't involved, but his brother, who just got out of prison, appeared to be the one responsible. Apparently, he blamed Jewel for ruining his brother's life. She was to blame for the plans he had to live off his brother when he got out of prison, believing that Lawrence was just raking in the money.

"So what is he doing these days? Cleaning toilets, I hope?" said Shelby.

"He manages some lowlife hotel on Seventh Avenue," replied Justin.

"So do they know where this brother is?" asked Shelby.

"The police are going to talk to Lawrence, and hopefully he will give them an address where they can find him," said Justin. "Look, I hate to cut this visit short, but I have to get Jewel back to my apartment so she can rest. She's had enough excitement for one day, and I'm sure her head is pounding. She hasn't had any pain medication for some time. Shelby, if you need anything, anything at all, call me or, call Clay if you can't reach me. Is that all right, Clay?"

Clay didn't say a word, just nodded. Jewel wondered why he even came up to the apartment; he never said a word the whole time. She was glad that Justin was cutting the visit short. She didn't know what part of her hurt worse, her head or her shoulder.

"Okay, thanks for stopping by, and by the way, your apartment will be ready for you on Sunday, just as planned," said Shelby.

"Please don't do anything. The apartment can wait. Take some time off," replied Jewel.

"Hey, that may work for some people, but you know me. If I'm not working, I'm going nuts. I need to stay busy, so if you're up to it Sunday evening, I think we should all meet there and celebrate, then you can congratulate me on the wonderful job I did and smile when I give you my bill," she said with a smile.

"Oh, I love you, you nut. We will be there, all of us, even smiley over there," said Jewel, pointing to Clay. "And yes, we need to celebrate and smile and sing joyfully."

"You think you can get him," she asked, again pointing to Clay, "to sing joyfully?"

"Well, if not, then we will just have to do it for him. Deal?"

"Deal," answered Shelby.

No one could see it, but there was a hint of a smile on Clay's face as they were leaving.

After Clay dropped Justin and Jewel, he decided to take a ride back downtown to that small restaurant he visited the other day, in hopes of seeing the man with the blue jacket, Willard Russell, but as luck would have it, he wasn't there. Clay ordered coffee and a sandwich and nonchalantly began to talk to the man behind the counter about odds and ends, the weather, baseball, the end of the football season, etc. He was trying to establish some type of rapport with him so it wouldn't seem odd that he was interested in anything specific. He asked about business, and the man, whose name Clay found out was Sal, said, "Some days good, some days not so good." Clay told him he was thinking of what he wanted to do when he got tired of driving people around all day and he thought about opening a little sandwich shop. Sal told him he would be better to stay driving. He told him how he had to come in early and leave late or they stole him blind; between the help and the customers, he was always short of something. He said he finally had to throw out a bum that kept coming in, ordering a sandwich and then running off without paying. Clay said he thought he was here that day and asked if the man wore a blue hooded jacket.

"Yeah, I think that was him. When he first started coming in, he was very nice, ate, paid his bill, left the girl a tip, and made no trouble, but the last few weeks, he looked like he never bathed, and he always looked hungover. My girl didn't want to wait on him anymore because he always got nasty with her. I finally had enough and told him not to come back."

"You wouldn't happen to know his name, would you?" asked Clay.

"No, but I think I heard someone call him Willy. Why? He owe you money too?" asked Sal.

"No, I'm just checkin' around for a friend. His brother is a little unbalanced and started living on the streets. He's been trying to find him, and this guy fits his description. Brown hair, brown eyes, about five ten, one-seventy, wearing a blue jacket," answered Clay.

"Yeah, that sounds like him, but I don't know where he hangs out. A few hang out back in the alley. Maybe you should try some alleyways or down on Ninth. He won't be coming back here anytime soon, unless he's got his self straightened up. I don't want no bums in here. Customers don't like it," he commented.

Clay finished his sandwich, paid the bill, and took Sal's advice, riding through some of the alleys. But he didn't see anyone fitting the description. "You had better be hiding good, you scumbag, 'cause when I find you, your ass is mine," Clay said out loud while he drove the alleyways.

Meanwhile, Justin and Jewel spent a quiet Saturday, and by Sunday, she was feeling much better and felt as though she could eat some breakfast.

"Do you have any English muffins?" she asked Justin.

"I was just about to go out for some rolls or bagels, but I think I have some in the freezer. Are you sure you wouldn't like a nice, fresh bagel?" he answered.

"What are you having?"

"I had planned to have a bagel with cream cheese and lox, but if you don't want anything, I'll just have a muffin with you," he stated.

"Well, I didn't want you to go out just for me, but since you'd like a bagel, then I'd like sesame with cinnamon butter, please," she said.

Justin said he would be back in a flash and she was to remain resting on the sofa. The phone rang, and Jewel answered it. It was Justin's mother, calling to see how she was feeling. She expressed her feelings for the crazy person who was doing this to her. Justin must have already spoken to his mother, for she already knew all about Lawrence's brother. She just went on to say how she hoped the police would waste no time in finding him and sending him back to prison and that Jewel would make a speedy recovery. She hoped they could come up to Connecticut for another visit. She said she had some new flowers just starting on one of her special lovelies, which was her way of describing her orchid plants. Jewel told her she would love to see the latest orchid to flower and would speak to Justin. Just after she hung up, Justin returned with the bagels.

"Oh, you just missed your mother," she told him.

"Did she need anything or just calling to say hello?" he answered, seemingly uninterested.

"She called to say hello and to see how I was doing and to inform me that she had one of her lovelies about to flower and wished we could make the trip up to see it. I told her I'd ask you," she said.

"I'm sure another one of her lovelies will be blooming again sometime soon. I have a much better idea for a trip," he answered.

"What kind of trip?" she asked.

"A trip that will get you out of the city for a week so you could soak up the sunshine, rest, and feel completely safe. How does that sound?"

"It sounds heavenly. Where is this place?" asked Jewel.

"Bermuda. It still may be a bit chilly mornings, but it would be warmer than here. I own a house there," he said nonchalantly, as if everyone did.

"You own a house there? Are you kidding me?" Jewel squealed with delight.

"I'm sorry, I thought I mentioned it," he said casually.

"No, I definitely would have remembered you telling me that," she said excitedly. "When do you go? Who takes care of the place? How long have you had it?"

"May I get our coffee? I would like to eat my breakfast," he stated.

"I'm sorry. Here, let me help you." Jewel put the bagels on a dish, sesame for her, plain for Justin with cream cheese and lox. Justin poured the coffee, checked his bagel to make sure the filling was evenly distributed. Satisfied that it was, he took a bite. Jewel was sitting on the edge of her seat, watching him. She hoped he didn't plan to eat the whole bagel before he told her some more about the house in Bermuda.

"I'm not exactly sure when Father bought the house, but I remember I must have been around fourteen. A few of his colleagues had homes there, and Father didn't like to be outdone. We started going down quite often, then less and less, till finally we only went down twice a year. Mother still goes twice a year, once in the summer, before it gets too hot, and then just after the hottest season is over. I myself haven't been there in, oh, I'd say three years or so. We have a couple who live in the apartment over the garage. They maintain it when we're gone and get it ready if we decided to come down. They're very good. So what do you think? Would you like to get away for a week? I'm sorry we can't stay longer. I have some important negations coming up, and I need to be in the office. I can't leave this to Celia. She is getting very good, but this one will need a little finesse. I've dealt with some of these people before, and they will only work with the highest level of office, and I'm afraid they consider associates as glorified gofers. So what will it be?"

"I'd love to go. It sounds wonderful! Oh, can we take Shelby? I really owe her, and this would be the perfect thank-you. Please? I promise to rest. I'll do whatever you say. Please say yes," Jewel pleaded.

"You promise to do everything I say? I mean it, Jewel. You've got an injured shoulder and a concussion, not to mention the stress you've been under from all this," he said.

"I promise, I really, really promise," she answered.

"Yes, all right, just as long as you remember, you are there for rest, not running around the island," he said.

"Don't I even get to walk on the beach?" she asked.

"If you behave," he answered. Jewel jumped out of her chair to kiss him. "This is exactly what I mean. Stop jumping about."

"I know. It wouldn't happen again, I promise. I'm just so happy. I've never even been out of the state except for Connecticut. Thank you," she said as she kissed him again.

"Remember your promise," he said again.

She kissed him softly on the forehead and promised she'd be good. "I'll ask her tonight when we go over to see my apartment. She's gonna freak. I hope she doesn't have any important jobs to do and can get away. It will be so wonderful if she can go. I think she has been just as frightened as I have these past few weeks. This will be good for her too."

The afternoon passed quickly, and Jewel couldn't wait to see the apartment. Shelby was going to call them when she was ready. She had put a bottle of Asti Spumante on ice, because she knew it was Jewel's favorite. Then as she was get- ting out the wineglasses and a plate of cheese and crackers, the doorbell rang. "I'll kill them if they're here already," she mumbled to herself but was surprised to see Clay standing there with a platter in one hand and something else in the other.

"Haven't you learned anything yet?" he grumbled. "Ask who's there before you open the door."

"I didn't because I saw it was you through the door peep," answered Shelby.

"Is that just a hole, or does it have glass in it?" he asked.

"Glass. Look for yourself," she said, slightly annoyed.

"Here, take this," he said as he handed her the platter. He came in, closed the door, and checked the door peep and the locks on the door. When he was satisfied, he turned and looked at the apartment.

"You did a nice job. It really looks great, sort of Oriental, nice and serene," he said.

"Thank you. That's what we were going for," she replied. "What's all this?" she said to Clay.

"Nothin', just one of those party platters. I didn't know if you got anything because of all the work you were doing, so I just got this. Is it all right?" he answered.

"Yeah, it's great. I just got some cheese and crackers, so this is fine," said Shelby.

"What's in your other hand?" she asked.

"Something I made for Jewel. It needs to be hung up. I brought the hook. Just tell me where to hang it," he said like it was no big deal.

"Can you hold it up for me?" asked Shelby. Clay obliged her request and carefully held the piece up so everything would unfold correctly.

"My God, that's gorgeous! Clay, did you make this? It's incredible!" said Shelby. "It's a hobby of mine. Whenever I have to go drive someone and it's near the ocean, I always walk the shore, looking for the sea glass to make these mobiles. Jewel and I talked about it once, and she gave me a glassful, so I said I would make her a mobile. And here it is. Where do you think we should hang it?"

"I know the perfect spot," said Shelby. "Over here by this window. It's so beautiful, and when this window is opened, there is just the right breeze to make it move."

Clay looked around and decided she had picked out the right spot, and screwed the hook into the ceiling, then hung the mobile on it. They both took a step back to see how it looked.

"It's just beautiful. As it moves, the sea glass takes on another color. Wow, Jewel is going to love this!" said Shelby.

Clay remained silent, hoping Shelby was right. He really hoped she liked it. There was something about the way he felt for Jewel, a connection. He wasn't sure what it was. She was strong and found silence comforting, as he did. She was bold and direct. Maybe that was why he felt this bond to her.

Shelby asked Clay if he would like something to drink, but he said he would wait for the others. Shelby tried to find something to talk to Clay about, but since she barely knew this guy, it was hard. What did he do in his spare time besides making mobiles? Did he like sports? Where was the most interesting place he had to drive someone? She just wasn't sure of what to say, and luckily, she didn't have to. Justin and Jewel had finally arrived.

"Welcome to your new digs, kiddo," said Shelby as she opened the door wide so they both could walk fully inside.

Jewel looked around the apartment, at the artwork on the walls, the furniture and its placement, the media center, the conversation area, the dining room, the kitchen, the bath, and finally, the bedroom, with Justin and Clay tagging along behind her.

She didn't say a word until she got back into the living room.

"Shelby, this is absolutely incredible! It's just what I envisioned, separate areas flowing one to the other, the color on the walls that magically changes shades. Oh, Shelby, I'm speechless! It's perfect, just perfect! I don't know what to say."

"Where in the world did you find these botanical prints? They go so perfectly with the feel of the room."

As Jewel turned around to looking at everything, her eye caught the mobile. She walked over to it and touched it slightly so it moved. She didn't say anything, just walked over to Clay and wrapped her arms around him. She could feel his body stiffen. She doubted if Clay had many people in his life that hugged him, and she always got the feeling that there wasn't anyone there for him and that was why he was so close to Justin, a brother he never had, possibly. Jewel had decided to stop wearing the sling, even against Justin's objections, because it just made her arm feel worse, so she was able to get both her arms around Clay. She let him go, and he took a slight step back.

"Thank you. It's beautiful," she said to him.

He never uttered a word, just gave a slight nod. She realized that in Clay "talk," it meant "Thank you" or "Okay." It was a good thing. Justin stood by and wondered what that was all about but said nothing. Then Jewel went to Shelby and held her close as she started to cry. She felt Jewel's tears on her face, and it didn't take long for Shelby to start too. The girls held each other without saying a word, while Justin and Clay looked on at both of them, each man looking perplexed. Finally, Shelby and Jewel pulled apart and looked at each other, both faces wet with tears.

"The place is perfect, Shelby. I don't know how you did it, but you've captured my very soul. It's magic! I love it, and I love you for making it magic. Thank you," she said to Shelby.

"You were my inspiration, Jewel. You guided me every step of the way even though you weren't here," she answered. Then to stop them from getting too maudlin, she said out loud so Justin could hear that it wasn't perfect until Clay hung the mobile he made. The three of them looked at the mobile, then at Clay. Justin was speechless; he had no idea that Clay had this much talent or that there was something in his life besides driving and bodyguard work. He was seeing Clay in a new light, and he was impressed.

"Clay," said Justin, "you made this?"

"Look, it's no big deal," he replied, slightly embarrassed.

"I disagree. It is a big deal. It's quite stunning, a remarkable piece of work," replied Justin. "How long have you been making these?"

"For a few years now. I started finding the glass when I took you to Connecticut. I liked to walk the shoreline, and I started collecting the pieces. Jewel had a glassful, and I said I'd make her one. No big deal. What's a guy have to do to get a drink here?"

They could see that Clay was slightly uncomfortable talking about himself and changed the subject, so they all went along. Shelby opened the Asti for her and Jewel. She asked the men if they wanted some bubbly or beer but already knew the answer and went to the fridge for the beer. When everyone had a drink, she raised her glass and offered a simple toast to Jewel and her new home.

As the evening went on, Shelby and Jewel got up to explore the apartment. Jewel was so impressed with the way Shelby had made the bedroom into a place to sleep and to work by hiding the mannequin and other sewing supplies in half of the closet and the rest of the supplies in a tall dresser near the closet. The other side of the closet was for her clothes. Jewel was thrilled with everything and thought now would be a good time to ask her to go to Bermuda with them, but she wanted to be by Justin so he could argue for her going if she refused. So she led Shelby back to where the men were, which was in the recliners, watching TV.

"Well, that didn't take long," she said to them. "Men, give them a beer, a recliner, a TV, and they're happy."

"Well," said Justin, "we weren't asked to join the tour, so we found a way to amuse ourselves."

"And I'm glad you did. I want you to relax and be comfortable. That was the idea behind the theme, and it looks like it works," said Jewel. "I wanted to ask Shelby something, and I wanted your support so she couldn't refuse."

Both men got up and walked to the dining room table, where both women were sitting. When they were standing close to them, Jewel smiled at Justin.

"Shelby, Justin and I are going to Bermuda for a week, and we want you to come with us. Justin has a house there, and with the ocean and the tropical feel, it will be great, just what we need. What do you say? You can put off work for a week, can't you?" pleaded Jewel.

Shelby looked stunned. *A week in Bermuda? Oh, heaven! That's just what this girl needs,* she thought to herself. Shelby remained silent for some time.

"Thank you. That's a grand offer, but no," she said, to the surprise of all.

"No? Did you just tell me no? I don't understand. Shelby, this would be so much fun! It's Bermuda! How many times have we talked about going to some island and doing nothing but lying on the beach? Whatever work you have surely could wait a week. Come on, please," Jewel pleaded.

"Look, you and Justin have been through a lot, and you need some time away, alone. You don't need me hanging around. Would that be two for dinner? No, three. You see, it would just be too awkward," answered Shelby. "Those kinds of trips are for couples."

"Please, Shelby. Justin, tell her," said Jewel, but before Justin could say anything, and to everyone's surprise, Clay spoke up.

"There is another option," he said. "I could go. Maybe we're not a couple, but I'd be glad to escort you around the island, since I've been there before, and we could have dinner together, the four of us, or just the two of us. I know I'm probably not what you envisioned going with when you thought about an island trip, but I think Jewel is correct. You have also been through a great deal, and a trip like this would be beneficial."

Justin was totally surprised, as was the rest of them, but he quickly spoke up and told Shelby that Clay was right. She, too, could use some time away from the city. Shelby looked at the three of them. Jewel, she loved like a sister-there was no doubt there but she also realized that Clay and Justin meant a great deal to her, too, and if Clay was willing to do this for her, then she had to accept. She thanked Clay for his generous offer and agreed to go.

"I don't know what the beaches are like there, but if we find any sea glass, I'd like a mobile too," she said as she smiled at Clay. Clay just nodded.

Justin said he thought they could leave as early as Thursday. He wanted to go to see his mother on Monday, then he needed to spend a few days in the office. If everyone agreed, then he would make all the arrangements. Everyone agreed Thursday was good for them. Jewel was glad Justin wanted to go up to Connecticut, for she had a surprise for his mother and she would have to speak to Clay about it, then she needed to see Celia and Kenneth and the boys. It had been so long, and she needed to see Rocky. She couldn't wait until she could bring him home. The boys would be sad, but they knew it wasn't going to be forever; maybe now they could persuade Celia to let them have a dog of their own. She thought of all she had to do. She would have to ask Justin's mother what clothes to bring on the trip.

Before they broke up for the evening, Jewel needed to speak to Clay.

"I can't thank you enough for offering to come on this trip with us. You're right in saying that Shelby needs to get away. I've known her for forever, and I've never seen her this tense. I know she jokes around and says she's fine, but she isn't."

"Rather like someone else I know," he said.

Jewel blushed but continued. "I know Justin will appreciate having you there to spend time with when he's had enough of us."

Clay didn't say any more, just gave Jewel that little nod. Jewel always took that to mean "All will be well," "Don't worry," and "I'll always find a bit of comfort in it." She told him that she would need to make a trip down to Twenty-Seventh Street Monday morning before they headed to Connecticut, that she had to pick up an orchid.

Monday, they got up early, dressed, packed, and headed downtown. Neither Jewel nor Clay told Justin why they were making this trip, and he didn't ask; he knew he would find out in due time. Jewel was always amazed by the lack of curiosity he had. If the roles were reversed, she wound never be able to stand not knowing.

Clay stopped at the address she gave him and jumped out of the car but was back in a quick few minutes, carrying what looked like to be nothing more than a clump of brown paper. She got back into the car gently, and when Justin asked what she had, she laughed and kidded him about his general lack of curiosity and said he would have to wait. He just shook his head. By now he knew better than to press the issue.

Jewel thought the ride to Connecticut seemed longer than usual, but she knew it was because she was so excited and couldn't wait to see the look on Evelyn's face when she saw what was in the paper.

They finally arrived, and Justin helped her out of the car and told Clay to pick them up at five. Justin held the door open for Jewel and her surprise package. Evelyn was there to meet them and tried to kiss Jewel on the cheek but was met with a wall of brown paper. Curiosity was not really her strong suit either, but she had to ask about the curious bundle. Jewel said they should really go into the greenhouse before she opened the package, making Evelyn even more excited. When they got to the greenhouse, Jewel set the package on the table and told Evelyn to open it carefully, as it was very fragile. Evelyn surveyed the package to decide the very best way to start; even Justin was getting interested now. When the final layer of paper was off, Evelyn just stood there, not able to utter a word. Justin just saw another one of those plants that took up so much of his mother's time and decided to go to the kitchen and get himself a cup of coffee, leaving the two of them to drool over the latest ugly plant. Evelyn stood transfixed as she gazed upon the marvel in front of her. Jewel reached for the stool behind her and placed it behind Evelyn and gently steered her so she was sitting down.

Jewel whispered softly in her ear, "Enjoy." Then she left Evelyn alone with her prize and went to find Justin, who was in the kitchen, having coffee.

"There you are! Do you think she liked it?" she said to him.

Sarah asked if she would also like a cup of coffee and asked what they brought up from the city that had Evelyn so engrossed she had forgotten her manners.

"It's all right, Sarah. Mother's having a moment she soon won't forget. Let's let her enjoy it. Jewel brought her one of the ugliest little plants you ever saw. I hope you didn't spend more than fifty dollars on the homely thing," he said.

"Never mind what it cost. Just remember the look on her face as she saw it for the first time," replied Jewel.

"Never mind. I know you. Just how much did that thing cost?" he said.

"What's the difference what it cost if it could bring your mother so much pleasure?" answered Jewel. "Besides, my grandfather always told me, 'Money is like fertilizer. It doesn't do a bit of good if you don't spread it around.'" And with that, she had Sarah laughing.

"Then I'm guessing it cost much more than fifty dollars," said Justin.

"Let it go, Justin. I'm not telling you. Besides, I'm sure there have been times you've gone way overboard when you wanted to please someone, so let's just say this was my time. Right, Sarah?"

"Sorry, love, I'm with Justin on this one. I don't understand the fascination she has with those things," replied Sarah, "but it was a very nice thing you did all the same."

Justin finished his coffee and said he was going to the study to read the paper. Jewel said she would stay in the kitchen and talk to Sarah and wait for Evelyn to eventually emerge from the greenhouse, which wasn't for another half-hour.

"There you are," she said to Jewel. "I'm so sorry to have left you alone. I didn't even ask how you were feeling. Here, let me look at you. There is still some bruising on your forehead, and your shoulder, how is that doing? You poor thing, I can't believe what you've been going through. It's just horrible! Have they caught the man yet? Do they have any new information?"

Jewel tried to get a word in, but Evelyn just kept rambling on. Jewel thought it funny. Evelyn was acting like a kid who just received the best present for Christmas. Eventually, Evelyn wound down and asked Sarah for some coffee. She filled Jewel's cup again too. When she had a few sips of coffee, she let out a large sigh and looked at Jewel.

CHAPTER 13

"You are the most incredible young lady I have ever had the pleasure to meet. Here you are, going through the most horrifying time, and you still can find the time to think of someone else. I am still in shock. Where did you ever find it? How did you know it would mean so much to me? It's like nothing I've ever seen before. It's glorious! A ghost orchid, a rare ghost orchid, Sarah. That's what this wonderful love has brought me. I don't even have the words to thank you. It's so grand, so magnificent. I shall be the envy of everyone in the orchid club! I can't wait to tell them, but you, what am I to do about you?" Evelyn got off her chair and made Jewel stand up so she could give her a proper hug. She asked Jewel if she was hurting her shoulder; she said no, and Evelyn continued to hold her close. Justin walked in at that moment and said that it was nice to see her out of her trance, and was the little plant really that interesting?

"Justin, if you don't marry this girl, I'll never speak to you the rest of my life," she said as she finally let go of Jewel.

"Thank you, Mother," said Justin. "Just so happens I'm taking the little lady here for a week in Bermuda, and I had planned to ask her that very thing. Now that that's out, what's for lunch?"

Jewel was stunned as she looked first to Justin, then to Evelyn, and finally to Sarah, who gave her a wink. Still too stunned to remark about what she just heard, she changed the subject and asked Sarah if she had any cake.

"Cake? That's not a proper lunch, especially when one's recovering from being banged around. I'll fix you a nice, hot bowl of soup. How's that?" said Sarah. Jewel said that would be fine but she really wanted something sweet. "What about me? I'm the one who asked for lunch," said Justin.

"Hold your pants on. I'll get to you," answered Sarah.

Jewel smiled and turned her head away. She didn't want him to see her laugh.

The day went quickly as Evelyn spent most of her time in the greenhouse and Justin in the study, reading his papers. Jewel was relieved when the doorbell rang and it was Clay, ready to take them home. Evelyn, still not over the surprise that Jewel had brought her, couldn't stop thanking and hugging her. Justin finally stepped in, took Jewel by the arm, kissed his mother, and out the door they went. After they were in the car, Jewel looked back and saw that Evelyn had tears in her eyes. *We must come up to see her more often, she thought to herself. She's such a lovely person, and despite her involvement in her women's clubs, she seems so lonely.* Jewel sensed that Evelyn missed her family, and that meant Justin; somehow she would have to figure out how they could spend more time with her. She needed them.

They got back to the city early, and Jewel called Kenneth at home to see if Celia was home yet and if she and Justin could stop by. Yes and yes was Kenneth's answer. The boys threw themselves at Jewel when they saw her and begged her to go to the game room with them for a while. She agreed, but just for a little while, because she needed to speak to their parents. Rocky also was overcome with excitement when he saw her. She knelt down as he kissed her face and told him one more week and he could come home with her. The boys were already moaning, but Jewel reminded them that she told them he was only staying until she got her apartment fixed and that now it was done and Rocky belonged with her. They were great boys and understood. Now she had to play some games with them, especially the new one they just got. They had to see if Jewel could beat them. They played continually for half an hour, and Jewel only won once, making the boys very happy. They ran upstairs, yelling that they had finally beaten Jewel. Jewel was yelling back that the match was unfair because they had more time to practice with the game than she did, and she promised them a rematch. Even when Celia told them to go upstairs to their rooms until dinner, they were still chanting, "We beat Aunt Jewel, we beat Aunt Jewel!"

Jewel asked Celia when the boys started calling her Aunt Jewel. Celia replied, "A few weeks ago, when they were asking why you hadn't visited in a while, and I told them it was because you were ill, they said they hoped Aunt Jewel was feeling better and couldn't wait to see her again. I asked them why they started calling you Aunt Jewel, and they said because they loved you and you were the best. Kenneth and I didn't see a problem with it and didn't think you'd mind, so we let it go."

"If you'd rather they didn't," said Celia.

"No," replied Jewel. "I love it. You know how I feel about them. If it's okay with you, it's fine with me."

Kenneth remarked that they missed her at work and asked her when she thought she would be back. Jewel told them that the doctor said to give herself a few more weeks' rest primarily because of the work she did and the strain on the injured shoulder blade. She told them of their planned trip to Bermuda for a week and of her completed apartment. Celia asked where they were staying in Bermuda, as she and Kenneth had been there many times and could recommend a very nice place. Jewel hesitated and looked at Justin for help. Justin told them that he owned a house there, and Celia's jaw dropped.

"A house? How wonderful!" she said as she looked at Kenneth.

"Yes. It's been in the family for some time. My father bought it when I was quite young. We haven't used it as much as we did when he was alive. My mother goes twice a year, but I've been so busy I haven't been there for a few years. Once we get this madman locked up and things return to normal, it would be most enjoyable if you and the boys would like to join us there," replied Justin.

"Thanks for the invitation, Justin," said Kenneth. "Sounds like fun."

"Yes," said Celia, "it does sound like fun. I could use a bit of sunshine."

"Good. It will give me a chance to get out of the office again," said Justin. "I will be in the office tomorrow and Wednesday, Celia.

I hope all parties are up-to-date on everything and that there are no major problems."

"Everything you laid out has been carefully followed, and so far, all is well," answered Celia.

"Excellent, then I'll see you tomorrow, Celia, and now I'd like to get Jewel home so she can rest. We drove up to Connecticut to see my mother, so it has been a rather-long day," said Justin.

They all said their goodbyes, even the boys and Rocky, and Jewel told them she'd be back soon for a rematch, making them chant, "We beat Aunt Jewel, we beat Aunt Jewel!" as they left.

Jewel wanted to stay in her apartment, but Justin said he would rather she stay in his until they returned from their trip. She was still recovering from a concussion, and he didn't want her being alone at least for another week. Jewel knew better than to argue with him on this one. She had to admit, the trip to Connecticut left her feeling weak. She hated feeling vulnerable. She promised herself when she was young that she would never feel like that again, and she hadn't until now, but now she had Justin to be her strength.

Thursday couldn't arrive fast enough for Jewel. She and Shelby packed based on what Evelyn had told Jewel, and Justin reminded them that they were only going for a week, not a year, so they were warned to keep their bags to a minimum. They drove to the South Street heliport and flew it to LaGuardia, where Justin had chartered a private plane to take them to Bermuda. The trip was smooth and faster than the girls expected. The ride to Justin's house was so enjoyable. The taxi driver was full of information about the island, and the narrow winding roads up the hills gave them a wonderful view of the pastel-hued and white-roofed houses. The abundance of verdant trees, colorful flowers, and warm breeze was such a relief from the chilly weather that they just left in New York. As designers, both Jewel and Shelby marveled at the profusion of different colors dotting the landscape, and they agreed they would love to go to the Bermuda Botanical Gardens to get a close-up look at some of the oleander and hibiscus, as well as some of the other varieties of flowers. The palms, ficus, citrus, and other tropical fruit trees, they could study by just walking the roads or renting scooters, which seemed to be the method of choice for most of the people.

Justin would probably object, but somehow she was going to take a scooter ride around the island.

His home was breathtaking, perched on top of one of the highest hills in St. George. Even though it was only twelve miles east of Hamilton, which was the capital, it was less populated and still held its old-world charm.

The housekeeper and her husband came out to meet them, greeting Justin formally. Justin introduced his guests, and the woman told him everything was prepared for them, including a nice light lunch. Her husband carried the luggage in and placed each bag in front of its designated room. Jewel's and Justin's rooms were on one side of the hallway, and Clay and Shelby on the other side. Veronic, as was the housekeeper's name, asked them to please check their rooms to see if they were to their satisfaction. The rooms were beautiful, florals in the women's bedrooms, and more subtle stripes in the men's. Jewel noticed an adjoining door to Justin's room. *How convenient,* she thought to herself. She had to wonder if it was strategic. After everyone freshened up and took a minute to unpack some of their things, they went out to the patio and had fruit and cheese and wonderful coconut biscuits. Shelby agreed she made the right choice to come and said she couldn't wait to hit the beach.

Jewel rested most of the day. She didn't want to let Justin know that she was still in some pain, so she told him instead that she just wanted to relax and soak up the sun. They had the whole week to see the sights. She walked to the edge of the patio to look down over the hill toward the beach.

"Justin, there's a pool down there!" she exclaimed. "How do you get to the pool?"

"From inside the house. Come, I'll show you," he answered.

"Wait, I have to get Shelby. I think she went to her room."

Jewel went to knock on Shelby's door. "Shelby, come out! There's a pool outside!" she yelled.

Shelby opened the door. "A pool? Where? I didn't see a pool," she said.

"Neither did I. Justin's going to show us. Come on."

Justin was waiting for them by a flight of stairs on the other side of the long living room. They followed him down, and at the bottom of the stairs, there was the most magnificent pool with gray and pink paved stones, a wrought iron railing, and huge pots of hibiscus surrounding the perfectly clear blue water of the pool.

"I'm sorry, I thought I mentioned it. There are two more bedrooms and a small kitchen down here also," he said.

"No, you did not mention it, or I would have been in it by now," said Jewel.

"It might still be a bit chilly," said Justin. "The water doesn't warm up for a few more weeks." Before he could say anything more, though, both Shelby and Jewel were feeling the water.

"I'd say just right. What about you?" asked Shelby.

"You know what they say. Last one in!" They took off to get their bathing suits on.

As soon as they got back down, which took less than ten minutes, Justin cautioned Jewel and to remember her promise not to be jumping around.

"Aye, aye, Captain," she promised as she eased herself into the chilly water. Shelby opted for the one-dunk method. The water was a little colder than they first thought, but that didn't deter either of them. Justin stood watching them for a few minutes and yelled to Jewel that she had ten minutes to swim, then she had to get out. He said he would be on the upper patio but would come down for her if necessary.

"This water's freezing, Shelby," said Jewel.

"Hush, or Father will make us get out now," replied Shelby, making both of them laugh as they splashed each other. They estimated it had to be about ten minutes by the blue lips they both had. They quickly ran up the stairs, yelling to Justin that they were going to change as they went by.

"Water a little cold, girls?" said Justin, snickering.

"No, just right," said Jewel, shivering.

"Yeah, it was refreshing," said Shelby.

"Right," said Justin. "Would you two like a blanket?"

"Yes, please," they said in unison.

Justin went into one of the bedrooms and came out with a large blanket and wrapped the two together.

"I hope it was worth it," he said to them.

Neither could talk from all the shivering, but they moved heads up and down to show that it was. When they were sufficiently warmed, Justin suggested they go and remove their bathing suits, and perhaps a nap would be good. That suggestion was specifically aimed at Jewel.

"I think you're right. A small nap does sound good. You coming, Shelby?" Jewel asked.

"No, you go ahead, kiddo. I'm gonna take in a little more sun."

After Jewel left, Shelby asked Justin if Jewel suffered more injuries than she was told, because it seemed to her that he was being very overprotective. Justin had no plans to tell Shelby anything, but since she asked, he decided to say something.

"We all owe you a debt of gratitude for saving Jewel the night of the brick throwing, but truth be told—and I'm swearing you to secrecy, Shelby, Jewel is not to know I told you. Do we have an understanding?"

"Yes, of course," she answered.

"Jewel didn't just bruise her shoulder. She has a slight crack in the bone of the scapula, and the concussion is a little worse than she was told. That's why she has the sling, which I can't seem to make her wear, and with the concussion, the doctors said she needed complete rest for at least another two weeks. Now, how do you propose I can make her rest properly?"

"Well, you could start by telling her the truth," said Shelby. "If you've learned anything at all about Jewel yet, then you know she puts honesty above everything. Did she hit her head that hard when I pulled her to the floor?"

"Yes, but Jewel didn't want to tell you. She said that you saved her by pulling her down to the floor and it was just an accident."

"I knew it," said Shelby. "I just knew it. To her it's just no big deal. That's our Jewel. She doesn't want me to feel bad when she's the one walking around with the concussion. You gotta love that girl."

"Yes, she's rather special," said Justin.

"She is, so you better tell her the truth," said Shelby seriously.

Justin gave it some thought and said that Shelby was right and he was going to remedy the situation right now. Justin went upstairs and knocked on Jewel's door, then opened it a crack. He saw that she was just lying on the bed, fully awake.

"Don't you think you should take a pill for the pain? And before you say anything, let me say this: Last night at dinner, you barely touched your wine.

That was because you had taken something beforehand, and when you got out of the pool this afternoon, you only used your right arm. So I know you're in some pain. I should have told you this before. Your injuries were a little more than you were told. I take full responsibility for that call, but I'm telling you the truth now. Your shoulder wasn't just bruised, it also has a slight crack in the bone, and the concussion was a little worse than you were told. The doctor said you could go home but you had to rest at least two weeks before you resumed any activity. I thought I could take care of you and that this trip would be the answer, because you could just rest. I was so worried about you I failed to remember whom I was trying to protect. I was treating you like a child. I meant well, but I know I was wrong to hold anything back from you. I'm sorry."

"I love you," she said to him. "I'm glad you're finally telling me the truth. I was wondering how long it would be before you told me."

"But how did you know?" he said.

"Just a bruise wouldn't cause that much pain, and my head wouldn't be aching like this, and you were trying to make me slow down all the time, so I guessed it was probably worse than I was told. But I don't understand why you didn't tell me the truth then."

"Honestly, I really don't know, and if it weren't for Shelby, I might never have told you. Jewel, I've never cared for anyone as I do you. I've never loved anyone as I do you. And deep inside, a voice keeps telling me to protect you always. Being in love for the first time, I'm afraid, has thrown my better judgment off. I'm so sorry."

"You just have to be honest with me, Justin. I told you before, I'm a survivor. I can handle whatever it is, if you just tell me the truth, and yes, I think I will take a pill. Now go out and read a paper and stop worrying about me. I promise I'll take it easy, and when I'm tired, I'll rest."

Justin got her the pill and some water, kissed her and pulled the coverlet over her, and left. Jewel couldn't help but laugh when she thought of how adorable Justin was when he was trying to express his emotions. She fell asleep still thinking of him and how much she loved him.

The following morning, Shelby told them that Clay was going to take her down to the beach. She especially wanted to see the pink beach. She and Jewel had spoken earlier, and Shelby knew that Justin told her the truth and that she planned to take it easy all day. If she did, Justin promised they could go to the botanical gardens tomorrow. Clay had the scooter out and ready to go. They said not to hold lunch for them because they might be gone most of the day. Jewel was glad to see Shelby so happy. She had worked so hard in school taking extra courses, then working at the worst places, trying to gain some experience so she would be hired by a high-end design firm. She had finally gone out on her own, and although it was tough going sometimes, she was starting to do really well. Her apartment was one of her best projects. A place you didn't want to leave. A place Jewel could call home. Except for the small house she bought for her quilt studio, she never really had a home.

Clay and Shelby traveled all over the island. Clay said he knew the island well, and he was right. He took her to some of the most unusual places—beautiful, lush floral and tropical locations, to the unusual rock formations on the north part of the island. They stopped at a small stand for lunch and had the best fish sandwiches Shelby ever had. Then they were off again, this time to the pink beach. The beach was a marvel to see, soft pink sparkling in the sunlight. They walked a mile up the beach, picking up whatever looked interesting. Shelby was going to wade in the water, but Clay warned her of the Portuguese man-of-war, a kind of jellyfish with long strands that float in the water and whose sting is incredibly painful. She thanked him for the warning and decided to do her swimming in the pool at Justin's.

The sun was getting lower in the sky, and Clay guessed it must be around three o'clock. Shelby sat on the sand and said she knew they wouldn't mind if they were a little late. After all, how many times does a girl get to sit on pink sand? Clay sat down with her and told her some other interesting things about the island, then he went silent. Shelby was a lot like Jewel; she also liked the quiet times and didn't feel it necessary to always have to speak.

After a half-hour or so, Shelby decided to break the silence. "You probably know that Jewel and I went to school together. I chose to take a few psychology classes to help me better understand what people wanted in the design of their homes. What people think they want is not always what they really want. So I have become pretty good at reading people. I've noticed that there seems to be some sort of a connection you feel toward Jewel. I know it isn't a romantic one, at least I don't think so. But you have feelings for her, am I right?"

"I admit there is something," said Clay.

"Would you tell me what, or am I crossing the line here?" replied Shelby.

"She is brave, stands tall, looks at you directly when she speaks. She speaks little but says much, and I feel connected to her somehow. That's all I know," answered Clay.

"Yeah, that's her, all right, but it could also describe you. I used to kid her about her being so direct, and she'd laugh and say it was because of her Cherokee ancestors," said Shelby.

Clay looked at Shelby and asked if this was true. Shelby said it must be because Jewel never lied. Clay got up and said they must go.

"Why?" asked Shelby.

"You asked Justin my last name once, and he told you to ask me, but you didn't. Why?" asked Clay.

"Boy, do you guys tell each other everything? I don't know why. I just thought there must be a good reason, and I wanted to respect your privacy," answered Shelby.

"Thank you, but I will tell it to you now, then maybe you will understand," he said. "My name is Shenendoah, Clay Shenendoah."

Shelby looked at him strangely, not quite knowing what to say. So his name was Shenendoah; that wasn't any worse than Goldman, which was hers. Then suddenly it hit her: his name sounded Indian. He was Indian, and the closeness he felt toward Jewel, the connection, had something to do with the fact that they were both Indian. Could that really be the reason he had these feelings toward Jewel? In her psychology classes, she learned that some things could not be explained but nevertheless some of the connections people felt for one another could be based on something as simple as that. Something to do with the chemistry we all shared but was ignored by most. Shelby said nothing further, knowing that Clay had to get back to Jewel. She wondered what he would say to her when he saw her.

The ride back to the house seemed to take forever, partly because Shelby was so curious and partly because they were on the south end of the island and Justin's house was closer to the north end. When they finally arrived, Clay put the scooter away and went into the house to look for Jewel. He found her with Justin on the patio.

"Mr. A, I must speak with Jewel, in private, please," he said.

Justin never asked why; he had known Clay too long and knew if he needed to speak to Jewel, then it must be important. Justin looked at Jewel and told her to follow Clay, that he had something to say to her. Shelby thought it strange that Justin didn't even ask Clay what it was all about. Was his trust in this man that strong? Jewel never asked either, and to Shelby, this was all so bizarre. Jewel followed Clay to the farthest point of the patio. The two of them stood looking out at the water, as if this scene was perfectly normal. Shelby couldn't stand it any longer and asked Justin how he could be so calm. Didn't he want to know what Clay wanted of Jewel? Justin answered that it was something between the two of them and they would know in due time. Shelby was annoyed with Justin, and she didn't know why; she just took the seat next to his and said that this was all too weird. She watched as Clay and Jewel casually looked out over the trees to the ocean below and then turned and faced each other. She would give anything to be closer, to hear what they were saying to each other. She knew why she was annoyed with Justin—he didn't show the least amount of curiosity in what was happening between the woman he loved and his friend. Did he already know?

"You know by now I am a man of few words, but since our first meeting, I have felt something for you that I couldn't understand. It is not the feeling a man has for a woman. Not the way Mr. A feels for you, but more spiritual, if that makes any sense," Clay said.

"It makes a lot of sense. The knowing that you were there for me never made me feel afraid. It is something I have felt also," replied Jewel.

"Shelby asked me about this feeling I have for you. She is very perceptive. I told her it was because you are brave, you stand tall and look directly at the person you are speaking to, but more important, you speak little but say much. She said I could be describing myself. Then she told me about your Cherokee heritage, and I knew. We are brother and sister."

"Because of our ancestors. You are Indian, aren't you?" Jewel asked, as if she already knew the answer, and it didn't surprise her.

"Yes," answered Clay. "My last name is Shenendoah. Your people are from the south, and mine from the north, but we have the same blood." Clay put his arms out, and Jewel walked into them without hesitation.

Shelby was beside herself and got up from her chair.

"Sit down, Shelby," said Justin calmly.

"How can you just sit there? Don't you want to know what's going on? God, you're annoying," replied Shelby. "That's my friend out there, and I want to know what's going on."

"Does she look like she is in any danger?" asked Justin.

"No, but what do you think they said to each other? When I mentioned to Clay when we were on the beach that Jewel had some Cherokee blood in her, we nearly broke the speed barrier getting back here. Do you think it has something to do with that?"

"We will find out soon enough," said Justin. "Now please try to calm down. What would you like for dinner, fish or steak? I must inform Veronic."

"How can you think about food at a time like this?" cried Shelby.

"Well, it looks as if we will find out shortly what is going on. Here they come now. And please try to contain yourself and let them tell us what they will," said Justin as he pulled himself out of the chaise lounge. He met Jewel halfway and kissed her.

"It looks as if the two of you are very happy," said Justin.

"That's it, you look happy. Is that all you can say? I swear, Justin, you make me crazy," said Shelby. "Look, you two, I know it's personal, but I have just got to know what was so important that Clay nearly killed us getting back here to talk to you. Jewel, we're best friends, remember? We tell each other everything, so unless this involves national security and Clay is a spy, I need to know right now."

Jewel looked up at Clay, smiled, and told Shelby Clay was her brother.

"Wait a minute, you don't have any sisters or brothers—at least that's what you told me when we were in school," said Shelby.

"Clay and I share the blood of our ancestors. That's why we felt a connection to each other. Our spirits make us brother and sister," said Jewel. "We would give our life for each other."

"Well, let's hope it never comes to that," said Justin.

"I need a drink," said Shelby.

That evening, after everyone went to bed, Jewel used the connecting door to Justin's room. She quietly tiptoed in and got in bed with him. With his back to her, she slipped her arm around him and moved as close as she could get to- ward him.

"What are you doing, Jewel?" he said softly.

"It's dark. How did you know it was me?" she answered.

"Let's see...Shelby, I think not. Clay, never. That leaves you. Now again I say, what are you doing?"

"I just wanted to be close to you, to feel your skin against mine," she answered.

"You know how much I want you, Jewel. This isn't fair."

"Turn around," said Jewel.

"You know that will make it worse," he answered.

"I don't care. Turn around, please," she said.

Justin did as requested and took a deep breath. He knew where this was going, and he couldn't stop now if he wanted to. He put his arms around her, pulled her closer, and began to kiss her, then stopped and pulled away.

"What's wrong?" said Jewel, confused. "This is what I want."

"And it's what I want, too, but I could hurt you. Your shoulder, remember? And you're not to be jumping around."

"All right, minimal foreplay, no jumping about, and you just have to lean to my right. How's that?" She laughed. "I just want to feel you inside me. Please do this for me, Justin."

"This will be over rather quickly, I fear," he said.

"I don't care. We'll have all the time in the world to practice when my shoulder heals. Right now, I'll settle for this," she said.

But she wasn't settling; she got just what she came for.

The remainder of their stay passed quickly. While Jewel was able to see a few of the things she had an interest in, for the most part, she stayed around the house and rested. She bought a stack of magazines and was content to browse through them, leaving all the running around to Shelby and Clay, who promised to take tons of pictures. Their relationship seemed to take a turn for the better after Jewel answered all the questions Shelby had about Clay and her. Justin joined her in the pool, and they took long walks together, but then he had to spend a great deal of time on the phone for business, which didn't upset Jewel. She spent the time designing, taking her inspiration from the flora and fauna around her. She felt confident Kenneth was going to be pleased with this collection.

The last evening was spent quietly, everyone silently wishing they had more time there. Clay was actually telling jokes and laughing at Shelby and Jewel's attempts to be funny. Justin sat and reflected on the entire week and smiled. He told them all at dinner that this had to be by far the most exhilarating and happy time ever spent in this house. He was deeply moved by the friendship they all shared and hoped it continued long after they left the island. He also said that he would like to make this a yearly occurrence. Everyone raised their glass and toasted to next year in Bermuda.

Clay asked Shelby to take one last scooter ride around town. She really hadn't thought about it, but by the way Clay was acting, she knew he wanted to leave this last night to Justin and Jewel. A short time after they had gone, Justin asked Jewel to come to the end of the patio so they could spend these last few moments breathing the perfumed air and looking out to the ocean, which looked slightly silver in the moonlight.

"This night couldn't be more perfect," said Jewel as she leaned her head on Justin's shoulder.

"It could be," he replied. He handed her a small box.

Jewel opened the box, and tears began to fill her eyes. The ring in the box was exquisite. Not what she expected, considering Justin's wealth; she expected that if he ever gave her a ring, it would be some gigantic stone with carats galore, but not this ring. This ring reflected who she was. Small in proportion, slightly old-fashioned, but the center diamond's shine was breathtaking.

"Will you do me the honor of becoming my wife?" he said softly to her and held his breath until she answered.

"Yes, Justin, I'll marry you. I love you so much!"

Justin removed the ring from the box and put it on Jewel's finger. It fit perfectly. Not just the size but everything about it said her name. They held each other in the moonlight, soaking up the happiness they were feeling. Finally, Jewel turned to Justin with a smile on her face and told him it was a good thing he asked her to marry him. He asked why, and she told him he risked having his mother never speak to him again. They both began to laugh, and Justin knew life with Jewel would be like a permanent holiday.

Clay and Shelby came back from their ride, and Shelby went straight to Jewel and asked to see it. Jewel asked her what she meant, trying to keep a straight face.

"Clay got me out of here so you two could be alone, and that could mean only one thing, so let's see the hand," said Shelby. Jewel raised her hand, and Shelby screamed that it was just stunningly perfect, as if it were made for her. She and Jewel hugged each other, and then Shelby hugged Justin, giving him a kiss on the cheek.

"Justin, my friend, I am incredibly impressed by your sense of style. This is classic Jewel. I always expected that one day you would hand her the biggest, shiniest, ugliest piece of rock they made. But you did good, better than good, and I love you both. Now we need some bubbly to toast."

But Clay was way ahead of her; while she was looking at the ring, he was opening a bottle of champagne, pouring out four glasses. When everyone had a glass, Clay was first to speak.

"To my newfound sister and my longtime brother, I wish you the stars and the moon, a long life, and many children."

"Hear, hear," said Shelby as she looked at Clay and gave a slight nod.

CHAPTER 14

Back in New York, Justin had to spend most of the week in the office. Jewel stayed in her apartment, resting and working on some of the patterns for the designs she drew in Bermuda. It was harder because her shoulder was still sore and stiff, but she worked anyway. Celia and Kenneth stopped by and were ecstatic to hear about their engagement. Celia thought the ring was perfect, and from Celia, that was high praise indeed. Kenneth congratulated her and wanted to know when she could come back to work; he needed her. All his people were imbeciles and didn't know what the hell they were doing, he said. It was as if someone gave them all stupid pills and he needed her to straighten things out or he'd be out of business. Kenneth always overexaggerated when things weren't going his way. She told him she would be back soon but she had to take care of some business upstate. There was a letter from the Wellers asking her to meet them at the house the next week. Justin protested because she was not fully recovered and he was afraid the stress would be too much, but she told him she needed to go, to finally get some closure. He asked her to call them and tell them she couldn't be there until Wednesday of next week. He would be finished with his contract negations and would accompany her. She told Kenneth that once she got back and got the okay from the doctor, she would be back to work. Kenneth just sighed.

Clay insisted on driving them upstate. Jewel told Justin she felt it would look odd arriving in a chauffeured limousine, so they rented a regular, midsize vehicle, but Clay still insisted he was driving them. Once they were out of the city and near the Catskills, both Clay and Justin remarked on the pleasant scenery. It was a short ride across the Rip Van Winkle Bridge and up Route 9H, and they soon arrived at Jewel's house. She wanted to go there first to see the girls that had worked for her. She had called Betty to let her know she was coming. Betty and Maria ran out as soon as they saw the car pull into the drive. Jewel got out by herself. She had told Clay beforehand that she didn't want him opening the doors for her; she didn't want to appear pretentious. Betty and Maria were so happy to see her. Even though they stayed in contact, it was wonderful to see her in person. Betty asked if her friends would like to come in, but Jewel told them that they hadn't even checked in to a motel yet, so they wouldn't be staying long, but she would be back tomorrow to see them. She told them she had to finish some business with Chris's parents and the vet clinic and that she had decided to sell the house. She told them she just became engaged to a wonderful man, so that meant she would be staying in the city. They congratulated her and told her that they wished she would have come back up here to live but wished her all the happiness in her new life.

The meeting with the Wellers was hard; it brought back so many memories, both good and bad. They were surprised when Jewel introduced Justin as her fiancé and legal counsel. They spent a few minutes going over good times, then got down to business. Chris's father told them that the new vet that Chris's partner hired, Evan Marshall, was going to rent the house, with hopes of buying it; he planned to continue the breeding program that Chris started. He said that Chase Cunningham, Chris's partner, knew Evan and his parents while they were going to school at Cornell, and they got along really well and hoped Jewel would consider selling her share of the business. Jewel said she was glad that things were working out and that Chris's breeding program would continue. Chris would be happy someone else saw the value in it. As for the practice, she would sell her share of the business to him after Justin reviewed the books and they could reach a fair settlement. As for the proceeds from the sale, she would like it to be used to buy some much-needed equipment for the clinic. Chris always said he could do more if he had an ultrasound machine. "I think having a room bearing Chris's name and the new equipment would mean a lot to the people who continue to bring their loved ones here to vets they know and trust," she said. She then asked if there was anything else they needed to discuss. It took Mr. and Mrs. Weller a few minutes to reply; both were surprised by Jewel's proposal. Mrs. Weller had tears in her eyes. Mr. Weller said, no, he didn't think there was anything else they needed to discuss, but Mrs. Weller wanted to say something to Jewel.

"What you're doing is so like you, Jewel. I remember the hours you spent driving back and forth to Albany, sitting at Chris's bedside half the night, never once complaining. The joy Chris felt when you were in his life, you made him so happy, and I will never forget what you did for his dad and me. You helped us through the worst time of our lives and never asked for a thing in return. I now understand why Chris left his share of the practice to you. I hope you will take the time once in a while and send us a note and let us know how you're doing."

"I promise I will, Mrs. Weller. Why don't I give you my address now?" Jewel wrote down her address and gave it to her; they all hugged one another and said their goodbyes. The whole experience was harder than Jewel expected, and she felt drained. She asked Clay to take her back to the motel while Justin was going over the books. She needed to lie down for a while.

Justin went over the books and spoke to Chase and Evan on Jewel's behalf. They agreed on a fair price for Jewel's share of the practice and told them that when the contracts were signed and the money transferred to Jewel's account, they should make a list of the equipment in addition to the ultrasound machine and they would have it as soon as possible. Both men were pleased with the deal and asked Justin to express their gratitude to Jewel. Chase asked how Rocky was and said to give him a belly rub for him. Justin said he would and left with Clay.

Jewel got a call at the motel from Betty and asked if she could stop by in the morning. After breakfast, they went to the house. Betty had coffee on and made some of her walnut sour cream muffins, which Jewel loved so much.

"Betty, if I knew you were going to bake these, I wouldn't have had all those pancakes," said Jewel.

"Oh, go on. You know you could always find room for one. Besides, you look like you've lost some weight, so eat up, sweetie," said Betty. "Gentlemen, would you like some coffee?"

Neither Justin nor Clay wanted any more coffee. They just wanted to be back in New York. They had had enough of the country. Betty and Maria had been doing well making their quilts and spoke to their husbands and decided they wanted to buy the house from Jewel. Jewel was ecstatic. She was so happy the girls were doing so well. She finished her muffin and coffee and told them she would get back to them as soon as possible. As she started to leave, Betty put the rest of the muffins in a bag and asked Jewel if she still had her bad dreams and longed for one of her muffins. Jewel laughed and said there was many a night she and Rocky longed for one of Betty's muffins. Betty just squealed with delight as they left.

Back at the motel, Jewel showed Justin a map of her property. Justin was surprised that Jewel owned more than seventeen acres. Jewel said she would like to sell them the half-acre the house stood on plus as much as was necessary for the driveway. The rest they would keep for possible later development. Housing developments were springing up all over the county, and Jewel had no doubt someone would want the property before long. Justin was very surprised by Jewel's business acumen and said he thought the plan was very smart. Jewel placed a call to the lawyer she used when she bought the house and asked if he had some free time to see her. She was selling the house and wanted him to act on her behalf. He said he could see her right after lunch.

They arrived promptly at one o'clock and explained what they needed done, a survey of the parcel she was selling to Betty and Maria and his handling the closing for her. After Justin explained in legal mumbo jumbo, the two lawyers shook hands and they went back to Jewel's house to talk to Betty and Maria. Jewel wanted them to be able to buy the house, so she gave them a price she knew they could afford. She explained the amount of land surrounding the house and the amount of roadway they would be getting. The two girls jumped for joy at the thought of them owning the place.

Everything had fallen into place perfectly, and all of it was settled. The lawyer would handle the contracts and everything sent to Jewel, so Justin could look it over before she signed anything. Jewel was overjoyed that it was finally over; her time spent here was good, but now she was eager to get on with her new life.

Once back in New York City, the first thing Jewel did was stop at Celia's. Celia was overcome by the news of their engagement but wished them much happiness. She told her and Kenneth about the meeting with Mr. and Mrs. Weller and that the girls were buying her house and everything was settled with the new vet. She didn't go into detail about everything, just a brief overview. They made plans to have dinner there on the following Saturday night. Jewel said she was taking Rocky back to live with her in her apartment and thanked them for keeping him. She knew it was going to be hard on the boys, so she was going up to speak to them. She asked them to really think about adopting a dog for the boys. They proved that they could be responsible and take care of one. Her talk with the boys was hard, but they knew from the beginning that the arrangement was only temporary, and they took it very well; they just asked that Jewel brought him over whenever she came to visit. She promised she would.

Clay dropped them off and carried Jewel's things in for her. Jewel could tell by the look on his face that he was sorry their time together would not be like the past few weeks. He enjoyed seeing her so often. He put her things down and said good night.

"Wait a minute, big guy," said Jewel. "Do you think you can just waltz out of here without giving me a hug? And remember, while I'm spending another week here at home, I expect to see you whenever you're free. Come for breakfast, lunch, or whatever, just come. Promise me."

"I promise, little sister," he replied and left.

Clay had a sense of uneasiness since they got back. He went to the small restaurant he visited before hoping to spot the same man that he thought was the cause of all of Jewel's problems but didn't see him, and no one else said they saw him either. Still, something bothered Clay. Clay decided to stay close to Justin and Jewel. He found himself driving around their neighborhood or parking on their street. A chill went up Clay's spine, and he couldn't remember a time he felt this uneasy.

Rocky ran through the apartment, smelling everything to acclimate himself with his new home. He especially liked the yard, which he could go out in, and made sure he marked every spot. Justin said he wanted to put his things away and would be back for their traditional Saturday-night pizza and bad sci-fi movie.

Since tomorrow was Sunday, Jewel told Justin to bring some things with him so he could stay overnight. Justin said that she should rest after her stressful trip upstate, but Jewel insisted she wanted him to stay.

Their lovemaking was adequate, but Jewel expected something more. She felt that Justin was holding back, and she didn't know if he was still concerned about her shoulder. Since she was always direct, even with him, she asked him about it. She asked if he was still concerned about her injuries. He said he was but was also thinking about her childhood and the horror she endured. He said he didn't want her to think about her past when they were making love; he didn't want to stir up any bad memories.

"Justin," she said, "when I'm with you, there is no past, only now, and what I want from you is to feel your love, your passion for me. You do feel passionate, don't you?"

"Do you mean how I want to grab you, rip your clothes off, have you in bed, on the sofa, the floor, the counters, anywhere, and everywhere? That kind of passion?" he said as he kissed her. Hard this time, not like he had ever kissed her before. They made their way to the bedroom and fell onto the bed. He unbuttoned her blouse and kissed her neck. Somehow, they managed to get their clothes off without their lips parting. He kissed every part of her. Jewel could feel herself ready for him, but he continued to ravage her with his kisses. As he looked into her eyes, he slid inside her, making her moan softly. She moved her body so she could feel him as deep in her as she could. Their bodies became one, with arms and legs wrapped around one another. He asked if he was hurting her shoulder. She said he wasn't as she turned to get on top. What she was feeling at this moment was more than she ever felt before with either Lawrence or Chris. As they turned back around, with Justin lying on top of her, she knew this was the time. As he penetrated her more deeply, they reached that point of complete elation, their bodies quivering together, holding each other closely. Justin moved to her right side, his leg still draped over her. He didn't want to put his weight on her injured left shoulder. His hand was resting on her breast, and both of them were breathless.

Pizza was ordered, and Rocky couldn't wait to have his slice; it just wasn't the same having it when he was with the boys. He missed Jewel. The movie was the typically bad sci-fi shown on Saturday nights, but to Justin and Jewel, it didn't matter. They were too deliriously happy. They made love again after the movie, then held each other as they fell asleep.

Sunday was much of the same; they were making up for all the times they thought about each other making love. As it got toward evening, Justin suggested they go out to dinner. Jewel said she would like to go to Josephina's. She wanted to tell them of their engagement. Justin wanted to go back to his apartment to shower and dress and would meet Jewel outside in forty-five minutes. Jewel quickly showered, dressed, and decided, since she had some time, she would take Rocky for a short walk so he could explore his new neighborhood. They walked up to the corner, with Rocky sniffing everything, even occasionally putting his mark over some other dogs. Jewel looked at her watch and didn't realize they were out so long; Justin would be coming out any minute. Jewel started up the three steps that led to the landing in front of her apartment house. Mrs. Shaw, the elderly woman who lived in the small apartment across the hall from Jewel, was sitting in her usual place with her webbed folding chair. She sat there every day, except when it was raining or too cold. Shelby would sometimes sit with her when she worked on Jewel's apartment, and Mrs. Shaw would tell her about her younger days, when she was a dancer in Las Vegas and how she met the man of her dreams and moved here to New York to be with him. Shelby suspected that she had a wonderful life even though she missed dancing onstage, but when she got to New York, she opened her own dance studio for children.

Jewel had started to say hello to Mrs. Shaw when she heard her name called. She turned around and was hit in the face and knocked to the ground. It took her a moment to clear her head and turn to see who hit her. As she started to get up, she was hit again; this time she went down hard. She tried to move but felt disoriented. She heard Mrs. Shaw yelling at whoever it was that was hitting her. Then she felt a kick in her side. Rocky was barking and went after the man kicking Jewel and grabbed his leg, biting with all his might, but the man pulled him off and kicked him two or three times. Rocky rolled to the ground, whimpering. Then the man continued his assault on Jewel.

Mrs. Shaw ran into the apartment house to get Aiden Murray. He was the cop who lived in the apartment behind hers, and she knew he was home, because he passed her earlier. The assault on Jewel continued. Clay was on his usual patrol around their neighborhood and came around the corner just as the man was kicking Rocky. He pulled up as fast as he could, left the car in the street, and ran to Jewel. He reached her just as Aiden was coming out. He saw Clay dive on top of the assailant and knock him to the ground. The two rolled on the ground, throwing punches at each other, but as Clay was so much bigger, he managed to pin the man down. Aiden had his handcuffs, and while Clay held him, Aiden put the handcuffs on him, but Clay continued to hold him down with his knee planted heavily on his back. He used his radio to call 911 for backup and an ambulance.

Clay ran to Jewel. Her face was covered in blood. He couldn't get a good look at her. She was curled up, with her knees to her chest and her arms around her head. He spoke her name, but she was too frightened and couldn't move. Justin was coming out of his building and wondered what was going on. Then he saw Clay, and he felt his heart starting to pound heavily in his chest. He ran toward him, praying it wasn't what he thought. If there was Clay, Jewel must be somewhere near. He quickly ran toward him. He was kneeling over Jewel. He saw another man in handcuffs and quickly surmised it had to be Jewel's stalker, Willard Russell. Justin was beside himself. This just couldn't be happening. *It can't be happening*, he kept telling himself. Even when he saw the blood covering Jewel's face, he still couldn't believe it.

"Clay, is she all right? Please tell me she's all right," cried Justin.

"I don't know, Mr. A. I just don't know. I don't want to move her until the medics get her, then we'll have a better idea what we're dealing with," answered Clay as he stood over Jewel protectively.

"How could this happen?" screamed Justin. He turned to the man who was being held by the cop and tried to get closer, screaming at him for what he did. Justin tried to punch him, but the police officer got between them and told Justin to back off. He had him in custody and personally witnessed the attack. He was just waiting for the patrol car to take him to jail. Justin pulled himself together and calmly told the cop who he was and how he had been terrorizing Jewel for months. As calmly as he could, Justin spoke to Willard Russell.

"I am a lawyer, and that woman lying on the ground is my fiancée. I will tell you now that I will use all my resources to see that you never see the light of day again."

The sirens from the ambulance were closer, and Justin had turned to go back to Jewel when he heard the prisoner say something.

"She got what she deserved for destroying my brother," he said.

Justin's anger overcame him, and he let loose with a punch right to Willard's face. Justin had never struck a man before in his life and couldn't believe what he had just done. The cop holding Willard never said anything about the hit; he just told Justin to see to the girl.

Jewel moved onto her back when she heard Clay.

"Did you get the name of that bus?" she said in typical Jewel style.

"No," Clay answered, "but we got the son of a bitch that did this to you. Try not to move until the medics take a look at you."

"Justin, where's Justin?" she said.

"I'm here, Jewel, I'm right here. Do as Clay said and don't try to move."

As if I could move, she thought to herself.

The paramedics asked them to stand back as they examined Jewel; they wanted to know exactly what happened to her, and Clay told them what he saw as he was trying to get to her. They took her vitals and asked if anyone was related. Justin explained that he was her fiancé and she had no relatives in New York. He supplied them with all the pertinent information they needed. After their examination, they called the hospital and relayed the information.

They placed Jewel on the gurney, but before they moved her, she grabbed Clay's arm and tried to speak even though she was in such pain and could feel her face swelling.

"Please, Clay."

Clay could barely make out what she was saying. He bent closer to hear her.

"Rocky, Rocky hurt bad, kicked many times. Please get to the vet. I'll be fine. Help Rocky, please." That was all she could say and then passed out. They quickly moved her to the ambulance.

Justin asked if he could go with her, but they said no. He told them which hospital she had been taken to before when she was attacked by this man and asked for her to be taken there. They had no problem with that, and Justin said he would be there as soon as possible if she asked for him.

Clay was already on his cell, first calling for a car for Justin, and then calling the emergency number for the animal hospital. Both arrived just minutes apart. Justin asked Clay to stay with Rocky and to let him know his medical status as soon as they could evaluate him. He knew Jewel would ask about Rocky before they determined what injuries she herself had sustained.

On the way to the hospital, Justin called Kenneth and Shelby. It gave him something to do rather than think about the possible injuries Jewel could have sustained. He looked down at his hand, which had begun to ache, and saw that it was slightly swollen. He was sorry that he only got to hit him once. Justin was not a violent man, but thinking about what that cretin had done to Jewel and he had no doubt that he would have hit him again and not been sorry for it.

Justin paced in the hall, waiting for someone to come out to tell him how she was. Waiting was tearing him apart. He needed to see her, to know she was all right. What would he do without her? The thought sent chills down his spine. He just couldn't stand around, doing nothing. He needed to do something. He phoned a friend of his, a criminal lawyer, and explained everything to him and asked that he do what was necessary to make sure this Russell character stayed in jail. He would update him on Jewel's injuries as soon as he found out something.

Clay phoned and told Justin that Rocky was going into emergency surgery. He had a ruptured spleen, and his right front leg was broken. They would set the leg after they stopped the internal bleeding. He might need a transfusion, and the hospital had the blood to give him. He would call back when the surgery was over, and he spoke to the doctor. He asked how bad Jewel's injuries were, but all Justin could tell him was that they were still working on her and he hadn't spoken to the doctor yet but that as soon as he had, he would call. He thanked Clay for being there, for without him, Jewel might not have survived the attack. Clay just said that was what big brothers were for.

The doctor finally came out to talk to Justin, and by the look on his face, Justin could tell her injuries must be serious.

The doctor explained that Jewel suffered a broken nose, a laceration over her left eye that would require stitches, a broken radius, which was one of the bones in her arm, several cracked ribs, and a cracked tibia or leg bone. She had bruising over most of her body, but there appeared to be no internal injuries. The plastic surgeon was going to set her nose, and she would require a cast on her left arm and leg. Since the ribs weren't fully broken, they would just wrap them. They were sending her up for an MRI because of the concussion she suffered just a few weeks ago. They needed to be sure there was no additional damage to her head. After the tests, she would be staying in the hospital for the next few days to monitor her condition. He could check at the desk later to see what room they were taking her to. Justin asked that she be placed in a private room, and the doctor said he could request it at the desk while she was getting her tests. Justin sighed. *At last, something I can do. I feel so useless.*

Why couldn't it have been me? he thought to himself. He tried not to think of what might have happened if Clay hadn't arrived when he did. He wondered why Clay was there, but he couldn't think about that now. How could he ever repay him for saving Jewel?

Kenneth and Celia arrived at the hospital and looked for Justin. They finally found him. Celia had tears in her eyes, and Kenneth didn't look much better.

"We came as soon as we heard," said Kenneth. "Is there any word on her condition?"

"I just spoke to the doctor," said Justin. "She has a broken nose, which the plastic surgeon is going to set, a laceration over her eye that will require stitches, a broken bone in her arm, some cracked ribs, and a cracked tibia. So far, they haven't found any internal injuries, and they are just taking her now to get an MRI of her head to check for concussion. I'm arranging for her to be put into a private room when they finish the tests."

"I can't believe any of this," cried Celia. "Why? Where were the police? They knew who the man was. Why didn't they pick him up before he had the chance to hurt her again? I just don't believe they let this happen." Kenneth tried to calm his wife, but she was having none of it. She wanted someone held accountable.

"Your message was a little vague when you called," said Kenneth. "Do we know the whole story yet?"

Just as Justin was about to tell them what he saw, Detectives Leeds and Beach showed up with Clay.

"Any word on her condition?" asked Beach.

"On her condition?" screamed Celia. "If you had done your jobs and arrested this...this Willard Russell, Jewel wouldn't be here getting stitched up and having casts put on her broken bones and everything else they have to do to her and all the pain she must be going through. How you can even show your faces here is beyond me. Kenneth, get me away from these...these so-called detectives, who can't even catch someone even when they know his name. No wonder the crime rate is soaring in the city."

"Calm down, Celia. Let's get some coffee. I'm sure they need to speak to Justin. Justin, can we get you some coffee? Would anyone like something?" asked Kenneth.

"No, thank you," answered Justin. The rest just shook their heads.

"I must apologize for Celia, gentlemen. She is very close to Jewel," said Justin.

"No problem," replied Detective Beach. "We've had worse. Besides, she's got a good point. How come we couldn't find this guy? Lowlifes like this one are good at getting lost if they want to, and this is a big city. Clay filled us in on everything. Anything you'd like to add, Mr. Angelis?"

"Not really. Clay was there before me, so I'm sure you have the entire story. Have you spoken with any of the people who live in the apartment house that witnessed the attack?"

"Yeah," said Detective Leeds. "We have statements from Mrs. Shaw and a few others as well as patrolman, Aiden Murray. All the statements are pretty much the same. Having Clay and Murray right there probably saved her life."

"Well, we have enough for now," said Beach, "but we will still need you to come downtown to give us your statement. With your being a lawyer, I'm sure you know how this works."

"I'll be there as soon as I can. I can't leave until I know how Jewel is. I'm sure you understand," said Justin. "Clay, how was Rocky doing when you left him?"

"He was good. Tough little guy. They had him slightly sedated so he wouldn't move around too much. I'm going back up as soon as I give them my statement," said Clay.

"Excellent! Thank you, Clay. I'll talk with you two later," Justin said to the detectives.

"You take all the time you need, Mr. Angelis. With Clay coming with us now and Murray on his way down already, you just come when you can," said Beach.

Kenneth and Celia were on their way back and passed the detectives in the hall. Kenneth warned her not to say a word as they passed by. Kenneth brought coffee for Justin, just in case he changed his mind. Justin took the coffee thanked him and told them what the police wanted and that they had very good eyewitness accounts of the attack. Clay was going down to give his statement, as well as the patrolman who was there to help Clay. He told them that one of the women who lived in the building and was sitting outside was the first to see Russell hit Jewel. She ran in and got patrolman Murray, who fortunately also lived in the building. By the time he could get there, Clay had tackled Russell and the two of them were fighting on the ground, but with Murray's help, they managed to subdue him. Unfortunately, Jewel had already sustained the worst of her injuries. Murray immediately called for assistance and an ambulance. Celia didn't want to hear any more; it was all too awful, so she went to find someplace quiet to sit and drink her coffee until someone could finally tell them how Jewel was. The wait seemed to take forever. Celia called the house to check on the boys. They were fine and wanted to know when they would be home. She told them soon but to go ahead and have their dinner. As Celia got off the phone, Shelby wandered in. She had been on Staten Island when she got the call from Justin.

Shelby went to sit by Celia, and Celia filled her in on what was going on. Now both women were in tears. Celia continued her tirade against the police, while poor Shelby just sat and listened, trying to understand how this could happen. It was all so awful. A week ago they were lounging in the sun, enjoying life, and now Jewel was fighting for hers.

A nurse finally told Justin that Jewel had been taken to her room but that the doctor had given strict orders that she couldn't have any visitors except him until he had all the test back and that they were keeping her slightly sedated for the pain. Justin's immediate thought was of Rocky; both he and the person he loved were being kept sedated. He meant to ask if Rocky had taken a good bite out of Russell. He hoped so. One couldn't help but have respect for an animal that would put his life on the line for the one he loved, and there was no doubt that he loved Jewel.

Justin told everyone to go home and that he would call if there was any new information on Jewel's condition. The women gave him a hug, and Kenneth told him that if he needed anything, anything at all, to please call, no matter what time it was. They all left, and suddenly, Justin felt so alone.

He decided to call his mother to tell her about the latest events. Somehow, even as old as he was, he always felt better after talking to her. They spoke for a few minutes, and then Justin went to find Jewel's room. They had her in the intensive care facility, which made Justin feel as though the doctor hadn't told him everything about Jewel's injuries. A few nurses were in the room, fussing over the monitors and making sure the IV units were set to the proper dosage. He asked them if she could hear him, but they said probably not because of the sedation meds she was getting. They all smiled and left the room, leaving him to gaze upon the woman he loved.

Her nose had been set with bandages holding everything in place. She had stitches above her eyebrow, and her beautiful face was now shades of purple and blue. She had a cast on her left arm, and while he couldn't see the rest, he knew she had a cast on her left leg and her ribs were wrapped. Looking at her now was more than he could bear. He held his head in his hands and cried and cried and cried. There was nothing he could do for her. His vast knowledge, his wealth and connections, none of it meant anything now. He thought about how happy she made him, and it made him cry harder.

A nurse came into the room and asked if there was anything he needed. He found that he was not embarrassed in the least having her see him cry. She laid her hand on his shoulder and assured him that she was in no pain and would sleep through the night and that maybe he should go home and get some rest himself. He thanked her for her concern but said that he was not leaving her. About a half-hour later, she was back and brought him a sandwich and coffee, saying that if he planned to stay with her all night, he would need to keep up his strength. He wouldn't be any help to Jewel if he let himself get run down. She wouldn't leave until Justin promised her that he would eat the sandwich. His first thought was that he couldn't possibly eat while Jewel lay there broken, but after taking the first bite, he realized he was hungry after all. The nurse was right; he had to remain strong, for there was no way of knowing how long Jewel would take to fully recover.

Justin fell asleep in the chair and was suddenly awakened by alarms and ringing and nurses running into the room. They asked him to please leave, but he refused, but he backed into the corner so he wouldn't be in their way. The doctor arrived and got the reports from the nurses that were attending to her. He checked her eyes with a small light and looked at the paper record from one of the machines. He looked somber as he explained to Justin that Jewel had slipped into a coma and that they were taking her down for another MRI. He had no explanation for the coma and said that she had been doing fine, her vitals had all been normal, and he could not explain this sudden turn of events.

A shroud of fear engulfed Justin. He couldn't breathe. He could feel his heart racing within his chest. His hands were numb. As they rolled Jewel quickly out of the room, the nurse who had brought Justin the sandwich stayed behind. Justin said he thought he might throw up the sandwich he had just eaten. She told Justin to sit down and put his head between his knees and try to breathe slowly. Apparently, she had noticed that he was hyperventilating. He began to breathe slower and could feel the pins and needles leaving his hands. He told her he was all right and was sorry for any inconvenience he caused. This time, he was embarrassed by his lack of control. *Strong, Justin,* he thought to himself, *you must remain strong.* He repeated it over and over in his mind until he felt it in his entire being. *Strong, strong, strong.*

Jewel was brought back to her room after having another MRI scan. Her doctor told Justin he couldn't understand why she was in a coma, especially since all her test came back normal. They suggested that maybe if they started to slowly decrease her pain meds, the pain might wake her up. Justin was uncomfortable with that; he couldn't stand to think of Jewel in pain. He suggested that they wait one more day, and if she hadn't awakened by then, they could start decreasing the pain medication. Everyone was in agreement to wait one more day.

Clay surprised the vet that was caring for Rocky by saying that he was prepared to sleep near him all night. The vet said that it wasn't necessary because they had a vet tech that remained through the night to monitor all the animals, but Clay insisted that Rocky needed someone he knew to be with him. The vet warned Clay that he was still worried about the possibility of his brain swelling, which could be very serious. Clay said he understood and that was all the more reason to have someone he knew with him, in case he took a turn for the worse. Shelby had agreed to stay with Rocky during the day, but nighttime, Clay would stay. Clay unrolled his sleeping bag and made himself comfortable next to Rocky. He opened the cage and put his hand next to Rocky's nose so he could smell him, then he stroked his head, closed the door, and talked to him softly. The vet tech that was monitoring Rocky's vitals was surprised when she saw that Rocky's breathing became more regular. Rocky had been sedated, but the little dog was still restless, but with the touch and smell from Clay, he seemed to drift off to a much more normal sleep.

After the second night, Clay felt good about Rocky's condition. He told the vet when he came not to worry about the swelling of his brain. He would be just fine. The vet asked the tech if Clay did anything to Rocky. She stated he did what he did every night, let Rocky smell him, stroked his head, and slept by him, talking softly. Clay brought food for Rocky, and the vet was surprised when the dog responded. The vet told Clay that maybe he was in the wrong kind of work; clearly, he had an incredible gift for dealing with animals. Clay just bowed his head and said he would be back again tonight and Rocky would be well soon.

Justin had been up for two nights. He was exhausted, and now there was a crisis in the office. Celia told the parties involved that Justin was out of the office but she would get ahold of him and call them back. Justin had been working too long on this project, and it meant a great deal of money for the law firm, so he had to handle it. He told Celia to tell them that he was flying back from California and could meet with them at six o'clock that evening in his office or early the following morning. Either way, Justin could go home and try to get a few hours sleep and still have some time to go over the prospectus for the new corporation. He was elated when Celia called and said they would prefer to meet in the morning. He would stay with Jewel until the afternoon, then go home and get some sleep. He asked Celia to bring him all the latest paperwork so he could go over everything at home.

Celia brought the papers to the hospital and told Justin he looked like hell and that he should go home and she would stay with her for a while. Justin agreed but said he would be back before evening and that he would look over the paperwork while sitting with Jewel.

Clay arrived at the hospital early and told Justin he had a car waiting downstairs for him and that he would sit with Jewel. Justin told him that there was no change in her condition. Clay tried to reassure Justin that Jewel was a fighter and she would come out of it soon.

At mid-afternoon, Evelyn appeared. She summoned Clay from the room and told him to explain to the nurse who she was. Since her name was not on the list of visitors, they were not going to let her into Jewel's room. Clay told the nurse Justin would want his mother to be at her future daughter-in-law's bedside and that he would take full responsibility for her. The nurse finally gave in and added her name to the list.

Evelyn was not prepared for what she saw and had to hold on to Clay for a moment.

"My god, Clay, what have they done to her?" she said. "What kind of monster could do something like this?"

"A monster indeed," answered Clay.

"I understand you were the one to save her. Well, I hope you gave him something he will remember for some time," said Evelyn. Clay said nothing specific but added that Rocky got in a pretty good bite.

"How is he? Justin said he had been hurt quite badly."

"Yes," replied Clay, "a broken leg and some cracked ribs. But he is a fighter, like his owner. They will both do well, of that I am certain."

"This coma business worries me," said Evelyn. "If all her tests came back normal, why won't she wake up?"

"Sometimes people don't want to wake up. Things from their past haunt them," said Clay.

"Things from their past, yes, things from their past. Clay, I think you may be right. Well, I'm here now, so if you have anything you need to do, go along, then," said Evelyn.

Clay left Evelyn in the room. He really didn't have anything specific to do but decided to call Shelby and see if she would like to have dinner with him before he went to stay with Rocky. Shelby suggested they meet at Jewel's apartment and send for takeout. Shelby needed to water the plants and make sure things were ready for Rocky. The vet said that he was making such good progress and would be able to go home in a day or two. Shelby planned to stay in the apartment to take care of him. It meant putting some work on hold, but she knew if roles were reversed, Jewel would do the same for her. Clay said he would stay with Rocky so she could continue working. They divided up the hours as they had dinner. Shelby was grateful that Clay could work around her schedule because she really needed to finish this job she was doing. Then she would have more free time for when Jewel came home. Clay was certain it wouldn't be long.

Evelyn moved her chair closer to Jewel. She wanted to hold her hand but hesitated because even her hands were swollen and bruised. A nurse came in to check the IVs and to turn Jewel slightly. Even though they had her on a special mattress, they needed to check her back for any sore spots. As the nurse turned Jewel, Evelyn got a better look at the extensive bruising. She couldn't help but tear up when she saw her injuries. Her back, her legs, there wasn't a place on her body that wasn't bruised or swollen. The nurse saw Evelyn wipe her eyes and tried to assure her that Jewel was young and strong and was doing much better than when they brought her in. Yes, said Evelyn, but she wasn't in a coma then. The nurse quietly left the room.

"All right, Jewel, time to wake up. I didn't travel all the way down here to stare at you sleeping," said Evelyn. "I think Clay was right when he said some people have pasts that haunt them. I think maybe you do, and that's why you won't wake up. I know about Chris and his death, and I know somewhere deep inside you still feel guilty about the day he died. You wonder if it would have been different if you had gone with him. No one could possibly know the answer. It was an accident, part of life. He might have died even if you were with him. You were not to blame. Even his parents didn't hold you responsible. You are not responsible for his death, but I'll tell you what you are responsible for, and that is my son's happiness. Justin loves you. I never thought he would find someone to love, but he loves you with all his heart. What happened in the past, you can't do anything about, but you can do something about the here and now. Wake up, Jewel, wake up and let Justin love you. He needs you, and you need him. Wake up, darling. Justin's waiting for you."

Evelyn noticed Jewel's reaction whenever she said Justin's name. Jewel seemed to be getting restless; she moved her hand, the one Evelyn was holding.

"Yes, darling, yes, open your eyes, Jewel," pleaded Evelyn.

Justin stood in the doorway of the room, listening to his mother.

"Hello, Mother," he said. "I didn't know you were here."

"Justin..." The word came out so softly neither heard it.

"Justin…" This time they both heard it and looked at Jewel.

"I'm here, Jewel, I'm right here," he said. "Jewel, can you open your eyes? Open your eyes, Jewel. I need to see those beautiful green eyes. Please, Jewel, open your eyes for me."

Jewel's eyes fluttered slightly. Justin asked his mother to go and get the nurse. As Evelyn was getting up, Jewel's eyes opened. Evelyn stood there, not able to move, tears running down her cheeks. Justin asked her again to get the nurse. Evelyn went running out the door to the nurse's station and asked someone to come quickly.

"Come quickly!" yelled Evelyn. "I think she's waking up!"

"Justin, I'm so glad you're here. I must have fallen asleep."

"Yes, but you're awake now," he said.

"Where am I, Justin? What happened? Is this a cast on my arm? What happened? I can't remember. Was I in an accident?"

"That can all wait, Jewel. I'll explain everything, I promise. Please tell me how you feel," pleaded Justin.

"I don't know. I'm not sure. My head hurts a little, and my back. Am I in the hospital? How long have I been here?"

A doctor and a nurse came into the room with Evelyn and asked Justin to step aside so he could examine her. He checked her eyes with his penlight, lifted her head slightly, asking her if it hurt. She replied, "Just a little." He asked her if she knew where she was, and she replied she thought she was in a hospital. He then asked her if she remembered coming to the hospital, and she replied that she didn't. He asked her what the last thing she did remember, but Jewel didn't answer. He asked her again, and this time she said she was in Bermuda. Jewel was becoming increasingly agitated. The doctor ordered a sedative for her and told Justin that it was not all that uncommon for people not to remember some of the past days, or weeks even. He told them not to worry. All her vitals were good, and there didn't appear to be any pressure behind her eyes. But they were going to take another CT scan just to be sure everything was normal.

Evelyn, who was usually so strong and whom Justin depended on for her clarity in situations like these, seemed to be falling apart. She was clearly distressed, and Justin made her sit down.

"Mother," said Justin calmly. "What's wrong? This is good news. She's finally awake."

"I'm afraid I may have done something wrong. Oh, Justin, I thought I was doing the right thing, but she can't remember. Maybe I pushed too hard."

"What are you talking about? Pushed her how, Mother? Tell me what you mean," he said, losing his patience with her.

Evelyn cried into her handkerchief, shaking her head.

"Mother, pull yourself together and tell me what you did," said Justin angrily.

Evelyn pulled herself upright in the chair, wiped her eyes, and looked at her son.

"I told her that she wasn't to blame for Chris's death, and if she was still feeling guilty, she should stop. It was an accident, and there was nothing she could have done. Terrible things happen in life, and we can't blame ourselves for all of them. I said she wasn't responsible for Chris but she had a responsibility now, and that was to you. I told her I didn't want you to be hurt and she had to wake up. Oh, Justin, if I said anything to upset her or make things worse, I'm so sorry. I meant well, my darling. Please believe me, I meant well."

"I know you did, Mother," said Justin. He took her quivering hands in his, and as much as he wanted to scream at her for possibly making things worse, he didn't. Instead, he told her everything would be all right. He tried to assure her that what she said probably didn't make any difference and that when Jewel got some proper rest and some answers to her questions, she would begin to remember everything.

Clay walked in as Justin was comforting his mother. He wasn't due at the vets' for another few hours. When he saw the bed missing and Evelyn crying, with Justin trying to comfort her, he immediately became concerned. Justin saw Clay and the expression on his face and thought he better tell him what was going on. Evelyn told Clay that she might have made things worse, but Clay told her not to worry; Jewel was strong and would regain her memory. He thought he would lighten the mood a bit and told them that the vet said Rocky could go home in a few days. He was eating well and, for the first time, tested out his plastered front leg by walking over to Clay. Clay told them about the arrangement he and Shelby made for when Rocky came home. It was great news, especially to Justin. When Jewel regained her memory, he knew the first thing she would ask about was Rocky, and he wanted to be able to give her some good news. Clay stayed a while longer, until Jewel was returned to her room. As the doctor said, everything was normal. Jewel was still slightly sleepy from the sedative they gave her, but when they finally got her settled comfortably in the bed, she looked at Clay.

"Big brother," she said.

"Little sister," replied Clay, smiling. Rocky's good, waiting for you."

"Tell him soon" was all she said, then she drifted off to sleep.

Justin and Evelyn both looked at Clay with amazement. Justin started to laugh. Evelyn insisted on knowing what he was laughing about and what all the "big brother, little sister" stuff had to do with anything. Clay tried not to laugh, but it pleased him to see Justin finally let go. Justin got up and walked to Clay, and the two men embraced each other, laughing. Clay could feel the tears rolling down Justin's cheeks, and he held him close. The bond they shared was greater now and would always be so.

Kenneth walked in on the laughing men and said that there must be good news if they were laughing. The two men pulled apart, holding out their arms for Kenneth to join them. He walked into their arms, and they told him that Jewel had awakened. Evelyn sat there feeling left out of something that was obviously important, but she decided to let the men have their moment.

The nurse came into the room and reminded them that there were too many people in the room and that Jewel needed her rest. Clay said he needed to go anyway to stay with Rocky, and Kenneth said that since Jewel was out of the coma and sleeping peacefully, he would go home and stop back tomorrow, hopefully when she was awake. Justin bade them good night and asked his mother if she would like to get a little dinner while Jewel slept.

CHAPTER 15

The following morning, Jewel was fully awake. They brought her a breakfast tray with some tea and toast. The nurse tried to explain to her that she hadn't had any food for three days and needed to take it slowly. Just about that time, Justin came waltzing in with coffee.

"I knew since you were awake, the first thing you'd be yelling for would be coffee," he said.

"Sir, I'm not sure she should have that yet," said the nurse.

"Nonsense. She would have it in her IV if you let her," he said and handed the coffee to Jewel.

"Justin, you're a lifesaver. Did I tell you I love you?" she said.

"No, I'm pretty sure you did not," he replied.

"Well, come give me a kiss and I will," said Jewel.

The nurse just shook her head and left the room, telling Justin that she would have to mark the chart that the patient had coffee and who gave it to her. Justin said she might take the tray but to leave the toast; he would make sure she ate some of it.

Justin went to Jewel and bent down to kiss her.

"I love you," she said, "and I'll have some toast, please." She smiled at him as she polished off the slice of toast and most of the coffee and said it was a good thing the cast was on her left arm, or she wouldn't be able to eat. Justin laughed and told her that if that was the case, he would gladly feed her. Jewel lay back, slightly exhausted. It finally hit her just how weak she felt.

"Feel better?" he asked.

"A little, but I'd feel much better if you told me what I'm doing here. You promised," she said.

"You remembered that?" he said, surprised.

"Of course. I remember everything you tell me—well, almost everything," she answered.

"All right, Jewel, but let's take this slowly," he said. "What is the last thing you remember?"

"We were in Bermuda."

"And then we came home," said Justin.

"Yes, then we came home and you had to go to work," she said.

"That's right, I had to go to work. Do you remember anything else?" he said, trying not to rush her. "Do you remember pizza night?"

"Pizza night?"

"Yes, pizza night. Your Saturday-night ritual, pizza and a bad sci-fi movie. Rocky eating his slice of pizza. Don't you remember?" he said, slightly frustrated.

"Oh, pizza night, you mean the night we made love. How could I forget that?" She laughed.

Justin felt his eyes begin to swell with tears. He bowed his head so she wouldn't see him crying.

"Justin, what's wrong?" she asked. "Why are you crying?"

"I'm sorry, I was just so afraid you wouldn't remember anything about us. When the doctor asked you what you remembered yesterday after you awoke out of the coma, all you said was Bermuda. I was just so afraid you wouldn't remember all the rest."

"I'm sorry, that was all I did remember, but I woke up last night looking for you, and it was all there, everything, up until we were going to Josephina's for dinner. I think I was waiting for you, I remember that, but I can't remember anything else."

"Yes, that was Sunday. I stayed over all day. Then we decided to go out for dinner, and I went home to shower and change," he said.

"Right, and you always take forever, so I took Rocky for a walk."

Jewel was beginning to breathe faster now and was getting restless. Justin thought it was enough for now, but Jewel insisted he help her remember. He warned her that the doctor said to go slow, that forcing the memories could cause a setback. Jewel was relentless; she wanted to know how she ended up in the hospital.

She asked if she had been hit by a car, but Justin said no, that it wasn't a car.

Jewel practiced what she knew best for calming herself down in unpleasant situations. She knew Justin would go no further if he thought she was getting excited. Slowly her breathing returned to a normal pace, and she stopped fidgeting with the sheets. When she felt she had eased Justin's concerns, she calmly asked him to tell her the parts that were missing. Justin got a short reprieve while the doctor made his evening rounds and was once again coming into Jewel's room. He examined her carefully, checking her leg cast and the rest of her body, while Justin took a short walk. Jewel was not prepared for what she saw when the doctor had the sheet off her legs.

"Should I guess that the rest of my body is the same as my legs?" she said calmly.

"You'd be guessing correctly. You are one gigantic bruise, a few cracked ribs, broken nose, concussion, and I'll bet you can guess why the casts are on," said the doctor.

"I'm thinking broken bones?" she replied.

"Right again. You are one lucky lady," he said. "I'm surprised there was no internal damage from the beating you took." The doctor's face froze. How could he let that slip? She had no memory of what happened. What would he do if she asked him about the beating? He just continued to talk about this and that, hoping like hell she wouldn't ask him anything else. He finished his exam and covered her up and told her he would be back in the morning, and then he practically ran out of the room, bumping into Justin. He quickly pulled him aside and told him about the slip of the tongue he just had while examining her. Justin asked the doctor if she asked him anything, and he said no. Justin told him it was all right; he had planned to tell her everything tonight. The doctor warned him again about taking it slow. Justin told him that with Jewel, you worked according to her schedule, not necessarily the preferred one. The doctor said he would return in the morning to see if she thought she was ready to get out of bed and sit up for a while. There was always the danger of blood clots when patients stayed without moving for long periods. The sooner they got her up, the better.

Justin went to the men's room to splash some cold water on his face; he knew the next half-hour was going to be difficult. He returned and noticed her calmness. He didn't like what he was feeling. He wished Clay were there with him. "I won't ask any questions until you're done, so just start at the place where I'm waiting for you, my last memory," she said.

"You were walking Rocky while I showered and changed. You remember that we were going to Josephina's for dinner," he said. He waited, but there was no response from Jewel, so he continued.

"As you were walking back to your apartment, someone called your name. You turned to see who it was and was struck in the face, knocking you to the ground. When you tried to get up, you were struck again. At this time, Rocky came to your defense and grabbed the leg of your assailant, giving him quite a nasty bite, but the assailant managed to free himself of the dog and kicked him a few times and sent him flying through the air. He lay there, too injured to get up."

At this point, Jewel began to cry. Justin knew she would as soon as he told her about Rocky's heroism and injuries, but he continued on.

"The assailant then turned his full attention toward you, and while you were still on the ground, he just began punching and kicking you. Fortunately, you were rolled up in a fetal position, so he couldn't kick you in the chest or stomach. So he kept hitting your back and legs, and your arm was broken when he kicked you. A Mrs. Shaw from the building had been sitting outside when it started and ran inside to get the policeman who lived across the hall from you. I think you know him, Aiden Murray. But before anyone could come to your rescue, Clay appeared out of nowhere, tackled the man, and fought with him, holding him down, until Murray came out and handcuffed him. He immediately called for an ambulance and backup. The police came and took him away, and the paramedics brought you here. At one point, they thought they lost you and had to use the paddles to restart your heart. You were brought into emergency, and tests were done to determine your condition. The plastic surgeon set your broken nose, and the casts were placed on the leg that had a cracked bone and your arm that had been broken. Some of your ribs were cracked, and those they just wrapped. They put you here in the immediate care room because they feared there might be some swelling in your brain. CT scans were done, as well as an MRI. Everything seemed normal. But then you slipped into a coma. The following day, they took another MRI, but everything was normal, and the doctor had no reason for the coma. And that pretty much covers it up until the point where you woke up."

"Where's Rocky?" Jewel asked.

"He's at the vets. He is doing well. He suffered a few cracked ribs, and his front leg was broken. You yourself told Clay to stay with Rocky and get him medical help before they took you away," answered Justin. "Clay has been sleeping with him every night so he wouldn't be alone, and Shelby stays most of the day. They even have a schedule worked out for staying with him for when he comes home, which will be later this afternoon. Clay said he really took a good bite out of the man who attacked you. Quite a loyal and brave friend you have there."

Jewel wiped her eyes and closed them as she lay back on the bed. She lay still and quiet for some time, and Justin was beginning to think that maybe he had told her too much too fast, but she opened her eyes and asked him who did this to her. Justin told her who it was and that he was responsible for everything. She asked why, and Justin explained how he blamed her for ruining his brother's life. He had just gotten out of prison and expected to be living high off his brother, who supposedly was doing so well. "Lawrence tried to explain that it wasn't your fault, but he needed someone to take his anger out on, and you were it. He is on parole and been charged with attempted murder, so he will be spending a very long time in prison."

Jewel said nothing for a while and then asked when she would be able to leave the hospital. Justin told her, now that she was awake and had regained most of her memory, he would guess in a few days. Justin was curious that she didn't ask a single question other than to ask about Rocky. Justin wished someone else were there to speak to her; maybe she would be more like herself. This calm and reserved demeanor was definitely not Jewel, and as if he could hear Justin's thoughts, Clay appeared. He looked at Jewel, and all he said was,

"Little sister knows," and she answered, "Yes." Clay put his hand on Justin's shoulder. Justin never understood the power that was in this man's touch. He felt more peaceful than he had in the past hours. Justin still hadn't asked him how he got to Jewel so quickly, and he didn't think he ever would. It didn't matter. What mattered was that he was there and had saved her life. Clay said he was going to pick up Rocky and bring him home. Jewel just responded with a nod. Justin didn't understand the silent communication the two of them shared. They never spoke actual words out loud, but they always knew what the other meant.

Jewel was tired; she had so much to digest. She asked Justin to please ask the nurse if she could have something for her headache. Justin left the room. Jewel didn't want him to see her anger. She pounded the bed with her good arm while letting out a mean growl, but she didn't cry. Justin returned with the nurse and something for her headache. After she took the pills, she lay back and closed her eyes. Justin asked her if she would like him to leave while she tried to sleep, but she said no; she just needed a few quiet minutes.

Evelyn felt so guilty for upsetting Jewel she just had to apologize again to her son. Upon entering the room, she saw Jewel lying quietly, as though she were sleeping, and she didn't want to wake her. Softly she called to Justin. He didn't hear her, so she called a little louder, "Justin." Immediately Jewel's eyes opened, and Justin became alarmed.

"What's wrong, Jewel? What's wrong?" he asked.

"The voice, it's the voice," she answered.

"What voice?" he replied.

"The voice that told me to wake up, the voice that I heard when I was asleep. The voice that said you needed me and I had to wake up," she said, slightly agitated.

"I'm sorry, Jewel, I didn't hear a voice," he said.

"I know I heard it," she said.

Evelyn, who was standing in the doorway and who couldn't be seen by Jewel, came into the room. "Justin, I just came by to apologize again," she said.

"Evelyn," said Jewel. "It was you. It was you talking to me, wasn't it? I know it was. I remember your voice."

"Yes, darling," answered Evelyn. "I sat and held your hand and told you how we were so worried about you."

"You told me I wasn't responsible for Chris's accident. That I shouldn't feel guilty because he was dead and I was alive. You said I was responsible for Justin's happiness, so I needed to wake up and prove I loved him," cried Jewel.

"Mother, how could you?" said Justin. "I'm sorry now that I allowed you to be let into the room."

"Please, darling, I meant well," said Evelyn, tearing up.

"It's okay, Justin. I had to hear it," said Jewel, "because on some level I did feel guilty for being alive. I know it was irrational, but it was there. I remember closing my eyes and being in pain and thought it must be my time to make amends for Chris's death that I would never wake up again. I heard the voice in my head, and I felt someone touching me. And I knew I wasn't dead. I thought it was an angel telling me to wake up. I kept hearing your name, and then I heard your voice, the voice that belonged to the only man I ever truly loved. And I had to see him. I thanked the angel for opening my eyes."

Evelyn stood next to Justin, crying and shaking so much that Justin got up and helped her sit down. He asked her if she was all right. Should he get a doctor? He had never seen his mother this emotional, not even when his father died. He wasn't sure what to do next: go to Jewel, who was still in tears, or help his mother? He decided to do nothing and let happen whatever was supposed to happen. Evelyn slowly calmed down and looked at Jewel for forgiveness. Jewel tried to pull herself up and put out her good hand to Evelyn. Evelyn was so happy; she took Jewel's hand in hers and brought it to her face. Jewel could feel Evelyn's tears.

"Thank you for telling me what I needed to hear. You are my angel, and always will be." Jewel pulled Evelyn to her, and they embraced. Justin watched as the two women he loved with all his heart embraced each other, and he cried.

Clay and Shelby rearranged Jewel's bedroom so the hospital bed Justin ordered would fit. He also ordered nurses around the clock, which angered Jewel, but she gave in when he promised her it would just be for the first two weeks, then depending on how well she did, they would renegotiate whether they stayed or not. Rocky was doing well, and they placed the large pillow bed Shelby bought for him by the side of the hospital bed. While Shelby made up the bed, Clay went to get Justin and Jewel.

Maneuvering out of the hospital bed into a wheelchair, then into the car, then being carried by Clay and put back into bed had taken its toll on Jewel. She was exhausted but would not rest until she held Rocky. Clay put the little dog next to her on the bed. Rocky cried, and so did Jewel. Clay put Rocky back on his bed next to Jewel. You could almost see the happiness he felt being united with her. Jewel took her pain pill and said she would see everyone later, then drifted off to sleep. It was the first really peaceful sleep she had after she and Justin made love. It seemed a lifetime ago.

A month went by, and Jewel had x-rays taken of her ribs and leg. The cast was removed from her leg, and the wrap-around her ribs was also removed, with the doctor's orders that she still had a long way to go and no to do anything strenuous and to use her cane when walking. Jewel was eager to get out of the apartment, but her bruises made it impossible to go anywhere without people staring at her, so for a while longer, she remained sitting in her little yard with Rocky. She spent the day sketching or reading. Her friends stopped by at sporadic intervals, and Justin had to work most days now but tried to come home early. Shelby and Justin took turns staying over so she wouldn't be alone. Shelby and Aiden Murray, the cop across the hall, started seeing each other regularly, and it was wonderful to see Shelby so happy. Clay would stop in occasionally just to see how she was coming along, but he never stayed long.

Halfway into the third month, the cast on her arm was removed. Jewel had amazing recuperative abilities, and when the doctor checked her X-rays, he was amazed that the broken bone had healed so quickly but again reminded her to take it slowly. Jewel was patient; she knew she would need all the strength she had.

At the end of the third month, Jewel asked Justin to accompany her to the doctor. Shelby had gone with her the last time without telling Justin. Justin was surprised that she needed to see the doctor again after such a short time. When they arrived at the address Jewel had given Clay, Justin was surprised that it wasn't her usual doctor. When he asked her about it, she just replied that she needed to have another exam to be sure all the female parts inside weren't damaged in the attack. Justin didn't appear to be surprised at all by her comment. Jewel was called in and had a short conversation with the doctor, and then she lay on the table. The doctor was about to perform an ultrasound of her abdomen. When the doctor found what she had been looking for, she sent her nurse to ask Justin to come in. Justin suddenly became worried; she had been through so much, and he hoped they didn't find anything else wrong. Justin entered the room and saw Jewel lying on the bed, with the doctor passing an instrument of some kind over her stomach. He asked if everything was all right, and the doctor, who was viewing a small TV screen with blotches of gray and white, said everything was perfect. She asked Justin if he would like a better look, but Justin said he wouldn't know what he was looking at.

"You're looking at your son," said Jewel.

Justin took a step backward, hitting the wall behind him. "Doctor," he said, "what am I looking at?"

The doctor pointed out a small peanut-shaped area and said, "That, Justin, is your son, and as far as I can tell, all parts are perfect, just the way they should be." It took a few more seconds for Justin to grasp what the doctor just told him, and when the shock was over, all he could say was "How?" The doctor calmly said, "In the usual way," and she and Jewel laughed. Justin's face turned red, and he admitted he knew how.

"But when?" he asked. Jewel said it must have been the day of the attack.

"But you had all those tests, all the x-rays. Are you sure it's all right?" he asked.

The doctor assured him that the tests she had when she was first admitted to the hospital would not affect the fetus, and after the first month, all the tests, especially the x-rays, were always done with a lead blanket over her in case she was pregnant.

"Did you know?" he asked Jewel.

"After the first month, I suspected I might be, so we took extra precautions when they did the tests," answered Jewel. "What do you think? Are you ready to become a father?"

"I don't know. I still can't believe it. Doctor, you're absolutely sure?"

The doctor laughed and said she was printing him a copy of the baby so there would be no doubt; he could look at it anytime he had doubts. The printer kicked out the copy, and she handed it to Justin. She had to point out the area that was the baby because all Justin said he saw were some lines. After he recognized the part that was his son, his face beamed with delight. He sat on the bed and showed Jewel.

"I'm having a son—I mean, we're having a son! Jewel, we're having a baby, a son. I can't believe it! How do you feel? Are you all right? Doctor, is she all right? I mean, after all she's been through, will this be too much for her?"

"I'll be fine, Justin, don't worry," Jewel replied.

"She was incredibly lucky with the injuries she sustained," said the doctor, "but she's fine, and so is the baby. She still has to take it easy for at least another month, though, so those broken and cracked bones knit well, but there's no reason to worry that she won't carry to her due date, which would put us at or around March 10. Justin, think you'll be ready by then? I'm just toying with you, but believe me, by the ninth month, you'll be crying for this to be over. Jewel, I'm going to give you a script for vitamins that I want you to take daily, and I'd like to see you in a month. That's it, guys. Congratulations." She wiped the gel off Jewel's belly and helped her up.

"Take good care of her, Dad," said the doctor as she started to leave the room.

Jewel was still sitting on the bed. She got up and moved to Justin. "I know it's quite a surprise. Are you okay?" she asked.

Justin felt like he had been holding his breath. No words would come out. Here was the woman he loved, the woman he wanted to spend the rest of his life with, and now she gave him the most wonderful news he ever received. All he could do was look at this beautiful person standing tall in front of him, and despite all the horror she had been through the past few months, she asked him if he was okay. He was better than okay; he felt like he owned the moon and the stars, and he wanted to tell her that, but all that came out of his mouth was, "Yes, I'm okay." Jewel gathered her things and walked out of the doctor's office, with Justin following slowly behind. He had to think to make his legs move. They waited for the elevator. Not a word had been spoken since they left the doctor's office, and Jewel was worried that Justin was having second thoughts about the baby.

Justin helped Jewel into the elevator, and suddenly, all the love and excitement that he had been holding inside finally found its way out. He moved closer to Jewel and wrapped his arms around her, being careful not to hold her too tight because of her ribs. He buried his face in her copper curls. She sensed that he had begun to cry. She pulled away and looked at him. He did have tears in his eyes.

"I thought I was the happiest, the luckiest man on earth, because I had you, and now I can't find the words to describe what I'm feeling. I have never been at a loss for words before, but you, my darling, you have filled my heart with such love. I stand before you, a man so in love, so enchanted, so joyful, and all I can say is I love you. I will always love you, as I will always love our child."

Jewel laid her head against his chest and could hear his heart beat. Soon he would put his head against her belly and hear his son's. They left the building, and Clay was waiting for them, standing against the car.

"Your firstborn," he said as Jewel nodded.

"How did you know?" said Justin.

"There is but one thing that can put that look on a man's face," he said. Clay held Justin close. Now he would always have to stay near.

The months would pass by quickly, and so many decisions had to be made. Once again it was Evelyn who had the answers. They had just finished dinner and were having coffee in the living room. Sarah insisted Jewel have tea. One cup of coffee was all she was allowed daily, and even that was decaffeinated. It took a little time, but she soon got used to it. Sarah had made her delicious apple pie, so Jewel didn't complain about the tea.

"Now, are we all comfy, cozy?" asked Evelyn.

"Oh no," said Justin. "Here it comes."

"Here what comes?" asked Jewel.

"Whenever Mother starts a conversation with 'Are we all comfy, cozy?' it usually means she has an idea for something that we have to sit and listen. Am I right, Mother? What is it this time?" asked Justin.

"Justin, don't be mean," said Jewel. "I'm sure your mother has given some thought to what she wants to say to us, and we should give her our full attention."

"Thank you, Jewel. I honestly wonder sometimes about you, Justin. Your lack of patience is appalling," said his mother. "Now, as I was about to say, with the baby coming..." They had told his mother the moment they arrived, and it took half an hour for her and Sarah to stop sobbing after they looked at the ultrasound picture. "Where was I? Oh yes, with the baby coming, have you given any thought to your wedding?"

Jewel, who was sitting on the couch with Justin, with Jewel resting against him, had to raise herself slightly to look at him. They looked surprised. Justin stated that with all that had happened and the surprise of a baby coming, they really hadn't given any thought to their wedding.

"All right, then, this is the first thing we should discuss. Would you like a large wedding or a small one?" asked Evelyn.

Justin looked at Jewel. "What would you like?"

"Small, just a few close friends. I always thought when the day came that we could be married here, maybe outside," said Jewel.

"Wonderful!" exclaimed Evelyn. "I was hoping you'd say that. We'll keep it simple, but elegant, perhaps a tent in the yard. The flowers will be at their best in a few weeks, so the yard will be perfect. We can serve fancy canapés and hors d'oeuvres, but we'll keep the food at the buffet simple. How does that sound?"

"It sounds wonderful," said Jewel.

"You'll need to pick your maid of honor and a best man, of course, and I'll have to come into town to help you find a suitable dress," said Evelyn.

"I don't think that will be necessary. I mean, you can come to the city, but I designed a dress sometime ago, and it's stored in a box at my apartment. I never sold the design to Kenneth because I wanted it for myself. I just hope it still fits. You can look at it and see if it's suitable," answered Jewel.

"I'm sure it will be. Your designs are so tastefully done. I would love to look at it, and it will give me a reason to do some shopping," she said. "I will need a list of guests as soon as possible. Unless you can think of anything else, I think that's done. You rest, and I'll take care of everything," said Evelyn. "I have been waiting for this day for so long, and it would give me the greatest pleasure to plan your wedding, unless you would like to plan everything yourself, of course."

"Evelyn, I can't think of anyone I'd rather have handle the arrangements for the wedding than you. I'm sure whatever you choose will be amazing," answered Jewel.

"Good. Thank you for your confidence, Jewel. I will do my absolute best for you and Justin. Now, on to other things," she said, getting very serious. "Justin, with everything you own, all the buildings, houses, financial resources, you could provide for your family very well, barely working at all, am I right?"

"Yes," said Justin. "Just what are you getting at?"

"Jewel shouldn't have to go through her pregnancy in the polluted city, and you certainly won't want to raise a child there, so I thought you could work from home, perhaps as a consultant. I realize you are far too young to retire. It's known far and wide that you are the best in what you do, in other states, even in other countries, and with all the electronic tools we have today—phones, fax machines, telecommunications—everything could be done from here. The study has a very good library, and the billiard room that is just collecting dust would be better served as another room for your office. All the equipment as well as an assistant could be put in there, and there would be very little construction to do to make it suitable. Then you would be here most of the time, watching your son grow. You miss so much when you're not around to see it. I remember your father saying to me once that his biggest regret was that he missed so much of your young years. I don't want you to go through the same thing."

"Justin," exclaimed Jewel, "is that possible? Could you work from here?"

Justin thought it over in his mind and realized that his mother's idea was a valid one; it was one that he had given thoughts to himself. He quickly thought of what would have to be done construction-wise, and with a minimum amount of work, it could be done quite easily.

"Mother," said Justin, "I like your thoughts about working from home, and I do believe it would only take a few small changes to turn the rooms into a splendid working office. And you're right about Jewel. I know it would please her to live out here in the country rather than stay in the city. Am I right, Jewel?"

"Justin, wherever you are is the right place for me, but if it's possible to do what your mother just proposed, I have to agree it would make me extremely happy. Just think, you'd be able to see him wiggle his bare toes in the grass as he takes his first steps. It would be wonderful, Justin, just wonderful!"

"And let us not forget you, my dear." She looked at Jewel. "We will have an architect come in, and you can plan the expansion that you will need to the carriage house for your quilting studio. I'm sure you will want to stay with the baby for the first few months, but after that, we will hire a nanny to watch over him, along with Sarah and myself, and you will be able to do the thing you love, making those incredible pictures with fabric. So I can tell by the look on your face that you are just as surprised as Justin was when I told him he could work from home. Tell me honestly, haven't you longed to go back to making those quilts? Don't they cry out your name just as my orchids do mine?"

Jewel was as surprised as Justin had been. She thought she might never be able to work like that again, especially with the baby coming. She would have to find a place to work, put the child in day care, or hire someone to take care of him, and she knew she would never do that. She had just about put quilting out of her mind, and now, here was the perfect solution.

"Evelyn, I don't know what to say," said Jewel.

"Well, you could start by calling me Mother," she replied.

"Mother," Justin said, "in less than an hour, you have found solutions for all the questions Jewel and I have been asking ourselves. You have surprised me yet again. I feel as if a great weight has suddenly been taken from my shoulders. What can I say but to thank you and to tell you how lucky I am to have you in my life? And I love you. Everything you proposed here tonight, with Jewel's okay, will be started immediately. Do I speak for you, Jewel? Are you for this?"

"I'm just overwhelmed, and yes, you do speak for me. I can't wait for this change to start." Jewel turned and kissed Justin on the cheek, then got up and went to Evelyn. "You brought me out of the darkness when no one else could, and now you have done it again. Your love for your son, your thoughtfulness, and your generosity, you possess all the qualities that make a great mother, and I only hope I can be half as good as you are. And I would be honored to call you Mother. I have always respected you as Justin's mother, and I love you as mine."

Evelyn brought Jewel closer, and with her hands on Jewel's face, she told her that she had always dreamed Justin would find someone spectacular, and indeed he had. "What a wonderful family we make!" she said.

Back in the city, Justin asked Clay if he would come up to the apartment for a bit, that there was something he and Jewel needed to speak to him about. Justin dreaded having to tell him about their new plans to move to Connecticut. This man had been through so much with him; how could he ever repay his loyalty? He was the brother Justin never had. Something about him always made Justin feel better, especially after they talked. Clay projected an inner strength and a quieting calm, and it was uncanny, the way he could tell what Justin was thinking or feeling. He owed him for saving Jewel, for holding him together after her attack, especially after she slipped into the coma. He owed him so much, and now he felt like he was deserting him. His stomach was in knots, but Justin knew the move to Connecticut was the right thing for his family.

The first few minutes in the apartment were awkward; Justin wasn't sure how to broach the subject, but before he could find the right words, Clay began to speak.

"We have shared many good times," Clay said slowly, "but sometimes a person needs to change what he does. Driving for people and being a bodyguard have lost their shine for me. I have chosen a different path for myself, one I have been contemplating for some time. I like the creative and passive side of myself and wish to nurture it."

Before Clay could go on, Jewel was in his arms, crying. Clay held her gently as she thanked him for being in their lives. Justin didn't know what to say; he just stood there, wondering what had just transpired between the two of them.

"Isn't it wonderful, Justin?" Jewel said. "Clay is moving to Connecticut with us. Our son will need a godfather to teach him how to remain on the path he is born to."

"All right, you two," said Justin. "Now you've got me totally confused. Would one of you please tell me what in the blazes is going on? I think I hate these silent conversations you two have. Someone please spell it out in English so I can understand."

Clay and Jewel smiled at Justin and felt slightly guilty for the frustration he was feeling.

"You'd better tell him, Clay," said Jewel. "I'm not sure he'd believe me."

"The glass mobile I made for Jewel's apartment, you said it was very good, remember?" said Clay.

"Yes, I remember," replied Justin. "I said it was quite good, and it was, but what does that have to do with this?"

"I had an idea for a small shop where I could make the mobiles and sell them, so I purchased a place that has a shop on the first level and a living area on the second floor. It is near the ocean that I love, and I think I will be happy there."

"I had no idea you were so unhappy in the city," said Justin.

"Like all things, change is inevitable, and it is time for me to go," replied Clay.

"So where will you be going?" said Justin.

"Not far, just a few miles from your house in Connecticut," answered Clay.

Justin was stunned by what he just heard. He looked at Jewel, then at Clay, and still looked confused.

"Let me get this straight, you are leaving the city and moving to a shop in Connecticut and plan to make glass mobiles and sell them. Is that what I just heard?" exclaimed Justin.

"And that I will be only a few miles from you, yes, that is what you heard," said Clay.

Justin had to sit down and get this all straight in his head. "Did you know about this?" he asked Jewel.

"Not until you heard it with me," she answered.

"But you seemed to know before Clay told us directly. How is that possible? And, Clay, how did you know we would be moving to Connecticut?" he asked.

Clay explained that he knew Jewel hated the city, and now that she was pregnant, she would want her child to be brought up in the country. She would stay in the city if she had to, but he knew somehow the two of them would find a way to live most of the time out of the city. He explained that he had been growing weary of the city also and knew the bond between him and Jewel was strong; the sense of family he felt with her made the decision easy. Jewel had no father or brother and needed him.

"Hell, I need you. I have no father or brother either," exclaimed Justin as he went to join the circle. "My son will need a godfather, and I can't think of anyone else I trust to be there for him. Thank you, Clay."

The wedding was wonderful. Jewel's dress was perfect. The honeymoon was incredible. One week in the English countryside, one week in Paris so Jewel could visit the Louvre, and three glorious weeks doing nothing but soaking up the warmth and beauty of Tuscany. Justin would keep his New York apartment. Shelby took over Jewel's apartment so she could be closer to Aiden. The sale of Jewel's land in Upstate New York provided more than enough money to start the quilt studio, and Justin was doing quite well working out of his office in Connecticut. Clay's shop was also doing well, and he often worked with Shelby in her interior design business, making custom glass mobiles for some of her clients. The emptiness Evelyn felt for many years was gone, replaced by the joy of her new family.

And now, five years later, as Justin and Jewel stood in the doorway, with Justin's hand on his wife's belly, waiting to feel the next kick of their second child, they watched outside as Clay, with Thomas Clayton Angelis (Thomas being Evelyn's father's name) upon his shoulders, pointed out the stars and told him their names and waited for Thomas to repeat them. Thomas and Clay had developed a silent communication between themselves, much as Clay had with Jewel. The sadness of Jewel's past was gone forever. This was her new beginning.

ABOUT THE AUTHOR

After a pretty severe car accident, she learned that writing masked the pain of having two spinal surgeries. Thirty days in a rehab hospital and she learned from a doctor that she was right. The brain cannot think of two things if you are concentrating hard enough. She spent eleven months to train her standard poodle to become a registered therapy dog so she could visit hospitals and nursing homes. The reward was wonderful. She did this for ten years, until the poodle passed away. Then she needed to write more and more. She and her husband have been married for fifty years and have two sons and four grand-daughters. Graduating from Ichabod Crane Central School in Columbia County and FIT in Manhattan shaped her into this person she is today. Writing is for her; it still takes the pain away as she goes through more procedures and tests. What does she do for herself? She writes and writes.